"A glowing portrait of a beautiful, if fatally flawed, world."—*The New York Times*

"This is the first book in another fine historical mystery series to add to your collection."—*The Charlotte Austin Review*

"Mary Jo Adamson has a winner here with her mid-nineteenth-century Boston reporter. The voice and the atmosphere ring true and transport you into a rewarding read."—Dianne Day, author of the Fremont Jones historical mysteries

"Vivid with period detail, its characters sharply drawn, *The Blazing Tree* is a compelling plunge into nineteenth-century New England. Historical mystery readers have reason to rejoice."—Stephanie Barron, author of the Jane Austen mysteries

"An exciting historical mystery. . . . The story line is crisp and fast-paced. . . . Michael is an intriguing character. . . . A delightful glimpse of a bygone era."
—Harriet Klausner

## Also by Mary Jo Adamson

*The Blazing Tree*

# THE
# ELUSIVE
# VOICE

A Michael Merrick Mystery

**Mary Jo Adamson**

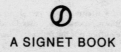

A SIGNET BOOK

SIGNET
Published by New American Library, a division of
Penguin Putnam Inc., 375 Hudson Street,
New York, New York 10014, U.S.A.
Penguin Books Ltd, 27 Wrights Lane,
London W8 5TZ, England
Penguin Books Australia Ltd, Ringwood,
Victoria, Australia
Penguin Books Canada Ltd, 10 Alcorn Avenue,
Toronto, Ontario, Canada M4V 3B2
Penguin Books (N.Z.) Ltd, 182–190 Wairau Road,
Auckland 10, New Zealand

Penguin Books Ltd, Registered Offices:
Harmondsworth, Middlesex, England

First published by Signet, an imprint of New American Library,
a division of Penguin Putnam Inc.

First Printing, September 2001
10 9 8 7 6 5 4 3 2 1

*For Vicki Schieber*

With sisters, love starts on a birthday and never ends.

William James's "frustrating law": "No case involving the paranormal is ever wholly convincing."

"Time has no objective reality; it is not an accident, not a substance, and not a relation: it is a purely subjective condition, necessary because of the nature of the human mind which coordinates all our sensibilities by a certain law, and is a pure intuition."—Immanuel Kant

## *List of Principal Characters*

**Michael Merrick:** narrator, Police News reporter for the *Boston Independent*

**Jasper Quincey:** owner of the *Boston Independent*, lives in Cambridge, Massachusetts

**Freegift:** manservant to Jasper Quincey

**James Hoggett:** investigative reporter for the *Boston Independent*

**Trapper:** Pequot Indian frequently employed by Jasper Quincey

**Dr. William Popkin:** retired physician and professor at Harvard Medical School

**Gideon Craddock:** professor of Greek at Harvard College and Quincey's neighbor

**Leonora Craddock:** sister of Gideon, who resides with him, and a devoted Spiritualist

**Emily Craddock:** niece of Gideon and Leonora, who resides with them

**Sylvie Singer:** a Spiritualist medium

**Julian Bock Bach:** a professor of chemistry at Harvard Medical School

**Newman Goss:** the new editor of the *Boston Independent*

**Susanna Bedell:** a wealthy widow, a good friend of Leonora Craddock's

**Dr. George Haskins:** a physician and a professor at Harvard Medical School

**Dr. Person Story:** a physician and a professor of Mental Philosophy at Harvard College

**James Cranch Meeker:** an eminent Boston cleric, noted for his preaching

**Mrs. Hingham:** Quincey's cook

**Mrs. Ticknor:** Craddock's cook and a sister of Mrs. Hingham's. Also called "Ticky"

**Osbert Davies:** owner of Davies Livery and Delivery, a stable near Quincey's home

**Josh Singer:** Sylvie's father, who worked at Davies as an ostler

**Goslip:** an ostler currently employed by Davies

**Portman:** Mrs. Bedell's butler

**Mrs. Rogers:** Mrs. Bedell's housekeeper

**Wilcox:** Dr. Bock Bach's assistant at Harvard Medical School

**Dookin:** custodian at Harvard Medical School

**Watkins:** Cambridge constable

# Chapter One

"**D**ied? At a séance?" In real surprise, I repeated Quincey's words after him.

He tapped the newspaper in front of him angrily; his bulging eyes narrowed. He shifted his heavy bulk, causing the sturdy leather chair to creak, and glared at the article. Even his wiry, graying hair seemed to bristle.

"Look at this, Michael. Look at it!" he gritted out, shoving the paper across his desk toward the edge.

It was the freshest of news, just off the press. The *Boston Independent* was wholly owned by Jasper Quincey. The afternoon edition, before it was hawked in the streets for a penny, was brought immediately to his Cambridge home, where I was staying while recovering from my injuries. When I heard the clatter of the hansom cab on the graveled drive, I'd put aside my own journal writing to get a copy. Just as I reached the hallway, Quincey threw open the library door and abruptly beckoned me in.

Wheeling my chair up to the desk, I hurriedly glanced at the lead paragraph on the front page. The deceased was a Dr. William Popkin, retired from Harvard Medical School. Suddenly in the midst of a séance he'd clutched his chest, gasping, apparently struggling for breath, tried to speak, and then slumped over onto the table. I didn't recognize his name. Quincey's reaction, which included no sign of personal loss, indicated he didn't know him, either. While Jasper Quincey could direct his prickly disapproval at almost anything, it seemed unlikely that he'd blame Popkin for dying.

I couldn't resist. "Perhaps the doctor was spirited away."

Not even a growl in response. Quincey was clearly annoyed. My eyes were still on the article, but I wasn't reading. I was thinking. Fast. Such ill-humor on Quincey's part usually stemmed from the idea that he might actually have to do something. He might have to lay aside his book, perhaps even stand up. Worse, his daily routine might be interrupted. That was out of the question. So, if he were forced to take action, he made sweeping plans which involved someone else actually doing it. I was the someone sitting in front of him. Of course, I was sitting in a wheelchair, but that wouldn't bother *him*.

He was still my employer—I was the police reporter on the *Independent*, although unable to do that work at the moment. Now that I'd received "a long-delayed inheritance from my father," as Quincey put it, I no longer needed the money, but maybe I needed the job. Empty days were not something I could allow myself. And I was his guest while recuperating. He'd insisted on that, possibly out of guilt, but he could probably convince himself that guests could be of help.

The last time action on his part was called for, I had to become a member of the Shakers, a very strict religious sect. They believed in hard work and celibacy. Now I was understandably wary. I looked down at the newspaper spread out in front of me.

But snatching it up, he jabbed his finger at the offending article. "It's next to the advertisements!" That was a choice spot on the front page. Merchants who wanted their wares described in that left-hand column were required to change the copy on a daily basis. People read the ads first. Moreover, this was a local story, and national and international news usually ran there. An account of the latest scandal in President Grant's administration. Or a three-week old account of the continuing negotiations following the Franco-Prussian war. The new editor, Newman Goss, had his own ideas on what sold papers.

Still, Quincey didn't often involve himself with such details. Maybe his indignation sprang from the fact that an article on séances appeared at all in the *Independent*.

His views on that subject were very clear. Quincey thought that those who conducted séances, called mediums, should be described instead as "charlatans" or, if he was in a kindly frame of mind, "self-deluded ninnies." I'd noted that his opinion was shared by a frequent contributor to the "Letters to the Editor" column, whose only signature was Truth Seeker. From what I'd read in other papers, the two of them were in the minority.

"That headline will sell a lot of newspapers," I pointed out, lifting a shoulder. Quincey was fond of money. I hadn't yet met Goss, since he was hired when I was sick with fever, but he must know what he was doing, putting the word "séance" on the front page.

A good percentage of Americans were caught up in the movement known as Spiritualism. People gathered around tables of all sorts, from the majestic oak ones of the rich to the scrubbed pine ones of the poor, clasped hands, and asked for advice and comfort from the dead. It appeared the spirits came, often ringing bells over the heads of the circle, playing unseen instruments, putting out candles with invisible hands, sometimes even tossing furniture about to make their presence known. They communicated through the medium, sometimes a man or a child, but usually a woman. In every article, someone mentioned a favorite medium and declared that particular person, referred to as a "light," was the very best at summoning the spirits.

From their pulpits, ministers thundered against the practice, declaring that evil demons were the ones being called up. One of Boston's most famous preachers, James Cranch Meeker, warned his flock that the Devil could appear in the guise of a deceased loved one. Skeptics—and Jasper Quincey was born into this group—said little. They threw up their hands and rolled their eyes. But now, for some reason, he wasn't showing even a low level of tolerance.

Suddenly he brought out, "Beautiful women are *always* troublesome. And this woman seems uncommonly clever, capable of all kinds of flummery."

Sitting up with interest, I tried to snag a corner of the paper so I could read it, asking, "Are you referring to the medium?"

He planted his elbows on the newspaper, dug his index fingers into his temples, and glowered downward. "Of course. But even such an adept one couldn't succeed if people didn't beg to be fooled."

"Hm," I responded neutrally. It was useless to bring up the appeal of Spiritualism. To think that those you loved were forever gone was unbearable. I knew. My mother and sister died in a fire when I was in college. Almost ten years had passed, but every day I felt the pain and loss, even though one could say I was used to it. Somewhere in my mind, I harbored the despairing hope that I'd see them again in an afterlife, but I couldn't believe I'd hear from them in this one. Still, if others could take comfort from these séances, I saw little harm in holding them. I could imagine that a young mother, half-mad with grief, hearing what she believed was the voice of her dead child coming from the mouth of the medium, might then be able to smile once more, sure then she'd hold that child again. If I'd brought up that idea to Quincey, he'd have labeled it "sentimental," which was for him a damning judgment. Reason was the only guide, every man's oracle.

I could make another point. After séances, those spoken to by loved ones "on the other side" insisted that only the deceased could have known that story or remembered that incident. This was accepted. So, in an America splintered by religion, here was something everyone could agree on: evidence of the immortality of the soul.

But I wasn't going to be drawn in to any discussion on this topic. I had several good reasons. All I wanted to know was why this article disturbed Quincey so much. His reaction was considerably above his usual hum of irritation. Also, I was intrigued by his description of the lady. Leaning over, I put my hand out on the desk for the paper.

He raised his eyes, but kept his elbows firmly in place on top of it. "Much of this stems from the fact that educated men have taken it into their heads to treat such stuff seriously." He stared over my head accusingly at the rows of richly bound books that lined his library as if they somehow should have prevented such an outrage.

"Was this Dr. Popkin a member of the Harvard Commission that studied Spiritualism some years ago?" I asked. Headed by the famed naturalist Louis

Agassiz, the professors had looked carefully into the subject but reached no conclusion. What was worse, in Quincey's view, was the fact that William James, a highly respected philosopher at Harvard and a medical doctor, was now a founding father of the Society for Psychical Research.

Most scholars agreed the movement started with the Shakers in upstate New York. A group of young girls at one of their villages suddenly began to quiver, stiffen, fall to the ground, and sing songs in unknown languages. They showed all the signs of classical possession, including preternatural strength. They claimed they were controlled by spirits, among whom were Jesus, Columbus, and George Washington, as well as the Indians who once inhabited the lands on which they lived. The belief in communicating with the dead spread rapidly among the some six thousand members living in Shaker communities from Maine to Kentucky and inland to Ohio.

"No, Popkin wasn't on the Commission, but he was in attendance at this affair last night, which indicates tacit approval!" Quincey drew in his breath sharply. "Then there was the irresponsibility of those upstate New York newspapers running those constant stories on the Fox sisters!"

Maggie and Katie, only fourteen and eleven, created the press sensation that ignited the Spiritualist movement. One night in 1847 the two girls and their parents began to hear strange thumps and knocks. Maggie and Katie found that if they clapped their hands, the rappings answered back. In response to yes-no questions and the spelling out of the letters to the alphabet, the spirit claimed to be a peddler murdered by a previous occupant of the house. When the cellar was dug up, human teeth, hair, and a few bones were unearthed. Even when the girls' hands and feet were tied, the rappings continued. No one could explain how this happened. Soon mediums all over the country found they, too, had the gift. Some, even under scrutiny, were impressive, as the Harvard professors said.

Spiritualism sped across the Atlantic to England faster than the new steamships. More slowly, but just as surely, the movement spread there. The noted British physicist, Michael Faraday, conducted investigations to try to verify supernatural phenomena. Eminent writers, respected businessmen, honored judges—all attended séances, just as they did here. The American press reported that members of the royal family had done so, too, although no one went so far as to admit that Queen Victoria had.

Hoping to divert Quincey, I latched on to his last remark about the press by bringing up our most despised rival in publishing business. "I see the *Courier* has raised its price to two cents."

"Were they to give away free, it wouldn't be worth bending over to pick it up," he responded witheringly.

Quincey had a point. He adhered to journalistic principles, although the *Independent* was also a "penny daily." Usually these newspapers were described as sensational, attacked for printing too many stories on crime and sex, and accused of bad taste, if not downright indecency. Frequently, it was the established six-cent dailies who condemned them. *Those* papers were bought by the educated class, the mercantile class. They rarely carried stories about financiers who embezzled, judges who took bribes, politicians who breached the public trust, clerics who didn't practice what they preached.

The penny press did. In large type. Such papers didn't support a party or a class. They tried to inform their readers—the porters, the draymen, the day laborers—men who wouldn't have heard of the crimes of those in power otherwise. To make their readers part with their hard-earned pennies, they also ran human interest stories.

Some of these sheets were guilty of every journalistic crime: Their facts were not checked, their articles were badly written, even their ads were dishonest. I couldn't have worked as a police reporter for any of them. They treated the trials of the wretches hauled up before the judges as comedy, making fun of their tongue-tied attempts to establish their innocence.

"Did you see the lead article in the *Courier* yesterday?" Quincey spat out. "It concerned a dockside madam who added some downstairs windows to her brothel. When a customer hung his pants on a chair by the window, a man hired by her could reach in, extract the wallet, and disappear down the street. The madam could seem horrified when she was told. Unfortunately, she hired a pickpocket who was so incompetent, he couldn't lift a wallet out of a pair of uninhabited trousers. Such stuff is not news of any importance and doesn't belong—"

I listened with half an ear. He was safely launched into one of his fulminations. Perhaps he'd shake his fist and I could slide the *Independent* closer toward me so I could read about this very attractive medium.

Despite my active disinterest in Spiritualism, I'd read a lot about it. Jasper Quincey seemed to think I ought to do so, although he was going about it in an underhanded way. Almost every day, several volumes from his well-stocked library in the east wing were brought to my study in the mansion's west wing by Freegift, the manservant, and piled on the table I used as my desk. These books were usually history or philosophy, and were ones, as Freegift quoted him, "that you'd enjoy perusing." Lately, there were articles on séances stuck in amongst the books. The headline on one announced that Cornelius Vanderbilt, one of the richest men in America, had his own personal medium, Miss Victoria Woodhull, who picked his stocks with spirit guidance. He'd done very well with their help. So had Miss Woodhull.

Quincey never asked for my opinion on the matter, which made me suspicious. While he might think those who attended séances were being gulled, I didn't see that as a real crime. I took some pride in my work, which was to keep the police honest by reporting on their activities. And this smacked of prying into the activities of private citizens.

". . . trivia that's hardly worthy of being in the paper at all, let alone on the front page. Yet the reporter trumpets that this exposure of the madam is another example of how the *Courier* protects the citizenry! Furthermore, the prose pussyfoots. The writer refers to the 'soiled doves' who work—"

I'd managed to edge more of the paper toward me. All I had to do was pretend to listen and nod in agreement. Quincey was often an interesting speaker, and he was remarkably knowledgeable on any number of topics. But there were three that we'd covered completely: Darwin's theory of evolution (which he approved of), Spiritualism (which he didn't approve of) and the duties of the press (which he was now expounding on).

We talked frequently. During my months-long stay, the two of us had sherry at eleven, followed by lunch. We dined together at eight. At meals, conversation was strictly limited to abstract topics so that digestion wouldn't be disturbed. No one else ever joined us.

Had they known about the cook, Mrs. Hingham, gourmands would have begged for an invitation. She could transform even a common dish such as chicken pot pie into a creamy, flaky work of art. Then there were her meltingly tender veal shanks. Her pork roast stuffed with sage and mushrooms. Quincey whole-heartedly agreed with Dr. Sam Johnson, who said, "A man who will not care about his belly will not care about anything."

Catering to what Jasper Quincey cared about was the major business of the household. The first rule was that nothing was to upset the placid routine of his days. He arose early, breakfasted in his room, and went immediately to the conservatory. It was an enormous, glass-walled room, heated throughout the winter by an ingenious system of pipes connected to an iron stove. Here, Quincey planted, harvested, and tended to an assortment of herbs, some of which looked like weeds to me. But all were remarkably useful, either for cooking or for medicines. He'd said he'd learned a great deal from the Shakers, whose prosperity was due in part to their excellent herbal potions, medications, and ointments. Sometimes I grew weary of his discussions on the properties of his plants, but much of what he said was interesting, and I had certainly benefited in my recovery from herbal medicines.

The rest of the day, when he was not eating, he was reading, or at least closeted in his library. He was not to be disturbed there, or in the conservatory. Not that there were visitors sweeping up his curving drive in their carriages. No one except deliverymen came, and they went to the side entrance. Quincey was a recluse. I suspected it was a choice on his part, but he made it sound as if it were an incurable condition. When we met, our working together forced him to leave his home. He still complained of the ill effects of the trip, made many weeks ago.

Freegift did once mention that Quincey had a good friend, Gideon Craddock, who lived next door. "A professor at the university. Of Greek Literature," he'd added.

"So he sees Craddock occasionally?" I'd asked.

"Oh, no." Freegift blinked in amazement at the thought. "But they correspond several times a week. I take the notes back and forth, although on Wednesdays, Mrs. Ticknor, the Craddocks' cook and a most obliging woman, brings one when she comes to tea with Mrs. Hingham, who is her sister. And there is an exchange of books and articles."

"But the two men never meet?"

Freegift thought a moment. "Several years ago, when we had that very wet spring and the Charles rose and looked as if it might flood the back lawns, Professor Craddock was inspecting the water level. Mr. Quincey had been keeping an eye on it as well and went out, and spoke a few words with him regarding that."

I suddenly realized that Craddock's name appeared in the article I was reading around his elbow. I burst out, "That séance was held at our neighbor's."

Quincey slapped his palm on his desktop. "It's not like you to dawdle so. Your attention must be elsewhere."

Now I heard urgency in his voice. Picking up the paper, I skimmed the rest of the front page story. The séance was conducted by a Miss Sylvie Singer. Gideon Craddock had attended with his sister Leonora and his niece Emily. I'd often seen her, a plump young woman, going to the summer house on the edge of their property, although I'd never caught a glimpse of her aunt and uncle. The next two on the list were not known to me: Mrs. Susanna Bedell and Dr. Julian

Bock Bach, a professor of chemistry at Harvard. The last person named was none other than Newman Goss, the *Independent*'s editor. Readers were referred to an article with further details under his byline on page two of this issue. I flipped open to that quickly.

# Chapter Two

*AMAZING MESSAGES FROM THE OTHER SIDE!*
The headline was in bold Italic script. The next
line, in slightly smaller type, read: **SÉANCE ATTEN-
DEES ASTONISHED BY AUTHENTIC WORDS OF
THEIR LOVED ONES.**

"Read it aloud, if you please, Michael." Quincey
sounded as if those first words had a nasty taste.

I did so. The writer, Goss, began in a tone that bordered on breathless. "This reporter has been present
at many gatherings to which the spirits of the dead
have been summoned, but never one where it was so
convincingly demonstrated that they'd come. While
the unfortunate demise of Dr. William Popkin is
much to be regretted, it is comprehensible. An elderly man, with a system weakened by age, doubt-
less he could not withstand a shock to the heart.
Those in attendance declared themselves astounded
at the detail, the particularities, mentioned in the
messages we received. We agreed that such messages could only have come from residents of the
next world.

"Let me say at the outset that I am a very experienced observer, not taken in by trickery or fraud,
and always disposed to doubt. On one occasion I
was privileged to be invited to a séance at the pala-
tial residence of the Duke of Devonshire, and it was

presided over by the famous English medium, Daniel Dunglas Home. Midway through the proceedings, live coals rose from the fireplace and floated about the dark room. While it was hard to imagine how that could be the work of mere mortals, even at the time I was not entirely persuaded that the spirits were there, were with us. Sad to say, such displays of 'physical' mediumship can be, and have been, faked."

Quincey's chair complained mightily as he moved. He interrupted. "Duke of Devonshire! While he was writing that, Mr. Goss was adjusting the silk scarf he uses as a cravat and brushing down the braided edges of his jacket lapels."

I couldn't imagine an editor for the *Independent* so over-dressed. "He wears a silk scarf? A suit coat trimmed with braid?"

"I don't *know*. I've never set eyes on him. His hiring was handled, of course, by letter. But he does."

Keeping my eyes on Quincey, I waited for the explanation. He gave me his usual impatient stare that indicated the answer was obvious. He finally came out with, "The man's writing style is flowery, and the content is self-aggrandizing. It follows that his clothing is dandified."

I thought it best not to reply to that. Although Quincey disliked ornate prose, our preachers and politicians preferred lofty, high-flown rhetoric. So did most journalists. Goss's style was not unusual. It was for the *Boston Independent*, though. I asked, "How did you come to employ him?"

"His qualifications were excellent." There was a pause. "I hired him, at a rise in salary, from the *Courier*."

"I see." And I did. The *Courier*'s readership had increased vastly. Merchants begged to place their ads in that left-hand column on its front page. If this was due to Goss, hiring him was a practical move. But it couldn't have been easy for Quincey to pay the handsome sum necessary to lure him away from the other penny daily. Perhaps it was just as well that the two hadn't actually met. I glanced again at the article. "Is he English?"

"Yes." He waggled his hand impatiently to indicate that I was to continue.

I read on. "Miss Sylvie Singer, who conducted the séance, practices only 'mental' mediumship. She uses no planchettes to spell out the spirits' responses letter by letter, nor does she engage in automatic writing, wherein an otherworldly hand guides the medium's. There are no table rappings. No filmy ectoplasm, supposedly a spirit taking shape, floats about the room. She asks only that the group be small and their interest genuine. In this instance, preparations for the gathering, held at the riverfront residence of Professor Gideon Craddock and his sister, Miss Leonora Craddock, were made exactingly. Chairs for eight people, the ideal number, were grouped about a round mahogany table in a spacious room, dimly lit by a candelabra set on a massive sideboard against the far wall. Chrysanthemums in large vases lent their spicy odor. A small fire kept off the chill of the autumn night. As she motioned us to be seated, Miss Craddock explained that, while many mediums insisted on absolute darkness because the spirits are said to shun the light, Miss Singer preferred to have candles burning. Furthermore, our hostess added, we should not be surprised at the medium's unconventional dress because Miss Sylvie, as she is called, believed that confining clothing inhibited the ability to slip into the trance state.

"Just then the medium entered, carrying a lute, and

her ethereal appearance reminded this observer of a painting of the Phoenician goddess Astarte, she of the golden hair and silvery feet, whose realm was the bright evening star. A young woman of absolute other-worldly beauty, her unbound fair hair fell over her shoulders and down her back in graceful curling tresses. Her white dress, with a high lace neck, was robe-like in its looseness. The sleeves were long and flowing, and not tight at the wrists as fashion dictates."

I could hear an exasperated rumble from Quincey, "Astarte!" But I went on without pausing.

"Miss Sylvie looked at each of us gravely, repeating our names as they were provided. Seating herself, she began to play the lute. Most of the airs were old English ballads, and the notes seemed to entwine with the murmur of the river outside. As the music flowed, peace descended on the room. Then she put the instrument aside and motioned that we should all clasp hands. She rested her head against the high back of her chair and closed her eyes. The hush in the room was absolute.

"Suddenly, although the voice was that of Miss Sylvie, I heard the unmistakable Yorkshire accent of my old nurse, Nanny Potter, speaking to me of what happened in my infancy. I was so stunned that I'm certain I all but crushed both the medium's delicate fingers and the soft hand of Mrs. Susanna Bedell on my right.

"Here let me beg the reader's indulgence while I provide some necessary background as a way of showing that there could be no chicanery involved, nor any question of prior knowledge on Miss Sylvie's part. I have never imparted this story to a soul, and I know that my dear Nanny never breathed a word of it before her death some twenty years ago. When she told me, she begged me to keep it as our secret. Even as a lad I was careful to do so since she explained she might then be dismissed as a fanciful old woman no longer able to look after me.

"My mother died of childbed fever shortly after my birth, and I was early weaned from the wet nurse and given to Nanny's care. She'd also looked after my father. I was a delicate infant, fretful, and she was often up much of the night, holding me in her arms, pacing the floor in an effort to calm me. One midnight she was at her wit's end because I was screaming as if in real pain. Although the nursery was on the third floor, she was anxious lest my wails disturb the household. She was sure of it when she heard footsteps coming slowly up the stairs. Putting me in the cradle, she hurried to the door and opened it, an apology on her lips. There was no one there. Stepping out into the hall, she looked down the staircase. Again, no one.

"Then, behind her, she heard the rustle of a silk skirt, the creak of the caned seat of the rocking chair beside my cradle. She spun around to see the crib gently swinging on its handle. The room was filled with the scent of the lavender talc my mother had used. My cries were instantly silenced. For some time, the crib went back and forth, back and forth. But no visible hand moved it. The wooden chair made a small noise, but it was empty.

"Poor Nanny cowered in the corner long after both chair and crib were still. At last she tiptoed over to see me sleeping peacefully. In the morning's light, she persuaded herself that she'd simply been overtired and, as she put it, her imagination must have run away with her. Soon she forgot about it.

"Then I came down with a hard case of the measles. The doctor said the illness must run its course; there

was nothing to be done. But in the early morning
hours, my fever rose so high that Nanny constantly
bathed my body with cool cloths. At last I lay utterly
still with open eyes. She put out the candle because
measles could result in blindness. Weeping in fear, she
sat with her head in her hands. That was when she
heard the slow, quiet footsteps again, coming up the
stairs. She was rigid in the darkness. It happened just
as before. The scent of lavender, the swish of silk, and
the unmistakable creak of the chair and rocking cradle. Early that morning, my fever broke and I recovered rapidly.

"Although my profession is writing, I cannot describe the effect of hearing that story from the
medium's lips, the words touched with Nanny's
North England burr. I can only say that for a few moments after, I was in a trance state myself, paralyzed
by the power of my feelings. When I finally realized
where I was—in a Cambridge parlor in America, and
not in my childhood home—I became aware that Miss
Sylvie was speaking again, this time of two lovers
parting. I vaguely recall the last sentence, a vivid
image of them on a bridge, her white skirt's hem
blown by the wind around the man's uniformed legs
as they stood together. Even in the flickering light, I
could see that tears glistened on one of the women's
cheeks and that her shoulders shook with the effort to
suppress her sobs.

"Then there was silence for some time. Only the
small fire's crackle could be heard. The medium's
hand in mine was unmoving and, when she began
again, I was startled at the bittersweet sorrow in her
voice. As nearly as I can recall, this is what she said:
'. . . end of summer. Closing up of the cottage. Most of
the servants gone ahead to the town house. Eight bed-
rooms already draped with dustcovers. Late after-

noon when the message arrived. One of the firm's partners coming. Urgent business. Be with us for dinner. Cook in a flurry of pastry making, covering the kitchen with flour. Everyone scurrying about, even the children helping. Almost twilight, but there were no flowers for the table. We rushed out, pulling up the velvety ones in the veranda border. "Choose the prettiest, my love." Those flowers. *Viola del pensiero*. English say "hearts-ease." Pansies. But no proper vase. Instead, just scattering them down the length of the cloth, laughing. They glowed like jewels on the white linen. After that evening, no one laughed again. Embezzled. Caught out. No more visitors. Furniture was gone. Oil paintings, too. Our bare walls said there wasn't any money.'

"Almost before Miss Sylvie finished that word, there was a choking sound, a strangled cry. I thought it came from her, but perhaps from Dr. Popkin, who was seated next to her. Either he or she brought out a few horrified words. I'm rather sure of the last one, since it was repeated. First, 'Killed! How? Why? The jade! The jade!' His hands flew up to his chest, as he panted hoarsely. He slipped sideways in his chair, then fell forward onto the table.

"For a few seconds, no one moved. Then everyone did. Amidst the noise and confusion, Professor Craddock summoned the manservant, who was speedily dispatched to the nearby residence of Dr. George Haskins, who happened to be an acquaintance of the stricken man. At this point Miss Sylvie, looking exhausted and shaken, excused herself. The rest of us were ushered into the drawing room and offered a choice of soothing tea or restorative brandy. So overpowering were our emotions that little was said, outside of a burst of remarks regarding the powerful effect of the messages we'd received. Eventually Dr.

Haskins stepped in to say that, after an examination, he could only tell us that Popkin's heart had given out. We all took our leave quietly. Thus it was that this most dramatic of evenings ended."

I let the newspaper drop.

# Chapter Three

Neither Quincey nor I said anything. Goss had put the story of a local man's death at a séance on the front page, and that headline would sell a lot of copies. Tomorrow's sales would go up because of his report on this amazing medium. The piece *was* signed, which indicated it was his opinion, but it was a most favorable account. All this must raise disturbing questions in Quincey's mind.

I spun my wheelchair a little to face him. "You looked into Goss's background? Heard from his previous employers?"

He nodded impatiently. "He's an experienced journalist. He worked for two prestigious London papers. As he said."

"So he isn't likely to allow even a face of . . ." I looked again at the article, quoting directly from it, "'absolute unearthly beauty' to sway him. At least to this extent."

Quincey growled. "He might as well have given her, free of charge, both advertising columns. Because of this puffery, she can raise her price considerably. And she'll have no shortage of eager customers."

"Could he be working with her? He praises her, perhaps does some research that gives her material to impress her listeners, and she gives him money under the séance table."

He pressed his lips together and shook his head decisively. "It wouldn't be worth his while for a share of her proceeds. Even highly paid women mediums make very little, at most five dollars a night. And I pay Mr. Goss a considerable salary. Which," he bit out, "given what he's written, he'd certainly lose should a connection between them be discovered. No other newspaper would hire him, either, because of that. Any claim of his to objectivity, on any subject, wouldn't be believed."

Drumming his fingers restlessly on his desk, he went on, "Moreover, it strikes me that his astonishment is sincere. Clearly Goss has followed Spiritualism for some time. He wishes to have his belief in it proven. He felt that happened last night."

That had been my impression, too. I suggested, "He could have told that nanny story, maybe some time ago, and forgot that he ever mentioned it."

Quincey inclined his head doubtfully. "Ye-es. But how did it come to her ears? This Miss Singer, I should mention, lived with the Craddocks for several years when she was very young, although she is in no way related to them. The odd thing was that the professor took an interest in her. I can recall being much surprised that Craddock would even speak to a child, let alone a female one. While discussing the development of the mind in one of his letters, he said he was teaching her Greek and she was a very apt pupil. She was, I believe, six years old at the time. Both his sister Leonora and he were very unhappy when her family—a large and indigent one—moved West and insisted she go with them. Now she is a young woman. Apparently she's returned. Very recently."

Quincey pushed himself back further in his chair, laced his fingers over his paunch, and stared at the ceiling as if for enlightenment. He mused aloud.

"Now, Craddock is a highly intelligent man. A solid scholar on the Greek tragedians, even if he has the curious idea that Euripides should be ranked as highly as Sophocles and Aeschylus." He stopped, as if reflecting. "He isn't usually a man to go against accepted opinion. Should he ever consider doing that, his sister Leonora would put an immediate stop to it. Still, he has . . . quirks. In his study, he insists on reading the Greeks while draping himself in their style of robe. Then, while perusing the Romans, he puts on a toga!" His eyebrows reached for the ceiling. "Of course he does that only in private. In our society one must conform in matters of dress." He glanced down with an air of satisfaction at his own severely straight jacket, long weskit, and butternut trousers. While his clothing was made of superb wool, the style would have been regarded as old-fashioned fifty years ago. But then, he thought that his own views were so entirely sensible that society ought to conform to him.

"Mind you," he continued, "he's a sound man, well read in many areas. He's never married, always lived with his sister. Their parents left them quite a comfortable income. And his salary from the university is reasonable. I believe it's well over three thousand a year."

He made a tent of his fingers and went on in a disappointed tone. "Now that he's in his sixties, one would suppose that he would not be considering . . ." That sentence trailed off. "But even men of his intellect can behave foolishly where attractive young women are involved."

"Yes." I didn't need to say anything else. In Quincey's view, if Miss Singer was a medium, she must be deceiving either herself or others. If the latter, he was concerned about Craddock. That alone made his explosive irritation this afternoon understandable.

A story in *his* newspaper had now praised the woman's powers.

"Was the professor caught up in this movement before her return?"

Quincey answered slowly, "I'd have said his thinking on Spiritualism was that of any rational man." By this, he meant that Craddock agreed with him. "Not that he actually expressed his own ideas. He mentioned that the Society of Psychical Research was composed of solid men, one of them a professor from the Mental Philosophy Department, Dr. Person Story, and that he thought highly of Story. The real problem is that Miss Leonora Craddock, his sister, is a devotee of mediums. Clearly she's a most impressionable woman and often comes home from a séance offering him 'irrefutable evidence' that there were spirits present. On several occasions, in my letters to him, I've put forth simple explanations that made nonsense of such 'evidence,' showing that what so impressed her was nothing but sharp practice and tomfoolery. I assumed that he repeats my words to her, thus avoiding the argument that would have ensued had he brought these forth as his own ideas."

"What did her evidence consist of?"

"Of the crudest tricks of the mediums' trade. For example, at the beginning of a recent séance, the medium played the zither and then set it aside. She asked all the people in the darkened room to put their palms down on the table in front of them. She brought her own down with a smartish clap, showing she'd done so as well, and asked that each person curl their smallest finger over that of the person sitting next to them. Yet, despite the fact that all had their hands touching at all times from the very beginning, as Miss Craddock averred, bells rang, the zither strummed sweetly, and ghostly fingers touched the cheeks of those present. Since all the people in the group were friends, and since there was no possibility of an accomplice slipping in and doing these things, she therefore insisted it was the actions of spirits." He blew out a disgusted breath. "It's obvious that it was an all too human person doing it." With that, he leaned back and closed his eyes.

Quincey rarely explains anything. It's an annoying habit. At least, it really annoys me. Whether he truly believes it isn't necessary to do so or whether he wants his listener to pry the answer from him, I've never been sure. I did what I usually do. I asked him, "How was it done?"

He raised his thick eyebrows slightly, pulling his lids up from their usual half-mast position. "You apply Occam's Razor to the problem."

I did remember William Occam, the medieval logician, from my Harvard days. He suggested cutting away assumptions to the absolute minimum, making the simplest answer the most likely. I thought a minute, then took the easy way out. I repeated my question.

Without looking at me, Quincey put out an open palm as if to say the answer was plain. "The medium was in the best position to do it all. She quickly withdrew her own hands and the two men on either side of her groped a bit, touched each other's hand, and entwined fingers, assuming they were clasping hers. Thus, she was free to ring bells, play the instrument, run her fingers down their cheeks. In the meantime, she further distracts those present by intoning 'spirit messages' that are so general that at least one of her statements would apply to someone seated at the table. In this case, the medium announced that a 'departed one' had come to say that the parlor furniture had been rearranged. A woman present fainted because she'd just done so. Then a message came that a bankbook had been mislaid but would be found. A man was reduced to tears that his 'darling Fanny was still watching over him so lovingly.'"

I ran the back of my hand down the side of my face while I thought. My newly regrown beard still itched. "Agreed. Every day people will misplace items and rearrange furniture. But you have to admit that Miss Singer's statements were by no means general. What about those pansies scattered down the table instead of being put in a vase? Under what circumstances would anyone bring that up in a conversation so that she might've come by the information?" I paused, then added, "Of course, she could have made that up herself. If the rest of the 'remembrance' was accurate, the person involved might think he or she had forgotten that detail."

Quincey sat back up, his gaze directly on me. "Yes. She must be far more clever than the usual practitioner. That whole story is troubling. It mentions a scandal."

"Blackmail." I nodded. That was what I'd had in mind. "She drops a few words at a séance to let the victim know she knows. Then she sends a letter offering to keep the secret for a sum of money. It'd work. And getting a share of a lot of money might make Goss willing to help her. "

"Indeed." Quincey's heavy lids usually gave him a sleepy look, but his stare now was focused. "We could back up the blackmail theory by noting that as soon as she delivers that particular 'message from the spirits,' Popkin clutches his chest and collapses."

I grimaced. "If that story applied to his family, it might well bring on a heart attack."

"We don't *know* that it was meant for him, however. Goss doesn't say, quite properly, whether anyone else claimed it, or which woman was shaken to tears by the parting lovers. Nor was he sure of those odd last words of Popkin's. Bah!" he burst out. "Without knowing more, all we can do is speculate idly. Miss Singer may be an accomplished criminal, a shrewd adventuress out to ensnare the professor, or a moon-eyed young woman who hears voices. All those present at that séance must be interviewed."

He pounded his fist sharply on the desktop. "If I'd never met Craddock, I'd be obligated to look into this. But the story about her was printed in my newspaper. And the devil of it is, even if Goss's honesty was above question, he can't be put in charge of any investigation. With his predisposition to believe, he isn't capable of objectivity. Nor is there a reporter on the staff with sufficient background. No. These are my neighbors, and the other attendees are people of substance. Mrs. Bedell is quite rich. And Harvard professors were there. Discretion is required. I shall have to take it over myself." The tragic tone of voice as he brought out that sentence would have suited the characters of Sophocles, Aeschylus, or Euripides.

I did feel some sympathy. His schedule would be disrupted, and he'd have to talk to a lot of people, some of them strangers. I offered crumbs of comfort. "Goss, though, is a good observer, and he'll be able to provide details not included in his article. Since you know the Craddocks, you can arrange interviews with them—and their friends—with no trouble. Perhaps their niece Emily might be a help. She could be a more impartial observer than her aunt. Has she been with them long?"

He nodded, adding, "She came to them some ten years ago because of the death of her parents. This was after Miss Singer left. At the time, Craddock mentioned in some disappointment that his own niece

was not as proficient at learning Greek as she'd been."
He heaved his eyebrows up again. "That Miss Singer
will have to be spoken to. At length."

I had a sudden image of the medium, golden hair
on her shoulders, dressed in her flowing white robe,
sitting in Quincey's austere parlor under his disap-
proving glare. Hurriedly wiping my hand down my
beard to hide my smile, I savored it. It'd be wonderful to see. But, no, probably not the robe for such a
visit. She might favor the oriental trousers that some
of the women suffragettes wore. They were called
"bloomers" because a Mrs. Amelia Bloomer of Seneca
Falls, New York, had introduced them in England
and they'd become immensely popular there with the
women who campaigned for the vote. Whether Miss
Singer was sincere or not in her belief in spirit communications, she'd have to give the impression she
was. So she'd be upright on the edge of a chair, balancing a teacup, and then she'd bring up one of the
several popular *scientific* explanations of how the
trick was done. If she did so, even if she delivered it
in perfect Greek, Quincey's eyes would bulge and his
fingers would be pounding a drumbeat on the chair
arms.

Given his tragic pose, the temptation to needle him
was irresistible. In a consoling voice, I said, "It'll be
most interesting to hear what she has to say. I can't
wait. In the articles you gave me, I noticed that many
mediums favor the telegraph comparison. Since Mr.
Samuel Morse has shown us that coded messages can
be sent along wires between Washington and Balti-
more, those 'on the other side' can speak to us as easily in their own tapping code. However, Miss Singer's
spirits don't tap, so she may favor terms borrowed
from science. The word 'electromagnetism' is used a
great deal. Some sort of invisible waves, I gather. Ap-

parently none of us can sense these. Then there's something called the 'Odic Force.' She may enlighten us on how that works. Or she may favor electricity as the explanation. That'd be wise. No one understands electricity, so she can say whatever she likes."

He only closed his eyes. When Quincey settles into thought, he becomes as still as a lizard. After a few long moments, he looked at me and spoke decisively, "You're right. The niece may be a resource. She and Miss Singer are close in age. Beginning with the Craddocks is best. Then Goss. Then the rest. Mrs. Bedell is a friend of the family. Bock Bach is a colleague, as was Popkin. Introductions, therefore, won't be a problem. Lastly, Miss Singer. Tomorrow I'll consider the questions that will have to be put to each."

As he spoke, he was arranging the papers on his desk in neat piles. I was surprised, but certainly relieved, to see that he was accepting what had to be done so calmly. There was not even a suggestion of a quiver in his jowls. He glanced at the tall clock in the corner, and it occurred to me that knowing he'd be spending the next few hours in his conservatory was a soothing prospect.

Looking up, he said, with some deliberation, "There'll be some inconvenience, Michael. The Craddocks will come to the house, as will their friends, but it's best to meet with Goss away from here. He'll be more relaxed in his office. Since you can be without your chair for brief periods, and a hansom cab will take you directly to the door, you'll be able to manage that with your canes. It is good of you to offer to talk to these people."

At those last statements, I started so abruptly that my wheelchair spun backwards a few paces. "Mr. Quincey, I didn't mean—Surely *you* should be the one to interview—"

"I? That isn't possible! Nor would it even be productive for me to do so. Consider. As his employer, I'd make Goss uneasy. He'll surely be more forthcoming with you, especially if you expressed an interest in the movement. Then, it would put a strain on my friendship with Craddock to question him closely on intimate matters. Miss Craddock knows of my critical attitude toward Spiritualism and would undoubtedly be tight-lipped. Also, the niece is not yet twenty. She'd be most unlikely to tell me what she'd openly say to a good-looking man of your years. You have an amazing capacity to listen sympathetically when women talk to you."

I swallowed, madly searching for the right way to refuse.

He frowned deeply. "While I'd contemplated articles on various mediums, *this* was not at all what I wanted. No. Here's what I had in mind. Having become aware of Leonora Craddock's naiveté in the matter of their practices, it occurred to me that the *Independent* should expose their deceitful methods. Instead—" He shoved today's edition onto the floor in disgust. "I wanted you to investigate and uncover their theatrical tricks! You must have noted that I'd been giving you background material, hoping to pique your interest. Now this. On our doorstep. Pfui!"

I opened my mouth and he held up his hand, saying, "First, let me explain. It occurred to me that your position at the paper had to be re-thought. Simply following the Boston Police about and reporting their activities, as the other papers' reporters do, offers little scope, although you yourself had widened it by including those suspicious fires which were invariably put down to accident or carelessness. Still, your talents were shockingly underused. Now I've conceived of the position of investigative crime reporter in Boston for you."

The clock began striking, and before the fourth melodious chime, he'd stood up. "But you'll have to begin with this. Here, you'll be invaluable. Tact is necessary. By tomorrow, I'll have a grasp of what you must ask, but other questions will occur to you in the course of your conversations. As well, you have an excellent memory. After hearing what you've gathered, I'll be able to analyze the new information and suggest your next step."

Opening the door, he gave me a concerned look. "Getting out will hasten your recovery, Michael. Writing is a good occupation for you, but it requires solitude. Away from your desk, you should spend more time in society. The young need to do this. Moping about the house depresses the spirits, and meeting all these new people will take you away from lowering thoughts. You look quite presentable now. Growing your beard fills out your face, which was too thin."

There was a touch of graciousness in his last words. "I'll make all the arrangements for you."

With that, he sailed out of the room.

# Chapter Four

I didn't sleep well after that. At first, I was just rest-lessly going over the conversation. While lying on my right side, I went over what I *should* have said to Quincey, and on my left I tried to come up with I *would* say to get myself out of this. On my back, I lay staring upward, hearing a cool inner voice tell me that Quincey really could use my help. He'd made a good case for that. He was obliged to look into the actions of Miss Sylvie Singer. Rolling over on my stomach, with a pillow over my head, as if that would shut out the voice, I argued back that it was *his* obligation—not mine. There were investigators he could hire to gather information, and he could then himself talk to his neighbors and these people of substance. Why should I do it? The chances for success were small. There were only three possibilities. If Miss Singer was a clever actress, adept at telling stories she'd heard from others, it'd be difficult to catch her out. If she was using her séances for blackmail, it could be hard to prove. If she really thought she was talking to spirits, I'd have to listen to her twittering on about her be-liefs, which I certainly didn't share. I counted the clock at two, then three, then four, listening to the chimes slowly dropping into the darkness.

Finally, I jerked myself upright. I'd have to make a decision. This morning. The idea of investigative crime reporting had appeal. I could try that. But starting with this case was altogether wrong. Failing on your first try didn't look good, even if failure wasn't new to me. I'd have to work with the just-hired editor, and Newman Goss clearly believed in Miss Singer. He'd put that belief in print, so he'd stand by it. He wasn't going to help me expose her.

I'd have to attend one of her séances. If she were as shrewd as she sounded, she'd check on my background because of my connection with the *Independent*. And finding out about me was easy. Cambridge might call itself a town now, yet it was still a village with farm land close to the Common. My father was a prominent businessman, and I'd grown up here. The blackened ruins of my family home, where my mother and sister died, still poked through the waist-high weeds on a lot not far from Brattle Street. When I was desperate for money, I'd sold the land, but the owner had never built there. Many of my former friends were still in town, although I never called on them. Some of the professors would remember my name. They'd told me I had brilliant prospects. A lot of people knew why these had never been realized.

I tried to imagine this séance. Suppose, sitting with those who waited with tense expectancy in that dark room, I heard my mother's voice or my sister's laugh, sounding as they did in my unreliable memory. Then, if a story was told from my childhood, one I'd have thought no one knew but them, would my desperate hope persuade me they were there?

No. While it was true that I'd had an experience with the Shakers that had shaken some of my convictions, it hadn't left me with any insights into why or what or how to believe. Of one thing, I was sure. The dead didn't speak to us. They did haunt us, but that was different.

The chill of the night air slid down the back of my neck and tightened my shoulders. I grabbed the heavy wool robe from the foot of my bed and muffled myself in it like a blanket, wrapping the sleeves around my throat. I decided to become practical. I could say that I'd like the job, but wasn't able to take on this case, and Quincey would purse his lips and nod, with a wounded look in those hooded eyes. But sooner or later, somehow or other, I'd find myself at that séance. I knew Jasper Quincey. And our daily meetings would be awkward. Over sherry, he'd trot out all the inconveniences he was suffering because of this investigation. Even the way he'd straighten the papers on his desk would be a veiled reproach.

It was best to move out. Since I had to find lodgings of my own soon in any case, why not now? While Quincey might halfheartedly continue his insistence that I stay, he'd been a recluse for years and couldn't find it pleasant to be faced with a guest at lunch and dinner every day. I'd long suspected that it was guilt on his part that was behind that insistence, although I certainly didn't hold him responsible for my injuries.

I considered how to live. Some boarding houses in Cambridge had separate apartments and provided meals. But there'd be stairs and hallways too narrow for my wheelchair, I'd guess. Here I had the entire west wing to myself with an enormous bedroom and study on the first floor. Since Quincey had long ago adopted the Shaker principle of absolute simplicity in furnishing, there were wide expanses of shining floor without any covering. He thought heavy carpets and area rugs were dust collectors, good for nothing but making you sneeze. All of the rooms were spacious. In some of them, chairs were hung on pegs along the wall to make floor cleaning more efficient and were unhooked as needed, Shaker-style.

Then there was food. I remembered the cooking of my former landlady, Mrs. Parker, who alternated meals of dry, stringy cuts of beef and dry, overcooked fish. That was probably the usual fare. In my years at Harvard, all the bachelor professors had a lean and hungry look. The women who kept boarding houses were not Mrs. Hinghams.

Hunching down in my robe for warmth, leaning back against my high-piled pillows, I realized I'd have to hire a man to help me. My feet needed regular bandaging if I were to wear shoes, and I could only stand for short periods, even with my two canes. Washing and dressing myself were still beyond me. What was he to do in a few small rooms when he wasn't helping me? Servants were always *there.* Observing you, if only to see if you needed anything. Because of the size of Quincey's mansion, I didn't often see some of the staff. Two women cleaned daily, but they didn't live in. I'd only caught glimpses of the small, stooped gardener who worked in the conservatory because he came and went through that wing's separate entrance. But a manservant was in constant attendance. You spent as much time with him as you did with any friend. I'd never find another Freegift.

My recovery, I knew, was based on his impeccable care. He knew the exact ointments and always had handy the boiled cloth strips to wrap my legs and feet. While I was still lost in my fevers, he'd looked over the clothes that I'd bought on my reporter's salary and disposed of most of them. Soon bolts of fine linen and broadcloth arrived from the Shakers for shirts, soft warm wools for jackets and trousers. As soon as I could sit up, a tailor appeared.

My inner voice, nagging and critical as always, pointed out the nature of my thinking. It asked if I were going to take this case simply because I was *com-*

*fortable* here. Suddenly I was angry. The heavy robe tightly wrapped around my shoulders and throat was stifling me like the dependency on Quincey that I felt. Since it's easier to be angry at someone else than at yourself, I shifted that emotion.

I began fuming over Quincey's high-handed way of dragging me into this. And I would, according to him, *benefit* from it. I was especially resentful over his last words. "Moping about the house," he'd said, implying that I was having "depressing thoughts." Well, maybe I was. I had good reason, quite aside from the slow process of recuperation. He knew my other problem. On an assignment for him at that Shaker village a few months ago, I'd met a woman who—but I tried hard to keep that out of my mind by day and at night. At that point I was thinking furiously that my mental state was no concern of *his*.

Then my inner voice turned venomous, suggesting that perhaps *I* should be concerned about it. It was only a little over a year ago that I was cured of my addiction to opium. That had begun with a terrible toothache. Laudanum, a tincture of opium, was sold by most druggists, a handy pain reliever for just such things, and a fellow student suggested it. I stopped in at a dusty little shop and bought some for a few pennies. Carrying the small parcel, I returned to my rooms at the university. Before, I'd been with my family in Cambridge, but after the fire I lived in Holworthy Hall, overlooking Harvard Yard, although "living" is probably not the word. I rose in the morning, dressed, attended my classes. I clung to routine, because the sudden death of those you love makes life unreal. But I no longer joined the other students drinking from the pailfuls of punch in the Yard, and I stayed away from the parties in one room or another.

When I took the laudanum, the grinding pain in my

jaw disappeared at once, although I don't think I even noticed that. What amazed me was the instant uplifting of the heavy grief I carried everywhere. That huge cold rock of grief was still in the room, but I was blessedly detached from it. Not that I sank into a stupor. Not at all. A vital warmth flowed through me, giving me new life. I sat down and wrote an essay that my professor declared was the best I'd ever done. It seemed I'd found peace of mind for a penny. After some hours, you do slip into a reverie. But even then, you're half awake. I always *heard* everything. The opiate, of course, wears off. But the ease of that escape proved impossible for me to resist. I kept returning to it, requiring stronger doses, until it took away my life.

Sometimes opium allows you to dream splendidly. The English poet Samuel Taylor Coleridge said that his work entitled "Kubla Khan, Or a Vision In a Dream" exactly described what he saw while taking the drug: "A sunny pleasure-dome with caves of ice!" There in Xanadu, "Alph, the sacred river, ran/ Through caverns measureless to man," and he smelled the incense-bearing trees growing in the fertile grounds, heard the music of the dulcimer.

Just as often, the visions are horrible. I stood, desperately alone, beneath a blank sky on a bleached shore. There was no way out. Behind me were pale, stony cliffs that offered no hope of climbing. The odd noise of the surf was loud in my ears. I looked at the ocean, and I suddenly realized it wasn't white-capped water. It was a billowing sea of screaming skulls, contorted with pain.

With that on my mind, I was instantly pitched into a black, airless well of memory. When I can't sleep, that happens. I try frantically to claw my way back up to the surface, but I can't. I'm condemned to re-live whatever I did during a particular time in my life.

Every cruel and stupid thing I did. None of the uplifting, sunshine moments come back to me. Now I was once again on the docks, lost in my addiction. That's the deepest well, and what makes it truly terrible is that I can't be sure I'd actually done what I recalled. I might be remembering an opium nightmare, just as vivid as if I'd in fact experienced it. Had I actually wakened once on an oozing pile of garbage, thrown out of a den for lack of money, and found the rats tearing the skin from my fingers as casually as from the last bits of meat on a pig's charred rib next to my hand? Had I beaten a man for his money, my fist slamming again and again into his mouth, not caring that the sharp edges of his teeth ripped my knuckles?

I'd inwardly scream back that my hands weren't scarred. They would have been. Had to be.

That didn't help. No sounds can escape these wells. And since that vicious voice fell in with me, it couldn't be drowned out. It kept pointing out exactly how disappointed in me my father—who died when I was young—would be. When I awoke, sometime after dawn, I was still half sitting up, propped up by the pillows, my robe around my neck, my mouth dry, my fists clenched.

After such a night, it's possible that late in the morning, as I was sitting outside in my wheelchair, I might have dozed off. The October air still had a slight touch of summer, and there was patchy sunshine. Freegift had draped a wool shawl over the back of my chair, and I felt its warmth on my shoulders.

But I wasn't drowsy. I was trying to come to some decision about what to say to Quincey. I can even remember what was in the front of my mind. Conducting this investigation meant I'd have to go into society. I'd certainly learned the rules from my mother. She'd read aloud from one or the other of her guides to manners: "The polite gentleman steps onto the street as if onto a public stage, with gloves and hat on. He's impeccably neat and clean, his collars and cuffs faultlessly white, and the clothes well brushed. One knows a gentleman by what he wears." Since my sister was always poring over books of fashion patterns, Celia needed no instruction in clothing. Instead, looking at her over her spectacles, my mother would recite from *Miss Leslie's Behaviour Book: A Guide and Manual for Ladies,* "All the information that a woman can possibly acquire or remember on the subjects of politics and finance is so small, in comparison with the knowledge of men, that the discussion of these subjects in men's company will not elevate her in the opinion of masculine minds."

Since I'd spent a few years dressed in whatever filthy rags I could find to keep out the cold, listening to the mumbled curses of the dockside sailors, which was all their conversations consisted of, it occurred to me I must have forgotten quite a bit about society's ways. And the rules were rigidly enforced. I'd recently read that a man in Cincinnati was ostracized because he'd said the word "corset" in mixed company.

With that in mind, I was about to spin my wheelchair right into my study and write out my resignation to Quincey. While it was in my power to recall all these niceties of behavior, I couldn't summon up the smallest bit of interest in caring about them. I was still surprised that in my time with the Shakers, I'd found I could care about people. Some of them. A few.

Then I saw her.

The courtyard where I was sitting overlooks a long grassy slope that ends on the banks of the Charles. Since the house sits on a rise, I had a good view of the river and the surroundings, which included the Craddocks' back expanse as well. To say that family lived "next door" is misleading as the two dwellings are widely separated.

The woman was standing near a small copse with faded, dun-colored leaves on the nearer edge of their property. There was a small gazebo in amongst those trees. I'd occasionally seen Miss Emily Craddock walking toward it, carrying a sewing reticule. But this wasn't the niece, who was short and round. This woman was tall and elegantly slim. Occupied by my own thoughts, I hadn't noticed her at first. Her dress was of the same silky gray as the river, and she was quite still. Her back was to me and she seemed to be staring fixedly at the water.

She was very fashionably gowned, and she looked out of place along those banks with the scrubby bushes and trailing willows. Her woven straw hat was tip-tilted forward, with a large dark satiny bow at the back and a lace fringe below it that hid most of the light hair massed beneath it. Her dress had a severely nipped-in waist and a wide overskirt bunched up in back into a bustle. The lower edge of yet another skirt ruffled around her feet. Her back was stiff and straight, no doubt rigidly held by a tight whalebone corset. The scene made me think of a French painter of the last century who drew people smartly attired for the boulevards and set them in luxuriant wilderness, where they really stood out. It was true that, once I saw her, she was all I could focus on.

I was trying to recall the painter's name when I heard her speak. But I couldn't have. She was much too far away, even for shouting. And the words were not at my ear but in my head, as if they were my words. But they weren't. This voice was quiet, that of a woman driven beyond endurance. Yet there was an edge of defiance in the tone. Somehow I was sure it was her voice.

She said: *I want to go. To the shining city. Away from here. Those stiff-collared men with their prodding fingers, poking at my mind. Always asking me "how." I want to shout at them. I don't know. Have never known. They know so many words, but it's the same question. HOW? But they'll pay me. Must do one or the other. If not them, then the trances. NO. I can't do that. I told Mother no, told Father no. Told Alistair I can't. I go so far down. I'm gone. So far down I can't hear what my mouth says. Down there, maybe that's where I hear HIM, his calling voice. He says, "Come to the shining city." But how can I believe? Familiar voice. Who is he? Who? What if HE starts talking to the people with my mouth? What might HE say? NO! I'll do the men's questions. NO! I can't bear it. Their fingers poking my secret places. I have to. The money. Take care of Robbie. Poor boy. Darling Robin. But now the dead man. Murdered. He knew it. Coming back up, so did I. Had to tell. Had to. Now what'll happen? Go away. Should I do that?*

The entire time my eyes were on her, she never moved, never as much as turned her head. Just looked at the river.

The next moment she walked into it. She didn't plunge in. Walked in. Fully dressed, in her stylish bonnet and wide skirts. It was as if she simply decided to leave dry land and go forward, wherever that took her. For a moment I only sat, open-mouthed, staring.

The flounces at the bottom of the skirt merged with the wind-ruffled gray water. Then the skirt's fabric—which had a pinkish sheen—belled up around her waist. At that distance, she reminded me of the dolls my sister made, using upside-down hollyhock blossoms for skirts. But she was real. Weighed down by the yards of petticoats, she'd sink rapidly, even if she could swim. Or would swim. She was still going purposefully straight ahead.

I started to jump to my feet, but the pain at that sudden lunge threw me back into my chair. I couldn't walk the distance to the river bank, let alone run. I whacked at the wheels of my chair, spinning myself forward, then realized that I could only go to the edge of the flagstones. I'd sink into the soft ground beyond. Frantically, I groped for my canes, which I usually kept in a holder at the back of the chair. They weren't there. Swiveling my head, I could see through the glass walls of the conservatory jutting out of the east wing. Quincey wasn't there.

And Freegift, at this hour, would be helping prepare lunch in the kitchen in the depths of the house. But he'd answer the bell. I had to get to the rope inside the French doors, pull it. Get my canes, try hobbling as fast as I could to the water. But it'd be slow going. At least I was a good swimmer. That wouldn't bother my legs. I spun forward to the doors, just casting one wild look backwards.

She was standing, quite dry, on the river bank.

# Chapter Five

For a moment, stunned, I stayed in that position, with my head yanked around over my shoulder, staring backwards. I blinked twice. Then again. She was just as she'd been, unmoving, on the shore, so still she might have been in that oil painting I'd had on my mind.

Letting out my breath, I circled my chair and wheeled back to the paved edge to take a closer look. Shakily, I put my hand on the cool marble railing of the balustrade to touch what must be real. Then it came to me. *I was dreaming.* I'd fallen asleep. That was it.

I began to relax, thinking it over. For centuries, the common belief about dreams was that they came from outside ourselves. They were usually warnings or portents. In the works of classic writers, the gods sent these messages from Olympus. Christians believed they were from God or the devil. But now many of my contemporaries had a different view. The poet Lord Byron suggested that dreams were creations of the mind and, if that was true, real events would be a part of them. Going over the words I thought I'd heard, I began working out how this particular one came to me.

Seeing a stranger on the Craddock property where the séance was held, I made the connection with the medium, even though this woman was dressed in the height of fashion and was probably a visitor from Boston. The women of Cambridge, the wives of professors or the squires in outlying manor houses like Quincey's, usually didn't aspire to being modish. I couldn't recall ever seeing any of them with such a stylish bustle. There was only a small group of people at the top, who considered themselves the elite, and most of them were careful with their money, even though they didn't have to be. Quincey fit right in. Outside of Beacon Hill society, following fashion was vanity, in New England eyes.

The notion that she was a reluctant medium—hating to go into trances—stopped me. Most of the mediums I'd read about were quite eager. They advertised in every newspaper in Boston, as well as in the Spiritualist papers, filling columns of print. Then I realized that my mind conjured it up because I myself, after the years on opium, was afraid of illusory states. *I* wouldn't trust a trance. The "stiff-collared men asking how" came from the articles I'd read on the study by the Harvard professors. A dead man, presumably at the séance, was from the story in the *Independent*.

Arranging it in this way calmed me. My breathing returned to normal, and my heart resumed its usual pace. I went over the rest of the words. The mysterious "he" who called from deep inside oneself, a "familiar" voice, was possible to guess at. Quincey had mentioned the medium might hear voices, indicating that was certainly a sign of untrustworthiness. Then there was my own inner voice, although I never confused it with anyone else's.

The names mentioned gave me pause. Where did they come from? "Alistair" and a boy named "Robin." Then it occurred to me that Quincey had mentioned that Goss, the new editor, was English. Alistair was a

British name. While I knew no one named "Robbie" or "Robin," the name was natural enough for a youngster who would of course have to be cared for.

It troubled me that the woman had to "go away" and then walked into the river. But, despite the desperate sound to the words, the voice was cool. I didn't think that was a suicidal impulse. It was more of a desire to leave problems behind that hadn't any acceptable solutions. After all, if one can fly in dreams and not fall, one could walk through water and not drown.

I wondered why the dead man mentioned was killed, rather than collapsing from a heart attack. There were the odd words as he died that Goss had recorded, but the journalist himself saw nothing suspicious about the death, nor did the attending doctor. But then the mind plays such tricks in dreams.

Satisfied and relieved, I leaned back in my chair and looked again at the woman in gray. Just then she turned sideways in the direction of a small, round woman hurrying toward her. Emily Craddock wore no hat, and the breeze, now brisk, pulled fine strands of brown hair loose from the bun at the back of her head, blowing them around her face. With one hand, she distractedly brushed these back. With the other, she held up the heavy folds of her muted brown dress so as to cover the ground faster. The tasseled ends of her shawl feathered around her. Fluttering forward, she looked like a plump sparrow caught in the wind. The other woman waited, still looking composed, although she was winding a small white handkerchief in her fingers.

I watched as the two of them talked. Or rather as Emily Craddock did. She was speaking rapidly, gesturing toward the house, and seemed to be urging her to make haste back there. I was too far away to catch their conversation, but it was clear that the other was reluctant to do it, shaking her head slightly as she answered, still twisting the handkerchief. Miss Craddock didn't give up. Half a head shorter, she craned her neck to look into her face, speaking earnestly. Neither glanced in my direction, but I was partially hidden by the marble balustrade that framed the courtyard.

At last, they turned toward the house, and just as they were about to move out of my sight, the woman in gray stopped, patting her skirt pockets, looking backwards, obviously having lost something. With a shooing motion of her hand, Miss Craddock waved her forward and, with her eyes on the ground, retraced her steps. Looking down myself, I saw a small white square lodged beneath one of my wheels. Perhaps it was the other woman's handkerchief she was searching for. I picked it up and, putting my weight on one of the armrests, half rose, holding up the cloth.

Seeing me, Miss Craddock rushed forward, one hand stiffly upraised in a clear command to stop. Then she patted the air, ordering me to sit. I lowered myself back down and smoothed the cloth over my knee, noticing as I did so that it was embroidered in one corner. It was an S-shaped curve made of unusual flowers that could only have existed in the mind of whoever did that exquisite stitching.

By then, my neighbor had reached the edge of the flagstones and began talking as soon as she was near enough. "Don't get up, Mr. Merrick, please. Please. Freegift says it still takes quite an effort for you."

Turning pink, she added as she stood in front of me, "I'm sorry. What must you think of me? Ordering you about . . . and we haven't even been introduced. I'm Emily Craddock." She didn't meet my eyes and seemed to be addressing someone slightly to my left.

Her words tumbled out, "Oh, dear, I didn't *mean* you were the subject of servants' gossip. It's just that Freegift was worried to tears when your fever was so high. And Dr. Haskins, who's a friend of Uncle Giddy's, kept saying that you shouldn't be treated with the Shaker methods that Mr. Quincey insisted on, which made us all so anxious. Dr. Haskins doesn't live far from here, and he teaches at the Harvard Medical School, so his opinion carries weight. But then your fever did break, so naturally Freegift and Ticky and Mrs. Hingham were trying to think of good things for you to eat so you'd get your strength back and it certainly seems as if you have because you look quite hand—" Out of breath, she stopped, half leaning against the marble rail of the balustrade, blushing even more.

Everything about Emily Craddock was rounded. Her acorn-brown eyes, the tip of her nose, her chin. And the bun at the back of her neck, although at the moment it was a little loose. While she must have been wearing a corset—my sister told me that every decent woman did—its efforts only gave her a slight impression of a waist above the billows of her skirt. The sleeves of her dress were wide, and the gauzy undersleeves ballooned beneath them to chubby hands, which were, I thought, quite eloquent. Her features were plain, but her animation was attractive. Quincey had indicated she was nearing twenty, although her manner made her seem even younger.

"Thank you for your concern," I said gravely. "Who is Ticky?"

"Our cook. Mrs. Ticknor. She's a sister of Mrs. Hingham"—her fingers danced in the direction of our kitchen to indicate our cook—"and when she'd come to tea with her on Wednesday, she'd bring those little fruit tarts that you seemed to like."

"I did. Very much. Please tell her so and thank her for me." I held out the handkerchief. "Is this what your friend was missing?"

"Yes, yes. I'm so happy you found it." Taking it, she looked at it with a little anxiety. "I did the embroidery. She always says how much she likes it."

"I can see why. It's beautifully done, and the flowers are unusual."

"I made them up. Aunt Leo says I must imitate the real, but the flowers I saw with my mind's eye were lovely."

"Artists," I replied, "are often criticized, but they don't have to listen to their critics."

Ducking her head, she smiled in confusion, now looking to my right instead of at me. "This could hardly be considered art. Just stitchery. But Mrs. Bedell says that some of the new floral patterns are quite fanciful and— But Aunt Leo, Aunt Leonora, I mean, is probably right. She usually is. It's just that sometimes it's hard to live up to her expectations."

As she said that, her voice was filled with a worried little sadness. It made me envision a small girl, whose parents had just died, coming to live with that formidable-sounding aunt. Maybe Mrs. Ticknor, the cook, had comforted her with the fruit tarts, and hence that affectionate tone when she mentioned "Ticky." Listening to Emily, I decided I was right in telling Quincey she'd be a help in the investigation. The shortest question led to a lengthy answer.

She'd already answered one without my asking. The fashionable woman in gray must be the Mrs. Susanna Bedell who'd attended the séance.

She'd been almost perched on the marble railing but now stood upright. Before she could leave, I said quickly, "Let me express my sympathy because of the circumstances of Dr. Popkin's death. It must have been distressing for you. He was a friend of the family's?"

"Yes. Oh, yes. I'd say so. He came to tea three or four times a week." She let out a sigh. "Why is it that when someone dies suddenly, I can think of all the kind words I *didn't* say when I might have."

She was distressed at that thought. I smiled and said, "Miss Craddock, although our acquaintance has not been longer than five minutes, I can't imagine you saying any *un*kind ones."

Her round eyes widened. It was clear that she wasn't much used to society, where polite compliments were handed out routinely. But what I said was true. Her openness, which was engaging, showed a generous heart. Her glance slid sideways as she said, "I *hope* I didn't, at least I didn't mean to, you know. It's just that I could've put what I did say—" She pushed her hair back on one side and then the other as she thought. "Most of the time I never could think of anything to say to Dr. Popkin at all. *He* didn't talk. He'd come so regularly to tea and just sit there. Aunt Leo insisted I pour and make conversation."

Trying to hide a smile at this picture, I said, "So you and your aunt conversed. Didn't he nod, gesture, show some interest in what was said?"

"He did make odd smacking noises with his mouth, pushing out his upper lip, but one couldn't tell what he meant. My uncle said that if you saw him at the university and greeted him, Dr. Popkin would just raise a finger and hurry on. Not say a word. Of course, Uncle Giddy avoided having tea with us. He said he didn't need to be there, that all the doctor wanted was the cucumber sandwiches and cakes. Which couldn't be right because he owns—owned, I should say—a great deal of land surrounding Cambridge, not to mention all that under the horse stable, but mostly he let to good farmers, so he could have afforded trays of tarts. Not that he had a cook. He didn't keep any sort of establishment—always lived in his rooms at the university, although that must have been a stretch because Harvard's Medical School is in Boston— Then my uncle started joking that Dr. Popkin was courting Aunt Leo. Only, it turned out, that it wasn't Aunt—" Now her complexion was a furious red and she was looking high up at our roof.

The elderly doctor had proposed to Emily. And she'd refused. Or perhaps her uncle did by indicating it wouldn't be a suitable match. There would have been forty years difference in their ages, given that he was already retired. Then, too, if Gideon Craddock dodged having tea with the silent, tooth-sucking Popkin, he'd have hardly welcomed sitting down to meals with him as a nephew-in-law. To save her further embarrassment, I changed the subject. "I understand that the medium at the séance, Miss Singer, once lived with your aunt and uncle. Have you known her long?"

She settled back against the railing of the balustrade. "It seems so because I'd always heard about her, but she moved with her family to Kansas before I came here. I've only really known her for a few months since her return. We've become great friends."

The warmth in her voice was obvious. It made me even more interested in Miss Singer. Both the aunt and the niece, who seemed very different, had taken to her.

"It was kind of your family to offer her their home. Were her own parents in some difficulty?"

Her forehead puckered, as if coming up with an acceptable answer was not easy. "They had so many children, you see. Mr. Singer tended to move about—

well, Aunt Leo says he was feckless, although Uncle Giddy says that he was very talented in some ways. In any case, he was quite good with horses, and at that time he'd just been hired as an ostler at the stable." She indicated with a graceful finger that she meant the one far down the road whose fields joined the Craddock property. "Mrs. Singer was often . . . confined and wasn't well, anyway. Naturally, she wasn't able to look after the children as she might have liked. One day, Aunt Leo heard Sylvie in the next field with the horses, and she was standing on a pile of dirt because she was very small, telling her brothers and sisters a story about . . . Well, that's not to the point. I'm sorry, I'm rattling on a bit. It's just that my aunt was surprised at her imagination. Some weeks later, Sylvie—who was then about five—came to the kitchen door selling apples, and Aunt Leo was there and told her to come in. She was going to scold her since those apples came from *our* orchard. But she and Mrs. Ticknor said they'd never seen any living person so dirty, as if she hadn't been washed since birth and—"

Emily stopped, blushing at the sound of her words. She hastened to add, "Of course, that wasn't Sylvie's fault or her mother's. You can see that playing outside all day, and the problem with getting enough hot water, living as they did above one of the barns. Anyway, her hair looked short and dark because of the dirt and the elflocks from not being brushed. It took Ticky and Gladys some time to wash and comb it out, and then they could see how beautiful she was with her long, fair hair. She had terrible chilblains on her feet—not having shoes, you know, and the mornings being frosty—and her toes were red and as swollen as sausages. It was clear it'd take some time for those to heal. Aunt Leo belonged then to a group that helped the deserving poor, and they gathered used clothing to give to them, along with advice. She decided to get some items to take to the Singers, shoes particularly. So she sent a note to Sylvie's mother asking if the child might stay a few days. Anyway, what with Sylvie taking them treats from the kitchen now and again, and bringing clothes, the Singers allowed her to remain. Aunt Leo paid for music and watercolor lessons, and Uncle Giddy tutored her. She was quite good, he said, at Greek, and he wouldn't have thought women could be. I certainly wasn't."

There was some sadness in her eyes as she said that, but then she rallied and added, "Although she wasn't adept at needlecraft, and she said that her art instructor despaired of her. She stayed for five years, but then Mr. Singer lost his job and they went West."

"A remarkable story. You two must be friends, having a great deal in common in terms of upbringing."

"Yes." She nodded vigorously. "Sylvie pays attention, you see, and never seems to think your ideas are queer, even when they are. And she is amazing at séances. A true 'light.' I know everyone claims that their particular medium is one, but she really is. Maybe you aren't a Spiritualist. Uncle Giddy says that Mr. Quincey is a complete disbeliever—a real 'bosh philosopher,' but unless you're one, too, I'm sure you'd enjoy meeting Sylvie."

"I'd like to make her acquaintance," I answered promptly, a little surprised at how smoothly the usual polite forms slipped off my tongue. But there was truth in the statement as well. I was content with my unriddling of my dream. I didn't imagine Miss Singer had any telepathic powers. But I did want to meet her. I asked, "Is she staying with you?"

"No," she answered wistfully. "That wouldn't be possible because—" She paused before going on.

"She's with Mrs. Bedell, a friend of my aunt's, a widow, who has a house in Cambridge on Brattle Street, on Tory Row, so even though it's in town, it's quite large. We do visit frequently. Sometimes, on class days, I go with Uncle Gideon, who sees me to the door. Or she comes when Mrs. Bedell calls at our house."

It occurred to me that before Sylvie Singer's return, Emily's life here on the outskirts of town with two elderly relatives must have been lonely. That probably accounted for her talkativeness, as well as her shyness.

Now she beamed and looked—almost—directly at me. "On Sylvie's next visit, perhaps you could come to tea and . . ." Then she cast a quick glance at my chair. "Oh, dear, that's right. It's quite a distance to our house from your door. Let me think of the best way. Ah! I know. Mrs. Bedell always brings her carriage when they come, and we could send that round for you."

"I'd enjoy that. It'd give me a chance to make your aunt's acquaintance as well."

She straightened up eagerly. "I'll make the arrangements now. Mrs. Bedell is always so obliging, and it'll give Sylvie something to look forward to later. Today won't be easy for her. Professor Person Story came himself to the house to try to persuade her to take part in the Society of Psychical Research Study, and she's hesitant. But he was a student of Professor William James, who, you know, has quite a name as a philosopher, even in Europe. Since he's abroad this year, his classes have been taken over by Dr. Story. He's quite insistent that he needs Sylvie's help and has persuaded Aunt Leonora that it would add to the advancement of knowledge on Spiritualism. He asked me to speak to Sylvie, too." Her fingers indicated the copse where she'd been talking to her friend.

Looking in that direction myself, I asked, "But that was Mrs. Bedell you were just speaking to, was it not?"

"No, no. Mrs. Bedell's—" Emily waved her hand in the air near the top of her own head to indicate a much shorter person. "And *she's* very near Aunt Leo's age. They'd been acquaintances for some years, but became quite friendly after Mr. Bedell's death. No, that was Sylvie."

Hearing that took me aback. Miss Singer seemed a woman of many incarnations. The ostler's barefoot daughter. The white-robed medium with her long, flowing hair. The stylish woman in gray.

And that information shook my carefully constructed explanation of the dream. Even after Emily left, I sat staring at the trees. But then I spun my chair around toward the house. *Sylvie* was the medium. How could I have any insight into *her* thoughts? It defied reason.

# Chapter Six

Freegift threw open the French doors as I approached. A small, spare man, he'd been raised by the Hancock Shakers and still clung years later to their style of dress. His long brown vest was buttoned to the top of his collarless white shirt, which had long full sleeves. He wore no cravat. His graying fair hair was cut in their old-fashioned style—straight across the front, short over the ears, and rather long in back. He'd absorbed their philosophy, too. Freegift was the gentlest man I'd ever met.

Removing the shawl from the back of my chair, he said, "I hope you had a nice rest, sir. And a pleasant talk with Miss Craddock. Seeing you with her, Mr. Quincey said I shouldn't disturb you, but he is waiting in the library. With the sherry. He's had a very busy morning—messengers coming and going." He blinked as he spoke, his colorless lashes almost obscuring his eyes. This was habitual, but there seemed little doubt that Freegift was surprised. Quincey was bestirring himself.

He was waiting at the door of the library as I wheeled down the hall. Shutting it behind me without saying a word, he went directly to the decanter, poured two glasses, handed one to me, and settled himself behind his gleaming desk. He didn't ask about my conversation with Miss Craddock, nor give me a chance to speak at all. Instead, tapping on the sheets of paper in front of him, staring at me over his half-glasses, he announced, "I have a report from Hoggett. You recall him? James Hoggett?"

The name was familiar, but I had to think. "Ye-es, occasionally I saw an article by him in the paper when I was working there. But I never met him. I don't think he was often in."

Quincey shifted his gaze slightly. "No, he rarely goes there. It was he who found you on the docks, but he may not have given his name. He usually doesn't."

Even if he had, I wouldn't have remembered. No doubt Hoggett scraped me up off the rough boards outside the opium den where I was probably in a sodden heap, having been shoved out for lack of money. I had no memory of much after that, either. I'd spent some time in the forest with Trapper, a Pequot Indian also often employed by Quincey, being cured of my addiction, but until I saw Trapper months later, I wasn't sure whether or not *that* was real or one of my really unpleasant opium dreams.

I simply shook my head, and Quincey went on. "Hoggett has a talent for not being noticed, and he collects reliable information—without giving any. Last night I sent a note round to him asking for some on the Singer family. He went to the stables down the road, the father's last place of employment before they ventured west. Both the owner and an old ostler remembered Josh Singer well. Very well."

He eyed the amber liquid in his glass, took a sip, leaned back, and said, "It seems he was one of those men competent at whatever he turned his hand to but not willing to stick to anything very long. And the owner, Osbert Davies, said Singer 'wouldn't be told.' I take that to mean he wasn't one to follow orders. Moreover, he'd disappear for weeks, although he didn't seem to be a drinking man, and he gave no reason when he returned. Davies said he kept him on partly out of pity for his family and partly because of his skill with horses, both in training them and taking care of their ailments. Hoggett writes that looking around this stable, that latter talent must have been useful. Most of the stock were spavined nags fit only to carry a Harvard student to Boston and back, although there were four sturdy horses used for deliveries. The old ostler, who'd been listening to the owner, added that Singer could fix more than horses. A stable patron had left a newish rifle saying it didn't shoot straight, but Singer tinkered with it and ended up being skilled at potting pheasants with it for the family table."

At this Quincey sat up, interrupting his narrative, saying, "Pheasant. I must speak to Mrs. Hingham. We haven't had one for some time. As I recall, she barded the bird with sliced salt pork, browned it, and baked it in a covered dish with apples, brandy, and soured cream. Very nice."

I glanced at the clock, although I didn't need to. It was bound to be close to lunch time, given Quincey's line of thought. In fact it was past it, which was surprising.

Taking a swallow of sherry, and noting with some satisfaction that there was still some in his glass, he went on, "In any case, Singer left his employment quickly. He'd sold a Boston man a pair of matched black horses. However, soon after, the man tracked him down. The shoe blacking had worn off, and it seemed one of the horses was a roan. That night, Singer and his family left for the far West. That was all Davies had to say. I gathered it was just as well since the man couldn't answer a question without quoting Scripture at length. But as Hoggett was going, the ostler caught up with him and said he knew of a man named Goslip, a wagon driver, who could tell him more about Singer. For a few coins, Hoggett also found out the name of a drinking establishment where Goslip might be found."

Quincey uncapped his inkwell, dipped in a pen, and jotted down a figure before going on. "A wise expenditure. This man had recent news of Singer. He'd done rather well in Kansas at first, 'having put his daughter Sylvie into mediuming' as Goslip phrased it. She was then about eleven, and I gather that girls of this age are supposed to have special powers. The farmers and their wives flocked to her séances." He paused for reflection, then came out with, "There must be an amazing lack of any form of entertainment in Kansas. But after three or four years, the girl absolutely refused to continue, despite her mother's pleas and her father's threats."

I sat my glass down rather too hard on the piecrust table next to me because Sylvie's words sprang into my mind. *I told Mother no, told Father no.* Quincey glanced up. I gave a slight cough as if to indicate the sherry had gone down the wrong way.

His eyes returned to the papers in front of him. "Hoggett's report is lengthy. I'll just give you the gist of it. Singer was not about to give up a steady source of income and, when he noticed that Sylvie was taken with an Englishman named Sandringham who'd recently arrived, he decided that perhaps a new husband could be more persuasive. The father felt entitled to half of Sylvie's earnings, and thought the bridegroom would share. Singer was much disappointed in that. Immediately after the marriage, Sandringham packed up his young wife and hurried her off to Chicago. I would guess she was about fifteen at the time. But the husband was also disappointed. The girl steadfastly resisted the idea of 'mediuming' and Sandringham, faced with the idea of having to work to support the two of them, left her and moved in with a well-to-do widow. How Sylvie supported herself after that, Goslip didn't know. She didn't return to her family, and they didn't know her whereabouts for several years, but at the end of this summer, she arrived here."

Quincey leaned back before adding, "You can see the source of Goslip's information. Josh Singer came back himself last week. Apparently, however, his daughter is still disappointing him in terms of handing over her income. Although she has obviously returned to her trade as a medium, when Singer called at the friend's house where she is staying, he was told on every occasion that Miss Singer was not in."

Trying to keep my voice steady, I interrupted. "This Sandringham to whom she was married, is his Christian name Alistair?"

He looked up. "Yes. Do you know someone by that name?"

Without meeting his eyes, I replied, "No. Does Goslip indicate whether Sylvie Singer had a child?"

"No. Why do you ask?" Then, peering at me over his spectacles, he said, "You look quite pale." He stood up. "Very pale. In fact, I think we should depart from custom and have a second glass of wine. It's nourishing. I apologize for putting back lunch a half hour so I could tell you about Hoggett's report."

While he refilled both our glasses, I didn't answer. At last, I brought out, "Some details of Miss Singer's history sound . . . familiar to me. Yet I can't see why they should. Miss Craddock told me of her youth, but nothing of the woman's recent past."

Quincey pursed his lips. Finally, he murmured

thoughtfully, "Those details came to you from Mrs. Hingham."

Dumbfounded, I stared at him before saying, "But I rarely even see her! I never go into the kitchen—" I gestured at my chair. "The steps down. And why, in any case, would she tell me such a story?"

"She didn't tell *you*, but she might have told it in your hearing."

I was shaking my head vigorously, but he put up his hand. "Let me explain, Michael. Your fever was very high for several days when we first returned from Hancock. Worryingly high. And you were delirious, drifting in and out of consciousness. We had a pair of competent women, but Freegift spelled them and indeed spent much time by your bedside. He was . . . overwrought. In fact, I don't think he was sleeping, and I doubt that he was eating. On several occasions, I saw Mrs. Hingham carry a full tray to your room. While she made sure that there was always honey water and beef tea by you in case you were able to drink anything, the food could hardly have been intended for you. I guessed that she was trying to tempt Freegift's appetite. She stayed in the room, I noticed, for some time. If she stood there, she knew he would swallow something. And, to distract him, she could have mentioned that Miss Singer had returned and repeated what she knew of her experience. Which Mrs. Hingham would have learned from Mrs. Ticknor who, in turn, would have heard it from Miss Emily. Several details, no doubt, lodged in your mind."

He nodded in satisfaction and took a healthy drink of wine.

I did, too. His explanation was believable. I sank back in my chair and thought it over, nodding myself. That was how I knew what I did. When I drifted off earlier, as I must have, what was stored in my memory sprang up and mixed with yesterday's events.

"You mentioned a child," Quincey reminded me.

"Yes. A boy named Robin. I'd like to know if his existence is also factual. While I can hardly ask Miss Emily, she might tell me. She's already said a great deal about her friend without prompting." I told him about our conversation outside.

Quincey began, "Miss Singer—and by the by, one can see why she resumed her maiden name. Her father has recently discovered that Sandringham already has a wife, very much alive, in England. The child, if there is one, is illegitimate. Goslip said Josh Singer was furious at being so fooled by the man. It's interesting that those who aren't above deception themselves aren't more careful in taking the word of—" At this point he was interrupted by a quiet knock on the door.

Freegift came in, and Quincey stood up quickly in anticipation, saying, "Luncheon."

The servant moved nervously forward, saying, "Yes, sir. It is ready. Quite ready. But"—he held out a large envelope—"there is a message for you, and the hansom cab driver has been told to wait for your reply."

Quincey frowned as he took it, looking at it carefully before reaching for his letter opener. The envelope was expensive, made of heavy vellum with a thin gold trim on the sealed edge. He read the contents and dropped down in his chair. Closing his eyes, he sucked his breath noisily in through his nose. At last he looked again at the paper before him. Reaching for his pen, he wrote just a few words on a piece of foolscap, folded it up, and handed it to Freegift.

After the man had hurried out, Quincey remained seated, tapping the envelope's edge on the desk. At last he said, "You won't have the trouble of going to Boston to see Newman Goss. He's coming here. He states that he must speak to me regarding business which involves the *Independent*." He tore both letter and envelope into pieces, which took some effort because of the thickness, and deposited them in the basket before going on. "In all the time I've owned the newspaper, not one editor has found it necessary to speak to me in person. A note has *always* sufficed. And he's bringing Professor Julian Bock Bach. You'll recall that man was also at the séance. They'll be here at three. You'll naturally want to hear what they have to say."

He slapped his palm loudly on his desk. "The damnable thing is that I will also have to listen." His quick movement sent the pages of Hoggett's report flying off into my lap.

He rose and strode out of the room, his back rigid.

I was staring at the scattered papers in my lap, where the investigation had just landed. I could have dumped those pages back on his desk, but I knew now that I wouldn't.

# Chapter Seven

"**M**urdered." His eyes on Newman Goss, Quincey pronounced the word with no inflection. His face was expressionless, too, and the droop of his heavy eyelids gave him an inattentive look. His bulk was spread over most of the brocade seat of the carved wooden sofa, but he was upright against the thinly padded back. None of the furniture in the parlor allowed much slouching. For all the beauty of the classic lines of the satinwood chairs, the tall mirrors, the square consoles, the functional side tables, and the rectangular clock, the room seemed stiff, excessively polite, not really welcoming. Perhaps that was the impression it was intended to convey.

It was the first time I'd ever seen the parlor actually used. By current standards, it was downright ascetic in its entirety. The floors were shiningly bare, and the ivory-silk drapes hung in slim folds, whereas the customary style here, as in Queen Victoria's England, was to envelop rooms in fabric. In the homes of the genteel, several layers of richly patterned carpets covered the floor; sets of thick velvet draperies shrouded the windows and hung at the entrance to rooms. Center tables, mantel tops, and pianos were swathed in fringed shawls and ornate throws. It had a cocoon-like effect, muffling the shouts and strife of the outside world.

But not even such a room could have softened
Newman Goss's statement that Dr. Popkin was deliberately murdered. I, hearing it stated as a fact when I
was convinced the idea was part of my dream, jerked,
almost dropping my cane, which lay across my lap.
Dr. Bock Bach, seated in the chair next to me, grimaced, although he must have discussed it with Goss
and was therefore unsurprised. Only Quincey was
impassive, flatly repeating the word. "Murdered."

This wasn't the response that Goss expected. Leaning forward, striking the heel of his hand lightly
against the chair arm for emphasis, he insisted, "Yes!
You can see that our readers will be attracted by this,
sir. It's *local* news and quite dramatic. Yesterday's
paper, carrying the account of the séance, was completely sold by six o'clock. Actually, by half five. And
I'd doubled the usual run." The editor straightened
and made a tent of his fingers. "I foresaw the excitement such a story would create. But solid evidence of
the murder came too late today to include it in the
regular edition. The only course, therefore, is an extra
edition, giving the information we now have."

His blond hair flopped slightly to the side over his
forehead, and his light eyes were intent on Quincey.
He was in his thirties, slim with a pale handsomeness.
His clothing looked as if it'd just arrived on a fast
steamship direct from London's Saville Row. His
lapels were outlined with black braid, as Quincey had
guessed. And he wore a black silk scarf under a
turned-down soft collar, which was unusual because
most American men wore stiff ones. His dark coat
was form-fittingly tailored, and his checked trousers
were tight, only slightly flaring at the hem. Over his
black shoes, he wore tan spats.

I disliked him immediately.

It wasn't entirely because of the up-to-the-hour

fashion of his clothes. When I was growing up, I'd see the Harvard upperclassmen on the streets of Cambridge. The students from Virginia and the Carolinas, particularly, were noted for their exquisite dress. Their high hats gleamed, their shirtfronts were pleated, their waistcoats embroidered, and the long swallowtails on their jackets were sharply pointed. Even on the playing fields, they kept on their hats and jackets. I so admired their dash, which they too seemed to truly enjoy. As a student, I had an evening suit, worn to balls, that was close to what they wore— swallowtails and all—and when I had that on, I felt splendidly turned out.

Before Goss came, I remembered Quincey's estimate of how he'd be outfitted and I changed to my new tan suit, made of the finest spun Shaker light wool. The tailor had taken some trouble because of the length of my legs—I'm almost four inches over six feet—and it wasn't easy because when he measured me, I'd had difficulty standing at all. But he'd done superb work. Also, I made the decision to walk down the hallway with only one cane, which I could do if I moved slowly and deliberately. When I saw Goss's attire, I was glad that I'd done this. Then I felt a flash of disapproval at myself because of my vanity. I transferred this to him.

Too, the assurance of Goss's manner and speech grated on me. He'd handed Freegift his high-crowned felt hat, his chamois gloves, and his gold-headed walking stick as if he were conferring a favor on him by doing so. As we were introduced, his remarks, which were courteous enough, seemed to have a condescending edge. The precision of his British pronunciation underlined his complacence. His smile bordered on smug.

Now, Quincey himself was arrogant. And opinion-

ated. Still, he could give you clear reasons for his
thinking, even when it was wrong-headed, and on occasion, I'd known him to change his thinking. Very
few occasions, of course. His devotion to logic convinced him that *his* view was correct since he'd arrived at it rationally. Other people's opinions were
fogged by emotion.

Looking at Quincey, I understood his dilemma. He
didn't want to rush to print with another article on
that séance. But because of the single word "killed" in
Goss's column, other reporters would hurry to pick
up on the story. If they could find Miss Singer, she'd
be besieged. Anything she said or didn't say would
make their headlines. **MEDIUM SPEAKS OF MUR-
DER** or **MEDIUM MUM ON MURDER.** Every man
on the street would buy a copy on the strength of either version.

As he thought over Goss's idea of an extra edition,
Quincey's hands, lying flat on each side of him, were
quite still, but I noted that his fingertips were pressed
into the sofa's brocade seat. At last he said with no inflection, "An extra. We've never done one. I can see
you would need my approval on that. What evidence
do you have that this man was murdered?"

Goss answered confidently, "I spoke to Miss Singer
this morning. She told me that although she was coming out of the trance at the time, she does not doubt
the words she heard, although she can't remember
saying them aloud. Those dreadful words, as you'll
recall, were these: 'Killed. How? Why? The jade, the
jade.' Nor, on thinking it over, does she question that
those were Popkin's words." A self-satisfied smile
touched his lips. "You must understand, sir, that I've
had much experience in the field of Spiritualism. In
fact, I would claim expertness in detecting any sort of
fraud. While I don't pretend to understand Miss

Singer's powers, they are real and they are formidable. She's going to be interviewed this afternoon on the Harvard campus by the Society for Psychical Research."

Settling back in his chair, he looked down at his hands, now clasped in front of him, and didn't notice that Quincey's fingertips were now digging so hard into the sofa that if it'd been covered with silk instead of brocade, the fabric would have ripped.

Perhaps Dr. Bach detected it. At any rate, he spoke abruptly, a Teutonic guttural tinge to his words, and his w's pronounced as v's. "Vait. I beg your pardon for intruding, but I must tell you this also. You can make of it vat you vill." The elderly professor was a small man, almost swallowed up in the wing chair, but he had a presence, the air of a man used to being listened to. His eyes were sharp in his bony face. A puckered white scar slashed across his cheek. He was dressed most unfashionably. I could imagine him wearing that high-collared straight coat in his student days in Leipzig or Leyden. In fact, the gold buttons down the front had what looked like the insignia of a dueling club, popular at some Prussian universities. His gray hair was pulled into a pigtail which jutted straight out in back because of the tall collar. Perhaps that style was also popular when he was an undergraduate. "This morning I asked Dr. Bonner, a man noted in the field of pathology, to examine Popkin's body. He says the heart vas healthy. In very good order, no matter his age. It is also true that there vere no detectable poisons and, in any case, the vay he died vas not typical of any common one, such as arsenic. Bonner could not say how he died, and vould not guess, but he saw no reason to think there vas any problem vith the heart."

Quincey gave him a long, approving look. Here

were facts he could grasp onto, none of these ghostly messages from beyond. "Such a dissection must be quite unusual under the circumstances, sir. Why did you take it upon yourself to request it? Was the deceased a good friend of yours?"

"Bah! Who could be a friend of Popkin's? His behavior was bad. Very bad. Alvays. He had no manners, no idea of how a gentleman should conduct himself." Bach waved stiff fingers, oddly stained with splotches of yellow and brown, probably from the chemicals he handled in the course of his work. "He vould spit out an insult at you one day and the next appear at your office door with no apology, vanting a favor. Often one that required you to use your time and even your money. His own he never spent. But he was a rich man. Still, most days he valked in snow and rain the eight miles to Grove Street in Boston to teach his classes at the Medical School, so not to spend the tram fare."

He paused, lifting a shoulder. "Perhaps all that valking was the reason his heart vorked vell. One of my colleagues believes that the old should move about, not sink into their chairs and rock. If Popkin heard that, he'd have valked hundreds more miles. Of late, all that vas on his mind vas living long. He listened to each new voice on how it could be done. When someone said a young vife increased one's years, off he goes to look for a young lady." He let out a bark of laughter before adding, "But Gideon Craddock pointed to the cost of that, and Popkin dismissed the idea very fast. He tried every new medicine—if it could be obtained cheaply. But"—he stopped himself—"you ask me how it is that I should order the body examined. The answer is that I am the executor of his estate."

The professor's straightforwardness was refreshing.

He struck me as a man concerned with truth, at least *his* truth, and one who saw the necessity of telling it now. The idea of speaking only good of the dead is honored. People bring up their deceased friends and relatives in conversation frequently, sometimes referring to them as if they were in an adjoining room. Death masks of them are often put in a prominent place; women wear mourning brooches embroidered with the loved one's hair. Still, I appreciated Bock Bach's candor. People are rarely killed for the good they do. The way he spoke held your attention as well. His use of American idiom lay lightly on the formal structure of his native tongue. And the ghost of Popkin, whom I'd first met in Emily Craddock's description, became solid in his words.

At Bach's last statement, Quincey's thick eyebrows went up. "I see. You felt it necessary to investigate the circumstances of his death, as far as you could."

"Ach. Yes. I had to do so. I do not vant later people going here and there saying I did not do right. In a vay I benefit from his death. Since he has no relatives, he has left his fortune in the form of a bequest to Harvard Medical School. I am to administer the bequest with the advice of two doctors on the faculty—George Haskins and Person Story—and James Cranch Meeker, a Boston minister." He threw one of his hands up as if to implore the help of heaven. "His vill calls for the money to be used to study how to increase man's life span!"

"As vague as that?" Quincey asked.

Bach jerked his head in a nod. "You see the complications. Let us say that most men die of a disease. To choose a disease to study, let us say tuberculosis, which strikes so many and causes most to die young, vere does one begin? To spend all the money looking for the cause of this disease? I am a chemist. Certainly

I could make the case that a better laboratory helps the search. And I *need* a better laboratory. Very bad. But it could be argued that the money should go to set up more sanitaria to cure those who have the tuberculosis now. In Europe, Dr. Mesmer set up magnetic baths in an effort to heal. Haskins is much taken with the idea of the hypnosis used there. He vants very much such a place of his own here. And he could side vith Story, saying that the mind influences the body and the vay we care for our health. Story is a medical doctor, but he is now in the Mental Philosophy Department, vich studies the mind. As for this preacher, Meeker, he has undergone treatments using herbs to increase masculine vigor, as he puts it. He vill think all moneys should go to this. The arguments! Bah! It vill take my time away from my vork. Already you see it does."

"Why," Quincey asked him, "did you agree to administer the bequest? You imply Dr. Popkin was not a friend."

"Harvard Medical School has no money. Ve are housed next to Boston's hospital, and ve are crammed into corners and crannies of the building. The doctors on the faculty take no money from the university, except their salaries. They all have good practices. And they do not vant Harvard College looking over their shoulders, so they do not ask for money. I am there because they need a chemist, but they do not vant to pay for a good laboratory. No. And the Medical School is a scandal. These young men have a total of only sixteen veeks of lecture and demonstration. Then they vait for a few years, vorking with a doctor who teaches them vat he has a mind to teach. Then they take this simple test. Ve turn out doctors not ready to practice medicine. President Eliot insists on reform, but this vill take time. Much needs to be done, and it all costs money. I buy out of my own pocket supplies for my students and pay my own assistant. I must do my own experimentation at night ven the laboratory is empty. Any sizable amount, however used, vill help."

He paused and slowly drew the tips of his finger down his scar. "Then, let me tell you this. A friend is someone you like, so you spend time together. Did I like Popkin? No. Did ve spend time together? Yes. Ve did. Ve were students at Leipzig together. Ve could talk about the past. Vell, I talk, he nods, sometimes speaking a name. Only *he* knew me ven I vas young. I vas a good fencer, very good, no matter that I had no reach." Bach's voice held a world of loss as his thin arm stretched out his walking stick, then gave it a flick with a still supple wrist. His gesture made you see the quick flash of a sword. He stopped now as if to hear the distant laughter of young men ringing over the clash of their steel.

"You see?" he went on. "And I vorried that, if I say no, he might give the money to someone else. He knew I vill be careful with it. With money I was alvays. At school he had money. I did not, although my lineage was very good, unlike his. He was a selfish man, even then. Maybe it vas in his blood. His father started as a small moneylender and in the end had a big bank. But once Popkin helped me. Once. I did not forget. At the end, he had no one else but me. It is too bad, vat he has done to the others at the Medical School. He made Haskins's life a misery over some small cabinet with curios that he thought he vasn't paid enough for. I don't know. But vat did Popkin do? Every day, he marched into Haskins's lecture room, sat himself in the front row, and stared at the doctor all the time the man spoke, sometimes pointing a finger at him. And yet he still vent into Haskins's office now and again and took the cough drops from the jar on his desk, and not so much as a 'by your leave.' As for vat he did to Story, a man much liked by his colleagues, it was a scandal throughout the faculty. Popkin shared an office vith Story, a former student of Dr. James and now on the faculty himself, and during the vacation he opened a locked cabinet of the young man's. In there, Story kept coca leaves he'd brought back from an expedition with Agassiz to Peru. Popkin chewed every leaf. He'd learned that the Peruvian Indians did that and they are said to live long. Story has a generous nature, but such an intrusion! Then, vat he said to Meeker, a minister admired by all Boston—Ach, vy go on? You see my point!"

Quincey was staring at the ceiling as Bach spoke. At last, he looked first at him and then at Goss and said, "So what we have is this. There is only negative physical evidence that the man was murdered. Dr. Bonner cannot say *what* Popkin died of. For motive, *if* he was murdered, he did possess a fortune, but no one directly benefits from this." He addressed the professor. "Even you would have to explain your expenditures to the others."

As he was speaking, Newman Goss moved restlessly in his chair, but Quincey ignored him, asking Bach, "You say he was universally disliked, but would you say he was hated by any one person?"

The professor at first shook his head so quickly that his pigtail bobbled a bit and he opened his mouth. Then he stopped himself, glanced to his left, thinking, and fell silent. Finally he slowly brought out, "I do not know. One man vill draw his sword at some remark, yet another might shrug avay the same vords and forget even they vere said. Some brood over an insult and grow angrier than ven the vords vere said." He paused again before adding, "If I knew *how* he vas killed, then I could . . . at least I might . . . say a name."

Quincey nodded in agreement. "We must consider how he was murdered, *if* he was murdered. You are a chemist. You must know a great many substances that kill."

"I think and think. The range of poisons is, as you say, great. The corrosive ones—sulfuric and prussic acid. The metallic ones—arsenic, lead, zinc. And the vegetable ones—atropine, strychnine. But I am troubled at the fact that he did not vomit, have seizures as one does vith most of these. If he vas poisoned, it must also be one that acts slow. Ve had dinner together in the Commons. He ate just vat I and all the students ate. His appetite vas, as alvays, good. Then we came together in the hansom cab. Mr. Goss"—he gestured at the editor, who was still shifting in his chair—"and I have talked and ve did not see him putting anything into his mouth but the tea ve all drank vile vaiting for the séance to begin. Ve—Bonner and I—ve looked through his pockets. Only keys, a handkerchief, small purse with coins, scraps of paper he'd written on. No tins of pastilles, nothing like that. I vill think more."

"Ye-es," Quincey drew out the word. "We both should do that. I myself am familiar with quite a few of the vegetable toxins. Besides the ones you mention, some of the common plants—autumn crocus, bittersweet, bloodroot, castor bean, henbane, hemlock, wintergreen—all can be lethal. And any number of garden flowers such as lily of the valley, foxglove, lobelia can cause death."

With his bulging eyes fastened on Bach, he abruptly changed the subject, asking, "Do you regard the medium as credible?"

The professor again lifted a shoulder. "She knows

things. That I know. I vish she didn't know." He stopped, then spoke as if with a dry throat. "Can the dead speak? Or is it the living that have talked to her?"

As he spoke, I fiddled with my cane, not wanting to look at him. Because of the emotion in his voice, I was thinking that the scandal involved his family. He'd said he was poor when he was a student. On the other hand, it could have been Popkin's family. His father could have recovered financially. But, given the subject matter, Bach could hardly be questioned, although I was sure that Quincey wanted to know the answer to that.

His next remark was odd. "I am assuming, sir, that Dr. Popkin was an American citizen, and you are as well, but neither of you by birth."

"Correct. Both of us born in Austria, as vere his parents and my father. My mother vas from Italy. Tuscany. From a very good family."

That seemed to satisfy Quincey, although I couldn't see why. No one had mentioned Italy before, but he clearly regarded that as settling a question in his mind. He then stated flatly, "You're a scientist. You question the evidence of your senses. Therefore, while you are willing to examine any evidence, you're not *convinced* Dr. Popkin was murdered."

To his real surprise—his raised eyebrows pulled up his heavy lids—this answer came.

Bock Bach said, without hesitation, "Yes. I am convinced of that. Yes. But if I had not been at that séance, I vould say immediately 'No.' Any heart can stop, as Dr. Bonner vould be the first to say. But I saw Popkin's face. He vas *angry*. Horrified, too. Surprised. *He* thought he'd been killed. No matter how. So I believe those vere his vords. That he should speak of a piece of mineral then, I can't guess vat that vould mean. I vas often in his office, in his rooms, I did not see anything like that. I vill look for it, but maybe ve heard that wrong. But not the first part. I am a man of science, and I agree vith the philosopher Descartes—our senses can deceive us. But I saw, I heard, and I *feel* it is true that he vas killed. That is all I can say." He ended with deep regret in his voice. "Popkin should not have died now. No. It is wrong."

Suddenly he repeated that, anger sparking *his* eyes, "It is wrong!"

Newman Goss couldn't bear the lengthy discussion any longer. "Sir, we must make a decision instantly on the extra. At the moment, only we know the whereabouts of Miss Singer. But the other reporters will discover that she is staying with Mrs. Bedell here in Cambridge because they both were at the séance. Miss Singer might speak to them. I sent a man at first light with a note asking her not to, but she sent no reply. Since she is meeting with the Society for Psychical Research at the university, and since Dr. Popkin was a faculty member, it might occur to them to start their search for her there. We must get the paper on the streets *today*. We're only a few steps ahead of our competition."

Quincey slowly turned his head toward the editor. His words were a statement, not a question. "You are assured that it was murder."

"Yes, of course." Goss's tone was edged with impatience. "I was at the séance. I agree completely with Dr. Bach."

"Have you considered then that further publicity might endanger Miss Singer? The murderer might be as sure of her vaunted powers as you are, might believe that she did not say all that she might have. And, in fact, there is a possibility that the murderer will be with her at Harvard College this afternoon."

It was plain Goss hadn't thought of that. With a nervous flick of his hand, he brushed aside the blond hair on his forehead. Still, he recovered quickly. "My article for the extra edition makes plain that she's said all she knows. I would argue that it'd therefore be a protection for her if we publish it."

Quincey snapped out, "Any piece printed in the *Independent* on this subject must emphasize that *she* is the source of your information and that she can say nothing further regarding this man's death. You may add that a respected authority has raised doubts that he had a heart attack since that is a fact. Under those conditions, you may put out this special edition, despite the expense." He pulled his lips in and thrust them out before going on. "However, since the paper will not appear until this evening, that affords Miss Singer no protection at the moment. Not only will she be out in public, but I'd suppose she'll still be in Harvard Yard after nightfall. No doubt one of the men on the committee will accompany her, but professors are not often men of action. Nor would he be alert, not being aware of any problem."

Quincey was needling Goss, I was sure, since he didn't for a moment believe that Popkin was murdered and therefore Miss Singer could hardly be in danger.

Yet I was suddenly afraid she was. I came out with, "I'll go to the university and I'll wait for Miss Singer and her escort and accompany them."

Dr. Bach turned in my direction, took in my size, and nodded approvingly. My beard and my new jacket hid my weight loss. Perhaps he thought the cane across my lap was merely one of the walking sticks in common use. He nodded again. "That is good. A precaution, although I myself do not see that she can come to any harm  here. I vill send a note to

Dr. Story that you are coming. Then I can return to Boston and my laboratory." There was a great deal of satisfaction in his voice at that idea.

Quincey looked at me, and his eyelids were no longer at their usual half-mast position. Although he didn't so much as glance at my legs, I knew he was thinking that I was being foolish indeed. He was right in terms of the doctor's advice.

I said, "You'll recall that this is the Feast of All Hallows. I remember from my time there that on this night the students are apt to be . . . boisterous. They drink a great deal of punch, make bonfires of the raked leaves, overturn the outhouses by the dining hall. Some of the Canadian students even feel that setting off Roman candles is a good idea. An additional escort can do no harm."

Quincey was about to reply, but just then the clock chimed four times. He stood up immediately, saying, "You will forgive me, gentlemen, but I must now leave." It was time to go to the conservatory. He didn't explain that. Nor did he wait for a good-bye. He went straight to the hallway, turned the corner, and disappeared.

I was glad to see him go. If he'd pressed me on why I was going to Harvard Yard, I'd have been hard put to stick to my point about student pranks on Halloween. I wanted to meet Miss Singer, but that could be done comfortably at a tea party at the Craddocks'. While Quincey was right that, if Popkin was murdered, Sylvie Singer might be in danger, I wasn't convinced that he had been, despite Dr. Bock Bach's sureness.

My reason had nothing to do with reason. I felt the back hairs on my neck bristling.

# Chapter Eight

He tried to walk through me as if I were a ghostly presence, as transparent as air.

I was making my way slowly through the Yard toward Harvard Hall. Since I was there at least on the pretext of protecting Miss Singer, I'd brought only one cane. I didn't intend to *look* infirm. Luckily, it was planted in the gravel at the moment he blundered into my back, his tall hat bouncing off my shoulder blades, then flying backwards off his head. As I turned around, he was scooping it up and begging my pardon at once. "Do forgive me. I was reading"—he gestured with a worn leather folder stuffed with papers—"and not paying proper attention. I'm so sorry."

Barely into his thirties, he had thick dark hair, a mustache, and a goatee, which he'd probably grown to cultivate a professorial look. He hadn't bothered to trim his small beard, and it dipped raggedly down to the carelessly tied black cravat beneath his starched collar. There was a noticeable stain on his lapel which he clearly hadn't noticed. His hazel eyes were intense in his young face as he continued to explain. "I find, you see, that when I get to the dull bits, I start to skim and then I walk faster without noticing. Whereas when I come across an absorbing idea, I slow down so that I'm barely moving. But"—he smiled ruefully—"this man's account of a séance is boring beyond belief. He might as well have been describing a woman knitting! Yet, actually being at such a gathering is exciting."

His name was pricked out in gold letters on the old leather case. Person Story. He was one of those named in Popkin's will to decide how his fortune would be spent. The man whose coca leaves had been filched by Popkin. The professor of Mental Philosophy who'd taken over the classes of the William James that Quincey so admired. I'd expected someone much older. "I'm Michael Merrick." I held out my hand. "Dr. Bock Bach was to send you a note regarding my coming."

"Oh, yes. Good of you to come." Pronouncing his first name as "Pearson," he started to extend his own hand, found that it was still holding his hat, replaced that hurriedly without popping out the slight dent, and shook mine. Taking in my height, he added, "Very reassuring to have you." He didn't comment on whether he thought Miss Singer could possibly be in danger.

Instead, he fell into step beside me, slowing his own gait to match mine and picking up the conversation as if we were old friends continuing a discussion. "But Dr. James"—he pronounced the name with reverence—"says that often these notes written after the séance are thin and insignificant. The vital heat is missing and only ashes remain."

"I haven't been to one. What happens?" I asked with interest.

"I've attended quite a few. As part of our study. To many scientists, psychic phenomena are no less 'real' than other invisible forces, such as gravity or electricity, and are worthy of intellectual inquiry. Mind you"—he waved his folder, and only his tight grip on it kept the papers from flying out—"many of the

mediums are such glassy frauds that one has to hide a
smile at their tricks. Before he went abroad, Dr. James
was telling me about a woman in Watertown and the
amazing reports on her abilities to levitate furniture.
Able to float pianos, it was said. On observing her,
however, he found that it wasn't psychic force that en-
abled her to do this, but a very powerful knee."

His left arm brushed sideways emphatically, just
missing a passing underclassman. "Let me urge you
not to waste your time with any medium who pro-
fesses to materialize the spirits. I've seen ectoplasm,
as it's called, in all its forms from spidery wisps to
full-figure manifestations. You'll find that it always
comes from some orifice of the medium's body, usually the mouth." He came to a dead stop, almost trip-
ping up a high-hatted upperclassman behind him,
who obligingly went around him without a backward
glance. He went on. "Once, I saw a white, ribbony
substance come drifting out of a medium's nose!"
Grinning, with one hand he made a smoke-like spiral
reaching from his mustache up to the sky. "It's supposedly the spirit forming itself from the substance of
the medium's soul or body, you see. For that reason,
one is told never to touch the ectoplasm lest the
medium come to harm. But if you actually do touch it,
you're likely to find it's very much like cloth—a
gauzy chiffon." He started walking again. "Very impressive, though, in a dark room or in a photograph."

"So the camera does lie?"

"Let's say that it shows what's before it, and ap-
pearances deceive." His smile faded, and he went on
with some solemnity. "Yet. Yet. I've been in one of
those dimly lit rooms when suddenly, with chilling
force, you feel a presence. A weight to the air. No
sound at all. You can even feel its reluctance to be
there, as if it only came because of an anguished de-

sire on the part of someone in the room. And then it's gone. Or the planchette begins to move—have you seen this device?"

I shook my head.

"It's a heart-shaped piece of wood mounted on three gliders. It's said to respond to magnetic forces passing through the fingers, which guide the point of the instrument to a letter of the alphabet, thus spelling out a message from the spirits. Dr. James wrote a review of a book on the subject in which he quoted a man saying, 'I refuse to believe such things upon the evidence of other people's eyes, and I may possibly go so far as to protest that I would not believe them even on the evidence of my own.' Yet, last year, one was in front of me, and I lay my hand lightly on it. It suddenly began to move rather quickly. As the letters formed words, I forgot to breathe. That message had to be from—" The professor stopped, drew in his breath, and continued, "Someone I knew."

Now he was walking so slowly that I had to lessen my pace. In a quiet voice, he added, "So often, these occurrences come quite unexpectedly. A few months ago I was in a lighthearted group, one that was bantering with the medium's spirit guide—a Hindu, in this case, as a good many seem to be—when all of a sudden a woman's voice came from the medium's mouth. She spoke musingly of a day in the past. A trivial event recalled—this was a visit to a lovely old Southern plantation—brought up as you might in a conversation with someone close to you. The man beside me became as still and stiff as marble. Afterwards, he said with a trembling voice that he and his wife had gone on a tour of the South on their wedding trip and visited that mansion, but he'd by no means been thinking of that, and in fact, the house was destroyed during the war. It was as if she, who was long dead, was remembering it."

This account was all the more striking because of Story's tone. Although there might have been an edge of emotion, he was speaking with scientific detachment as if he were questioning even as he spoke.

"Let me explain this, too," he continued. "I began my career in medicine. But in my practice, I was impressed again and again with the way the mind could cure. Or not. I knew then I had to begin my studies over. Fortunately I started my new work with Dr. James. He has an amazing ability to hold opposing ideas in his mind comfortably. Of Spiritualism, he remarked, 'Either there exists a force of some sort not dreamed of in our philosophy, whether it be spirits or not, or this human testimony, voluminous in quantity, and from the most respectable sources, is but a revelation of universal human imbecility.'" Story added, "So interesting."

We were then nearing the entrance of Harvard Hall, and he fumbled out his pocket watch. It had an unusual small fob, embroidered with bright red hair. "I suspect I'm late again. Yes, I am. They'll be all assembled and waiting. I'm sorry not to be able to ask you to attend this meeting of the Society, but it's a closed one since we'll be talking to Miss Singer about working with us. I'm most impressed with her, and all the others are equally so with the reports we have of her. So many of the mediums we've interviewed, although infinitely obliging, are not able to express themselves. Miss Singer is intelligent and articulate. We shouldn't be all that long, though. We wouldn't want to tire her or Mrs. Bedell, who's come as a chaperone. There's some chairs in the small adjoining room and reading material, as I recall. I'll look for you there afterwards."

With a warm smile, he sprang up the stairs and

hurried through the wide doors. I followed him more slowly.

The room he'd indicated was a remembrance of Harvard's Calvinist past—straight-backed wooden chairs, bare floors, and shelves of dusty historical tomes. It was designed to remind all the young "limbs of Satan" who attended that they'd better sit uncomfortably upright because otherwise they'd have a hard struggle to escape eternal damnation. Too tense to settle in any of those uninviting chairs, I walked to the window.

Staring outside, I wondered what threat could be *here?* The wide expanse of Harvard Yard, the lawn crisscrossed by paths, was surrounded by solid buildings of mellow brick, some draped with yet unwithered ivy. It could have been a castle courtyard built to keep out intruders. Above, the solid clouds were a sheltering ceiling on the mild last day of October. Students, freed from their classes and recitations, were everywhere, ignoring the paths, rushing, strolling, in groups and alone.

And where could danger come from? I glanced up at the mullioned windows of residence halls and then down at a group of laughing young men hurrying by. Had a wild-eyed killer rushed through the Yard, bent on hurtling toward Miss Singer with a knife, he'd have been tripped by a heedless underclassman who then would have picked him up, retrieved his weapon, and apologized profusely before running off.

All I could do was keep a careful eye out. If Popkin was murdered, his killer was resourceful. And *he* might see Sylvie Singer as a threat, not knowing she was a fraud. She was. I had to agree with Quincey on that. She'd gathered information on the people who'd be attending the séance, no doubt by talking to the artless Emily Craddock and others in Mrs. Bedell's circle. While sitting and drinking tea with their friends, most people were not as silent as Dr. Popkin. And while Newman Goss wrote that he'd never mentioned the ghost in the nursery to anyone, he probably had. It was a good story, and he wasn't the sort of man who'd keep it to himself.

Just then, I realized that I, a reporter myself, was being influenced by what he wrote about this woman! Astarte. I was even attributing a mysterious, dark inner voice to her. Shrugging, I blamed it on my drifty state of convalescence. She had a handsome figure and was probably of average looks, but I'd allowed Goss's description of her, exaggerated to make a better story, to slide into my imagination.

"Sir!" A sonorous voice suddenly filled the room.

Turning from the window, I took in the man standing just inside the door. Dressed in a fitted dark suit with a soberly rich gray-silk weskit, he was not overly tall or broad, but his presence made him seem a larger man. He doffed his tall hat, revealing silvery hair swept back from a broad forehead, inclined his head an inch, and asked, "I beg your pardon. I wish to attend the meeting on magnetism. Is it in this building, do you know?"

"The only gathering I'm aware of is the Society for Psychical Research in the next room."

"That some of our ablest men here at the College are engaged in such a pursuit!" A small, painful line creased his expansive brow. "Even some of my flock! No, the group I seek are conducting a genuinely *scientific* inquiry into a new method of healing, led by Dr. George Haskins of the Medical School."

He stepped in and sat down on one of those hard chairs. "Forgive the intrusion. A friend will be coming here to meet me, and he'll know the location of the lecture." As he laid his hat aside, I noticed again that artful sweep of hair and recalled a newspaper wood-cut. This was James Cranch Meeker, another of the men mentioned in Dr. Popkin's will.

The article that came with that etched drawing gave an account of a lecture by Cranch Meeker against Darwin's theory of evolution. After he spoke, he stood to the side of the backlit stage. Two men rolled in a draped box. With a dramatic flourish, he uncovered it to reveal a caged ape. The frightened animal screamed, gibbered, slobbered, and threw itself at the bars. All the while, the minister, wearing a flowing white choir robe, his majestic head held high, stood silently beside it, his eyes on the open Bible in his hand. Everyone in the hall agreed it was a complete refutation of Darwin's ideas.

Slipping a newspaper from beneath his arm, he snapped it open disapprovingly. It was this afternoon's extra edition of the *Independent*. He caught my eye and commented, "Yet another article on this medium. She's a shameless woman. The theatrics she indulges in! Yet she's worse than a common actress, appearing in a gown that's little more than a nightdress, no doubt exposing much of her body, with her hair loose. The point of it all is to seduce men! And the dangers of this movement that she espouses! There's no doubt that insanity, prostitution, and Spiritualism go hand in hand. I shall have to bear witness even more strongly from the pulpit against this evil."

While there was nothing of the soapbox or revival tent about Meeker, his outer polish didn't hide the zealotry in his words. He went on, "I can hardly credit that this Miss Singer is admitted to society. Moreover, a member of my congregation informed me she's a fallen woman, having lived with a married man. How she can have access to the proper circles baffles me."

That remark explained why Emily Craddock said it "wasn't possible" for Sylvie to stay with them. I replied, "I understand Miss Singer is a guest of a Mrs. Bedell, who lives in Cambridge."

Meeker's face cleared. "Mrs. Walter Bedell? She often attends our church. A woman of substance. Ah, well. No doubt she sees this as a Christian act. She's a widow and has no one to guide her properly."

It seemed clear that he wasn't going to criticize anyone in Mrs. Bedell's social position. If *she* wished to have a medium on the premises, that would be acceptable.

I didn't answer, but I wondered what this man would suggest Sylvie do to support herself. As he indicated, marriage was out of the question, and what wife would hire her as a maid? She could put herself, as the saying went, "under the protection" of a rich man, presumably one already married. I thought about that. She'd have empty days and nights. This man would be busy with his other life. None of his peers would censure him, but everyone would condemn her. There'd be no callers. Respectable women would shun her, and they wouldn't allow their husbands to even glance at her. There'd be none of the pleasures that lighten a young woman's heart. There'd be no point in beautiful gowns. No dinner parties, no balls, no evenings at the theater. She would simply wait in the elegant house he'd provide until he came. Perhaps he'd bring a jeweled necklace for her. But no one else would ever see how it graced her. Anyone's sense of worth would crumble in such circumstances.

I shifted my gaze uneasily back out the window. I couldn't afford any more sympathy for her. She'd have to be exposed. By me.

After a few moments, another well-dressed man bustled in, spilling apologies because of a misprint regarding the time and place of the lecture. The minister stood up quickly, nodded a farewell to me, and the two hurried off.

Pacing the room, I had my pocket watch out every five minutes. A long hour dragged by. The new skin on my feet and legs was being stretched, but I couldn't sit for long. I kept ending up at the window, staring out restlessly.

Suddenly, the side door to the adjoining room opened and Dr. Story came out, deep in conversation with Sylvie Singer. She was wearing the flowing gray-silk dress she'd worn in the morning. She didn't glance at me, but I was staring at her. I was sure I knew her. I stood absolutely still, shocked by the recognition. I tried to imagine where we could have met or under what circumstances. And then I tried to imagine how I could have forgotten a woman that beautiful.

# Chapter Nine

As she moved nearer, I let out my breath. I knew why she was familiar. Sylvie Singer had the face—heart-shaped, flawless—of Botticelli's famous portrayal of Venus. If I described her that way to Quincey, he'd snort and ask if she'd been standing on a scallop shell. He'd question anything else I said about her, sure that I couldn't be objective. But she could have been the Italian painter's model.

I tried not to stammer through the introductions, but I've no idea what I said.

She took my arm as we set off sedately down the steps from the hall. Mrs. Bedell and Dr. Story were behind us. I kept glancing at Sylvie sideways, still struck by the resemblance, which might have ended with her face. I couldn't tell. Her light hair didn't flow around her shoulders in clinging curls. It was hidden in front by the forward slant of her stylish bonnet and in back by a satin bow. Over her high-necked dress she now wore a flowing cloak of Scottish wool in gray and heather colors. Those colors emphasized her cool composure. The narrow width of the ruffled skirt beneath her bustled overskirt required her to take small steps on the uneven path of Harvard Yard.

Her beauty distracted. It was luminous, like the silver shimmer in the gray silk of her dress. Moreover, in the portrait, the goddess is looking sweetly down, whereas Miss Singer kept her blue gaze fixed on my face as I spoke. I couldn't recall any other woman doing that because society would have considered that bold and unlady-like. Even a man wouldn't continue to look so directly at another under ordinary circumstances. But it was immensely flattering in this case.

Still, I was unlikely to become infatuated with Sylvie Singer because I was already in love with someone else. She was a Shaker, and Shakers are celibate. Nor would she leave the Society. So I had to distance myself from that love. I refused to think her name. That didn't help. Her image rose in my mind, and I could suddenly see her, dressed in her sober beliefs, walking down her narrow, shining path. It took an effort of will to thrust her out of my mind.

I cleared my throat. All I could come up with was, "The pleasant October weather has continued to the end of the month."

Sylvie's eyes were again on my face, and she nodded, but the very clarity of her eyes hid her thoughts. Her reserved demeanor added to the elusiveness of her mind.

Any attempt to think clearly was further confounded by that insistent prickling down my back. I kept glancing up and sideways.

Behind us, Dr. Story and Mrs. Bedell were conversing, or rather exchanging comments. She'd mentioned Boston's rapid growth. He replied, "The project of filling in the Back Bay, which will add land, seems to be going well, no doubt due to the fine weather."

The brief introduction to Mrs. Bedell in the anteroom in Harvard Hall made me think that mundane topics were probably the safest conversational course to steer with her. She was a small, nervous woman with darting eyes, whose movements were quick

twitches. The high, white-feather cockade she was
wearing in her dark-red turban, fluttered jerkily. And
she was given to sudden unexpected outbursts. Perhaps she felt she was uninteresting and tried to make
up for it by being dramatic. As we waited for the
cloaks to be brought, I'd asked her about her interest
in Spiritualism. She said it was recent because her delicate health meant she was often confined to her
home, explaining, "Dr. Haskins says that he has *never*
before seen such a case of weakness of the nerves. I
have tremors, tears, and headaches caused by, as he
puts it, 'feelings tender to a fault.'" She described
these in some detail, adding that the doctor begged
her to spend as much of the day lying down as she
could. Then she exclaimed, "But those dear to me
who have passed on are always with me! I feel the
footsteps of pale spirits treading as thick as snow on
my sofa and my bed, by day and night." It was hard
to know how one should reply to that.

Catching the quiet murmur of their voices, I decided that Dr. Story had a calming effect on her, despite the fact that his energy was what struck you on
meeting him. His warmth of manner was appealing.
Escorting Mrs. Bedell out the door of the Hall, he took
her arm as if he'd been hoping all day for the opportunity to walk with her.

Miss Singer had fastened on mine with what seemed
relief. From the strain around her mouth, I gathered
that the meeting with the professors had tired her. She
didn't need any more questions. Nodding in the direction of Holworthy Hall, I said that I was lucky to
have been housed there. It was the first of the residence halls to abandon the medieval monk system of
one very small room per scholar. Besides the bedroom, I'd had a pleasant study overlooking the Yard.
As I spoke, I remembered the mornings and after-

noons reading there. She listened, unsmiling, but with such care, as if my casual remarks were of real interest to her.

Halfway to the gate by the Common where Mrs. Bedell's carriage waited, we stopped to let a procession of underclassmen in their visor caps cut across the path in front of us. They were running, laughing, carrying loads of leaves in their arms to the bonfire, dropping quite a few of them. Behind them strolled a few upperclassmen in their top hats, who were carrying nothing. They slowed their pace even further as they approached us and managed to stare discreetly at Miss Singer. As we stood, she remarked on the sweetness of the autumn air. The tall elms were now surrounded with their drifting leaves, which had a scent of sun-warmed brown earth. Glancing across the still-green lawn of the Yard, where scattered scarlet maples blazed in the twilight against the graceful facades of the Federal-style buildings, she went on, "This is like an elegant park, isn't it? It must have been a wonderful place to study."

Agreeing politely, I was suddenly swept up in a memory of strolling on this path with my father when I was just a boy. Since I grew up in Cambridge, the two of us often came this way on a summer evening. I was smiling as I told her. "My father wasn't so lucky. He said—of course, this was almost fifty years ago when he was a student here—the Yard was almost treeless and cluttered up with a brewhouse, stored wood, and a good-sized pigpen." I left out the privies dotted about that he'd mentioned. Outhouses that were often tipped on Halloween. "Sheep from the Common next door wandered over to graze, and the squeals of the pigs waiting to be fed would interrupt classes. Then President Kirkland took office, and by the end of his administration, he'd managed to change all that. My father pointed with as much pride at the growing trees and green grass as if he'd planted them." As I spoke, I could almost feel his large, comforting hand wrapped around mine. He'd died when I was only eleven, and I still grieve for him. With tightness in my throat, I concluded, "He'd enjoy seeing it now."

With sympathy, she said, "It must have been hard to lose him when you were so young."

My arm jerked beneath her hand, and I turned quickly to look at her. Servants' gossip couldn't account for her knowing when my father died.

Her smile was almost a wince. "No, Mr. Merrick, my assumption that your father died early in your life is not a medium's insight, but a simple mathematical computation. I'm sure you're not yet thirty. If he was a student here fifty years ago, when he was near twenty, then you must have been born when he was in his forties, or nearly. If he were alive, he'd be in his seventies. Yet if he'd died recently, you wouldn't have had that world of regret in your voice because you'd have considered that at least he had a long, full life. And," she finished, "he'd have seen the Yard in its glory."

I stammered slightly as I said, "Of course."

"That is one of the problems with working in my 'trade'—I suppose you could call it that. People seem to feel that spirits are constantly whispering in my ear, that I know things that I don't. Even during the most ordinary conversation, they're apt to scrutinize my simplest remark for some meaning, look at me oddly, as if I were not 'one of them.'" She stopped for a moment and then went on, "When I was young in Kansas, there were covered wagons that would go from town to town in the summer. The drivers would hastily set up a canvas booth, and those in the wagons would emerge with sheets draped over them and go directly into the booth. Once inside, the sheets were removed and they sat in chairs around the cloth walls. They were malformed, deformed people, known as 'freaks.' One man had flippers growing from his shoulders instead of arms. Two men were twins conjoined at the back. One woman's face was so scrunched together that she looked like a pug dog. The townsfolk would pay their pennies to come and stare at them. Sometimes I feel quite as much on display as they were."

I would have expected bitterness in her voice at such an observation, but there was a cool matter-of-factness instead. I didn't know what to say. I wanted to reply that she had a right to any complaint about being on display because no doubt that was how she had felt answering the professors' questions. But on such a slight acquaintance, I could hardly express such a sentiment. She didn't seem to want sympathy, let alone pity.

Her next remark was equally unexpected, especially because she spoke so gravely. "Do forgive me," she said. "It's just that I couldn't bear that *you* should be influenced by my occupation as most others are. I feel as if I know you, probably because Miss Craddock spoke so highly of you. She's making plans for a tea party for us, and I'm quite looking forward to it. Usually on social occasions, I confine myself to simple statements, the tritest of observations, but I'm hoping that we can talk as friends do."

That implied compliment was certainly graceful. I could see why she charmed everyone she met. I could also see a self-interested motive in all she'd said to me this evening. It was an effort to make me believe she was a misunderstood but genuine medium, even though she didn't enjoy her work. She wanted to erase any question in my mind that she practiced deceit in her craft. Emily must have told her quite a bit about their neighbor, Jasper Quincey, and me. It was certainly in Sylvie's best interests to enlist us as supporters. The power of his newspaper and his friendship with Gideon Craddock made him quite an ally. And I provided access to him. She was a beautiful, bright, and very calculating woman. I decided that I had to keep that in the front of my mind. Having arrived at this conclusion about her, I wanted to change the subject. I took her last statement as a signal to do so and I waited to see what she'd say.

Her voice was low and soft. "I feel you're performing an act of real friendship coming this evening. This walk can't be easy for you." Yes, I thought, Emily had told her all about me, including the injuries I was so vainly trying to hide. But her next remark caught me up. "You think there's a possibility of danger, don't you?"

I took in a deep breath. She hadn't had a chance to speak to Goss, nor would he or Bach have told her of our discussion this afternoon. So she might have her own fears. She was too intelligent to accept a denial from me. I hesitated.

Looking up at me, she continued unsmilingly. "But perhaps I presume too much. It's just that Miss Craddock mentioned you were still recovering, so I thought you must have a purpose in coming when it involved such exercise. And then your eyes are never still, Mr. Merrick. You are watchful."

Her left arm shivered in mine, but she waved her right hand dismissively. "I'm probably being influenced by the calendar. A hallowed evening. Tomorrow is All Saints Day, isn't it? The day we honor the dead. But I think this night's feast of disembodied spirits arouses anxiety. Probably that's why the young engage in pranks and making noise."

Just then, as if to underline her point, there was a bang, a sizzle, and a Roman candle arched upward in the darkening sky. We all stopped to follow its fiery red-and-gold trail. Cheers and loud shouts rose throughout the Yard, and there was a rush toward the high-piled leaves near us. A sharp odor of kerosene, and then the fire sprang to light. "Not yet!" someone hollered. A heavy-set youth carrying a huge basket of leaves raced across our path, yelling back, "Yes, yes. We've got wood, too. We can keep it going for hours."

At that moment, Dr. Story touched my arm and asked apologetically, "Sir, would you mind seeing the ladies to the carriage? I seem to have left my papers back at the hall, and I'd planned on going over them tonight. I'll have to go back for them."

Before I could respond, Mrs. Bedell broke in. "We'd be happy to wait for you, wouldn't we, Sylvie? I so enjoy a bonfire, and there may be more candles set off. This is quite delightful. There is nothing here that could possibly offend a lady. Even my dear Walter, who is always near me in spirit, would not object, I know. As for the night air being injurious, it is still early in the evening." She didn't wait for an answer, putting a gloved hand on my elbow. There was more than a trace of a satisfaction in her next words. "My carriage is large and seats four comfortably. My coachman will drive you and Mr. Merrick to your residences after taking us to Brattle Street." She nodded her head so firmly that the high feathers in her wine-red turban swayed.

After that, I could hardly do anything but agree, but I knew I'd be much more relaxed when they were safely in that carriage. Story hurried off in a rather awkward trot. The three of us turned to watch the students getting in one another's way as some added to the fire and others danced about, stomping on scattering sparks. A knot of them some twenty yards from us were bending over something on the ground. One broke away, shouting, "I'll get the pole." Another called out before he disappeared, "And more rope, Ted."

It wasn't long before he returned, holding aloft a thin, stripped log taller than he was. A length of rope dangled from one end. His friends surrounded him, heaving up a burlap bundle, cinched in the middle, and tied again near the rounded top. They fastened it to one end of the pole, although their laughing and pushing made the process slow. It was very roughly the size and shape of a man. "Who's got the sign? Who's got it?" Several of them were shouting at once.

"Whatever can they be doing?" Mrs. Bedell asked.

"Some unpopular professor is going to be burned in effigy. We won't know who until we read the sign on the 'body.' Perhaps it's the President of Harvard College," I answered with a smile.

Her reply came out in a shocked whisper. "The President! Mr. Eliot! How disrespectful! He must be a scholar, a highly intelligent man, to have such a post. I'm sure he cares a great deal about these young men, and he certainly would know what's best for them." She elaborated on this idea for a full minute, pointing out that while she had never met Mr. Eliot, all the better people of Cambridge spoke highly of him.

I didn't interrupt her to explain the intense political maneuvering that went on in choosing the man for that post. The Massachusetts legislature had to approve and, since the university was divided between Calvinists and Unitarians, each of those groups wanted one of their own. Occasionally, a superb leader emerged. Occasionally. Perhaps this time.

Several students were whacking at the burlap figure, and Mrs. Bedell drew her breath in sharply. "Whatever could they find wrong with what he does?"

I was watching the scene with nostalgic amusement. I tried to explain briefly. "Possibly they're unhappy, not with the President, but with college policy. There were many protests until the compulsory evening prayers were abolished. Then, I remember that the students campaigned for a long time to have modern languages taught, as well as Latin and Greek."

"How foolish of them! A gentleman only needs a command of the *ancient* languages. And they can't be that difficult to acquire. Sylvie, who's a woman, was taught Greek by Dr. Craddock, and he said she learned with amazing quickness."

Miss Singer, who was holding my opposite arm, may not have heard that. She was staring intently at the fire's leaping and the joyful commotion around it. Mrs. Bedell had her eyes on it, too, although her expression was a frown of disapproval.

Still, she said, "Let us go a little closer. Perhaps we'll be able to read the sign and tell who they're burning. The ground is quite dry, Sylvie, and won't ruin our slippers." Clutching my left arm tightly, she darted straight ahead, almost pulling me along and Sylvie with me. We stopped just this side of a thick-trunked oak. We were now directly in front of the fire, although some ten yards away. Mrs. Bedell leaned across me, her plumes of feathers almost tickling my nose, and asked, "Dearest Sylvie, would you very much mind coming round and taking my other arm? That way I'll have the advantage of the warmth of your cloak."

Addressing me, she said, "Really, the moment I saw that garment—imported from Scotland, and I do

think the colors are all misty as that country is re-
puted to be—I knew that I had to acquire it for Miss
Singer. It so suits her. And, of course, the Celts are
known for their second sight. She is partly Celtic."
Without responding to that, Sylvie took her other
arm, draping the cloak over it.

Two loud pops, one right after the other, burst on
our ears, and two Roman candles scorched skyward,
one on each side of the bonfire. At that, the burlap figure was raised to thunderous yells and applause. A
chant began. "Hang him high. High. High." The students holding the pole advanced toward the flames,
and I craned my neck, without success, to read the
sign.

Just as the bottom of the burlap caught fire, there
was another sharp crack. I looked up. There was no
sign of fireworks. Jerking my head in the other direction, I saw that Mrs. Bedell's turban was pushed
down on her forehead and its feather cockade was cut
in half as if by a bullet. It took me a second to realize
it *had* been slashed off by a bullet.

With one long stride, I yanked both women behind
the oak's trunk. In my rush, I almost lifted Mrs. Bedell
off her feet and she was indignantly protesting, all the
while trying to straighten her hat with her free hand.
"Mr. Merrick, *whatever*—"

A second burst of noise and the rope holding the
burlap effigy snapped, sending the figure down into
an upleaping burst of flames. "Great shot!" one of the
underclassman cried out, looking over his shoulder at
the hall behind us. He threw his visored cap in the air.
"Hurray!" he yelled. Those behind him all spun in
that direction, too, and when they saw the glint of a
rifle barrel in one window of Holworthy, sent up a
roar of cheers. The gun was abruptly withdrawn.

Sylvie, who'd jerked her head upward when they

did, saw it, too. She dropped her hold on my arm and pressed herself against the rough bark of the tree for support. Mrs. Bedell, still sputtering, was only occupied with settling her turban properly and at last patted it in place. Then her fingers touched the ruined cockade. "What happened to my feathers? Why, why, they've been . . . taken off!"

The students near us were marveling at the expertise of the rifleman, calling out their compliments toward the second-story window where the gun had appeared. One upperclassman doffed his top hat and bowed in that direction, saying, "Perfect shooting. Cut the rope in half, by George. Full marks, sir!"

"Mr. Merrick, why is there all this talk of shooting?" Susanna Bedell was almost babbling.

"It's over, ma'am." My words came out of a very dry throat. "It's all right. Some young man just letting his rifle off to make noise. No one was hurt."

"A gun? A gun, you say? So my feather was shot. The feather on my hat. That's what happened. They could have hit my—"

Her hand on my arm slipped away. She didn't sway but crumpled immediately downward in a faint. I only managed to catch her limp body before it hit the ground.

# Chapter Ten

"Someone . . . is trying to kill me." Mrs. Bedell's voice was quivery, and her breath came out in shallow gasps. "It's the only explanation. A woman of my social position, knowing so many people, can quite unwittingly . . . offend someone. I *must* have done so. That is the fact of it, my dear sir." She clung tightly to my hand, her eyes on my face. She was reclining on a maroon velvet chaise in her front parlor. The dark red of her turban, with its sliced-off feather, emphasized her pallor. Her housekeeper was rushing about in search of medications, her maid was draping her with warm shawls, and the butler was going out the door to summon her doctor. Sylvie stood behind the chaise, chafing her other hand. Although Story gently advised her to rest and lie quietly, now that Mrs. Bedell had come out of her shocked silence in the carriage, she clearly preferred talking.

"It's obvious," she went on, "that this . . . person has been following me for some time. Seeing his chance tonight, he fired at me. I shall never . . . forget this horrible evening, Mr. Merrick, but I shall always remember that it was you who saved my life by your quick thinking." She tried to draw in air. "My dear Walter, ever watchful over my welfare from the other side, must have guided you to me. My nerves, of course, will never recover, but I shall always be grateful to you."

Throughout all this, Sylvie didn't even glance at me. I couldn't guess whether she too believed that Mrs. Bedell was the target. Yet I'd seen her right after the shooting, eyes wide-staring, dark blue in the dusk, filled with surprised fear. What was odd was that she hadn't turned her head, didn't look to see where danger might lie. She'd stood perfectly still, as if listening. A few seconds later, she was by my side as I bent over her friend, telling me that there'd be some smelling salts in Mrs. Bedell's purse.

Story had come running up when he saw us. It took the efforts of both of us to get the distraught older woman to her carriage. I knew that right then was the time to rush to Holworthy, question anyone who might be in the Hall, and ask bystanders what they'd seen. But getting the two women out of the Yard was first. I'd come back as quickly as I could.

Prying a name out of Susanna Bedell, should she have a particular person who wanted to kill her in mind, couldn't be done now. Nor was I going to be allowed even a few private words with Sylvie. That would have to wait.

Observing that the women were in good hands now, I said, "You both must be in need of rest. Please allow me to call in the morning to inquire after your health." Story echoed my sentiment. Throughout our farewells, Sylvie never met my eyes.

Quincey needed to hear about this immediately. That rifle could have been aimed at Sylvie. Getting the gun wasn't impossible. Any number of fowling pieces might be kept by students in their rooms. But someone would have to know which room. Too, only a few people knew she'd be in the Yard about that time. Or where in the Yard.

Dr. Story, of course, knew exactly where she'd be, and he'd left us waiting there while he disappeared.

His work would benefit from the distribution of Popkin's fortune. If those shots were aimed at her, he'd head the list of suspects who had opportunity as well as financial motive. And Bock Bach had mentioned that relations between Story and Popkin were strained. Any man, no matter how good-natured, would react strongly to the ransacking of a locked drawer and the taking of coca leaves he wanted for research.

Quincey could talk to him, ask him detailed questions and assess his truthfulness, while I hurried back. Story accepted my invitation to the house. He seemed as unsettled as I was. Although he was quiet in the carriage, he was combing his ragged goatee with gloved fingers and riffling the edges of the papers he clutched in his hands.

Outside the curtained windows of the carriage, the night was loud. Students were in the streets, yelling, calling to each other, and hansom cabs rattled by. But, shoving the curtain aside, I could see only shadowy figures in the scattered gaslight. Even Mrs. Bedell's spirited white horses couldn't move quickly down Brattle Street, clogged as it was. The slowness of our progress made me even edgier.

Turning to Story, I asked him directly if he thought Miss Singer was in danger.

His answer came slowly. "Whatever the explanation for those gun shots, I'm not at all easy in my mind that she's perfectly safe. I don't mean that any attempt on her would necessarily have a connection with Dr. Popkin's death. What I'm saying is this. Because of the articles in the *Independent*, something unpleasant, if not dangerous, could happen to her if she becomes the focus of the general intolerance aimed at the Spiritualists."

He added, "I don't like to bring this up before Mr.

Quincey, since that is his newspaper and it might sound as if I were criticizing the inclusion of stories about her. But some of their opponents are zealots, fanatically opposed to the movement. When a newspaper in New York ran an article on a man who was trying to design a machine to harness spiritual electricity, a mob broke into his home and smashed it to bits. His life was threatened as well. If at all possible, Miss Singer's name should be kept out of the press." He spoke apologetically, but insistence lay behind his words.

"Mr. Quincey is sure to agree," I said dryly. "But I don't quite see why so much feeling is aroused by this topic. Basically, the Spiritualists are asserting that the human spirit survives, which all our religions maintain. Is it the fear that devils appear instead of loved ones, as the preachers have it?"

"That's often the text of sermons, but it goes much deeper, Mr. Merrick. Much. This movement's beliefs call into question the role of women in our society. Most of the mediums are women. For centuries, you know, they've been excluded from the 'higher mysteries.' Yet in a sense, they're serving as priestesses at the séances. That's quite clear to the hierarchies of the established religions, who are all men. They're strongly opposed to the idea that women should presume to take over their role. Perhaps it stirs up ancient memories when women had that power. I find it interesting that, on seeing Miss Singer, a comparison to the Phoenician goddess Astarte sprang to Mr. Goss's mind. Think of the Greek Oracle, or the Vestal Virgins of Rome who kept the sacred fire."

"Do you think they're aware of that ancient connection?" I asked doubtfully.

"At some level, yes," he returned. "But then you have to consider, too, that these women are being

paid. Not large sums, but it gives them some economic choice. A wife who can support herself might
leave her husband, especially if the man is a drunk-
ard, one who harms her. Then we'd have a dissolved
family, done by a woman's choice. This threat may be
behind the law in Alabama that forbids the practice of
mediumship. In addition, there's an outspoken group
of women who regard marriage as a prison and who
advocate free love. All of its members are Spiritualists."

Story held his hand up abruptly. "Not that the other
way around is true. Most people involved in the
movement wouldn't defend the idea of free love."

I wondered if Sylvie Singer had been asked at his
meeting if she espoused that idea. I was about to ask
but, scratching his mustache thoughtfully, he said,
"The specter of divorce rises up at another, more
widespread Spiritualist precept. The idea of an 'eternal union,' which is as old as mysticism itself. It goes
like this: The infant was born married, and somewhere or other is the exact half of his nature, waiting
to be united to him. This 'true marriage' is necessarily
indissoluble. A divine matehood. If this spiritual
counterpart is discovered after a 'transient marriage'
has been undertaken, a divorce should take place because there wasn't a true union and it would interfere
with the 'reunion' of the counterparts. Some even say
that divorces are natural until the harmonial plane is
reached. Those who hold to the idea of reincarnation
go further. This eternal union lasts throughout time.
The two soul mates may even switch genders."

The papers he was holding slipped out of Story's
fingers, and he fumbled on the floor picking them up.

When he straightened, I replied, "I see your point.
Every cleric would denounce any such threat to the
family. And they could arouse their congregations."

"Then, simply because Miss Singer is most attractive, she might become a target for this anger and fear." Story stopped and added musingly, "Do you know she reminds me a good deal of Botticelli's painting of Venus? Moreover, she dresses fashionably, conventionally, and she's quite well spoken. In that way, she's like Miss Victoria Woodhull, and you know the bitterness, rancor, and abuse directed at her."

I'd read about her. "You have to admit, though, that *she* actively courts the press. I suppose she has to as she's declared her candidacy for the Presidency of our country."

"Even if women had the vote, Miss Woodhull could hardly be elected because of her radical ideas. Have you seen those newspaper drawings of her, invariably with Satanic horns? No doubt she's portrayed that way because she espouses free love."

That was just the opening I wanted. "Do you know Miss Singer's opinion on that?"

I could hear the smile in Story's voice. "I believe that several of the men on the committee this afternoon very much wanted to know. But with Mrs. Bedell, who would hardly approve of the question, sitting primly beside her, no one had the courage to ask. I did bring up the idea of eternal union. I don't think she'd mind my repeating her answer. She looked kindly at Mrs. Bedell and said, 'I'm sure love survives time. But it seems to me hard enough to find a compatible partner without having to search the wide world for your exact counterpart.'" He drew in his breath. "Miss Singer looks at you so candidly when she speaks that she gives the impression she's replied fully and honestly to what you asked."

"But it'd be useful, wouldn't it, in trying to assess her powers, to know her opinions on these Spiritualist

beliefs? And she seems unwilling to hold séances.
Maybe she'd give her reasons if she were alone."

He shrugged. "That's unlikely to happen. Mrs. Bedell or the elder Miss Craddock would always come
with her. I'm unmarried. Cambridge is a small town,
and Miss Singer must be 'protected' against any hint
of gossip, particularly since something of Miss Singer's
history is known. She has a child and no husband."

"She does have a child? Do you know the name?"

Story thought for a moment. "Yes. She mentioned
the boy. Robin."

I pushed back against the carriage seat. So I was
right about that. I wanted to tell Story about my experience in the courtyard. But I didn't. I couldn't rule
him out as the rifleman. In fact, he might have
brought up a danger to her from fanatical opponents
to Spiritualism as a way of disguising his own in-
volvement.

The muffled sound of the horses' hooves meant
we'd left the cobblestoned streets behind and were
now on the country road that led past the Craddocks'
to Quincey's house. I let out my breath with relief. I
was hoping that, in talking to Story, he could draw
something useful out of him.

The man was likable, and in his defense, it was
hard to imagine him as a crack shot. That required a
steady hand and a good eye, even with the best rifle.
Too, reloading quickly took adroitness. Story seemed
to have a handful of thumbs, and he kept forgetting
what his body was up to.

He was saying now, "The Spiritualists, of course,
are much influenced by Swedenborg's idea that
there's no gulf fixed between this life and the one beyond death and—"

The cab pulled up before Quincey's wrought-iron
fence, and the gate was, for a wonder, open. The

lanterns atop the two brick posts on either side lighted the path to the door and pushed back the shadows of the huge elm trees on either side of the path. The Georgian front of the three-storied house, with its balancing shorter wings on either side, faced the road with cool certainty. Tonight, the lamps shining in the twelve-paned windows mellowed the brick and took away the usual austerity of the facade.

I hustled Story out of the carriage as quickly as I could. He stumbled on the way to the door, but that didn't have to indicate nervousness. He was still talking about Swedenborg.

# Chapter Eleven

"It was criminally careless of that student to fire at the effigy. Reckless in the extreme. Any bystander might have been hit." Quincey rumbled this out, standing by the library fireplace filled with crackling applewood logs, his hands clasped behind his back. That was his theory, and I could see he was going to stick to it.

As soon as I introduced Dr. Story, explained what happened, and brought out my intention of returning to the Yard, he held up a hand. "We should send Hoggett instead." He rang for Freegift and began writing, saying as he did so, "You'll seriously slow your recovery if you continue walking, Michael. In addition, if *you* question those young men, they'll give vague answers, fearing they could cause trouble for one of their fellows. Hoggett, dressed as a groundsman or a janitor, can act as if he's simply agog with curiosity over the excitement. They'll tell him the true story. And he can wander through the hallways, ostensibly checking the gas jets, and find his way to the right room, perhaps even locate the gun. By this time, the punch will be taking effect and the students will be talking freely to each other."

I pressed my lips together hard. Was he also in-structing the reporter to ask if those students saw Dr. Story in the hallways of Holworthy? Or for that matter, any strangers who looked out of place in a residence hall? I knew he wasn't. Quincey's theory held real charm for him. It was convenient. It fit in with his assumption that, since Popkin died of a heart problem, no one would have any reason to make an attempt on Miss Singer. But I couldn't bring up these matters in front of Story. Just as soon as he left, however, I surely would.

After dispatching the message, Quincey moved to the decanters. He filled our glasses with Madeira, murmuring, "This is restorative." Then, leaning on the mantel, his eyelids at half-mast position, he listened, with only a question or two, to the rest of what we had to say. Now he was delivering his judicious opinion. He was just as stubbornly attached to his explanation as Mrs. Bedell was to hers. He was the very model of the level-headed, hospitable, nineteenth-century American gentleman, wanting to make his guest comfortable and solve any problems that he could. It was quite a performance, put on for the professor's benefit, and it was plain there would be no penetrating questions directed at Story.

Now Quincey was saying, "As La Rochefoucauld notes, 'Youth is the fever of reason.' The idea that he was endangering someone simply didn't occur to this young man. He was over-confident of his marksmanship, even though the light was poor."

I persisted. "If Hoggett fails to find the culprit, other avenues should be explored. I suppose we can't rule out an attack on Mrs. Bedell by someone pursuing her, yet it concerns me that a number of people knew that Miss Singer would be in the Yard. Dr. Story raises the issue that she could be the focal point of militant opponents of Spiritualism."

Quincey got the point about publicity. He fixed his bulging gaze on the professor. "While it's true that she was again mentioned in my newspaper this evening, the editor's intention was to announce that Miss Singer knows nothing more than she said at the séance. I see no reason why her name should ever again appear in the *Independent*. I've expressed this hope to Mr. Goss."

Story nodded in approval. Maybe that reassured him. Not me. While Quincey's word may have been law to previous editors, the smug self-assurance in Goss's manner was fresh in my mind. But even if she wasn't mentioned again in the newspaper, I wasn't convinced Sylvie was safe. Under the circumstances, it was a very odd coincidence that a bullet came so near her. Bock Bach's certitude that Popkin was murdered impressed me. If the two events were connected, the man behind them was clever, fast, and dangerous.

My expression must have given me away. Quincey narrowed his eyes at me and said, "To imagine that *this* was a deliberate attempt on Miss Singer's life would be foolish." He waved that idea away imperiously with thick fingers, adding magisterially, "As we'll see when we hear from Hoggett."

Story seemed calmed by such certitude, or perhaps it was the wine. His color was better, and although he still held on to the papers on his lap, his fingers were still.

I turned to him, asking, "As you were coming by Holworthy, did you see the rifle? Note which window?"

Story shook his head guiltily. "I didn't. The path was crowded and I was trying to hurry. Until I saw you bending over Mrs. Bedell, I thought the noise was a Roman candle, and I wasn't aware of anything amiss."

"Do you catch sight of anyone nearby whom you knew—"

Quincey interrupted. "This sort of thing can safely be left to Hoggett."

Luckily, the stem of my wineglass was thick cut glass. I was clenching it tightly.

When I looked at him, he was looking at Story, and he was almost beaming. His next words were even more surprising than his expression. "We'll surely have his report soon. Would you join us for dinner?"

Apparently, Quincey would go to any lengths to prove he was right. And he wanted the professor to witness it. He reached for the tapestried bellpull.

Freegift must have been just outside the library door. Quincey ordered, "Serve dinner as soon as it is ready. There will be three of us. Then, see that Mrs. Bedell's coachman is properly fed while he waits for our guest."

The manservant was quite still, other than his fast-moving eyelashes, managing only a shocked nod before disappearing.

After refilling the wineglasses, Quincey called Story's attention to the painting above the mantel, saying, "By an American artist, sir, that I wasn't familiar with—Martin Johnson Heade." It was a magnificent work showing a thunderstorm on Narragansett Bay. One could almost hear the lightning crack above the black water, dotted with the ghostly sails of hurrying ships. Yet in the foreground, a returning fisherman moved leisurely along the strip of shore lit by the disappearing sun. "The contrast between light and dark I find especially pleasing," he went on. "While paintings of the Romantic School don't often attract me, this one is an American masterpiece. Should Harvard ever have its own art museum, I'd happily donate this work." Now he was Jasper Quincey, patron of the arts.

Holding his head to the side as he scrutinized the picture, he asked Story, "Doesn't this bring to your mind some of William Turner's landscapes?"

"It does, sir," Story replied. "I've seen many of them because, as a young man, my parents often took me to Europe, and I traveled on my own there later. That sky particularly puts me in mind of his masterful 'Rain, Steam, and Speed.'"

"Yes." Quincey bent a benign glance of approval on the young man. "Although here Heade doesn't call up the English painter's brilliant, hazy light—"

They went on in this fashion for some time. I refrained, just, from drumming my fingers on the armchair, but it would have relieved my tension.

At last Quincey ushered us into the dining room, as if having a guest was routine. After a quick look at the table, he frowned, asked us to be seated, and walked out.

I could see nothing wrong. There were three covers correctly set with silver to hand, ivory napkins on the ivory-linen cloth. Each place had its small round salt-cellar and a matching silver dish with cracked pepper. As usual, there was a flowering herb as a centerpiece and tonight it was the evening primrose with its ferny leaves and small cups of yellow. The tall candles on the table were already lit as were those in the tripod candlestands in the corners. A light scent of mint, infused into the tallow, touched the air. Quincey didn't like the odor of oil lamps.

Story commented on the airy spaciousness of the room. I agreed. It didn't have the parlor's spare elegance, yet the furniture had well-proportioned lines. Nowhere in the house were there any of the massive pieces—all weight and substance—that were in fashion, but here a couple of sizable pieces stood against one wall. The four-door walnut breakfront cabinet, filled with thin crystal and china, was high and wide but not festooned with heavy carvings of fruit and flowers. The sideboard, Georgian in its plainness, showed only its gleaming wood. The tall clock— Quincey always had to know the time, and there was one in every room—had a graceful curlicue on top, but the front was of simple inlaid mahogany. The burgundy drapes were thick, but the pattern of climbing vines and intricate flowers was muted. And, what pleased me most, the dining-room chairs were comfortable with wide, upholstered seats and broad slat backs. Since one spent long hours at the table, it never made sense to me to choose chairs that pleased the eye but made the guest wish the best meal over well before dessert was served.

Everything seemed in order. The small coals in the fireplace gave out a pleasant warmth. The gilt frames of the pictures—nicely drawn still lifes—were perfectly straight. There wasn't a speck of dust on the parquet floor. I couldn't imagine what displeased Quincey. Or why setting it right should take all this time. At one point, I could have sworn the heavy front door opened and closed, although quietly. I wasn't sure. Even the sound of the solid door knocker would be muffled here.

Almost squirming in my seat, I was wishing the meal over, and we hadn't begun yet. Where *was* Quincey?

Just then he came sailing back into the room.

# Chapter Twelve

**H**is face smooth, his manner unruffled, Quincey murmured only a brief apology. Freegift followed him in with the fish course.

Once we'd started on that, Quincey showed how far he'd go to give Hoggett time. He brought up a subject sure to disturb his digestion. He turned to the professor and said, with apparent interest, "I understand you are taking Dr. William James's classes whilst he's in Europe. Craddock has, from time to time, sent me writings of his. Impressive. Tell me why such a clear-thinking philosopher as he is—and I understand he's a medical doctor as well—should inquire into Spiritualism."

Story replied with animation. "Because, sir, as a scientist, he regards all 'facts' in the universe as needing to be tested. We don't *know* that the dead can't speak to us. He insists, of course, that all reported instances of such messages, or of the many accounts of the dead appearing to the living, be rigorously investigated to rule out fraud or mistake."

He speared a succulent oyster from the cream sauce, managing to splatter a few drops on his lapel, and swallowed it before going on. "As he says, borrowing language from the professional logic-shop, a universal proposition can be made untrue by a particular instance. If you wish to upset the law that all crows are black, it's enough if you prove one single crow to be white."

Logic was Quincey's barricade against chaos, and he was nodding in agreement as Story spoke. I had the odd image of Sylvie Singer as that white bird, her head cocked as she heard the voices the others could not. Perhaps Story had something similar in mind. He was smiling; his earnestness now lightened.

The door opened and I glanced up involuntarily. Freegift came in and removed the fish course.

Obviously an ardent disciple, Story continued quoting from William James. "Then there is the problem of what he calls 'wild facts.' He states that the ordinary academic and critical mind is very slow to acknowledge facts that have no pigeonhole to put them in or that might threaten to break up the accepted system. Mr. Darwin noticed that the small finches in the Galapagos had beaks of different sizes and shapes. And he began to wonder why that was so. His theory of evolution grew up around that."

Quincey was still nodding. I grew restless just thinking about how long dinner could drag on if they started on Darwin.

Luckily, Story continued, "I admire Dr. James because of his extraordinary receptiveness to ideas. Admittedly, I fear that he allows some people to waste his time. We have a student, a very mechanically minded one, who asserts that some day we'll be able to send our voices through the air and be heard by others at great distances who have some sort of small box. Without the use of Morse's telegraph wires. It sounds absurd, but Dr. James hears him out. He has the faculty of listening with enthusiasm. And he is very interested in thought transference, sometimes called telepathy, the idea that one mind can speak directly to another."

This time when the door opened, Quincey's glance also strayed sideways. Freegift brought in the game course. Roast breast of duck with chestnut stuffing.

Quincey chewed slowly and swallowed. Then he went back to the original point. "All very well, sir. But you can measure the beak of a finch. In the world of spirits, how do you know you *have* a fact?" He grabbed a fistful of air to demonstrate his point before going on. "An experiment is a question science asks of nature. It must be formulated so that the answer can be duplicated each time the experiment is run. Then we know we've wrested a truthful answer from nature. How can you do this with a medium? How can you hope to prove that the answer to the question asked her came from a spirit and not from some knowledge she herself had of the deceased person?"

The professor sighed in agreement. "Exactly. Dr. James has outlined seven ways a medium might herself know the answers. Five of them are quite natural: common gossip, indications unwarily furnished by others at the séance, lucky chance hits, acquaintance with the deceased who mentioned an incident in her hearing, and related to this, such information stored in her trance memory, but out of reach of her waking consciousness. The other two ways he terms 'supernatural': telepathy, that is, the tapping of the mind of someone at the séance or of some distant living person, and last, access to some cosmic reservoir." He let out a discouraged breath again. "And we aren't sure that we've eliminated those first five in any of our attempts so far. Dr. James has already formulated a frustrating law: No case involving the paranormal is ever wholly convincing."

As he talked, I was coming up with questions I could reasonably put to Story over the after-dinner port. While he might slide around his own uncordial relationship with Popkin, what would he say about the feelings between the doctor and the other two men?

This time when the door opened, all three of us looked up. Freegift came in pushing a trolley with a huge platter containing a fragrant, herb-encrusted leg of lamb and several side dishes. He placed the meat in front of Quincey and took away the game dishes. As he began carving, Quincey said to the professor, "Pray go on, sir."

Story paused, apparently trying to remember what he'd been saying. "Ah, yes. Dr. James worked with the medium Mrs. Piper for some years. Her comings and goings, the people she talked to, were monitored by the Society for Psychical Research to rule out any question of prior knowledge. She was a reputable housewife, apparently quite an ordinary woman, but she sometimes astonished the Society at séances. Once, after Hodgson's sister died in Australia, she described the house, down to the leaning picket fence, in precise detail. While she spoke, it was as if she were studying a photograph, although none had been taken of the place. And Mr. Hodgson, who is Secretary of the Society, swore he'd never mentioned the appearance of his sister's home to anyone after his visit there. Indeed, why would he?"

Story looked first at his host and then at me, as if waiting for an answer.

Quincey fixed his gaze on me pointedly, reminding me of my continuing silence. I tried to gather my thoughts, coming out with, "Maybe, at some social function, a lady or gentleman asked Hodgson, after his return, about housing in the as-yet unsettled country of Australia. It's especially likely because in the recent past several American newspapers carried articles pointing out gleefully that newly arrived Britishers

built homes there with southern exposure to catch the
sun as they had on their own gray island. However,
they'd forgotten they were in the Antipodes and
should have built homes facing north. But in answer
to a casual question along these general lines, Mr.
Hodgson might have described his sister's dwelling,
including the detail about the collapsing fence as an
example of the fact that there the necessities of living
had to take precedence over the amenities. This conversation was repeated in Mrs. Piper's hearing and
stored in her memory, whether she was aware of it or
not."

"Quite possibly," Quincey said. He served the juicy
pink slices of lamb, saying, "That's an example of Dr.
James's point of a story repeated in her hearing and
stored in her memory. I could illustrate another of his
points: indications from the sitter at the séance, although the person isn't aware of giving those signs.
Let us say that Mrs. Piper sits, supposedly in a trance,
but looking blankly at Mr. Hodgson. She knows
where he's been and whom he visited. She thinks of
the bleaching effects of the sun in that part of the
world and brings out that the house has peeling paint.
His eyes widen. She sticks with the fierce weather
there, the winds, and comes out with a leaning fence,
a shutter that is askew. Mr. Hodgson, who doesn't remember the condition of the shutters, shows how impressed he is by pressing his lips together. And so
on."

Taking a sip of wine, the professor continued. "I
should add that Mrs. Piper did repeat messages from
spirits the content of which was far beyond her edu-
cation. Still, such messages were unusual. Most were
trivial. A spirit would report that an aunt in Ohio was
doing well or comment on the buying of a new chair
or some such. As Dr. James said in exasperation,

'What real spirit, at last able to revisit his wife on this earth, but would find something better to say than that she had changed the place of his photograph?'"

With real curiosity in his voice, Quincey asked, "With such evidence, *why* does the good doctor persist in his study?"

"Because, as he repeats, in some psychic phenomena *something* happened even though it's still impossible to know precisely what or how. A thing is not necessarily untrue simply because it conflicts with known principles of science. I have to remind myself of that whenever I speak with our student who believes in the wireless sending of our voices." He sighed with pleasure, saying, "Excellent lamb, sir. I've never had better."

Quincey answered, "I'm glad that you enjoy it, sir. The rosemary is fresh since I have a shrub in my conservatory, necessarily placed where it has all available sunlight since it is a Mediterranean herb. I have some bushes outside as well, espaliered on the east wall. Rosemary has been used for centuries, mentioned by the ancient writers. And you'll recall Shakespeare's reference to it in *Hamlet* as a symbol: 'Rosemary, that's for remembrance; pray, love, remember.' Also he refers to it in *Romeo and Juliet*. As for its medicinal uses, the herb is used to cure headaches, relieve rheumatic pains, and increase circulation. It's known to be an effective aid to digestion. In Europe it's always added to the spas' bath water, and they've found rosemary is absorbed through the skin quite easily and that improves . . ."

His discussion on horticulture carried us through Freegift's entry with the ginger fluff. All three of us carefully avoided paying attention to his entrance. It was one of my favorite desserts, but I hardly noticed its spicy lightness. My aggravation with Quincey was

now intense. He must know that, by now, the students would either have drifted to their rooms to
sleep or set off for Boston to celebrate further. Hoggett
had found out nothing. We needed to talk to Story.

I was haunted by that look of fear in Sylvie Singer's
eyes. Did she feel she'd gone too far in insisting Popkin was murdered and now realized it? *She* didn't
think that shot was accidental. I wanted to know more
about her, and I wanted to hear what Story might say,
whether he was guilty or innocent. Quincey could
have asked how she compared to this Mrs. Piper as a
way of bringing up the subject. It was he who wanted
to unmask her deceptions. But the opportunity to discover anything was being lost in a lecture on horticulture. The only thing I could do was wait for the
after-dinner wine.

Finally, Quincey stood up, saying to the professor,
"Please join us in the library. I have an excellent port."

Story shook his head with regret. "I'd enjoy that, sir.
But I need to go over my notes while they're still fresh
in my mind."

Quincey accompanied him to the library to get the
papers, and then the two of them went down the long
hallway to the front of the house.

Closing the door to keep in the heat, I flung myself
into one of the wing chairs before the fire. Its fragrant
logs were now ashes, but I didn't add any more. I
wasn't going to be there long, and I was warmed by
my angry resolve. While I intended to pursue the investigation to ensure Miss Singer's safety, I could do
that on my own. I'd have nothing further to do with
proving her a fraud. Story's account of mediums convinced me that she could be one of those who un-
knowingly record incidents in conversation in their
minds and that this information could come out in a
trance state. To continue to do anything else would

smack of persecution. She had no respectable way to support herself. And she might have cause to be frightened.

There was little point in telling Quincey any of this. His mind had snapped shut at the very beginning. Therefore, there was no need for discussion. My decision was final. As soon as he returned, I intended to tell him *that* and march out the door.

To my surprise, it inched open just then. Deciding that he must have hustled Story out to the carriage with unconscionable speed, I jumped up, ready to speak my piece. But my legs and feet, already sore from the day, collapsed under me. In two seconds, I was back in the wing chair, pressing my lips together in pain. I directed a baleful look toward the slowly opening door.

# Chapter Thirteen

Freegift came in, nudging the door open with his foot, since the huge silver tray he carried took two hands. He didn't even glance at me since he was holding the tray with as much care as if it was a saint's relic paraded in an Italian street. On it was a wide-bottomed crystal decanter with diamond facets that caught the fading firelight, glinting and flashing on the sober shelves of books. It was filled with a dark, honey-colored liquid. Beside it were three thin-stemmed goblets. With his eyes still fixed on the tray, he murmured, "Sorry not to knock, sir, but I didn't want to chance setting this down. Not wanting to stir up dregs, should I have missed any when I decanted it. This is the vintage port from Douro."

"That's port?" I muttered through my gritted teeth. Usually what we drank was a deep, rich red. At the moment, however, I was concentrating on what seemed a thousand cuts in the healing skin of my legs and feet. This morning it'd been smooth and pink; at the moment it felt as crackled and crazed as old glass.

"Yes." Letting out his breath with a sigh, he slid his burden onto the library table. "Mr. Quincey just told me this was what was wanted or, of course, I would have brought it out while you were at the table." He was still looking at the wine, as if it might cloud up the instant he took his eyes off it. Then he turned, went back out, and reappeared almost immediately holding my felt slippers and thick white stockings. Before he shut the door, I heard a horse's quick snort in the drive. The carriage apparently still hadn't left.

Freegift blinked at me reproachfully before kneeling to ease off my shoes. Beneath his thinning hair, his scalp gleamed pinkly. "We'll have to do this now, and here, as Mr. Quincey said you'd be up for some time tonight. While some exercise is recommended, sir, it isn't to be overdone, as you know. And today you—" Seeing the stains on my stockings, he stopped and gave his head a quick sideways jerk and pressed his lips together. He held out the clean ones, saying, "I've rubbed the ointment on the inside of these so there's no need to touch the skin. I was afraid of this, I was. You'd best slip these on yourself lest I do any further damage."

As I inched them over my feet—which didn't look as bad as they hurt—I asked, "Did he say why *he* is staying up?" I stressed the singular pronoun.

"I assume he still expects a reply from Mr. Hoggett. Quincey said that I should retire after putting out the port, that he would get the door when the bell rang."

Freegift's eyes were on the ceiling, and he added with a distinct quaver in his voice, "I'm apparently not needed further tonight. It's beyond my understanding. What with all the comings and goings today, not to mention standing outside without an overcoat as he is— It can't be right. To be staying up beyond the usual hour as well. None of this can be good for *anyone's* health." Noticing that I'd put on my slippers, he hurried to pull over a footstool. He gestured for me to lift my legs, stooped, slid the footrest beneath them and went right on. "I don't see that I'm overstepping any boundaries by saying *that*, sir. If he's over-tired, Mr. Quincey will hardly be able to

ready himself for bed on his own, and in the morning
he'll certainly be in no state to—"

It was clear that he didn't like his routine interrupted any more than his employer did. Worse,
Freegift's feelings were wounded. For him, it was necessary to be necessary. Growing up with the Shakers,
the concept of usefulness had been ingrained. He
stood before me, plucking at the cuffs of his wide
white sleeves, spotless as always. His gray-white hair
lay neatly across his forehead, and his long brown
waistcoat had not one wrinkle. But his face was crumpled in distress. I couldn't bear looking at him.

So I broke in, sounding for all the world as if I knew
what I was talking about. "You're right. Mr. Quincey
isn't going to be fresh tomorrow. *You* will have to be
the clear-thinking one in the morning. It'd do no good
to have all three of us half awake. The situation, you
know, is serious. And as it involves the Craddocks,
who are such close friends, extraordinary measures
have to be taken."

He glanced sideways, his brow smoothing, and
then nodded. "Ah, of course, sir." Turning immediately to the fire, he laid extra logs on it with some
care. He checked the decanter and then held up each
goblet to make sure there were no spots. Touring the
room, he slid a volume more precisely into its place
on the shelf. He squinted at each of the gas jets on the
walls. At last, adjusting the footstool by the wing
chair next to mine, he looked pointedly at my feet.

"Much better," I said, "much better. Thank you."
Actually, the salve was very cooling.

He let out his breath and said, "I'll wish you good
night then." He left with a military back.

It was a full five minutes before Quincey burst in,
cold air following him. His wiry gray hair was standing up, and his sober jacket, cut straight in the old-

fashioned style, was buttoned over his vest. Undoing it, he marched to the fireplace, rubbing his hands briskly before it. An almost satisfied expression lurked around his mouth as if he were sure he'd done his duty, well above and beyond the call in fact, and could now relax. Then his eye lit on the decanter and he went straight to that and poured two glasses. Before handing one to me, he held the amber liquid to the fire's brightness and nodded with satisfaction. "Perfect. You'll enjoy this, Michael. Nothing quite like it. You'll note the slight suggestion of walnuts in the taste, although—" He stopped to lower himself into the chair next to mine.

"Hoggett is very late," I said brusquely. He was not going to get away with it.

"I was sure we'd hear from him by now. I deliberately drew out the meal." He didn't meet my eyes. "But he had several tasks."

"What were they?"

"First, to go to the Yard, of course. Depend on it, that young man will have boasted about the shooting to his peers over the punch. He'll do so even knowing that should his name reach the authorities, he'd face a severe reprimand, perhaps even be sent home. To be able to sever that rope—even on the second try—took skill of a high order. He'll want applause." Saying it aloud seemed to reinforce the truth of the statement, at least as far as he was concerned. Quincey lifted his glass with an air of things being settled.

"And what if this student's discretion is equal to his marksmanship and he says nothing? As you pointed out earlier, it was extraordinarily irresponsible to fire into a crowd. *That* might have occurred to him after a few minutes."

He set down his glass resignedly. "As well, Hoggett is to find out if anything that occurred was out of the ordinary. After all, the sight of a professor in a residence hall is unusual. Someone would have noticed that."

"So you at least entertain the possibility that Story, or one of the others on the committee—"

"Obviously not Dr. Story."

"Why?"

Quincey didn't turn his head in my direction, but he lifted an impatient eyebrow. He spoke succinctly. "He had the papers with him. When you set out, he didn't. But he wouldn't have had time to both fetch them from Harvard Hall and nip up the staircase at Holworthy, fire two shots, and get back to you in the time you indicated when you described the incident. And I took the liberty of inspecting those papers. They were as described—notes he'd taken regarding Sylvie Singer. I needed to see them—another reason I had to ask the man to stay to dinner." He took a sip of the wine with an air of self-congratulation.

But he went on with discontent. "You can see how useful it'd have been if Story had heard definitely, this evening, that the shooting had nothing to do with a medium or a séance. Since he was on the scene, he'll be repeatedly asked and he could give a clear account."

Setting down his glass, he brought out more slowly, "Hoggett was also to go to the stables and find out the movements of Josh Singer. One has to consider that he might have been the rifleman."

"Sylvie's *father*? Why would he try to kill her?"

"Not kill. Frighten. You recall that his friend told Hoggett that she refused to see him. Singer probably needs money. The newspaper—*my* newspaper—has informed him that she is now holding séances again. If he can pot a rising pheasant, he could probably take off Mrs. Bedell's upraised feathers. And, knowing her own father, Miss Singer would probably understand that message."

Resting my head against the high back of the chair, I blew out my breath, feeling more sympathy than ever for Sylvie. I picked up my glass, unthinkingly sipped the wine, and set it down again.

Quincey craned his neck around the upper curve of his chair, and asked eagerly, "Well?"

"What?" I asked, startled.

"The port. Do you not note the depth of it? Each day's sun adds a slight touch of ripe sweetness. Does it not have a taste that will linger, not just in your throat, but in your memory?"

Taking another sip, I tried to nod thoughtfully. "It truly has. Walnuts, yes."

He stretched out his legs in obvious disgust. "You *are* distracted. Tell me what you discussed with the professor whilst I was gone."

I did so.

"Dr. Story needn't worry that Miss Singer's name will appear regularly in the *Independent*. But, as I supposed, your talk centered on her. 'Who is Silvia? what is she,/That all our swains commend her?' Shakespeare's *Two Gentlemen of Verona*, Act IV. He actually said she resembles Botticelli's Venus? I can hardly credit it. He must be besotted to make such a remark."

I'd have liked to cross one knee over the other and remark urbanely, "Indeed." Instead I said bluntly, "She does. That is merely a statement of fact. I am not besotted. Nor is he. I think the professor is genuinely interested in researching her *mind*."

He let out a snort. "Recall how you felt about that Shaker woman. You're sure of your feelings in this case?"

I wanted to say that I didn't make a habit of being besotted every other month. Instead, I replied firmly,

"Yes. I'm fascinated, though. She's a most . . . unusual woman. She doesn't speak or respond at all as you expect her to, and I don't know what to make of her. One moment, she has all the manners and mannerisms of a woman of fashion. She brings up acceptably boring topics of conversation. And she has an excellent command of the giving and taking of polite compliments. That's the way Miss Singer begins. But then she says something of substance. In this case, she spoke of how she felt about being a medium, and it was a candid comment on her life, all the more believable because she sounded . . . detached. Let me tell you about our conversation in the Yard."

When I finished, he sat in silence, his lips pursed as he thought. "Umph. Candid, you said. There is one thing that strikes me. While I find it impossible to imagine a serious conversation with a medium, I'd like you to consider this. Now Goss mentioned Daniel Dunglas Home, the medium who was taken up by English society. If you and he were sitting here over port and he spoke to you as she did—denying that he understood his 'powers,' in fact minimizing them, and even using the comparison of being regarded as a freak of nature. Her description of those poor people being at first draped from view and then having their deformities put on view for money catches the imagination. How would you have regarded him?"

After a moment I replied, "I see your point. I'd have begun imagining the difficulties of such a life. And I would have been halfway to believing that he was not a fraud. Nonetheless, my guard wouldn't have dropped. I'd still have been alert to the possibility of a stratagem on his part, a deliberate attempt to enlist my sympathy. The goal would have been to persuade me that he was genuine, had real psychic abilities.

What confused me, you believe, was that a *woman* would talk to me so frankly."

"Yes." He spoke firmly. "I see it as an excellent ploy in these circumstances. She wants you on her side. She's a woman of deep artifice. If she'd fluttered her lovely lashes at you, perhaps shed a small tear and claimed to be a poor woman who was totally misunderstood, she'd have gotten your pity. But that's not what she wants. She wants your support; she wants you to remain open-minded on her abilities. She's seemingly honest. As you noted, that's effective if a man does it, and it's doubly so if a woman does because it's not a device you'd expect from one and therefore you're less likely to regard it as a trick."

Because that was what had gone through my mind, and I believed myself to be more open-minded than he was, I became irritated. "But in fairness—" I began, wanting to point out that Story studied the mind, and he obviously felt that some people had genuine powers.

He held up a hand, palm toward me. "Yes. You are going to defend her." At that point, it occurred to me he might have condemned her so strongly to get my reaction, to see if I were able to be dispassionate about such a beautiful woman. Quincey avoided any display of his own emotions, unless you consider aggravation an emotion, but he always wanted to know what feelings lay behind the words of others.

He pulled in air through his nose. "But you do seem able to regard her with a degree of dispassion, which is necessary. I do not understand women, Michael, and I must depend on you." There was a certain stiffness in his statement that persuaded me he might mean it. On the other hand, he must have sensed my desire to get out of the investigation and he was using this blatant appeal for help to persuade me to continue. He was underhanded.

"And I was going to add that—" He stopped. The doorbell had rung.

He stood up with alacrity. "That'll be Hoggett or a note from him." It was clear Quincey was sure that his investigator had found that daring student.

# Chapter Fourteen

"If it were not for the exceptional circumstances, you must realize I'd never intrude." The man's voice was agitated, high-pitched, precise in enunciation. "Not at all. And *never* at this hour. Again, I apologize."

I decided that couldn't be Hoggett speaking, and as soon as the visitor entered the room, I knew it. Quincey had remarked that the reporter went unnoticed everywhere. Not this man. His weedy eyebrows sprouted above his eyes, and he had an unforgettable beard. His shock of white hair darkened as it grew down his cheeks, jutted out in slight points at jaw level, and then merged with the dark peppered beard that cut straight under his chin. It was as if his face—high forehead, beaky nose, and clean-shaven upper lip—ended in a shadow box. Tall and slightly stooped, he was dressed in a long striped sack coat, with bulging pockets, and loose checked trousers. The narrowest strip of a cravat was tied under his short, stiff collar.

Glancing around at the shelves and shelves of stately books, and then down at Quincey's wide mahogany desk, he burst out, "Gad! I envy you having a desk in your library. I *cannot* persuade Leonora of the necessity of that. She merely comes out with what she sees as the unarguable answer: 'But you have a desk.

Upstairs in your study. One needs only *chairs* in a library. A chaise as we have is permissible, and occasional tables to hold the oil lamps. That is all. That is what people expect to see.'"

As he spoke, he picked up a volume from the desk. "Ah-ha! You have William Cullen Bryant's new translation of Homer. As you'll note, it's rubbishy stuff, even if he's got a reputation as a poet. He takes such liberties. If one feels compelled to translate the godlike Homer for those too lazy to learn Greek, one *must* do so literally. And he even mistakes one of the verb forms—"

At this point, he spied me by the fire and rushed over, saying, "Don't get up, young man. If you're Michael Merrick, you'll already have had an exhausting day, saving Susanna Bedell's life." He cackled as he finished and grasped my outraised hand, saying, "Gideon Craddock."

I began, "I am Michael Merrick, but I assure that I in no way saved—"

He broke in. "But you'll not persuade Mrs. Bedell of that. And since my sister received a note from her this evening, just a scribble outlining the 'attempt' on her life at the Yard—from which she so barely escaped because of your heroism—there's been no peace at our house. Women, you know, have excitable natures. Leonora is in a twitter, unsure whether she should worry or not. First, she reminds herself that her dear friend tends on occasion to 'overstate,' but then she recalls seeing the Bedell carriage going down the road to your house—and staying there—and she can think of no explanation for that happening other than some cataclysmic event. As soon as she heard the carriage again on its return, Leonora begged me to come and ascertain the truth. I was reluctant, of course, given the rudeness of such a call, and I'd thought merely to have a walk down the road and puff on my pipe and then return and tell her the house was dark. But not only was the house lit up, so were the gate lanterns. Hence, my presence here."

Two things occurred to me. The professor was gabbling because he was ill at ease. In his view, this call was a shocking breach of manners. But there was bright curiosity in his eyes. He'd come because he was interested, and he was using his sister's palpitations as an excuse. As he spoke, his fingers twitched at the pipe outlined in one of his coat pockets.

Quincey said nothing, impassively gesturing toward the third chair drawn up by the fire. He fetched another glass from the fold-down drawer of the secretary, and filled it. Seating himself, Craddock almost gasped when he saw the contents. "The vintage port? Gad. Since you recommended it so highly, I told Leonora to order some, but she returned with a vinegar mouth and said, 'Why, I could get quite a fancy new frock for the cost of one bottle!' "

When he quoted his sister, he let his voice slide up the register a notch, and the image rose of an angular, prim-mouthed woman who resembled him exactly, except for the eyebrows and the beard. "Not," he said, turning to me, "that she ever does buy a fancy frock. The expense of it would take away any enjoyment for her. No. Somewhere in Boston there must be a shop that, despite all the decrees of fashion, still sells cheap, serviceable, dull brown stuff. Leonora has all her dresses, and Emily's, made from that, as far as I can tell."

Quincey lowered himself into his chair, and we all raised our glasses and sipped. There was an ensuing silence, followed by their murmured, reverential comments on the wine. The word "complexity" recurred, as well as "mellowness." After what he apparently judged as a decent interval, Craddock sat forward, fixed his inquisitive gaze on the two of us, and said, "Now then, what did happen?"

I left the answer to Quincey, and he duly brought out the explanation of the brash student aiming at the rope holding the swaying effigy and, on the first attempt, clipping Mrs. Bedell's feathers. As in talking to Story, he spoke as if not one Thomas could doubt, as if Hoggett was even now busily lining up witnesses. I could see the wisdom of his taking that course with Craddock. It was hard enough to separate truth from speculation. Adding gossip to it would make it worse.

Craddock's reply was a chortle and then a head-shake. "Mad-brained young devil. And with an eye like that, he could have put the arrow in Achilles' heel. Hmm."

He was about to go on, but Quincey slid in with a question. "How did it happen that my editor, Mr. Goss, was invited to the séance at your home?"

The professor pressed his thin lips together, which made them disappear altogether. At last he answered, "I shall have to think. Leonora made all the arrangements, of course. She had some difficulty talking Sylvie into it. Because of that, my sister wanted all the formal rules followed. I gather there are a lot of them. Eight attendees are the ideal number, and they should be divided equally by sex. Then there's the question of the temperament of those attending. Apparently, one wants opposite ones, as positive and negative, and definitely not a person of a strong magnetic character as that has the tendency to quash the spirits."

I decided that the tendency to long digressions ran in the Craddock family. Like uncle, like niece. Quincey was shifting in his chair, but he kept eyes resolutely on the fire.

"Hmm. Leonora wanted men from Harvard College, and while I gave in to the pressure to attend—on this subject, she brooks no disagreement—I left it to her to invite whom she would. The Theology Department, you know, frowns on this sort of thing. They expelled one of their students for having a séance in his room. That was some time ago, but they've never come round. Not that this would trouble men from other fields. Some might come simply because those in Theology disapproved. She didn't want Story because she felt his attitude would smack too much of the probing intellect. That, like bright lights, is anathema to the spirits, as she says. Hmm. Why she decided on *Popkin* is a mystery. I'd rather thought he was the author of those vituperative letters against spiritualism in your paper. The ones signed 'Truth Seeker.'"

Quincey looked up at that. "Perhaps he came intending to attack the proceedings in his next letter."

The professor blew out his breath and shifted uneasily in his chair. "Good thing he died, then. Leonora would have been most displeased. Let's see, I think Bock Bach came as a favor to Story. But Goss? Now, he had some business dealings with Popkin—"

"What kind of business?" Quincey interrupted.

Waving a vague hand as he crossed his right leg over his left knee, Craddock said, "Something about some land that Goss was interested in purchasing from him. I gather your man fancies himself as a country squire and wanted a place for the weekends. It didn't go through. Popkin apparently hadn't mentioned that this acreage was given to flooding at certain times. So I doubt that he— Ah, I have it. Leonora met Mr. Goss at a séance. He is quite interested in the subject."

Quincey didn't respond immediately, which was a mistake. Craddock returned to the subject that interested him. "But about your thinking on this gunfire in the Yard, sir. Leonora will certainly remark that there's More To It, as she is wont to say. She'll not suggest that anyone would attempt to shoot Mrs. Bedell, a harmless creature, but she'll put it about that the man who killed Popkin is now trying to shoot our Sylvie, standing next to her. You may depend on her saying this, Quincey, particularly after your extra edition proclaimed that an autopsy was performed on Bock Bach's orders. He's not a man who chases wild hares."

With an audible sniff, as if the answer were obvious, Quincey addressed his neighbor's last words. "Ah, but as executor, the good doctor must at the outset make sure there is no idle talk about murder, so he properly took that step. As for the rest, you'll recall Vergil's words in *The Aeneid : 'Fama volat parvam subito volgata per urbem.'* As the poet says, small towns are filled with fast-flying rumors. Cambridge is a small town."

The professor drew his wispy eyebrows together for a moment. "Ah, yes. That line is from Book VIII, is it not? Hmm. I actually had to stop and think where it was. Ah"—he pulled at one of the dark triangles of his beard—"I see why I had a little trouble remembering. I've been neglecting my Latin. A case of overlooking the 'grandeur that was Rome' for 'the glory that was Greece,' in Mr. Poe's words. I shall remedy that."

As he said that, I had a vision of our neighbor, alone in his upstairs study, dressed in his toga, all naked knees and calves, one bare, skinny arm upraised, as he intoned stately Latin phrases. Then I wondered what he wore, if anything, while reading Ovid's lewd and bawdy verse. Maybe he stuck with the epics.

He returned to Quincey's last words. "But you

make a point with Vergil—the danger of rumor in this case. Still . . ."

Quincey moved in for the kill. "And, as you've sometimes suggested in your correspondence, Miss Craddock is apt to be credulous, particularly in any matters that have to do with Spiritualism. Then, it must be repeated, as you noted, women are high-strung and imaginative. They prefer lightweight gossip to solid truth."

Making circles in the air with his right foot, Craddock was silent for a moment, apparently trying to decide how to get around that. It was apparent that he refused to go home to Leonora without a piece of news. "It's damned queer, though, you'll admit. Sylvie spoke of murder and then a bullet whizzes by her head. If you have any doubts at all on the matter, Quincey, you should come out with them. My sister and I feel we have a responsibility here. Living with us as a child, Sylvie—" He interrupted himself, running the back of his hand beneath the exactly trimmed square under his chin. "She was amazing. Leonora took her about quite a bit, and strangers congratulated my sister, assuming she was her offspring, saying how beautiful the child was. And quick! Why, she need only look at the conjugations of Greek verbs and could then repeat them back to you. Give her any book, and she'd not glance up until she'd finished it. Mind you, she had some strange ways. You'd catch her sitting, still as a cat, and she said she was listening to the voices. Leonora fussed about that until I reminded her Joan of Arc heard 'em, too, and she defeated the English handily at Orleans. Couldn't have been all that crazy. But that didn't reassure my sister. Probably shouldn't have brought it up."

With a start, I recalled the words I dreamt in the courtyard, imagining why Sylvie was afraid of her trances: *I hear HIM, his calling voice. Familiar. Who is he? Who? What if HE starts talking to the people with my mouth?* I asked him, "What did Sylvie say about the voices?"

"Not a word. Once she saw it upset my sister, she didn't speak of them again. But here's another odd thing. A few weeks before she came to our door with those apples, Leonora was inspecting our garden borders one day and heard her telling her the other young ones a story. Standing atop a dirt pile, black as an imp, she was saying that she'd been a princess. But it was not pretty fairy-tale stuff. She talked about the huge open fireplaces and the bitter cold rooms of the castle, of rushes on the floor, and then she made them all laugh by saying that when the gentlemen scratched their codpieces, bugs jumped out! My sister said she was sure that the child actually used the words 'rushes' and 'codpiece.' She couldn't have been above five, so how could she have known such things?"

"Ah." Quincey had a forced patience in his voice. "But as she lived above the stables, she might have heard the patrons talking while they waited for a horse to be saddled. A professor might have recounted that. You mention that she has an excellent memory."

Pulling at the dark points of his beard, Craddock replied, "Hmm. Possibly." He didn't sound convinced. He added with a touch of asperity, "But Story, and he's good man, thinks Sylvie's mental powers are worthy of study." Swallowing the last drops of wine, he added, "And, by Jove, she's grown into a decorative woman. Not at all like my niece Emily, who was a stubby child and is now a pudding-faced sort of girl. Furthermore, *she* is quite unable to learn Greek. You would think that one's own kin— But that's the point I was making, Quincey. My sister and I regard Sylvie as kin. If she'd been allowed to stay with us, she'd have been spared all these difficulties. As Leonora points out, *we* could have found her a fine husband. Perhaps we couldn't have looked as high as Beacon Hill, despite her beauty—society there is rather fussy about one's background—but a good, steady man, perhaps of the mercantile class. Not like that rascally Britisher who ran off and left her. And now we find he was married previously. She was quite alone, you know, while delivering the child. It took some time, and the room was quite unheated. That's what happened to the boy. Robin—silly name—has health problems."

Despite the painful details of this account, the professor sounded merely disgruntled that matters hadn't turned out as he would have wished. Although he was a man well versed in ancient tragedy, he didn't seem able to understand others' griefs.

Again I heard the desperate words as I was sitting in the courtyard: *Take care of Robbie. Poor boy. Darling Robin.* I cleared my throat. "Is the child able to talk? To walk?"

"Certainly he can *walk*. He's always slipping away from whatever servant is put in charge of looking out for him. Why, one day he climbed up the outer staircase to my study—I had that put in especially so I could have a pipe, walk in the garden while thinking—and when I looked up from my desk, there he was, staring at me with those peculiar eyes. I all but leaped out of my chair. He can talk quite properly, but he says very odd things. And he falls asleep wherever he is. Sylvie dotes on him."

Quincey made a noncommittal sound in reply. He raised his eyes to the thundery landscape above the fireplace and then said, "To answer your question, Craddock, I have no facts regarding this incident. In an effort to garner some, I've sent a man to the Yard to investigate." Turning his head slightly, he glanced at the corner clock. It was past eleven. "Given the lateness of the hour, I suspect it'll be morning before I hear from him. Should he have confirmation of the student's identity, or even a strong pointer toward it, which would settle the matter as far as I'm concerned, I'll notify you immediately."

That was a clear invitation for the professor to prepare gracefully for departure. But he made no such move. Drumming his fingers thoughtfully on the arm of the wing chair, he said, "I was at the séance, you know, and ever since I've been puzzling over Popkin's words at the end. 'The jade, the jade.' I'm damned sure that's what was said, but why at such a time would he have green stones on his mind?"

"That mineral," Quincey replied, finishing his wine, "needn't be green, although it commonly is. It could be white or even blue. Alternately, he may not have meant the stone. It can be a contemptuous name for a horse, a worn-out one. You'll recall that in *Taming of the Shrew*, Shakespeare refers to a man in that sense. But today in England—and Dr. Popkin would have learned the language from an Englishman—'jade' is still a term of reprobation for a woman. It usually indicates she's a scold or unchaste, but it's a strong word of condemnation." He ended, "Perhaps Popkin thought his killer was a woman."

"Absurd, sir!" Craddock burst out, leaning forward and planting both feet on the floor.

"If the man was murdered, the means had to be poison," Quincey answered, emphasizing his words. "Women can kill with it as easily as men. I believe you all took tea before the séance."

"But—" The professor was sputtering. "That was my sister's home-brewed herbal concoction."

"Yes, yes, but anyone in the parlor might have added something to Popkin's tea. Were not people moving around the room?"

In his agitation, Craddock stood up. "Well, they were, now that I think of it, talking to different people about previous séances. I see that it *could* have been done. But to think of that—in one's own house—and such respectable people!" He ran shaking fingers through his hair. He'd been delighted with the titillation of the rumors of murder, but he was horrified at having its ugly reality occupying *his* parlor.

Quincey rose and put a firm hand on the professor's shoulder. "We have yet no proof that such a thing occurred. We must consider every possibility, however. I think we can rule out a woman using that rifle tonight, of course. If nothing else, her presence in a residence hall would be remarked. It's well to keep in mind that the shooting and Popkin's death probably are quite unrelated." He used his hand to guide Craddock, who was nodding in confused agreement, toward the library door. "Tomorrow I'll send a note regarding the results of my investigation. There's nothing else to be done tonight. Michael has offered to go to Mrs. Bedell's in the morning and inquire after her health and that of Miss Singer. Perhaps by then he'll have solid news for them. Please give Miss Craddock my regards and assure her that this matter has my full attention."

Ushering his guest down the hall, I could hear Quincey still referring to the incident as a Halloween caper. But when he returned, he glumly replaced the stopper on the decanter and glanced at the clock, then at me. With deep feeling, he said, "Confound it!"

Resuming his seat, he held up a finger, saying, "In the past, my long-standing friendship with Craddock consisted of an exchange of books, articles, and notes, some of which were lengthy. He writes clearly and sensibly, and his ideas interest even when I can't agree. I enjoyed reading those communications. Any conversation was excluded. After this evening, I am determined that he and I *must* resume our previous arrangement."

# Chapter Fifteen

"**A**h, Mr. Merrick," the butler said, glancing at my card and bowing as low as he could, given the substantial paunch beneath his white weskit. "Please come in. Mrs. Bedell asked that you be brought to her without delay." As I walked into the vestibule of the Bedell residence, I heard the glittery sound of women's voices shimmering from the parlor into the spacious entry hall. I slid my eyes sideways, heart sinking. The massive hallstand on my left was heavy with fur-trimmed cloaks, and its base clutched a number of umbrellas in crook-shaped paws. And every visitor had apparently brought flowers. Huge vases filled with trumpeting amaryllis, elegant chrysanthemums, and tall stalks of gladiolus stood on every table and stand. Their insistent scents surrounded me.

I followed the liveried butler across the marble floor toward the parlor with unwilling steps. He too walked slowly, with a pigeon strut. As I went, I hurriedly straightened my hair and smoothed my beard.

This was not at all what I'd planned on my way here. When I came down to breakfast, Quincey was already in the conservatory. Only after I'd finished my poached eggs, potatoes, ham, and johnny cake did Freegift hand me his note with a few acerbic lines. "Hoggett is continuing his questions. He hasn't as yet found a student who resides in Holworthy Hall who was actually in residence during that time of the shooting. One claims he was in the library, which makes him suspect indeed. Six students who claim to be very reliable observers have pointed to four different windows at which they sighted the rifle. Josh Singer and Osbert Davies were separately making deliveries in the neighborhood of Harvard Yard. You can lay your mind to rest on one point. Hoggett has sent a copy of the announcement of Dr. Haskins's lecture on magnetic rods, and he'd have been speaking at that time."

That meant I had no news to deliver. I'd thought about that as the cab turned onto Brattle Street with the mansions of Tory Row, so called because the original owners were staunch followers of King George during the Revolutionary War There were seven of these, with lands and formal gardens that stretched all the way to the Charles. The newer residences, like Mrs. Bedell's, mimicked their dignified elegance. Hers was a three-story brick with white Ionic pilasters, a white roof-rail, and side piazzas which overlooked wide lawns. But the architect had decided to improve on the classic design. He'd stuck a very short portico over the front entrance, and it jutted out into the circular drive. While this sheltered those stepping out of carriages on their way to the door, it took away the sweep of the wide, pillared front.

Getting out of the cab beneath that, I'd decided to simply put my card—the right-hand corner of which was properly folded to indicate a personal visit—on the butler's silver salver. Then I was going to murmur a few words about returning the next day. Mrs. Bedell, I'd told myself, would surely be confined to her bedroom under her doctor's orders. But I'd planned then on asking if Miss Singer were in, assuming that the two Miss Craddocks would be in attendance so propriety would be observed. I hoped that I could at least get a few words with Sylvie regarding last night. Instead, I was going to get an audience with Cambridge society looking on.

The entrance to the parlor was framed above by swags of burgundy velvet drapes and gold tasseled cords that intermingled with the heavy folds of fabric on the sides, much like the curtains on either side of a stage. No sooner had I stepped onto the thick, flower-emblazoned carpet than the nearest group of women, none of whom I knew, fell silent. They were too polite to stare, but I felt their oblique glances. The entire room, twice the size of the ample sitting room I'd been in last night, was filled with imposing pieces of furniture, all with small knots of visitors gathered around, almost all female.

I looked over a sea of hats topped with feathers or flowers or ribbons or all three. Some of the women were seated on armless chairs or straight-back settees, balancing teacups. Others were standing by the ornate fireplace, or near a ceiling-high mirror with a baroque stand beneath it, or by the be-draped entrance to the library on the right. Apparently Mrs. Bedell had found the strength to write about her narrow escape, not only to Leonora Craddock, but to every woman of her acquaintance. Every one of them had come. All had braved the November drizzle seeping from a stony sky that pressed down on the treetops. They'd have attended with a nor'easter blowing. None would miss a chance at getting the story of the shocking incident last night in Harvard Yard.

I was going to have to walk past all of them.

At the far end of the room, I glimpsed a scrap of lace on a graying brown head framed by the upward swoop of a chaise back. A tall man beside her was bending low so he could hear her words. Since the butler was making his stately pace in that direction, I assumed he was heading toward his mistress. Equally slowly, trying not to lean on my cane, I came behind. Several times, I heard my name murmured after I passed.

As we neared, I saw three women on a curved settee on my right. In the center was Sylvie, and I couldn't stop looking at her. She was wearing a round-necked dress of iridescent blue, a fabric with a sea-shine to it. A circlet of pearls was at her throat, and her fair hair was pulled back from her face into a high cluster of curls that then coiled luxuriously down the back. She had an air of sitting alone, of not being a part of these surroundings, although her eyes were on the face of the woman beside her as she listened to her. What she was wearing was quite proper for this event, so maybe I had that impression of her apartness because such beauty never does fit in. It attracts, but it also distances.

"Good morning, Mr. Merrick." Emily Craddock saw me first, touched Sylvie's arm, and gave me a summer-sky smile. Her triangular hat had a white plume that curved stylishly toward her cheek. Her fine hair was fastened neatly in a bun in back. The antique lace collar of her dress relieved its prosaic brown. She looked as fresh and wholesome as a ripe fig. Her uncle's unkind description of her as a "pudding-faced girl" sprang to my mind. I wondered if he also overlooked her generous spirit. In her affection for Sylvie, there was no trace of envy. Happy to see her, I smiled back and bowed.

The third woman turned, and I would have recognized her as Leonora Craddock anywhere. But she wasn't the angular, thin-lipped female version of her brother that I'd imagined. Not at all. Her resemblance to Emily was striking. The roundness of the features and face were identical; their coloring, their height, even their dresses were similar. But there was an enormous difference. Emily was plump. Her aunt was obese. She filled two-thirds of the small sofa. Her fleshy forearms strained at the seams of her sleeves; her waist didn't exist. Her face was moon-round; her cheeks looked stuffed. Her eyes were almost swallowed in fat, giving them a small meanness. Or perhaps that was always there. Her mouth was permanently puckered with disapproval, even now when she nodded graciously at me to indicate she knew who I was.

The butler stopped behind the broad-shouldered man bending down to Mrs. Bedell, and I waited as well. He was saying, "—truly unfortunate that another doctor had to be summoned. *I* should have been here last night. You know I'd have come post-haste had I received the message. I was with another patient until quite early this morning. But her case hadn't the seriousness of the shock to the nervous system that you suffered. Still, I'm sure that Dr. Simmons did what he could. Nonetheless, I'm leaving the proper medicines for you and for Miss Singer with your housekeeper. Simmons is very young and inexperienced. Since your health is so fragile . . ."

He let that sentence trail off, as he shook his head in concern, before adding, "In any case, the powder I sent to you at first light will prevent any lasting deleterious effects. I'm persuaded of that because your pulse is stable. Of course, when my magnetic rod treatment is available—which will be soon, although I've not yet found the funds—you will be amazed at the difference in your health. For now, I only wish all my patients had your recuperative powers."

His voice held such calm authority that it was hard to imagine that anyone who heard him would ever question anything he said. Tall, strongly built, he was standing in slight profile, and it occurred to me that he appeared to be one of those sound-bodied, sane-minded, wholesome men that the expensive Boston dailies extolled as the ideal man of our times. He was in his fifties, and his graying hair was thinning in front but thick on the sides and marvelously well trimmed. In fact, everything about him was in good trim. His dignified suit was pressed, his shirt front immaculate, and his dark shoes shone with polish.

Just then, Mrs. Bedell saw me towering over her butler. Being so tall makes you too visible. She stretched out a hand covered with a lace fingerless glove and uttered, "Mr. Merrick." Then she paused dramatically. "You've come." Raising her eyes to the other man, she said, "I must introduce the two of you. Without this man's quickness and courage—and your superb care, Dr. Haskins—I'd not be here. I'm most certain of that. My dear Walter, watching from above, sent you both to look after me. I am the most fortunate of women."

Haskins's eyes, slightly red-rimmed from his last night's vigil, didn't smile, although he stretched his lips as he shook my hand. I gathered he wasn't used to sharing center stage. Then I recalled that it was his advice that Quincey ignored in the treatment of my legs and feet, relying instead on the Shakers' herbal treatment. I believe Dr. Haskins had favored amputation. I thrust that out of my mind.

At least his bedside manner couldn't be faulted. He bowed toward her as he said to me, "In saving Mrs. Bedell's life, you've earned the gratitude of all of us. I admire your prompt action, particularly because I'd have assumed the shot was a Roman Candle. I was myself in Harvard Yard to give a demonstration on the effects of magnetic rods to an interested group. The noise of the fireworks was distractingly loud. And I'm most relieved to hear from Miss Craddock that Mr. Quincey, whom I've met, is vigorously pursuing the young fool who fired into the crowd. He should be hung."

Turning to his patient, he took her bird-like hand between his two large ones and said, "Dear lady, to my regret, I've another patient to see this morning. But I'm confident that after you take the pills that I've given you, you'll soon be in the rosiest of health." He looked at her closely, adding, "Although I must admit that if I didn't know what you suffered, I'd believe you are in that state now because of your bloom."

That was true. A near-miss by a bullet had done wonders for Susanna Bedell. Attention was being paid. Overnight, she'd become an interesting woman. Her small, pale face lost its pinched look, and her color was heightened. Oddly, the excitement seemed to have calmed her abrupt, agitated movements. She was almost tranquil, although the small piece of lace on her head fluttered a bit, after Haskins took his farewell, as she turned here and there to see who'd arrived. Her eggshell-colored gown, heavily trimmed with the same lace, seemed chosen to underscore her delicate health, which somehow made an attempt on her life all the more reprehensible. Propped up by satin pillows against the high curve of the chaise, she gestured for me to be seated toward its end, which had no back at all. "Now, finally, Mr. Merrick, we shall have a chance to *talk*."

There was nothing to do but ease myself down near her feet. "Leonora," she began, in a hushed voice, "tells me that she *cannot* accept—try as she will—the idea that the shots were aimed at the effigy. Nor, as you know, do I. I know that Mr. Quincey is a brilliant man. A genius, as Professor Craddock says. Still, he is not acquainted with me or the extent of my connections. That person who fired wishes to kill me. You, who have saved my life, must help me determine who this is, or I shall never feel safe again. I beg your assistance."

Her eyes, fastened on mine, were pleading. She was twisting a heart-shaped tortoise brooch, and the gold filigree edge had silvery brown hair entwined in it. Then she lowered her lashes. "Here is what I propose. I will employ a person to watch the house, but clearly he cannot be included in social functions. It will, of course, be some time before Dr. Haskins would think of allowing me to be out and about, but I'm so hoping that Sylvie and I might depend on you for an escort when I'm strong enough to venture to musical evenings and dinners at the homes of my friends."

Hearing that, I started talking fast, desperately hoping that some excuse would come to me before I stopped. The thought of whiling away long evenings in Sylvie's company was very appealing, but that wouldn't be the case. At dinner I would always be seated next to Mrs. Bedell, presumably to fend off any attacker leaping from behind the ferns in the dining room. That meant that I'd be spending very long evenings listening to *her.* I plunged in. "Hiring someone to watch the house is an excellent idea, especially because it would assure all of us of your safety. It would certainly set your own mind at ease. Since the only time you'd be in danger is getting in and out of your carriage, the person watching over you could effectively be on guard. I'm know that, were he here, your husband would advise—"

"But of course." Her hands flew to her cheeks. She almost shrieked the words out. "Why didn't I think of that? We must ask Walter! He is watching me from the other side. In this instance, I'm sure Sylvie would be happy to conduct a séance. Mr. Merrick, you've once again done me a great service by the suggestion.

We've tried to contact him before without success, but this time, knowing of my danger, my dear husband will be sure to get through to tell—"

Suddenly, she became very still, staring at the person who was following the butler into the parlor. "Do see who has just come in! *He* has heard of my terrifying experience and has come here—to my home—to console me. And today, when all of Cambridge is here. Everyone will notice and see that I've been so honored! That such a man, renowned throughout all of New England, is visiting me is beyond all imagination." Her voice had an ecstatic tremble. "How good of him! While I attend his services faithfully, weather and my health permitting, we have only the slightest acquaintance."

Following her gaze, I saw James Cranch Meeker, dressed in a solemn black suit with a flowing gray jacquard cravat, stop every few feet to greet one woman or another. As he spoke, he spread his two hands wide as if in blessing. Or perhaps he was framing the face of his listener, as if she was all he'd want to see. He bent his magnificent head with its silvery-blond mane forward as if sharing a secret with each woman as he addressed her.

I recalled an article in the *Courier* which noted that the minister's frequent sermon topic was God's all-encompassing love for His created beings and the way we must both receive it and share it. The unnamed reporter wrote that this notion was most appropriate because when Cranch Meeker preached, his audience often included twenty of his mistresses. The minister never deigned to reply to such assertions. Maybe the article even increased the number of those in attendance on Sundays.

Watching his triumphal procession down the room, with the butler pausing each time to wait, I felt a

sharp rush of sympathy for Dr. Bock Bach. In distrib-
uting Popkin's estate, the purpose of which was to increase the human life span, he'd have to work with
men of widely differing views: Story, Haskins, Meeker.
Why did the dead man choose two doctors and a minister at a time when science and religion were squar-
ing off for the right to explain our existence? And why
choose Story, who was studying Spiritualism, and
Cranch Meeker, who abhorred it? From what I'd
heard of Popkin, he hadn't a sense of humor. Perhaps,
if he was the writer of the vituperative letters against
Spiritualism in the *Independent*, as Craddock suspected, he was trying to cover all possibilities. The effort to reach agreement with those men would surely
decrease Bock Bach's life span.

Suddenly, in agitation, Mrs. Bedell sat straight up,
leaned forward, and clutched my arm, whispering urgently. "We mustn't mention our plan to speak to
Walter while Dr. Meeker is here. He believes very
strongly that we shouldn't attempt to contact the spirits. Something about the Devil sending them. Although why *he* should do so, I cannot fathom."

Striding up to the chaise, not waiting for the butler
to murmur his name, the preacher thrust his arms
skyward and turned to face the assembled visitors.
Despite his light hair, he had dark brows, and beneath
them pale, compelling eyes. Middle age had given
him solidity but had not softened his firm jaw. He
rolled out his words. "Almighty God, for sparing us
this woman, we give You our gratitude. Now lend us
her gracious presence here for many more years." Despite the polite thanks at the beginning, his last sentence sounded rather like an order. But there was no
denying the fervor in his voice as he continued his
praise of God's love. Throwing back his splendid silvery head, he called out, "Amen!" Some of the

women repeated the word; others, wondering whether it was the expected thing, kept silence.

With a flourish, hands spread wide to include the entire chaise, he turned to the beaming Mrs. Bedell. "My dear lady, what degraded times we live in that violence should come near you. You, who are so—" He paused here, perhaps for effect, or maybe he was searching for an adjective other than 'rich.' He continued with, "—gentle, kind, and generous in your dealings with your fellow man. And to think that I myself was nearby and had not a premonition that you were in danger."

There was no doubt that he was going to continue but, at that moment, Mrs. Bedell's brimming eyes spilled onto her cheeks. She groped for a handkerchief, more lace than linen, beside her on the couch, covered her eyes, and wept. Cranch Meeker moved closer to lay a consoling hand on her shoulder. I saw the chance to escape.

Since I'd risen at his approach, I bent a little and said quietly in his ear, "Sir, permit me. I'll send someone with tea for Mrs. Bedell and for you."

Luckily, neither of the two uniformed maids who'd been serving were anywhere near. I hurried the length of the parlor before I saw one near the hall entrance. As soon as I explained, she set off with her tray and heavy silver pot toward the other end of the room. Seeing that Mrs. Bedell was still overcome, I decided that a formal farewell needn't be made and I could leave. Then I noticed that Sylvie was making her way in my direction. I changed my mind. I waited.

Just at that moment, there was the crash of the heavy outer door being thrown open. Then a thud, and a loud, angry voice boomed out.

# Chapter Sixteen

**P**ushing aside the drapes, I plunged halfway down the hall, taking in the scene before me. The butler was sprawled on the floor, gaping in astonishment. A burly man dressed in a weathered Stetson hat and a rough leather jacket with fringed sleeves stood over him, shaking his fist. "I won't be told agin she's not in when any fool can see she must be 'cuz she ain't come out all mornin'!"

"Sir!" I barked out the word. I planted my feet and lifted my heavy cane. "As you were not invited in, you should leave. Now."

He jerked his head up, took in my size, saw my held-out stick, and said in a much lower voice, with a trace of conciliation, "Wa'al, now, there's no call for any fuss. None atall. I got ever' right to be here. M' daughter's here." He leaned down, thrust out a thick hand, and pulled the even more surprised butler to his feet. Taking a tentative step forward, he burst out, "I jist want to see—"

Sylvie stepped around me and advanced toward him, stopping midway between the two of us. Her tone was even, but there was an edge of sharpness. "Father, there's no call for such an intrusion. I'm a guest of Mrs. Bedell's. She has visitors."

Josh Singer swept off his hat, revealing slicked-down hair that looked as if it'd been touched up with the same shoe blacking he'd used on the roan horses he'd sold. He had a bloated face, which made his eyes and nose look crowded in the middle of his face. The puffiness didn't take away his air of menace. His cheeks were pockmarked, and there was a dark stubble on his chin. Scratching his head carefully so as not to muss his hair, he kept his eyes on his daughter.

"I'm right glad to see ya, Sylvie." His vowels were as flat as Kansas, despite the fact that he'd lived for years in Cambridge. He must have a good ear at least for the sounds of others' speech. Whether he heard what they said was a different question. "And . . . and you look purty."

With a furtive upward glance, he took in the vault of the ceiling with its carved ropes and golden tassels and sculptured furbelows. He slid his eyes downward to the veined gold of the marble floor. He squinted at the tall mirrors that reflected only each other and the stiff, gorgeous flowers.

As still as she was, Sylvie might have been one of them. She made no move closer to him, nor did she ask him into a private room where their conversation couldn't be overheard. Her head erect, her back straight, she remained about five feet from him. Standing behind her, I could see her profile in one gilded mirror. Her face was composed, and her hands were clasped at the waist of the lustrous blue dress. Still, I decided that it'd be a very good idea to stay just where I was. I was going to back any decision she made.

Not one of those well-bred ladies as much as peeked around the heavy velvet drapes by the parlor entrance, although those nearest would have heard Singer's noisy shouts.

Now he managed to sound both abashed and defiant. "See here, girl, I been in town mosta' week and

I'm havin' trouble makin' ends meet. I figgered you'd hook up agin with them Craddocks, but that ol' man, he comes to the door when the girl fetches him, sticks his nose up, and says you wasn't stayin' with 'em and if I'd jist leave my address, he'd give it to ya. Add-ress," he snorted, drawing out the word, and swung his head aside as if to send out a spray of spittle.

But he cast a quick, uneasy look at me and seemed to reconsider that. "Wa'al, I looked up Goslip, but he's a bit short hisself and he's been bunkin' under the canvas in his wagon. At first, Os Davies says he cain't let me doss down in the loft in case Popkin came round. Os still rents from 'im and that man never'd give me a good word, even when I was workin' there reg'lar. Treated me like horse—" He clamped his lips together and then finished, "Manure." He made a hawking sound in his throat. Then he brought out a sly, delighted grin. "'Course, then he died, din't he? Right unner your nose. At a séance. Os seen it in the newspaper, said it was a judgment on him for goin' to one."

His smile died and his expression turned hangdog. "But, Sylvie girl, it ain't much better fer me. I got me a place to stay at the stables long as I help Os out a bit lookin' after the horses and takin' the odd package. But his business is slow so I ain't got proper eatin' money. And you been havin' the séances agin. So *you* got some."

Sylvie let out her breath in a sigh. "One séance. *One*, Father. I used the money to buy medicine for Robbie."

Josh banged his hat against his knee, spraying water drops from its wide brim onto the marble floor. He almost yelled in frustration. "You din't! Sylvie, you cain't be tellin' me that. Ya gotta know it ain't gonna do no good. Boy's not been right since birth, and there ain't nothin' you kin do about it. How could ya be such a darned fool?"

Her shoulders flinched, but her voice didn't tremble. "The doctor said—"

"Doctors! Now you lissen ta me fer once. Mebbe the ones here smell better than ol' Doc Carter, but they do the same thing. He'd grind up some stuff—mebbe he got from some ol' Injun, or mebbe from his back patch—throw in little bits of one or 'nother in some syrup. He did know the names of plants, I give 'im that, but that's *all* he knew. Now and agin I'd help 'im mix 'em up. Mebbe he'd try it out on his wife, and if she says her rheumatism was some better then it's Hallelujah time!"

Singer thrust his arms up with his hat and hands over his head, waggled his fingers, and twirled around in a heavy-booted dance. "Now's he got a miracle cure. He writes up the label and the stuff's supposed to cure not jist the rheumatism but everythin' from headache to hangnail. You 'member when I was sellin' his pills, his ointments outta the wagon goin' to Kansas! I even brung some of it with me here. I'll give it to ya' free, and it'll do jist what those pills ya got from that fancy doctor here'll do. Which is to say *nothin'*."

At that, I moved slowly but purposefully toward him. Sylvie's father or not, I was going to grab him by the scruff of his neck and pitch him through the door, whether it was open or not.

Taking two steps backward, he held up his hand to me. "Wait. Just wait a minit. I still got somethin' to say."

He twirled his hat brim in dirt-encrusted fingers, looked down at his cracked boots, and then in a wheedling tone, he asked, "Sure you ain't got a little bit of money left?"

"No, I haven't. But if I give another séance, I'll send you some money in an envelope in care of Mr. Davies. Os is an honest man, and he'll see you get it."

He raised his voice, blustering again. "Better be soon, girl. I need it. And ya don't want nothin' else bad happenin'—"

At this point I stepped quickly up to Sylvie's side. My tone was blunt. "Mr. Singer, now that you've gotten that assurance from your daughter, it's time to leave. The weather might worsen, you know. We could have a nasty day. The butler will see you out." I looked over his head. The servant was peeping around the wall of the vestibule.

Sylvie raised her voice, perhaps to preserve the illusion that he hadn't overheard the conversation, which he certainly had, and said, "Portman, would you be so good? My father is leaving."

Singer whacked his hat against his leg, glared, but said nothing as he spun on his heel and marched toward the vestibule. The butler opened the door quickly, standing well behind it, and Singer shoved his hat on his head and disappeared into the gray drizzle.

Lifting her face to me, more of a weary grimace than a smile on her mouth, Sylvie said, "Thank you for remaining, Mr. Merrick. I'm sorry that you were put in the uncomfortable position of witnessing a family matter. But my father—" She lifted her shoulders and let them fall. "You heard him. I'll not make excuses for him. He bullies when he can, cajoles when he can't. I had no wish to see him privately."

Her voice was steady, but I could see that her clasped hands quivered. As if she'd followed my glance, she clutched them together more tightly and pressed her elbows into her sides. Before I could answer, the door at the far end of the hall opened and the housekeeper, whom I'd glimpsed last night, came forward. No doubt she, like the butler, had been listening. "I beg your pardon, Miss Sylvie," she said, her eyes kind in a plump Irish face, "I was just in the parlor and thought it quite warm with all the visitors. So I put a tea tray in the morning room. Perhaps you'd enjoy a cup there."

Nodding twice, saying nothing, Sylvie put a hand on my forearm and held it quite firmly as we followed the housekeeper.

# Chapter Seventeen

Sylvie Singer and I sat in silence while the drizzle outside turned into a noisy sleet that pinged against the windows. The housekeeper had poured the tea and left. I had a lot to say, but I waited.

The room we were ushered into was empty, although it was certainly full of furniture. Small tables, all draped with fringed silk shawls, were scattered about beside plumply upholstered wing chairs and next to sofas with small hills of decorated pillows. Two colors dominated—green and gold—and the effect was soothing. There were all the shades of green from summer apple to winter pine. And all the golds from pale jonquil to deep saffron. Glints from these were reflected in the hammered bronze curlicues of the fireplace screen behind which huge logs glowed warmly.

Every surface, from the mantel top to the jutting wall shelves to the tables, was covered with bric-a-brac. Coming in, I walked carefully—putting my cane down precisely—lest I nudge a table and knock over a photograph, souvenir, etching, or china ornament. The room was meant to seem intimate, a place where the hostess and a close friend or two could chat in the morning. Unlike either the sitting room or the parlor, which opened onto that echoing hall, this room was closed off by solid doors, ensuring privacy. With such a large staff, Mrs. Bedell might have thought that a good idea.

I did. The questions I had to ask were personal in nature. While Sylvie could on occasion be open, she was normally reserved. Of course, if she was the woman of deep artifice that Quincey saw, could I even believe the answers if I got them? At the moment, I assumed she had to be uncomfortable, embarrassed by the scene with her father. Her elegant head didn't droop, but she was very pale, withdrawn, barricaded behind that beautiful face. Her transparent eyes gave away nothing of her feelings. Nonetheless, I was going to try to find out who Sylvie was, or at least what she knew.

At last, she took a deep breath, put a plate of ginger biscuits nearer me, and said, "You were right about the day turning nasty, Mr. Merrick. But then, given its beginning, one couldn't hope for clear skies."

"True, and if Mr. Quincey were here, he'd quote some gloomy Roman philosopher to the effect that hope is a snare and a delusion. However, he'd be wrong in this case. All my hopes for the day are being met. Not only am I having tea and crumpets with you, there is a table here. Few men are born with the talent of balancing a teacup, and I'm surely not one of those happy few. Moreover, Mrs. Bedell seems comforted by the company of her friends. You look well, but it'd be impossible for you to look otherwise." I brought out that last sentence in a hurried monotone to indicate that I hoped that was the end of the stilted pleasantries.

Sylvie managed a slight smile. "You have all my admiration, Mr. Merrick. You took my proper, if dreary, comment on the weather and turned it into a graceful compliment, all with good humor. And your tone indicates relief that all that has now been gotten out of the way."

"How are you really? Did you manage to sleep last night?"

"I didn't sleep well. Eventually, I took a sleeping draught, which I don't like to do, but it seemed to work."

"Mrs. Bedell is still convinced that the shot was meant for her because she's offended someone. Do you believe that?"

"No." Her answers, like her face, told me nothing. Apparently, all I was going to get today were careful replies.

"Do you accept the idea that a student was aiming at the effigy?"

"That's certainly a likely explanation." She picked up her teacup.

I set mine down and said pointedly. "Miss Singer, while we were walking last night, you said you hoped we might talk openly." I decided to jolt her off balance. "Now, Mr. Quincey suggested to me that your father might have fired that gun—I understand he's a good shot. He wanted to see you, and you were not willing to see him. So he shoots, but deliberately misses. A warning, perhaps. You'll recall that he just told you that you wouldn't want anything *else* bad happening."

Instead of the strong reaction I'd expected, she simply sat and thought for a moment. She carefully adjusted her necklace, whose pearls were the same pale ivory as her skin. She thought some more. At last, she answered, "My father is capable of doing that. You met him, and you're a perceptive man. You must have noted the envy that clawed at him seeing that vast hall, seeing the fine things that he'll never possess. His humiliation at always being judged by his poverty.

The sharp sense of need that drives him to beg. And, to be honest, sometimes to cheat. I say you noticed it because of the way you handled him, getting him out the door without humbling him further. You can't have a high opinion of him, but—"

As she paused, it occurred to me that was a real understatement. But more, what surprised me was her detachment. She was neither surprised at his behavior nor angry. He could have been a character of some interest in a novel we'd both read. She went on, "I don't believe he did shoot at me. I don't know what he meant by those words. Nor can I even guess at the name of a person who might try to kill me." She paused, swallowed, and said, "If that was what was intended."

We looked at each other. Neither of us spoke. I was determined to outwait her.

Finally she said, "Mr. Merrick, you think I'm not being forthcoming with you regarding my view of that . . . incident." She didn't phrase that as a question, and I didn't reply. Because of what she'd just gone through in that scene with Josh Singer, I really didn't like pressing her, but I was going to. There might not be another chance to talk to her alone. If she was in danger, I had to know more. For her sake. I was thinking of that shock of fear she showed last night. That was genuine fear. For herself. She must know something that called it forth.

Her gaze was direct, and her eyes more blue because of the deep sea hue of her dress. She said straightforwardly, "It's hard for me to say what I think because of your lack of trust in me. Your glance at me is as watchful as it was last night when you were alert to a threat."

It was a flat statement, with no hint of reproach. Equally bluntly, I answered, "You know why. The practices of many mediums, I should say most, have been exposed as fraudulent."

She nodded calmly. "Yes. I was taken aback when I read recently that even one of the Fox sisters, those little girls who started the movement, has admitted that those inexplicable rappings, which supposedly came from the spirits, were caused by her and her sister's ability to crack their toes loudly." With a faint smile, and a glance at her tightly fitted shoes, she added. "I assure you, I can't do that."

I had to smile back before going on. "Still, I can believe that not all mediums are frauds. Dr. Story mentioned the possibility of genuine psychic powers by which you—"

"Please, please, Mr. Merrick, don't ask me how it happens. That's the right phrase. It happens. I go into the clairvoyant state, as Miss Craddock phrases it." She stood up abruptly with a swish of silk, turned her back, and stared out the water-streaked window. "I slip into a trance. I don't know how. I've never known."

At her words, a chill went down my back. Her inflection, her tone, were exactly what I'd heard the day she stood beside the river, her back to me then as now. I sat, as motionless as if I were mesmerized. How could any dream so reflect reality?

Without facing me, she went on, "In Kansas, I once saw a man suffer an epileptic seizure. He couldn't have told you anything that he did during that time. Nor can I when I'm in a trance state. On both occasions when Dr. Story asked how it happened, sitting there so carefully taking notes, I told him this, but he simply rephrases the question! I say that I'm not aware of my surroundings when I'm in a trance." She turned and drew herself up, stroking her chin as it a goatee grew there, and mimicked the professor's intense voice, 'Miss Singer, when you're in such a state, do you feel a cold sensation?' "

Without a trace of a smile, she remarked. "I know why he does that. Very often, if one goes over the same ground, one might recall a fleeting impression that didn't surface at first. Or, if the person being questioned is lying, a constant barrage of similar queries might cause her to forget what she said the first time." Her tone was as neutral as she brought out the last sentence as it was at the first one. And she remained standing, her back perfectly straight. She seemed to have an inner corset on her feelings that was as rigid as the outer whalebone one she wore. She ended with a sigh. "And I shall have to talk to him many, many more times."

I put up a hand. "Wait. I wasn't going to ask you for an explanation. I was trying to explain why *I* was hesitant to trust." I stopped. While I believed that she was telling me part of the truth, I couldn't forget my imagining, if that's what it was, of her thinking: *Down there, maybe that's where I hear HIM, his calling voice. Familiar. Who is he? Who? What if HE starts talking to the people with my mouth?* Could that be accurate, even if I couldn't see how it could be? I put off the question of that voice in the inner darkness, asking only, "Would you mind telling me what you *did* tell Dr. Story?"

She came back to the table and sank down into the chair. "I don't mind. Our first talk, at the Craddocks', was brief. He asked me to recall what people told me occurred during the séances. You must remember that almost all of these took place when I was much younger. A child, really. Still, I did recall some of the 'messages.' One in particular I can't forget because the woman who heard it followed my family all the way to Kansas. We were traveling west then, and she was in our group of wagons, planning to leave in Ohio and stay on with a relative. But she attended one of my séances. She'd lost her little son Jem, and apparently in the trance I'd mentioned his favorite toy. An odd one. A stuffed elephant his uncle had brought him from India. No one at the séances had ever seen a picture of such an animal, they said. The mother had buried the toy with the child. She swore she'd never said another word about it, that she couldn't bear to speak of it. Wherever I was, she'd find me and stand before me crying and begging me for another message."

Sylvie slid her eyes, which looked unnaturally bright, toward the water-streaked window. "That woman's face remains with me. As far as I know, I never repeated other words from Jem. Nor did I have any messages from my baby brother who died with the measles on the way west. My mother so wished for one. Just a few words. That's all she asked for. But nothing came. As I grew older, I refused to continue with the séances."

When she began speaking again, though, her voice was calm. "Then, the second time, Dr. Story asked me to go over those earlier messages again for the assembled members of the Society for Psychical Research. And to repeat my description—which makes me sound like a simpleton—of the trances. He ended by asking me if I shared certain beliefs held by some of the Spiritualists. That is as far as we've gotten."

"Which beliefs?"

Straightening her pearls again, she answered, "He brought up the question of the 'eternal union.' The idea that we have an exact half in this wide world, and we should look for this spiritual counterpart."

There was the lightest irony in her tone. I could tell

where she stood on that, but I pushed her anyway.
"How did you reply?"

"Very briefly. I don't *want* to believe that. It's an ancient theory, older than Plato, as Dr. Craddock would
say. But if it were true, it'd be a cruel joke. Suppose
this person were born in another country, or died as a
youngster before you were born. Now if one accepts
the concept of reincarnation, which would give you
world enough and time, one might eventually discover one's ideal mate." Despite the warmth of the
room, she seemed to shiver slightly and then said
firmly, "Or so I imagine."

"And you rule out multiple lifetimes?"

Her gaze was directly on me, a wry twist on her
mouth. "Except, perhaps, for a rare Thursday when I
recall a distant glimmer of being somewhere that I've
never visited. Everyone's had that experience. And
everyone who's been at a deathbed has had that powerful sensation that between one heartbeat and the
next, the body before you is suddenly uninhabited.
The spirit has gone." The mocking irony left her
voice, but there wasn't a tinge of wistful hope. She
shrugged a graceful shoulder. "We could return to
this life, I suppose."

I had the immediate sensation that what she'd said
earlier about not wanting to believe was entirely true.
What went through her mind on those "rare Thursdays"?

"I find reincarnation hard to believe," I said. "Like
most people. I suppose it's because death is such a
painful fact in our lives and we're afraid that we're
only cheering ourselves up by denying it exists. Of
course, Mr. Quincey would say there's no evidence
for it."

"I could say to him there's no evidence against it,
either. Millions of people in Asia accept it." From her

tone it was obvious that one woman in Cambridge
didn't. She lifted her teacup, but set it down immediately. The bone-thin china must have felt cold to her.
Her lips curved, and her eyes lit with sly humor.
"Besides, Mr. Merrick, on the question of eternal
matehood, everyone says, when they fall in love,
that they feel this 'supernatural sympathy' for the
other person, as if they've found their other half. I
believe that impression usually fades, sometimes
very, very quickly."

She'd carefully shifted our discussion back into an
unemotional badminton match. I served; she flicked
her wrist in an easy return. At this rate, I'd never
learn what I needed to know. So, although it was a
rude question, given what I'd heard about her life, I
asked, "Everyone says? Have you never felt that kind
of 'sympathy'?"

She was quite unruffled, and her answer indicated
that she knew I was quite familiar with her past. "No.
When I met Alistair, we were living in Kansas. Because I wouldn't continue the séances—and I was, at
fourteen, the breadwinner—my parents were always
angry. My life had become"—she glanced toward the
gray rain outside—"a constant November. Alistair
was a handsome, blond, sunny man. He told wonderful stories, lightened all our lives. He wanted everyone to be happy and tried to make them so. He gave
every impression of warmly agreeing that I shouldn't
have to continue as a medium. So, I saw marrying
him as a way out of my dilemma. And I liked him
very much."

She gave a quick sigh. "Poor Alistair."

I sat upright abruptly. We were talking about a man
who'd married her illegally, who'd then abandoned
her, pregnant and penniless, who had left her to go
through labor alone, on a bitter day in a cold room.

The words came out before I could stop them, "Poor *Alistair?*"

Sylvie's glance swept the room. "How can I explain? We had no money. He was wretched because of that, and he can't bear that feeling. It hurt him to see me so miserable. But if he'd had to take a job, say as a bank teller, he'd be unhappy every day, a prospect he couldn't face. He kept pointing out to me that I could become quite famous as a medium and we could travel about, have pleasant days for a few nights' work and more money than we needed. But I refused. At last, he couldn't bear his pain. So he left. I'm sure he was very sorry about doing that."

Clamping my lips together, I just kept looking at her. And she looked back at me with those mermaid eyes. For all I knew, there could have been boundless rage behind them, but I couldn't tell. I had only her words in my ears.

"I should add," she said meditatively, "that I can imagine feeling that love, but from what I've seen, it isn't ever 'free,' is it?" Her eyes were still on mine. "Certainly not for a woman. And rarely for a man, if it's genuine."

And that answered that question, if not in the way I'd put it. But there was one more I had for her. "Earlier you used the word 'messages.' Has Dr. Story asked you if you yourself believe those are from spirits?"

She shook her head. "No. He's approaching the question of my opinion, as opposed to genuine knowledge, slowly. Perhaps he wishes me to keep an open mind as we discuss possibilities. I wonder what I'll say when he does ask." Suddenly, she shuddered. "It still frightens me to think that the dead might speak through me. It terrified me as a child. I thought that if they could talk to me, they'd come into my room at night. Just bare bones and grinning skulls. Their feet would clack on the floor as they came slowly closer and closer toward my bed. I thought they'd lean down and press those gaping mouths against my ear to whisper messages."

As I listened, I remembered my childhood dread of skeletons. I saw a picture of one in an anatomy book of my father's and I couldn't get it out of my mind. It was only much later that I realized I lived with my own skeleton. After Sylvie's experiences with séances, anyone would be reluctant to hold another.

At this exact point I made up my mind to believe her. Quincey's suspicions be damned. He'd say that Sylvie was shrewd to come up with that grieving mother and that horrifying nightmare, just to win me over. But, because of what she said and the way she said it, I thought she was being honest. Maybe not completely open with me, but honest. In fact, she struck me as being a truth-teller. Such people are always asking themselves how they know what they know. They're afraid to lie because the untruth might stick in their heads and confuse them.

Whether or not this was a murder case, I was now convinced it *wasn't* a case of fraud.

I chose my words as carefully as she chose hers. "I accept that you don't *know,* and in a scientific inquiry such as Dr. Story is conducting, you are right in being cautious about voicing your opinions. But," I said flatly, "now that you're older, you don't *believe* it's the dead speaking through you."

She searched my face for some time before she replied. She began as if she were musing aloud. "I don't know why you seem like an old friend to me, Mr. Merrick. Maybe it's because you're sympathetic. Your eyes can be hard, but you have a sensitive mouth. An expressive face. It's in my own best interests to tell you because you wish to protect me, should I be in danger. Yes. *I* accept that I don't know. I'll tell you what I believe, although I've never told anyone else. Never."

After that, she sat in silence for some time, staring at the cold rain that slid down the window.

# Chapter Eighteen

When she finally spoke, I thought I heard the faintest quiver, but she showed no outward sign of agitation. The tiny tendrils of hair on her forehead, pulled loose from the elaborate curls on the top of her head, were not damp. Her hands were folded in her lap. Her tone became firmer. "However, I risk my livelihood by answering. I trust you not to repeat what I say. No, I don't hear the dead. But while I desperately hope I never have to give another séance, I may have to. People won't flock to a medium who doesn't believe in her work. Nor would the Society of Psychical Research continue to pay me. All those men want reassurance that the soul survives. While Dr. Story would be willing to work with me as an opportunity to learn more about the powers of the human mind, to try to discover how I know what I know, the others really wouldn't be interested. And even he, who lost his fiancée just before their wedding, has such hope in his heart that he'll hear from her."

She shook her head slowly and with real regret. "What happens to me when I'm *not* in a trance state may throw light on what happens when I am. I have a strange ability. I must tell you first about that." She stopped, and it was clear she didn't want to go on.

I prompted her. "You can read people's thoughts?"

"It's telepathy of a kind. But make no mistake, as I

sit here, I have no idea what you're thinking. What I can do, on occasion, is feel your feelings. I can sense almost anyone's emotions, although not at any given time. Women are supposed to be intuitive. From birth you and I were told that. It's said that if women were educated, they'd lose that delicate sensibility. But I'm not talking about mere intuition. Nor do I mean the ability to decipher the language of another's body. Coupled with that person's words, men too can know a great deal, as you could by observing my father. No, I mean I *physically* feel another's emotion. Growing up, I assumed all women did. One always hopes one is normal, like others. But in the last few years, I've decided I'm different in this regard."

I stared at her, really uneasy that anyone could feel what I might be feeling. "So you have empathy raised to a high degree."

She grimaced. "Compassion is desirable. We all need more of it. But this is a cursed gift. I must always be watchful so I can separate my emotions from those of others because I feel them as my own. I hurt just as they do."

Her eyes fell to her hands clasped in her lap. I should say 'clenched' since her knuckles were white. "One evening, Mrs. Bedell and I were in the sitting room, reading. I was engrossed in one of Miss Austen's novels. As I recall, she was describing a wedding. The next instant, I was consumed with grief, a terrible sense of loss. It was all I could do to hold on to the book so that I wouldn't cry out in pain. Mrs. Bedell had her eyes on a fashion magazine, but her dead husband was on her mind, in her heart. For a moment, I was inconsolable at the loneliness, the emptiness that comes when one loses a lifelong companion, something I've naturally not known."

Shaking her head slowly from side to side, she

seemed to be trying to empty out that thought. "The hardest part, I find, is that I can't judge people harshly, perhaps even when I should. Their foolishness, their thoughtlessness, their unkindness become too understandable when you know why they act as they do. It blurs my thinking."

I let out my breath. "You can feel all emotions?"

"No. Not at all. It has to be a very strong emotion or a deep memory of it. I'd describe it as a primal one. Rage, fear, despair, desire, for example. Not just a fleeting feeling. And, again, not everyone's. It's not something I can control. Sometimes I'm talking to someone, and nothing comes to me. Other times, I feel battered, shaken, but I don't even know the source— that is, whose feeling I'm experiencing. It does have to be someone in the room, as far as I can judge."

"So thoughts themselves don't enter into it?"

"I don't think so. Perhaps *I* translate the emotion into my own words."

Then, to my surprise, she smiled wanly as she said, "Some don't need translating. When we were walking in the Yard last night, I distinctly felt your real love for a woman. A woman you admire and respect, as well as desire. And I was aware of your aching, your piercing sense of loss because she won't marry you."

Even my ears felt hot with embarrassment. I recalled too clearly the wave that overtook me when I was thinking that it protected me from Sylvie's attraction. Lust and love come together. Hurriedly, I slid my hand down my beard, hoping it hid my flushed face. The thought of talking about it made me take out my handkerchief and wipe my perspiring forehead.

But I'd asked her to be straightforward. It was my turn. Clearing my throat, I brought out, "Yes, that's true. She's a Shaker. Celibacy is a tenet of their religion."

"Was she raised in that faith?"

"No. She wasn't. But their sureness in the soul's immortality is very strong. I think she *wills* herself to believe. As long as she's with them, she doesn't doubt either. Every day she sees her delighted spirit, freed at last, rushing down a road by flowery fields, imagines seeing again—" I stopped. I was reliving pain.

After a moment, she said, "I see. I'm sorry. You feel you can't ask someone to give up a hope of heaven."

We needed a change of subject. After a longer moment, I asked, "What would you guess happens to you in the trance state?"

"My self disappears. So there's no filter. That person's feelings come out as thoughts directly through my mouth. Understand, I can only guess at this, based on what others have told me after the séances. I don't *know*."

I considered that: the loss of the self. In my nightly dreams, the sense of my psyche being present was always there, if only as an observer. Slipping into an opium reverie, blissful or terrible, there I was, most of the time, although I didn't want to be. I was trying to escape the pain of life without dying. It couldn't be done.

For Sylvie, this absence of self would be hard. She clearly felt the need to be in command of her own emotions because of her "strange ability" to experience those of others. Probably she constantly suppressed her own. You could see it in her stiff posture, her reserve, her remoteness. Perhaps, too, she saw self-control as necessary because she had so little over her life. It was understandable that she'd dread slipping into a trance.

With real curiosity, I asked, "Do you ever hear voices when you're not in a trance state? Last night I heard—"

I intended to finish by repeating Craddock's words regarding her childhood experience.

But I had no chance to finish the sentence. For the first time, Sylvie Singer dropped her guard. She stared at me in amazement, her hands gripping the table, her face a white mask, her words spilling out. "So *you* heard him, too! His words came through me! Out of my mouth. I've always been afraid of that."

"Who? What did he say?"

Suddenly, she relaxed a little, but her eyes were still enormous. She let go of the table edge and let out her breath. "Oh, I see. I must have repeated the words aloud. That's all."

"What words? What did you hear?"

Her shoulders hunched a little, as if she were gathering herself inwards. She clenched her hands; her lips were pressed together.

"Sylvie, tell me." Her first name slipped out.

She didn't look at me when she spoke. "When I was a child, I heard voices. Singing, laughing, whispering. After a time, I realized it was always the same voice. His. He seemed young then too. He told me stories, but as if he were reminding me of things I already knew. When he spoke, pictures came to mind, strange scenes that were somehow familiar. So was the sound of his voice, as if I'd heard him before, knew him before. But I didn't think he was dead. Only gone. Somewhere else. I soon learned that other people didn't hear such things. Insanity is an ugly word."

Now she glanced at me quickly, a worried frown between her brows. My expression seemed to reassure her, but her next words came out fast, as if she wanted the subject over, closed. "I . . . stopped listening. Maybe he spoke to me when I was in a trance state, but I never remembered it. While waking, I didn't hear him. Well, perhaps only a sentence, a phrase, at odd times. Not often. But last night he was shouting at me, shouting from inside me. 'You're in danger. In danger.'"

"You've never had such an experience before?"

"No." She crossed her arms in front of her, gripping her elbows. "No. But last night, I couldn't sleep because he whispered from every corner of my mind. Sometimes he'd just sigh my name, saying 'Sylvie' over and over again. I couldn't drown him out. That's why I took the sleeping powder."

She was in real need of reassurance. I brought out, "Let's think about this. My sister Celia had an imaginary playmate. She insisted on an empty chair next to hers at mealtimes for her friend. I've since heard that's not uncommon for children. When I teased her about it, she no longer talked about it. Suppose you had a similar experience, but you were made to feel deeply ashamed. You pushed the idea down, away from you. What happened last night was shocking, terrifying in its suddenness. That could shake loose all sorts of unconnected fears."

Leaning forward, I put my hands over hers, which were still clutching her elbows. "It seems natural to me that you wouldn't be able to push these aside immediately. Too, after such an experience, the agitation in one's body affects the mind. As you become calmer, the voice will disappear."

There was doubt in her eyes, but her brow smoothed. "You are a kind man, Michael," she said finally.

Then there was another voice in the empty room. We both heard it. A small one, saying, "Aah. Aah. There you are!"

# Chapter Nineteen

Sylvie sprang up, turned her head, looking distractedly around the room. Then she bent quickly before the shawl-draped table about three feet from us. Throwing back the cover, she knelt on the floor, her feet behind her. "Robbie," she said. "Come out, please."

Curled up on his side beneath the wide table legs was a little boy of about three, his head resting on a sofa pillow. At first, it was hard to make him out because his green velvet suit merged into the deep-green patterned carpet. Then he sat up slowly and sleepily. With a mother's automatic gesture, Sylvie put her hand on the top of his head lest he stand abruptly and bump it. Beaming, he crawled out instead, climbed into her lap, and his smile became one of delight. "Mama, here you are." He snuggled his head against her shoulder. His golden ringlets shone against the silk of her blue dress.

"My dear," she said, trying to put a note of stern reproof in her voice, but not quite succeeding, "you've run away and hid from Nanny Doris again. You shouldn't. She wants you to be safe, and you need to be with her so she can watch out for you. Otherwise, she worries. And if you're not with her, so do I because then I don't know where you are."

"I find *you*," he answered reassuringly. She shook

her head slightly at him, but since she was smiling back at him, it couldn't be considered a scolding. Medieval and Renaissance artists never tired of painting the Madonna and her infant, always trying to capture that look of love a mother turns toward her child. It says so clearly that she sees no flaws. Sylvie obviously saw none. Absorbed in him as she was, she relaxed her tight shoulders, curved her body around his. Here was an emotion she knew was hers, was genuine, and she needn't hide it.

She brushed the curls up from his forehead, delicately trying to feel for any sign of fever. He lay very still against her, obviously content, and showed none of the restless energy of a small boy. His small hand, splayed like a starfish against her dark dress, seemed mostly bone. The heavy velvet of his suit didn't hide his body's thinness. His velvet knickers ended at the knee, and his calves were encased in thick green stockings. But I could see his legs were as narrow as saplings and looked barely able to support his light weight.

He turned his head to look at me and regarded me intently. He was a beautiful boy, but his pale oval face hadn't the round-cheeked look of a healthy child. His eyes were an odd color. Surrounding his light gray pupils, there was a silvery tinge. It emphasized the clear whiteness of his eyeballs. There was curiosity in his gaze and, I thought, a touch of apprehension.

Sylvie said to him, "This is Mr. Merrick. He lives next door to Aunt Leo and Uncle Giddy." Her smile was pleased, proud, as she added, "My son, Robin."

"How do you do, Robin?" I said politely, trying to avoid that fake heartiness that often seems to infect adults' voices when they address children.

He stared at me for a second longer, and then said, "Feet hurt."

"I'm sorry to hear that," I replied. "Where do they hurt? Your toes, your heels? Or all over?"

He glanced down at his brown shoes, clasped over the arch with a strap and buckle on the side. Moving his ankle in a slow circle, he scrutinized his foot, then shook his head. Abruptly he pointed a small dimpled finger at me. "Not mine. Yours."

Taken aback at first, I stared back at him. Then it occurred to me that, although he might have been drifting off in sleep as we came in, he could have heard my halting steps despite the thickly carpeted floor. Or, while visiting the Craddocks, he could well have seen me in the courtyard during the last month. While he wasn't in good physical health, there wasn't anything wrong with his mind.

I nodded at him. "They do hurt. For a while yet, I have to use a wheelchair, and that helps. It's a good one, made especially for me by a friend at the Shakers. You just touch the wheels," I demonstrated with my fingers on the arms of the chair, "and you spin forward fast. Have you seen mine?"

Almost dreamily, he moved his head back and forth against his mother's shoulder, his curls brushing against her cheek. "No. I'll have one. A good one, too."

"Robbie," Sylvie protested hurriedly, "you can walk. And soon, one day, you'll be able to run. You won't need a wheelchair."

He hummed for a long time, sounding like a drowsy bee, before saying, "I will, though."

Then, with only the sketchiest of knocks, the side door flew open. A round-faced, red-haired girl, her face wrinkled with worry, stuck her head in. Letting out a loud sigh of relief, she came in, bringing out apologetic words as fast as she could. "I'm so sorry, Miss Sylvie. Truly, I only took my eyes off 'im fer a

minit. We were up by the attic window, lookin' at all
the carriages comin' round the drive. He was happy
as a clam, sittin' on my lap, and makin' horse noises
as they pulled up. But the gray carriage pulled by
those gray horses came, the fancy one, you know,
with the snakes on the stick painted on the door—"

She stopped. Clearly she was avoiding saying a
name. But the caduceus on the door she mentioned
could only have referred to a doctor's vehicle.

Putting out a freckled hand in explanation, she
went on. "So Robbie got real nervy and I decided to
take him back to the nursery. I was gettin' out his little
soldiers, and the next second, he's gone. I been turnin'
the house upside down. I won't let it happen agin.
Honest."

"I understand, Doris. I know how fast he can move.
And then he hides and falls asleep." Sylvie kissed her
son's ear lightly and murmured into it, "You see, my
dear, how worried Nanny Doris was. And if I hadn't
found you, I'd have been so afraid myself. You *must*
stay with her." Like all mothers, she believed that repeating her point would work.

Like all children, Robin was making an entirely different point. His tone was patient, reasonable. "Doctor came. Had to look for Mama."

"Oh, Robbie. The doctor wasn't coming to see you.
He was visiting Mrs. Bedell. She wasn't well last
night."

The boy sat up in alarm. "Give her medicine?
Shouldn't take it!"

Patting his shoulder comfortingly, Sylvie glanced at
me and said in explanation, "Robbie doesn't like the
powders Dr. Haskins prescribes for him. Even when
we add blackberry syrup, the mixture doesn't taste
very good."

Lifting his face to his mother, as if he just remembered something, he said, "Man looking for you, too."

"Who?" Sylvie asked.

He looked back at me, studying my face. He shook his head as if it were heavy on his neck. His light eyes with their silvery ring slid left and right as he thought. At last, he said, "Did know but can't remember."

Maybe from the attic window he'd seen Josh Singer across the road, pacing, watching for his daughter to come out, perhaps taking cover from the drizzle under the bushes that overarched the fence of that house.

Setting Robin on his feet, Sylvie held his waist until he seemed steady on his spindly legs. She stood up and smoothed the folds of her skirt. "Now," she said, "Nanny Doris will take you back to the nursery. It's time for lunch. If you eat your soup, you can have ginger biscuits and milk afterwards. Maybe you'd like to play with your soldiers then or listen to a story. Wouldn't that be good?"

He grasped the silk of her skirt tightly. He pleaded, "You come, too."

She leaned down, the long curls of her back hair falling forward. "Robbie, Mrs. Bedell has guests. I should go back to the parlor."

Still clutching the shining fabric of her dress, he said winningly, "Eat all my soup if you come. Even if I don't like it. You come, just to the top of the stairs."

Sylvie smiled, loosening his hold on her dress, taking his hand. "All right then." She looked at me as she added, "I'll have to return to the guests after that. Mrs. Bedell is probably tiring, and perhaps I can persuade them, one by one, to take their leave. I do hope we can talk again soon." Although the nursemaid behind her would have considered that a sedately proper remark from Sylvie, I heard the friendship in her last words. "Good-bye, Michael."

I stood up regretfully. As she, the nanny, and Robin left, he was still bargaining to keep her with him. "You come up all the stairs. Down the hall to the nursery. To the door."

Sylvie's warm laugh floated back toward me as the morning room door closed behind them. It was the first time I'd heard her laugh.

She hadn't had much reason to do so in her life. Sinking back down onto the lyreback chair by the table, I thought over what she'd said in that light. Rescued briefly from the impoverished misery of her childhood, she'd been thrown back into a hardscrabble existence, jounced in a wagon in searing heat and brutal cold across the prairies. Along the way, she'd been exploited for money, holding séances that brought her pain. I could imagine the effect of all this on a highly intelligent, sensitive, and imaginative girl.

I couldn't sit. Weaving my way around the cluttered tables and overstuffed chairs, I tried to grasp what Sylvie had just told me. I didn't doubt *she* believed she had a "strange ability" to feel other's emotions. It even seemed to make her patient with that scoundrel of a father. She'd clenched her hands instead of pitching a heavy vase of flowers at his head. But did she really experience such things in a rarefied form of empathy? Or did her mind create vivid fictions to which her body reacted? When reading a description of a wedding, maybe she noticed, but didn't quite notice, a tear slide down the widowed Mrs. Bedell's cheek. Anyone might sense that pain. As for knowing my unhappy love, she might have heard that part of my story. Who knows what I cried out in delirium while Mrs. Hingham and Freegift were at my bedside? If Sylvie saw a flash of longing and despair on my face, she could guess the cause.

I paced back toward the door, careful not to bump into the piecrust table that held a small shrine to Mrs. Bedell's husband. There was a photograph of him in his coffin and two thin vases on either side with one lily each. A gold ring in a glass box was in front.

Sylvie's trance states. Maybe somewhere on the unbearably long road to Kansas, she'd succeeded in slipping away inside. Dr. Mesmer and his followers hadn't any trouble getting patients to slide into such a state, so it might be possible to do so on one's own. While "sleeping," Sylvie's amazing memory might bring up things she'd heard. As Dr. Story said, our understanding of the vast potential of the human mind was limited.

The explanation I'd put forth of the dark inner voice could be accurate. I twiddled my cane between my palms.

Edginess was tightening my body. I rubbed the back of my neck. I was as tense as Sylvie. No matter my soothing words to her, I still felt she was in need of protection. The bullets were real. Then the thought jumped into my mind that I'd heard something in the parlor that troubled me. From Mrs. Bedell? No. The idea of the upcoming séance would by itself disturb me, but that wasn't it.

What I needed to do was figure out how to keep her safe. Trying to understand her was useless. I wasn't going to solve the mystery that was Sylvie. I was hampered at the start because whenever I looked at her, some painting or other sprang into my mind. I didn't mean to turn her into an object, no matter how beautiful. But I did. I couldn't seem to close the distance or get any nearer.

It occurred to me that if I told Story some of what

she'd told me, he might make sense of it. I could ask him general questions, anyway. He'd said he'd visit this morning and might be in the parlor. I grasped the knob and stopped. I wasn't going to be able to face that again. No, I'd sneak past that crowded room and out the front door.

Then I heard an imperious question coming from the hall. "Where is Miss Singer?" I wasn't going to get away so easily.

# Chapter Twenty

"You must understand, Mr. Merrick"—Leonora Craddock leaned forward, her corset creaking beneath the dull-brown fabric of her dress—"that I've gone more deeply into the nature of the spirits than any woman of my acquaintance and, I daresay, most men. In Summerland—messages we've received from the other side refer to it that way—spirits exist as a more highly perfected form of matter. But they still enjoy the refined pleasures of this world, of course. Good music, tasteful books, well-prepared food, wine—although certainly not cigars, as one man has written."

She drew her breath in impatiently. "As for the idea that they go without clothing, as some have seriously suggested, that is *not* to be considered. They *cannot* have so forgotten propriety. Their descriptions make it clear that the next world is much like ours, although more desirable in every way. The mansions in which they live are quite elegant. I envision them as set in surroundings much like one of the better parts of London. But Nature makes no leap, even over the grave. Why would the spirits behave differently there than they did here?"

Although I was returning her gaze with an expression of bland politeness, I was recalling a remark by the author Henry David Thoreau to the effect that, if those rapping spirits' reports were accurate about the quality of the future life, he'd exchange his immortality for a glass of cold beer. Leonora and I were having the discussion on Spiritualism that I'd really hoped I could avoid, although I'd always seen it looming darkly on the horizon. But, after asking where Sylvie was, she'd thrown open the door of the morning room. Her eyes were narrowed into half-moons of suspicion. It was clear that she surmised as she'd marched up to the door that some rule of proper conduct was being violated behind it. If nothing else, I certainly shouldn't be having a private interview with Sylvie, with whom I was barely acquainted. I introduced myself, apologizing because I hadn't had the opportunity to do so sooner, and explained that Miss Singer and Doris had at last taken Robin up for his lunch, leaving the impression that the boy and the nursemaid had been with us all the time. Mollified, she sailed into the room, meekly followed by Emily, who ventured only a timid greeting but smiled shyly at me behind her aunt's back.

Rigidly upright, the two women were perched on the edge of the sofa. The piles of pillows and their bustles made it impossible for them to sit farther back, and both looked quite uncomfortable. Emily edged a little sideways, but that pulled the fabric of her sober brown dress slightly above one ankle and, blushing, she hurriedly rearranged her skirt. Her aunt shot her a frowning sideways glance, but that movement allowed more room for her and she took it. Settling in, Leonora had immediately addressed me on the subject of a séance. "Advising Mrs. Bedell to consult her dear husband Walter on her fears was *most* wise of you. Now, we'll have to make preparations today—"

This time I clamped my teeth together because, although I wanted to explain that Mrs. Bedell had truly misunderstood me, I could see that interrupting this woman was beyond my powers. Probably beyond anybody's powers. Having her think I was inclined to her beliefs was much easier. Conversations with true believers of all sorts go better if they're one-sided. And I was likely to get out of here faster that way.

"—since the séance, conducted by Miss Singer, of course, will be held at my residence. This is agreeable to me, as it will be to my brother Gideon." I sat up at that news. She obviously hadn't asked Sylvie if having one at all was agreeable to her, wherever it was held. I didn't like the idea any better than she was going to. My objections centered around her safety.

"Miss Craddock—" I began firmly.

"I do know what you're going to say, sir." She waggled a finger at me. "You're going to ask why it would not be held here since Mr. Bedell lived in this residence for many years. Now, some *would* say that our chances of communicating with him specifically would be greater in such familiar surroundings. This is nonsense. You must let me explain this fully. Sylvie is such a 'light,' as we term a genuine medium, that she can serve as a channel for any spirit wherever the séance is held. You're aware, no doubt, that it was I who raised her during her formative years."

I settled back in my chair, deciding to wait until I had her full attention. She shifted her position, trying for a little ease on the sofa, and her corset complained again. A recent ad in the *Independent* proclaimed that the best of such undergarments were now supported with ivory. Thinking of tusk of elephant and rib of whale, I found myself wondering why women should wear such things. The bones of dead animals digging into their soft skin, making it hard to breathe. Were they afraid of the way their own bodies moved? Or was it some man's idea? Couldn't have been. Well, maybe a revival preacher.

Pressing on the tight bun at the back of her neck, Leonora was continuing, "The truth of it is, Susanna prefers not to hold a séance here lest the report of it reach the ears of Dr. James Cranch Meeker, whom you saw just now in the parlor. He is a minister of world renown, true, but he's unenlightened about Spiritualism. He actually fears that a lying devil or angel—yes, an angel sent to discourage us from endeavors to communicate with the beyond—might impersonate one of our loved ones."

Her eyes, puffed underneath, opened as wide as they could. "Preposterous. As if we experienced attendees couldn't tell the difference. But Dr. Cranch Meeker doesn't understand—as yet—the scientific underpinning of our movement. At a lecture I attended recently, the speaker emphasized the important contribution we séance-goers are making to empirical science. We are slowly opening a door to the other world that people thought was forever closed. Some find that impossible to believe. Yet the telegraph was once considered marvelous. My father was stunned by the idea of receiving immediate news from many parts of the country, when it once took months. He said he couldn't get his mind around it. Now we take the telegraph for granted. Science has reduced it to a completely understandable accomplishment. This will happen regarding our communication with those who've passed on."

Leonora tried again for comfort on the sofa. When Emily made a slight movement also, her aunt said sharply, "Don't squirm. It's most unladylike."

Ignoring Emily's painful blush of embarrassment at her criticism, she continued, "Admittedly, there are those amongst us who are willfully ignorant of the scientific aspects of Spiritualism. For example, they mock the fact that at some of our gatherings, the table moves, without being touched by any in the room. Before the last one, my brother Gideon remarked that he hoped our domestic furniture wouldn't attempt such impertinence, as he put it. I had to explain the obvious to him, despite the fact that he's a highly educated man. The movement is caused by a redundancy of electricity. Moreover, some have tried to make the point that, as the spirits are bodiless, they have no hands to knock on the table. These raps, of course, are caused by an electromagnetic discharge from the fingers and toes of the medium."

Brushing the air with a pudgy, emphatic hand, as if to wave away any arguments, she added, "As a lecturer noted, those who are unaware of the daily intrusions of the invisible world into the visible are truly blind."

Turning to me with a narrow smile, she said, "Now, as to the séance. Although Susanna and I have only exchanged a few words on the subject, we agreed that Wednesday next would be the best date." She frowned as she thought aloud. "Today is Saturday. Invitations will have to be issued at once. Then refreshments and flowers need to be procured. You will see to this, Emily. We have the Java burner, which is ideal for the frankincense." She rounded on her niece. "And this time, because of the cost, do *not* use quite so much."

Without listening to Emily's hurried apology, she continued with her plans. "But the most important decision will be in regard to those we invite."

As she paused to go over her mental list, I said quickly, "You're being a good friend to Mrs. Bedell by having this gathering. I can appreciate that. However, it occurs to me that because of the ill-fated end of the last one, perhaps Miss Singer might be reluctant—"

"I assure you that won't be the case," she broke in firmly. "Sylvie will do anything in her power to comfort Mrs. Bedell, who has been a very good friend to her. Susanna's nerves are much affected because of the outrageous incident last night. Dr. Haskins is concerned. She needs her mind set at rest, the sooner the better for her health's sake. If there is the slightest chance that Walter can get through, it must be attempted."

With equal firmness, I said, "Miss Craddock, I'm concerned about Miss Singer's safety. If Dr. Popkin was poisoned, his killer might believe that she knows more—"

Leonora shook her head decisively. "Sylvie has said— and her statement was published in Mr. Quincey's newspaper last night—that she doesn't. As for protecting her, all the more reason to hold the séance at our residence, where she will be quite safe. A hired person will escort Susanna and Sylvie to and from the carriage. *You* will be at the séance, and my brother says you seem quite fit now. And this further thought probably hasn't yet come to your mind. Perhaps Dr. Popkin himself might send a message. We'd then know the truth of the whole affair!"

I ran an open palm down my beard and then kept my hand over my mouth to make sure it stayed shut. I might as well try to stop an oncoming locomotive with a stiff arm. Emily's eyes were on mine, and she gave a sympathetic wince.

With the satisfied air of having settled minor matters, Leonora returned to the list of invitees. "We'd best plan on having only six, plus Sylvie, of course, because we don't wish to bring in another woman who's unfamiliar with our circle. I'll be one and then Susanna and Emily. As for the men, there is a problem because my brother Gideon returned last night from his discussion with you and Mr. Quincey vowing that he'd never attend another séance. I'm not sure what

was said that so disturbed him. He kept muttering
about my herbal tea being served. It was, and will be,
because it's light and soothing. However, we'll have
you, Mr. Goss, and Dr. Story. I just spoke to the professor in the parlor and he's most eager. Should Mr.
Goss fail us, and I'm sure he will not—"

Leonora was interrupted by a sharp knock on the
door. The butler opened it and muttered an apology.
"Sir," he addressed me, "there's a gentleman at the
door with a waiting hansom cab. He says he needs to
speak to you urgently."

After a reminder about the time on next Wednesday, Leonora bowed her head graciously, excusing
me. I made my farewells to both women and followed
the butler. Whoever was waiting for me, I was going
to be happy to see him.

# Chapter Twenty-one

"**D**r. Bock Bach has disappeared from the face of the earth." Newman Goss delivered this news with a melodramatic air that was decidedly un-British. His tone was solemn, but there was excitement in his light eyes. "I've been to see Quincey. We must return to Boston to the Medical School to see if there's been any further news." He was standing under the portico, holding the half-door of the hansom cab open for me as I emerged from the Bedell residence. We set off immediately, the icy rain slanting in against us through the open front.

Wearing a wide-caped overcoat, Goss sat on the edge of the seat. The driver clipped along at a good rate, but the way the editor leaned forward showed that our pace wasn't nearly fast enough for him. Even his tall, gray-felt top hat, its narrow brim turned down in front, tilted onward in the direction we were heading. He gave a good imitation of a well-dressed pointer hot on the scent. After we passed the Cambridge Common, the horse-drawn tram, also going to Boston, rumbled along beside us, making conversation difficult.

As we crossed the West Boston Bridge, the city seemed to swallow us up immediately. Whereas Cambridge still had open spaces, here the buildings were crammed together. An older colonial nestled against a

solid Federal six-story brick, which was jostled by the
pillared front of the next in classic Greek style. Fog
curled across their fronts, seeming to merge them together more tightly.

Goss settled back and told me what he knew. It
seemed that he was guilty of exaggeration. While
Bock Bach was very possibly somewhere on the
planet, he hadn't as yet been located in the Boston-
Cambridge area. Hearing that lessened my worries a
little. True, he'd missed an appointment with Goss, as
well as two chemistry tutorials. His landlady, Mrs.
Hawkins, said he apparently hadn't returned to his
lodgings last night. His bed hadn't been slept in, and
he hadn't come down for breakfast. But she'd told
Goss that did happen occasionally. The professor had
an office next to his laboratory at the Medical School.
If he worked late because of an experiment in progress,
he stretched out on a cot there.

He'd made arrangements to give Goss a copy of the
written autopsy report on Dr. Popkin at eleven, but he
wasn't there when the editor arrived. The graduate
assistant, a young man named Wilcox, told him that
he'd been puzzled at first when he'd had to send the
tutorial students away. Then, as the morning wore on
and the professor still didn't arrive, Wilcox became
worried. Eventually, he'd gone through the entire
building, thinking that Bock Bach had a mishap of
some sort, maybe fallen on the back staircase going to
the basement for supplies. There was no sign of him,
nor had any of the few doctors there seen him, either
last night or this morning.

Goss's tone could only be described as portentous.
"Wilcox said the professor was most punctual always.
In the three years he'd worked with him, he'd never
canceled a lesson, much less missed one. Very precise,
too, in his work habits. Yet last night, before leaving,

he'd cleaned up so hurriedly that he'd put the alcohol jar on the wrong shelf and hadn't properly washed the glass beakers, which he was most particular about. The young man was so taken aback by what he called the disorder in the lab that he insisted on showing me around. Said he couldn't even find the latest experiment book. Mind you," Goss added, "the whole place looked quite tidy to me. Then Wilcox checked with the hospital, which is the next building, but no one matching the professor's description had been admitted. As soon as I reached Cambridge and learned he hadn't returned to his lodgings, I sent word to Wilcox to set off for the police station and then"—he paused for effect—"to the morgue."

He shook his head carefully so as not to disturb the precise angle of his top hat. "I'm much afraid we won't have good news about him when we get there. And, mark my words, his disappearance is a direct result of his attendance at the séance."

The assurance of his statement irritated me, or maybe it was his high British vowels. I could think of a number of other explanations. I began speculating. "The professor could've heard of the shooting in the Yard last night and rushed off because he'd gotten a garbled report making it sound far more serious. That'd account for his departure from his careful routine at the lab."

"But then, being in Cambridge, why not return to his lodgings?" Goss countered. "Let's even suppose that he went to the home of a friend afterwards and spent the night. If he were then somehow unable to come to the Medical School this morning, he'd surely have sent a note to Wilcox. No. It smacks of foul play, no question."

I *was* worried about that, although my concern didn't have any connection with the séance. If Bock

Bach had arrived at the Yard, heard the explanation of the over-excited student letting off his gun and therefore decided to return to Boston late at night, he might have been bashed over the head and robbed. You didn't have to be near the docks to be in that kind of danger. As police reporter for the *Independent*, I'd often gone down those refuse-heaped back alleys near North Grove Street. The professor's body, shoved out of sight, would stay there until it smelled. And even then it might not be noticed. Certainly, the police weren't going to take his absence of a few hours seriously. It'd be a few days before they started looking and then only if a formal report was filed.

Suddenly Goss turned to me. "It just occurred to me. I may well have been the last person to speak to him! Yesterday, after we left Quincey's, we shared the cab back to Boston. We barely talked. He was preoccupied. Of course I had the extra edition on my mind, which I had to hurry back to get out, with the news on Popkin's autopsy. That account was sparse—although the headline was eye-catching—and I thought I might get a tidbit out of the written report to use in today's paper to keep the story fresh. Had the devil of a time getting him to agree to give it to me. In the event, we didn't need it since the lead article today will be the shooting in the Yard. None of the morning papers had much on it. Didn't know the names of the women, you see, or the connection with the séance. So I ordered another double run, and even so we'll sell every copy by six. I—"

At that I interrupted. "In today's paper, did you imply that Miss Singer was the rifleman's target?"

"Of course not," he answered huffily. "I heard about the gunfire while at dinner, and I immediately sent a reporter to the scene. He saw Hoggett, who told him that Mr. Quincey was convinced it was an excited student who fired at the effigy. And *that* was what I gave out in today's article, adding that the College authorities were investigating."

I eyed him narrowly for a moment. "But I want to know what you *implied*. Might you have said, for example, something along the lines that it was a curious fact the bullet narrowly missed Miss Sylvie Singer, the medium at the séance where Dr. Popkin met his end?"

Goss blew out his breath. His indignation indicated that that was exactly what he'd done. When he caught my black expression, he burst out, "Really, old chap, you can't rule out a connection. My man on the scene said Hoggett found no evidence either way. You were a reporter. You know what has to be done to sell papers. And," he went on defensively, "Mr. Quincey will be pleased at the number sold."

What concerned me was what else he'd do to keep that story fresh in his reader's minds. Print all the wild theories that were bound to pop up following his article? My next question was, "Mr. Quincey hadn't seen today's edition when you spoke to him?"

"No. It wasn't ready. Still isn't. I'm holding it up in case we have something solid about Bock Bach. I left a space open on the front page. Which I can fill with an advertisement. But why Mr. Quincey still insists on putting them on the front page, I can't think. It isn't done any more by the better papers. None of the up-to-date ones. And they've all become morning papers. Much better. As for the name! The *Independent!* We should have something more striking. Hmm. *Voice of the People.* Or better yet. Just *The Voice.* Not that he'd consider it."

Glancing out the window, he seemed to be considering the domed, granite top of the Bulfinch Pavilion of Massachusetts General Hospital poking through the fog in the distance. He added, as if it were an afterthought, "I didn't actually speak to Quincey this morning. The manservant with the odd name said he was at lunch and couldn't be disturbed. So I told *him* about Bock Bach, and he told me you were at Mrs. Bedell's. Said he didn't feel he was overstepping any boundaries in giving out your whereabouts because the case was serious."

I glared out my side window at the rain-slicked cobblestones instead of at him. He'd *implied* that it was Quincey who wanted me to go to the Harvard Medical School. Still, if Quincey had known, he would have sent me there so it didn't matter. Goss hadn't had time to do more than the obvious in terms of investigating.

Returning to what he'd said earlier, I asked, "Didn't Wilcox talk to him after he left you yesterday afternoon?"

"No. He said the professor only nodded, took off his coat, and went right to the lab. He got busy getting out materials right away, and Wilcox didn't disturb him. Now that I think of it, Bock Bach seemed in a hurry when he got out of the cab. He muttered again that Popkin's death was wrong, jumped out, and headed for the door of the building. I had to call after him to remind him that I'd be by at eleven. He didn't turn round but he must have heard."

I thought a moment. "Remember that he said yesterday at Quincey's that if he knew what poison was used, he'd be able to put a name to the person? Suppose in the cab something occurred to him. As executor, he had a key to Popkin's office and went to look. Suppose what he found convinced him he himself was in danger. And he just left."

"Why not leave a note?"

"Saying what? His evidence would have been

flimsy. He needed time to think. Maybe to come up with a way to protect himself."

"Didn't strike me as the cowardly, cut-and-run sort." Goss had a stiff-upper-lip sound in his voice that made plain that was not what he himself would have done.

I returned blandly, "However, Bock Bach is a highly intelligent man. And not young." I recalled his sad look as he flicked his wrist holding an imaginary sword. He knew he couldn't defend himself as he once did, with or without a weapon. It'd be a hard realization for an aging man. "Anyway, I had the impression that as he talked to Quincey, the professor was reconsidering what happened at the séance. Maybe he'd seen something that he hadn't noticed at the moment, but now—"

"Remember, old chap, that I too was there and I'*m* an experienced observer. Had there been anything noteworthy, I'd have surely taken it in."

I closed my eyes for a long moment. I distrusted self-important men who saw themselves at the center of everything. They missed too much on the edges. And he was vain. And I was stuck with him in a cold rain, being jolted across cobblestones in a cab whose roof protected our heads but whose large open sides did little to keep the water out. Moreover, my overcoat dated back to my days as police reporter. While still serviceable, it was becoming sodden while his, of much thicker wool and with an additional cape, was not. On Monday, I planned on ordering a new one.

Still, Goss wasn't a fool. Summoning up a scrap of patience, I replied, "Bock Bach had a lifelong acquaintance with Popkin. Maybe talking about the different meanings of 'jade' stirred an idea that hadn't come to his mind before. Or, I don't know, telling us about seeing the man's face as he died could have made him think again about Popkin's color, suggesting a specific poison."

"Hmm. I did, of course, have the same idea myself yesterday at Quincey's. I mean, that the professor had a vague stirring that he wasn't going to bring out then. I should have pressed him on it during our ride, especially because even at the time I . . ." He gave his head a slight but meaningful shake. His voice deepened. "Now, with the shooting and his disappearance, my suspicions are being realized. I fear we have a Spirit Killer in our midst."

My jaw dropped open. It took me a minute to get the words out. "You think a dead man is killing the people who were at the séance?"

"No, no. I choose the name Spirit Killer because it'll fit so well in a headline. Were I to refer to him as the Spiritualist Killer, it wouldn't leap out at the reader, you see. Too long." His tone became weighty. "But I do think someone is intent on murdering those who were there."

"Why?"

"Someone feels he's on a mission from God. I don't think that's putting it too strongly. A very unstable individual stirred up—maddened, I should say—by all the fire-breathing sermons against the Spiritualists. He feels that this killing of us, one by one, is a cleansing of the demons. And it'd be a warning to all others to turn away from what he regards as heresy. I'd judge him to be fundamentalist in his beliefs, extremely conservative, a man who can't bear any deviation of his understanding of Christian doctrine."

Our cab had been gradually slowing because, although the rain had stopped, a fog was blotting out the buildings and blurring the way ahead. Goss only noticed that we were creeping along and not why. He impatiently thumped the roof with the head of his walking stick. Then he thrust the stick out over the splashboard in front of us so the driver could see it from where he sat on the dicky seat behind. Goss twirled his cane to indicate more speed. Sensibly, the driver ignored him.

"A fundamentalist?" I asked. "You're imagining some poorly educated man, fresh from the revival tents—"

"That's a possibility. The man who runs the stables down the road from you, Osbert Davies, believes every word of the Bible must be true. You can't possibly hire a horse from the fellow without having Scripture dinned in your ears. And he rented the land from Popkin, who might well have swallowed some new pill that Davies gave him, thinking that it'd restore his youthful vigor."

He adjusted his already perfectly fitted chamois gloves before going on. "And, as I discovered to my sorrow, he's fanatically against the movement. Not long ago, I was looking at some property in Cambridge and needed a horse. Inadvertently I left a copy of *The Banner of Light*—the Spiritualist paper—behind at the stables. When I returned, Davies came lumbering out, carrying it. In it, there was an article on the Old Testament, pointing out that angels and spirits were quite the same, and noting that an angel/spirit appeared to Abraham, Lot, Hagar, Jacob, and Joshua. On the next page, another writer referred to Jesus as a medium, giving examples. He healed under spirit influence, walked on water upheld by spirit hands, exercised clairvoyant gifts and, after the crucifixion, appeared as the Christ spirit.

"Davies jabbed a grimy finger at that page and asked me quietly enough what I made of it. Now, my thinking on Spiritualism derives from philosophers such as Swedenborg and Goethe. I'd say my views encompass, but transcend, Christianity. When I brought out some of this, he started shaking his head from side to side and finally said, 'Yes or no? This true, you think?'

"Unfortunately, I said yes. My word. The man became incoherent with rage. Spittle flecked his beard, which is as bushy as any Old Testament prophet's, and he ranted on. I made my escape on foot instead of waiting for a cab."

It was possible. Hoggett would have to go back to the stables and see where Davies was last night. And try to find out whether he was a good shot. Many of the street-corner preachers I'd seen on the docks seemed like very angry men. "But," I objected, "how could that fit in with Bock Bach's disappearance? A man like Davies couldn't draw him into a conversation, much less lure him away."

"But the Spirit Killer needn't be at all like Davies, you see. I heard Dr. James Cranch Meeker condemn the movement with such passion that he could have roused the meekest of men to take action. He's a magnificent orator, although quite mistaken in his understanding of Spiritualism. He mocked our evidence of the presence of spirits as mere table-turning." Glancing at me, Goss smiled smugly. "I myself could have turned the tables on the good minister by pointing out that a religion that depended on the correctness of historical anecdotes about mysterious events in a foreign country in a remote period could hardly lay claim to real evidence."

Chuckling at his own observation, he then added, "But what I'd like to direct your attention to is that the men in his congregation are all well dressed, well spoken, and many of them attended Harvard College. Not that *that* means they were truly educated, in the largest sense."

I knew, if I asked him, he'd tell me he himself was at Oxford. He probably had been. I didn't ask.

He went on, "Obviously our beliefs threaten the established churches. A letter in *The Banner* noted that, saying we had to appreciate that it's a sad thing for the worshippers of dead forms and ceremonies and mummied creeds—and the ministers at the altars of such—to find that the spirits speak through ordinary people, moved as the first Apostles were. Of course, at the first Pentecost, tongues of flames appeared over their heads. *We* are like the original, the ancient, Christians. The idea infuriates and frightens those ministers, and they all ignite their congregations against us."

He seemed to take some satisfaction in that, as though such opposition underlined the truth of his own views. He added, "We ourselves in the movement have followers who can't truly grasp the invisible world, the existence of which we now have proof. Instead of an entirely different kind of universe next to ours, which is how I see it, they imagine it as a place of tasteful mansions and clean streets. The women take great comfort in such an idea, thinking of their loved ones who've gone on as well as their own future in such surroundings. And, after all, some mediums channel spirits who describe things that way. They're trying to explain the ineffable to people of this world, so they speak still in their terms."

I changed the subject quickly. "Do the letters to the *Independent* against the Spiritualists sound as though they come from unbalanced men who might be tipped over into violence?"

Goss shrugged. "Many of them are mere scrawls, full of misspellings and unprintable words. I can't run them. Now, those signed Truth Seeker, which you may have seen in the paper, are equally condemnatory but well written, the work of an articulate man. Several times I've wondered if Cranch Meeker does them."

"Why would he send them anonymously to the *Independent*? Several of the owners of the six-cent dailies must sit in his church. They'd be happy to let him give his views and be eager to have him sign his name."

"But suppose he wishes to reach working-class blokes who can only afford a penny for a newspaper? In the interest of fairness, despite my own convictions, I always print them exactly. Besides," he added with a sly smile, "those letters are long, boring, and full of words our readers don't understand. And Mr. Quincey quite approves of my running them."

"Do our readers go to séances? The men, I mean?"

"Oh, yes. Every neighborhood has a housewife who insists she's psychic. Wants to earn a little money. Then, too, at their gatherings I understand there's quite a bit of knee-squeezing under the table in the dark. A lot of the old slap and tickle. Blamed on the spirits, don't you know. Entertainment. Harmless in the end. The movement welcomes all who seek in the truth. It has nothing to do class divisions. Extraordinary things can happen even amongst people of that sort. There might be a medium here or there who's the genuine article. Not in the same category as Miss Singer, of course. She amazes."

I didn't comment. "Have you any idea why this man would decide to start murdering at *her* séance?"

"I do," he replied, nodding judiciously. "Consider who was there. Three professors from Harvard and the editor of a newspaper. Men who are educated and in a position to sway opinion. That would enrage the Spirit Killer. He'd think *we* should know better. And he'd garner publicity."

"Why give it to him, then?" I burst out.

"He'd get it anyway." Goss waved a gloved hand airily. "And have you thought of this? He might start writing to the paper. What he says and how he says it would tell us a lot about him. We'd have a much better chance of catching him."

Looking at Goss, I wondered how seriously he took his own theory. He was clearly enjoying spinning it out, but his voice was so calm that I wasn't sure he appreciated what followed. "If this is true, you yourself are in some danger."

"Yes." He gave me the stiff upper lip again. "But I'm prepared." He held up his cane. "Sword in this stick, don't you know. As well, I have a pistol in my drawer at the office. A brand-new Colt .45. Just out on the market. Called the Peacemaker."

I simply nodded, not pointing out that neither would be effective against poison or a rifle. Instead, I brought out, "By the way, this morning Miss Craddock told me that she plans another séance on Wednesday next. Mrs. Bedell is anxious to contact her dead husband. You're invited, of course. You'll have to be especially careful, if your assumptions are correct."

The cab driver took the corner of Fruit Street rather sharply just then, throwing me against Goss. My height gives me real weight. Perhaps that's what took the breath out of him. He looked pale and shaken. He said nothing as we went toward North Grove and the Harvard Medical College, its carved limestone exterior looming up out of the by-now thick fog.

# Chapter Twenty-two

The fog followed us in through the heavy doors, and a misty ribbon of it drifted ahead of us down the long, cold corridor. Only a few gas jets were lit along the walls, and their small flames did little to lighten the gloom of the November afternoon. The heavy molding above them seemed to swallow up what there was. The dark paneling on the walls beneath them was dusty and scarred. The building, which seemed deserted, was old, with planked wooden floors that made our footsteps echo.

Goss seemed to know where we were going, and we made for the wide staircase at the far end. On my right were closed doors with small brass plaques with the doctors' names engraved on them. I could make out a few: Bigelow, Holmes, Haskins, Marler. Bock Bach had said that all the men who taught here had profitable practices, and they paid the expenses of the Medical School. Since they didn't take money from Harvard College, they could run things as they chose. Apparently, upkeep of the building wasn't of much importance to them. We passed a lecture hall where the seats in the back row had stuffing spilling out. But the doctors would see their patients in their homes, or in the hospital, not here.

"Chemistry lab is on the third floor. Wilcox should be there," Goss said, as I followed him up the staircase, a relic of the building's better days. The smooth wooden banister swooped up gracefully, and the balusters supporting it were intricately carved. The newel caps at the end of each half flight were heavy wood globes sculpted in the shape of some exotic fruit. But they were useful for guiding your steps. When your fingers touched the globe, you could tell you'd reached a landing. The only lit jet flickered feebly in the shadows somewhere above.

Glancing back at me, Goss saw me grasping the banister, as well as leaning heavily on my cane as I made my way up. "Can you manage, old chap?"

"Quite all right," I answered testily.

"These stairs are a bit of a poser." He pointed up into the darkness. "The Dental School is on the top story. Hmm. Shouldn't like to try to get down after having some teeth pulled by a beginner. Still," he said, groping for the next newel cap, "the patients don't have to pay much."

On the third floor, we went round the corner and into the lab. The long room was filled with rows of high tables and stools. Cabinets with bottles and jars took up all the available wall space, and more shelves laden with glass beakers stood over the two sinks in the front. The windows along the far wall were now rectangles of gray fog, so nothing of the back of the room could be seen. The sharp smell of napthol, which I recalled from my chemistry classes, hit my nose. It didn't bring back pleasant memories.

A young man was seated at a desk beneath a window, an oil lamp illuminating the ledger in front of him. As we came in, he stood up immediately and asked, anxiety in his voice, "Have you any news at all?"

"I'm afraid not," Goss replied, before introducing me to the assistant. "And you?"

Wilcox shook his head, adding, "Although in my case, I'd say that's good news. At the morgue, they showed me the corpse of an older, gray-haired man who had drowned." He averted his eyes at that thought. "But it wasn't the doctor." His dark hair was brushed back, revealing a widow's peak in front. With his bright, round eyes and the merest suggestion of a nose, he looked like a clever small mammal. He was wearing fingerless gloves and, as he spoke, he rubbed the backs of his hands. It was a nervous gesture, but he might have been doing it for warmth. I could see several layers of sweaters beneath his knit-wool outer one.

Catching my glance, he said, "It's usually warmer in here. Big furnace in the basement, and the heat comes up. But on Saturdays, they don't stoke it because no one comes in on Sunday. Even *he* didn't . . ." His voice trailed off as he glanced helplessly around the room. "I can't imagine him not leaving a note as to what work he wanted done! It's he who pays my salary, not the College."

Coming round the desk, he walked over to a door set against the nearest wall and threw it open. "See here. The latest lab tests haven't been marked for Monday, when the students come in. I didn't like to begin without his approval." There were papers, piled neatly enough, across the scarred wooden desk in front of the window. An opened text lay next to the quill pen and inkwell in a stand.

The rest of Bock Bach's office was Spartan and functional. Bookcases lined with heavy, forbidding tomes, their weight causing several shelves to sag, filled the walls. A cot with a thin pallet mattress, a small pillow, and folded blankets was pushed out of the way beneath some shelves. His gold-headed walking stick, which I recalled had the same crossed swords on its top as his buttons had, leaned forlornly in the corner.

Gesturing toward it, Goss said, "Had to have left in a hurry. Forgot his stick."

"And not to have left out the experiment book!" Wilcox was squeezing the fingers first of one of his hands, then the other. He hurried back into the lab and tapped the top of the first table. "It should have been here. He'd write up what he'd done, the results of that, and instructions for the next step. That way I could have everything he needed set out. I don't even know what he was working on last night."

"Have you found anyone who saw him leave?" I asked.

Wilcox's worried face tightened further. "No. The custodian locks the front doors at six. The doctors have usually left before that on their rounds. Their lectures and demonstrations here are earlier in the day. The professor was often here much later, and usually left by the side door off the basement. There's a back staircase that leads to it."

"Did the custodian see him before he left at six?"

"He says not. And Dookin isn't likely to have noticed. "

"Has Dr. Bock Bach any relatives nearby to whom we could send inquiries?"

"No. He has a sister in Maine, and he spends vacations there, but no one nearer. Her address is in the office, top drawer." His eyes slid to that room as if he hoped that suddenly his employer would materialize in the doorway.

"Was Dr. Bock Bach a well-liked professor?" I asked, recalling my own too long hours in the chemistry lab as an undergraduate, while my instructor criticized behind me. There were days when, as we all foot-dragged toward the lab, had we heard the instructor had gone missing, we'd have celebrated.

Wilcox hesitated. "He was . . . respected. But he insisted on things being done exactly. If not, the work would have to be done over. And over. And you see, most of our students have no background in chemistry and aren't familiar with the basics, which meant a lot of redoing. So—"

I interrupted. "But they'd have had classes before at the College. It's a requirement for graduation."

"Most of our medical students aren't graduates of Harvard. In fact, some of them haven't even finished high school."

Goss, obviously impatient at what he thought were my irrelevant questions, was peering at the labeled bottles on the far wall. At that statement, he turned around in amazement. I stared at Wilcox.

The young assistant added hastily, "President Eliot is requiring changes. That's how the professor came to be here three years ago. He'd always taught Chemistry at the College. In Cambridge, I mean. He isn't a medical doctor. But at that time, one of our graduates practicing in Quincy gave the wrong dosage of morphia to three patients. They all died. So Dr. Bock Bach was sent here, over the strong objection of Dr. Bigelow, head of the Medical College. He still gets quite red-faced on the rare occasions when he comes up here. He says there's no need for all this"—Wilcox waved the length of the lab—"because medicine is an art, not a science."

"Could failure in this class mean a candidate wouldn't get his degree?"

"Not exactly. You see, our students are only required to pass five out of the nine examinations. The tests are very easy. Most can't do the Chemistry, but they can do well in most of the other eight. Still, several have failed five. The system itself isn't good. The professor was always demanding it be changed, although Dr. Popkin was his only ally. As it is, the medical students have sixteen weeks of lectures and demonstrations. But it's three years later when the examinations are given. During that time, the students are to work with an established practitioner. Now, that doctor often gives them little to do but basic tasks. He wouldn't want his patients to become attached to anyone else. By the time the young doctors return for the viva voce, they've often forgotten what they did learn here."

Thinking about that, I could see that both students and faculty were suspect in Bock Bach's disappearance. Any one of those failed young doctors, who'd spent over three years learning—or not learning— might have focused his rage on the chemist. The red-faced Dr. Bigelow, with the others solidly behind him, would be overjoyed if Bock Bach didn't return. President Eliot was determined to make changes, and they'd have regarded the professor as his agent. How angry were *they*?

Also, I could now understand the odd terms of Popkin's will. He'd intended to control his money from the grave. And there was more than a touch of malice in the conditions he'd set. He'd given his fortune to the Medical College but made Bock Bach the executor, a man the others saw as an outsider and whose ideas they'd reject out of hand. Then he'd picked Story, who was a medical doctor but who was in the Mental Philosophy Department at Cambridge, and therefore not one of them. Haskins was a faculty member here, but he was possibly chosen because, involved as he seemed to be in his magnetic rods— whatever they were—he'd go along with the chemist if some of the money came his way. Cranch Meeker's reputation as a minister made him an unimpeachable arbiter, but one who probably wouldn't want any part of the impassioned arguments the will would stir up.

"What was that?" I asked suddenly. It sounded as if a door down the hall had been quietly closed.

Goss waved the noise away. He was getting even more restless at my questions. He was so set on his Spirit Killer theory that he wasn't going to waste time on any other. And it was clear that his hole in the front page wasn't going to be filled with news of the professor. He burst out, "The pressmen are waiting. It's already past time the paper was on the street. I'll have to go."

"Good idea," I replied heartily. "Wilcox and I can go over the next step." Not that I had any idea what it would be.

Goss tipped his hat, murmured something meant to soothe the young assistant, and was gone.

But thinking about Popkin made me ask if Wilcox knew where the key to his office was. He shook his head, adding, "The professor would have that with him. He never locked his own office, so he wouldn't think it safe to leave it here."

I wanted to see that office. "Perhaps he went there before he left and in his hurry found he was holding that missing experiment book you need. He might have left it there."

The young man shook his head. "He'd have brought it back. Dr. Popkin's office is just down the hall, off the anatomy lab."

Casting another dejected look around the lab, he said, "Dr. Bock Bach often sent me away early on Saturday. But I shall wait. Just in case. Even if I don't know what to start on. Twice this year, he told me how reliable my work was."

From the expression in his eyes, I could tell that if the professor didn't return, he'd have one real mourner.

"I wouldn't wait, you know," I answered. "It's late in the day for him to be starting anything, especially if he never comes in on Sunday. By Monday, we'll have located him. Mr. Quincey, the owner of the *Independent*, will use all his resources." I supposed that took in Hoggett and me. I handed him my card.

"Yes. Yes. You're right. He's so exact in his habits. He'll be back on Monday." Wilcox nodded, trying hard to believe his own words. He took off his outer sweater, hung it on a hook, and shrugged into his overcoat. "I'll have to lock up here. Would you be needing anything?"

"I doubt that. But this custodian, Dookin, would have a key to all the doors, wouldn't he? He'd need to clean after hours."

The young man thought that over. "I suppose so. You'll have to look round for him. He's probably on the first floor."

"I'll find him," I said.

# Chapter Twenty-three

**A**s Wilcox's steps retreated down the staircase, I glanced the other way, thinking the door I'd heard shutting was the custodian. But the corridor was a straight path into darkness, and he'd surely have turned on the gas jets. I listened, but the building was full of noises. It was noticeably chillier inside and, as the furnace cooled, the walls and floors made the twig-snap creaks of an old man's bones.

It wasn't until I slid my fingers around the last newel cap on the way down that I caught sight of the custodian. A giant of a man, his back to me, he was mopping the wood of the first floor. He was halfway to the entrance, swabbing a path down the center, ignoring any part that wasn't in easy reach. He'd nudge his bucket forward with his boot, plunge in the bundle of tied rags, splatter gray water, and push his mop ahead. He kept his eyes forward on the door as if on a distant and unreachable goal. Although he must have heard me, he didn't shift his gaze.

I finally stopped just out of the range of his mop and said, "Pardon me, I'm looking for Dr. Bock Bach and I need your help. We haven't been able to locate him anywhere."

He swiveled his head and looked at me for a long moment, as if he needed time to mentally translate that to another language that he could understand.

Under his old tweed cap, his huge face blossomed as knobbily as a cauliflower. He had round, blank blue eyes, a small nose, and a disgruntled mouth. His old tweed jacket, made for a much smaller man, strained across his broad shoulders and had sleeves that ended halfway down from his elbow, displaying three inches of a dirty flannel shirt. Plunging the mop into the bucket, he nodded to show he'd heard me, but he said nothing as he swirled the rags around in the water.

I tried, "Wilcox tells me that you didn't see him yesterday and—"

"Nor today neither. No point in askin'. Can't help." He returned to his splattering and swabbing, adding, "Ever'body askin'. Still ain't seen 'im. Not last night. Not today." His voice was curiously reedy coming from such a big man.

"Mr. Dookin? Right?"

His eyes narrowed as if he couldn't imagine how I'd come by that information, but he nodded.

"I'm Michael Merrick. Dr. Bock Bach came yesterday to consult Mr. Quincey, the owner of the *Boston Independent*, on a serious matter, and we're now very worried about the professor. I was thinking that maybe last night he went into Dr. Popkin's office and could have taken ill. Have you been in there today?" I had to give some excuse for looking at it.

Dookin shook his head. "Don't go in there atall. He don't want *nothin'* touched. Did the lab floors last week. Never do 'em on a Satiddy. Do the hall floors then." He started pushing his mop forward, his eyes again on the front door, the tip of his large pink tongue moving from side to side as he concentrated.

"You do have a key? We should check that room."

His head jerked up in astonishment. "It's up on third! I still got these offices and this here to finish. I stop at six. Got to be quick to get done." He sidled forward, speaking with satisfaction because a reason not to do it occurred to him. "And it wouldn't be 'lowed. Popkin's dead. So I can't be openin' the door."

"But Professor Bock Bach might be there. Slumped forward on the desk, unconscious. Near death's door. Needing our help." I thought that was a nice touch of verisimilitude.

Unmoved, he mopped.

I tried, "The doctors here would want you to check." More mopping. Reaching into my pocket, I pulled out some coins and held them out to him. "I'm sorry to interrupt your work."

He stared at my outstretched palm as if I'd managed some particularly adroit magic trick. He licked his lips, muttering, "Well, I never. Jist make up the difference, it would. Exack'ly. Why, this way Mother wouldn't never know I spent any on the beer. I could put that in the envelope with the rest of the sal'ry, go home, and hand it over to her like reg'lar."

Suddenly, he looked up at me, suspicion turning his blue eyes hard. He squinted at me from under his cap's frayed bill. "Could be you come from the Devil. I sinned last night buyin' the beer from the pay packet. I did. God wouldn't be helpin' me."

Tired of holding out my hand, I shoved the money in his upper jacket pocket, reached into my own, pulled out two more coins, and added them, saying firmly, "God is merciful. He forgives. Let's go upstairs."

Nodding to himself, as if turning that over in his mind, he felt the coins in his pocket. Apparently it was a hard decision. But fear of nagging won out over fear of the Devil, although deep-grained laziness seemed a close second. He stuck the mop in the bucket. As he came back to me, he said, "We jist look in and leave. Then I got time to finish." He stopped, considering, "I can do it all right. Today is Satiddy so I don't have to do the boiler. Take out the ashes on the Monday, is what I do, 'afore I shovel in the coal. Only got the two office floors down here yet. See, the doctors down here, too, they don't want nothin' moved about on their desks or shelves. Clerk does it. 'Course he jist waves a duster. Ain't as if he's savin' me—"

Putting the point of my cane down sharply, I wheeled and headed for the stairs. When he caught up with me, I asked, "Who was looking for Dr. Bock Bach?"

He scratched at his lumpy chin as we walked. "Lemme see. Couple strangers today. Couple of the doctors yestiddy. Bigelow. Maybe Haskins. Bigelow, though fer sure, 'cuz I was in his office so's the clerk could gimme the pay packet. Usual way, I git it ever' Satiddy, but seein' as how it was the last day of the month, the clerk wanted to do up his books."

Having accepted the money, he seemed determined to tell me every single thing he knew. He toiled up the stairs behind me, going as slowly as I was, his thin, penetrating voice trickling up. "That's how I fell into sin. Got home and the wife already gone to the prayer meetin'. But to git there, I had to go by the tavern. 'Course, this mornin' Mother din't ast me for the money, thinkin' it won't be until today. Which is the usual. And I couldn't think what ta tell 'er tonight. All day I been tryin' to come up with somethin'. If she knew it was for the beer, I'd never hear the end. Not in this vale of tears. Our chapel, we don't hold with the drinkin', especially Mother. And then, you come along with jist the same money. I can't figger it out. I—"

"Who *else* was looking for the professor?"

"I'm turnin' it over in my mind. Hm. Today Dr. Bonner ast me. He does the dead. In the basement 'cross from the boiler. But I don't do up his room. No. One of them students does it. I won't do it. Cuttin' up bodies ain't right. Come the Judgment Day, there they're goin' be, missin' parts. Dr. Bonner, he comes in while I was shovelin' the coal, and I tells 'im that Wilcox is lookin', too. Then I'm goin' up to third and purty soon Dr. Story catches up with me. I know him 'cuz he used to be here. Stop and talk, he would. Never give me money, though."

"What time did he come?"

"If I was goin' up to third, be past mid-mornin' but not that near lunch. I don't recall bein' hungry. Mother does do a nice sandwich, even at the end of the week. Cheese and pickle. 'Course if the pay packet was short, I'd be lucky to get bread with a bit of lard on it on Satiddy. So if you din't come along, I—"

To my relief, we'd reached the third floor. The hallway ahead was as dark as the staircase. The fog outside curtained the few windows.

"Who else?" I asked wearily.

"Don't know the name. Never seen 'im afore. But he had a queer beard." Here Dookin displayed some talent for physical description, making his body taller, thinner, more stooped, then pulling a hand out from either side of his chin in points. "Dark at the bottom it was."

"Could his name have been Craddock? Gideon Craddock?" What could he have wanted with Bock Bach?

"Can't say. He come after Dr. Story did. I was already up here, but Wilcox was lookin' round the building, so I was the one told him the perfessor warn't here. Real upset, he was. Then, another stranger." Here, he gestured to indicate a portly, broad-shouldered man, and he tossed his head as if it were covered with a thick silvery mane instead of a squashed tweed cap.

"Do you know if that was a minister named Cranch Meeker? Has that big church near the bottom of Beacon Hill?" After all, both he and Story had reason to talk to Bock Bach, perhaps wanting to press their claims for some of Popkin's fortune as early as possible.

Dookin looked offended. "Wouldn't know. Me and Mother are Chapel, I tole ya. We don't hold with them fancy churches."

We'd passed the chemistry lab, and the custodian took out his keys, saying, " The 'natomy room is right here. Office is in a front corner."

Unlocking the door with a heavy key, he felt on his ring for a smaller one. He turned to look at me as if to make sure I was still there. "Don't like comin' in here late. I clean it in the mornin'. See, the thing is—"

I couldn't stand another word about his schedule. Brusquely, I waved him forward. He shuffled into the room, stopping at a high lectern, and turned the knob on an oil lamp on a nearby large table. That unexpected glow cast the end of the long room in even deeper shadow. Unlike the chemistry lab next door, here there were writing desks in rows facing the lectern. Dookin cast an uneasy glance around the room, even narrowing his eyes to peer at the back. He gestured to a paneled door.

But as Dookin was about to insert the key, we both saw it was off the latch.

He wiggled the knob, saying, "Now that ain't right. Allus kept it locked. Particklar 'bout that. See, what happened once was, some of the students got in here for a joke like, don't know what they did fer sure, and what I heerd I don't credit. Well, who would? Settin' up that thing on the privy! So even I never been in.

'Course he's dead, but the perfessor woulda locked it. What he's got in here is—"

He swung open the door, but never finished the sentence. Dookin took one look at what was coming toward us, let out a muffled scream, and with a low moan, crashed to the floor.

# Chapter Twenty-four

The skeleton slid quickly nearer, head bobbling in greeting, jaw clattering, trying to speak. The arms waved loosely, and the fingerbones rattled and clicked as it came closer out of the darkness of the office. The legs swung back and forth in a rhythmic walk. With the dead weight of Dookin across my feet, I couldn't move. But my legs had gone numb in shock anyway. My heart pounded in my dry throat. I raised my stick and was about to bring it crashing down on the skull.

Then I stopped and stood there, feeling foolish. We were in an anatomy lab. Popkin had no doubt used this upright collection of bones in his classes. As I stepped closer, even in that dimness, I could see the hook at the top, attaching the skeleton to an iron rod, and the metal base that supported that. The wooden wheels of the base clunked on the uneven floor, rolling toward me. Probably he'd slid the skeleton around as he lectured, perhaps even pushing it down the aisles between the desks so the students could see clearly the intricate spine, the shield of the ribs, the clever sockets of the hips.

Dragging Dookin out of the way, I closed the office door. He didn't need to see the skeleton as he came out of the faint. Then I had a second frantic thought. Maybe he'd had a heart attack instead. I clapped one hand on his throat and relaxed at the ragged pulse beating beneath my fingers. As I knelt down to do that, I heard a metal thunk in one of my overcoat pockets and felt to see what it was. That was a welcome find. I hadn't worn this coat since last winter and, as a police reporter, I always carried a flask of brandy. Not for me. But a lone constable, standing guard at the scene of a crime on a bitter winter night, rarely said no to a warming drink. It was a great tongue-loosener. In this case, just the sharp, sweet scent of it might reassure Dookin. I gave his cheeks each a quick slap, uncorked the flask, and waved it several times right under his nose.

His lashes fluttered. After a blank stare, alarm filled his eyes. "It was comin' right at us! Where—" White-faced, he jerked his glance from one side to the other.

"It's all right. I pushed it back in the office. It's just a . . . teaching aid for Dr. Popkin's classes. It's on wheels so he could move it around the room."

Scooping one arm under Dookin's thick shoulders, I brought him up to a sitting position. His head immediately slumped forward onto his knees, and he muttered, "I never seen it afore. Never want to see it agin." He let out two shuddery moans.

When he lifted his head, I held out the flask. "Take a little drink of this. Might help. It was the shock of it coming forward that way that got to you."

He took a sip, choked, looked at the small bottle in surprise, and took another, much longer one. I recorked it, shoved it in my pocket, stood up, and held out a hand. "You sit at one of these desks for a minute until you get your legs back."

When I got him there, I turned on a gas jet above his head, and headed toward the office.

"You goin' in there? With that . . . thing?" His voice was incredulous. "Might be somethin' else—"

"I'll take the lamp. I'll do fine." In fact, much better without him, I thought as I closed the door and slid the skeleton back against the wall.

Holding up the lamp, I could see that Popkin's office, although it looked cluttered, was as functional as Bock Bach's. The plain pine desk took up one side of the room. On its top stood a lamp, some thick texts between wooden bookends, the quill pen in its holder next to an inkwell, and a sharp blade beside that to trim the pen. On all the walls, instead of books, there were pieces of human bones spread out. Stepping closer, after a quick look, I decided they were ranged in order. Finger bones, wrist bones, arms, shoulders, pieces of the neck. A gap-toothed skull in pieces. Long rows of individual teeth, from small to large. Below those, spread out on the shelves were the ribs, thighs, calves, and foot bones. Some were nicked and jagged, perhaps from knife cuts or fractures. Powdery dust coated them and the spaces between them.

Other than the unlocked door, there was no sign of Bock Bach's presence. Then I held the lamp near the skeleton and decided there was. Next to it was a heavy coat rack, and one of its claw feet might normally anchor a wheel of the base to keep the skeleton from rolling forward as it had. A thick tweed jacket was on the rack, but someone might have searched the pockets and in doing so changed the coat rack's position slightly. Going through the pockets myself, all I could find was a folded handkerchief. Bock Bach had every right to look and, if so, had taken out any contents.

I pulled out the desk chair and tried the drawers. The first one held packets and packets of papers, all neatly tied. They were rental receipts, the top ones signed with a scrawled "Osbert Davies." So these were for the stables. The second and third drawers held identical receipts for other properties, each neatly torn in half, with the top apparently given to the renter. The other sides yielded only stacks of student papers, and the middle drawer held a collection of pins, loose keys, string, scraps of paper, and some nails. Shoving that shut, I let my eyes rove once again around the room.

Then it struck me. Quincey said jade could be white. What if Popkin had a valuable piece of it, perhaps carved into the shape of a bone? Say, a Chinese antiquity? The best place to hide it, and yet be able to enjoy seeing it, would be on those shelves. Picking up the lamp again, I went back. After only a minute of studying the bones, I decided that, while that was a good idea, I couldn't tell a small sculpture from the real thing, even if I looked for hours. But then, at the very end of a waist-level shelf, I noticed what wasn't there. In the thick dust, there was a clean round circle. Something had been taken.

I heard the timid scrape of a desk on the wood floor and realized Dookin might be sitting there in dread. Opening the door, I called out reassuringly, "Nothing here." I grabbed the lamp and shut the door. As I neared him, he stood up; he was still swaying a little on his feet. Hunching his shoulders, he held out a small key on his ring. "Mebbe you'd jist lock that there door?" As I retraced my footsteps, he called after me, "Tight, now. Make sure."

I turned the key in the lock and jiggled the knob to check.

As I returned, he was huddled near the lamp as if for warmth. He was very pale still. I asked, "Are you feeling all right?"

He gave his head an uncertain shake.

Neither of us apparently was sure. I said, "Look, I'm going to take this lamp downstairs with us. There's no point in turning on the staircase gas jets because you'd just have to come back up to turn them off." I had another use for the lamp but I wasn't going to mention it now. "It's almost the end of your day. You should lock up and go home. If there's anyone else in the building, can they get out by the back door?"

"Yep. Door's got a wooden bar on it. Falls down when you go out. Key's kind a lever that lifts up when you want in. Don't work too good, but Dr. Bonner's 'bout the only one who comes in that way. Brings in . . . things. You know, the dead ones. Some of the other doctors go out that way, though."

He smacked his lips together and waggled a finger toward my pocket. "Kinda dry. Mebbe I could have another swaller of that?"

"Yes." I headed toward the door, adding, since he still looked shaky, "At the bottom of the stairs."

He locked the lab door, trying the knob three times.

I went ahead of him down the staircase, holding out the lamp to light both our steps. I was going slowly since I couldn't use my cane. When I glanced around to make sure he too had a tight grasp on the banister, I could see he was looking backwards. His face was full of fear as he turned around.

"There wasn't nothin' in that office, was there, 'cept that—" His sentence trailed off in a quaver.

"No. Dr. Bock Bach had been there, since it was unlocked." I continued talking, hoping the sound of my voice would reassure him. I didn't want him fainting and sliding into me or we'd both go down under his weight. "Something seemed to be missing, though. Did Popkin have an assistant who would know—"

"Did you hear that? I heerd a noise up there. I did. It could maybe get out, even if you locked up." His loud whisper had an hysterical edge.

"All old buildings have noises," I answered firmly.

My words echoed as if to underline that remark. I decided to give him something else to think about. "Do you live far from here?"

"No, 'bout half mile is all, on— There! I heerd some . . . walkin' up there. Din't you?"

"Dookin, here's what we're going to do," I said firmly. "There'll be a hansom cab by the hospital. I'll drop you off at home before I return to Cambridge." That was the inducement I was offering, plus the brandy. "But before we go, I need to take a look around the basement."

"Ya don't want to do that! No, sir. Me, neither. Ya won't be able to see nothin' much with jist the lamp. And what's there ta see?" He was babbling. Dookin didn't want to go into the building's dark bowels. "Dr. Bonner's place takes up mosta the room, and I ain't got a key 'cuz I don't clean it. Then there's jist the boiler, the furnace, the closets fer the—"

Suddenly, he grabbed the back of my coat. He whined, "You gotta' heerd that! The screechy noise." We were both on the landing, and I had my hand on the carved globe on the newel, about to start down the last flight of stairs.

"Let go," I said in sharp exasperation. I had my foot poised above the next step. "We're almost—"

He didn't let go, his fingers clutching and twisting the wool.

Then, from high above, a newel cap came down like a cannonball, cracking and splintering the wood of the stair I almost stepped on. Thunder-loud, it caromed further down, smashing and crashing the stairs as it jounced. Stunned, I watched it roll. I could still hear its clunky spin going down the long hallway at the foot.

Not breathing, I looked at the broken wood, imagining my split skull. Then I raised the lamp upward. I could only see the turn of the banister and blackness reaching beyond that. I heard nothing at all.

Dookin had released his hold on my coat. He was sprawled in a dead faint on the landing in back of me.

Dumping the lamp down beside him, I bounded upward three stairs at a time. I strained my ears as I ran, hearing only my own loud steps. On the second floor, I glanced to the left at the windowless hallway to the other staircase, but I saw nothing in that gloom. I raced upward. On the third floor, my fingers touched the edge of the raw wood where the cap had stood, and I slid them into the narrowing hole with its grooved sides. No noise. No sound. I couldn't tell if the cap had been deliberately unscrewed or if it'd been loosened by the constant touching and had toppled off.

Then a scream split the silence. A tortured yell from above. It ended abruptly, but its echo wailed downward. Grabbing for the banister, I dashed up one more floor. There was a square pane of pebbled glass lit up in a door halfway down that corridor. I leaped toward it and yanked at the knob.

Blood was running down the raised arm of the short, muscular man before me. He was holding up a thick pair of pliers, looking at what it held. Turning toward me, he asked hopefully, "An emergency, sir?"

Blood was dribbling from between the fingers of the man in the chair, whose hand cupped his mouth. His eyes were wide in shocked pain. Setting his pliers down on a splotched table and releasing the tooth, the dentist flicked it into a nearby waste basket. He wiped his dripping fingers on the front of his once-white jacket and beamed at me. "I can see you right away. We're just finished here, aren't we, Mr. Jenks? Isn't that better? It was a nasty one, but that one won't trouble you anymore."

With that back staircase in my mind, I nevertheless brought out, "Is there anyone else still on this floor?"

The pleasant-faced young dentist shook his head. "Doubt it. It's after hours, and usually we don't wait on a Saturday. Most people convince themselves that their pain will ease by the Monday." He looked closely at me. "It doesn't, though. Much better to have the tooth out."

"You didn't hear—" I began.

"Oh, that banging a bit ago? Don't let it trouble you. Probably the custodian dropped his bucket again on the staircase. Clumsy person. Now, are you sure—"

I raised a hand, backed out the door, and went down the staircase to Dookin.

# Chapter Twenty-five

" **A**bout eight inches in diameter, almost round, carved like some odd fruit." I was gesturing with spread fingers to show the shape and size of the newel cap to Quincey. "Lead-heavy. It had a long wooden base that screwed into the hole in the banister. One at each landing and each new flight of stairs."

"Deliberately dropped?" Quincey's expression was so hard that his jowls disappeared.

"Could have been. The custodian who was with me insisted he heard noises above us, although the building seemed empty." I stopped, recalling the punch of fear as I'd watched the thick wooden stair splintering right at my feet. Then I'd been sure it was hurled down with deadly force. Still, I added, in an effort to be objective, "On the other hand, everyone who goes up or down those badly lit stairs fumbles for the caps to help them find their way. And, since the Dental School is on the top floor, I'd bet the fingers of those patients would be sticky with sweat. Being touched and spun might loosen the base and it might teeter and fall. And, as we came down, Dookin was clinging to every inch of the banister for support."

Quincey snorted. His bulging eyes were half closed in disgust. "Inconclusive, therefore. Like every other aspect of this investigation. In Dr. Popkin's case, we have a body. He might or might not have been murdered. With Dr. Bock Bach, we now have no body. Miss Singer, who might or might not have genuine psychic powers, may or may not have been the target of a rifleman. This gunman might have been aiming at her because she's a medium or because she'd implicate him in a murder. Perhaps if you recount the events of your day fully, something might occur to me. Or might not."

I took a sip of Madeira. My first had been more of a gulp. But sitting here in the quiet of the library with the rows of sedate books, where even the fire's crackle was muted, I was becoming calmer. When I'd come in, I'd told Quincey that, while the professor wasn't at the Medical School, I was lucky not to be there—rigid, cold, stretched out in the pathology lab with a crushed skull. On the long cab ride back from Cambridge, I'd had a hard time keeping that picture out of my mind. Now I decided that going over what happened might help me put things in perspective. I started with the morning at Mrs. Bedell's, describing the guests and repeating the conversations as exactly as I could. He jotted down a word from time to time, but didn't stop me. Occasionally, I interrupted myself.

"Seeing that Cranch Meeker came himself to call on Mrs. Bedell leads me to believe that she's far richer than I thought," I mused. "As for Haskins, what are those magnetic rods that he regards as a cure-all?"

With a shrug, Quincey answered, "It stems from an idea in ancient cultures: A magnetic fluid supposedly permeates and links all human beings. An energy, if you will. The Japanese term it *ki*, the Chinese call it *ch'i* and the Hindus *prana*. You've heard of Dr. Franz Mesmer. He first worked with magnets to draw out illness, but then decided that the healer himself could transmit healing energy to the patient through touch or with the help of iron rods. At the end of the last century, Mesmer's procedures were discredited, but the idea remains."

"So why would Haskins need a lot of funding for those rods? Can't be that expensive to buy a piece of iron, can it?"

"Ah, but the surroundings would be important in the cure. Mesmer made a fortune and his perfumed rooms were lit with low light, decorated with crystal objects, mirrors, paintings, and elegant furniture. In addition, he had huge, round, wooden bathtubs filled with 'magnetized' water with iron rods protruding. Now, if Haskins also 'mesmerized' the patients— putting them in a sleep induced by his suggestions— and then introduced the idea that they were cured, he'd be very successful."

"With hypochondriacs, you mean."

"Certainly, but Mesmer had startling success with all kinds of illnesses. He had no shortage of patients. At the end, he maintained he could cure anything, and that was his downfall. The Medical Academy in France was against him, and they sent a doctor with a false illness. Of course it couldn't be 'cured,' yet he insisted he'd done so. If Haskins has a powerful personality, as you indicate, and sets up an impressive establishment, half the population of Boston will beat on his door. A good few of them will even get better. The mind plays an important part in illness and recovery, but it's hard to measure the effect. As medicine moves toward science, which requires exact measurements, the practitioners will move away from the mind's influence. But the idea will return."

He waved an impatient hand as he went on. "On that basis, Haskins could make a good claim on Popkin's fortune in terms of increasing longevity. As could Story, coming as he does from the Mental Philosophy Department. Maybe Cranch Meeker believes prayer will work. And you tell me he was in Harvard Yard at the time of the shooting. But Haskins can be eliminated because of the lecture he was giving. We can also exclude Story, because he had the notes of his meeting with Miss Singer."

"Can we?" I asked slowly. "Did you notice a date on them as you flipped through them while we were at dinner?"

"No." His brow drew together. "Why?"

"Because she mentioned this morning that she'd had *two* meetings with him—the first at the Craddocks'—and he wrote throughout both of them. Suppose he planned the shooting very carefully, hid those first jottings ahead of time somewhere nearby—"

Quincey slammed his open palm down sharply on his desk. "That was a possibility I should have taken into account! When I saw the care he took of his papers, I became convinced of his innocence. That could have been part of his scheme, and leaving them behind so I could inspect them yet another part. I leapt to a conclusion at the start. Unforgivable. He can't be excluded. I should never have asked him to dine."

Instead of letting him fret over the idea that someone, somewhere, might be cleverer than he was, I decided to take his mind off it. I skipped ahead in my chronological account and brought out Goss's belief in a "Spirit Killer" who specifically targeted those who attended the first séance. I expected another loud explosion at that, but instead he listened calmly, making an occasional note, and remaining silent. I ended, "If we're to accept this, Osbert Davies at the stables must be suspected."

"Your tone indicates considerable skepticism regarding the whole idea, Michael. You can't reject a theory simply because it comes from Mr. Goss. Whom you don't like."

While I couldn't recall saying anything to that effect, I nodded abruptly.

Quincey leaned back and made a tent of his fingers, which he rested comfortably on his belly. "In reading Hoggett's report about the Scripture-quoting Mr. Davies, that same idea occurred to me. While most of those who insist that every word of the Bible must be literally true are honest, God-fearing people, their view of the world is now under severe attack. Mr. Darwin's theories about evolution contradict the account in Genesis. Some of the more unbalanced ones are filled with an aggressive anger that this should be questioned. Craddock suggests a good Greek word for such a feeling: *paranoia.* It describes a feeling of systematic persecution, not based on objective reality. It could easily cause an individual to take arms against this sea of heresy, as he'd regard it, which would include the Spiritualists and their communication with the dead. Hoggett will have to check into Mr. Davies's recent movements."

"Well, this Spirit Killer, if he exists, is going to be afforded another opportunity very soon." I explained my misunderstood remark to Mrs. Bedell, who'd immediately come forward with the idea of a séance in a few days with many of the same people attending.

Quincey blew out an exasperated breath. "Yes, I already know of that plan. This afternoon I received an urgent note from Gideon Craddock. He's adamantly against having this gathering at his home. Apparently, the idea I brought out last night—that people might suspect poisoned tea was served—quite upset him. However, his sister will prevail. She always does. Knowing that, I pointed out some precautions that could be taken, as a way of reassuring him. Obviously, no refreshments should be served. In terms of guarding against an intruder, Mrs. Bedell has unfortunately already made her own arrangements. Since she has two men from the Pinkerton Agency watching her house, she's hiring three more to be stationed at entry points around the Craddock home on Wednesday evening."

"The Pinkertons," I repeated with no enthusiasm.

"I agree entirely. Some of those detectives may be trained in such duties, but I doubt they are well trained. According to Craddock's note, one will be at the top of our road, and the other two at the far east and west stretches of the Charles, guarding against any entrance through my property or the edges of his. I suggested hiring Trapper, but Mrs. Bedell wouldn't be persuaded of his amazing abilities. She doesn't trust Indians, apparently, although that can't be based on her own experience. But then, she has never shown any sign of the ability to think clearly."

Trapper was the Pequot who worked with us at the Shakers and separated me—that's the best way to put it—from my opium addiction. I had the highest respect for him. Were he watching the Craddocks' house, the most elusive of riflemen would be caught.

"I'd be glad to pay him myself," I burst out. "The peace of mind that would buy would be well worth it."

Quincey snorted and shook his head. "Keep in mind that the Pinkertons will be armed. With pistols. Trapper would be in danger from *them*. Since I value him highly, I won't have him anywhere nearby. Grazing cows won't be safe. At least *you* will be in the house, able to keep a good eye on those there."

That remark ruined any chance of my having peace of mind. I opened my mouth to suggest that he himself might attend, at least sit in the living room while we communed with the spirits, but he waggled his fingers at me, saying, "Continue with your report."

I proceeded with an account of Josh Singer's blustery entrance into the Bedell home. Quincey just stared over my head at the bookshelves behind me, his eyes at the customary half-open position.

When I began on my conversation with Sylvie, I chose my words more carefully. She'd asked me not to repeat her disbelief in her powers at calling up spirits, but she hadn't said I couldn't mention her sense that she felt the feelings of others. That, after all, threw light on how she might have come up with Popkin's last words. Too, since Craddock had already mentioned her childhood remark on hearing voices, I felt I should include what she'd said this morning regarding that. Several times, I caught his glance on me, but I continued reporting. He made no comment at all.

I was grateful for that. His habit of telling me what I think, based on my expressions and tone, always irks me. That he is commonly right makes it worse. Nonetheless, I wanted his reaction to her ideas on her "strange ability," or as she also put it, her "cursed gift." But before I could even phrase the question, he was gesturing for me to go on. He was clearly more than usually irritated.

Throughout my description of Robbie, he kept his eyes on the ceiling. I did detect a twitch of a smile at Leonora Craddock's pseudo-scientific descriptions of the table moving. There was no doubt of the intensity of his interest when I went over the events at Harvard Medical School. He looked directly at me as I went over the contents of both offices. When I described the clean circle in the dust of Popkin's bone shelf, he let out a "humph." Otherwise, he just pursed his lips until I finished.

For some time, Quincey sat in silence, leaning back in his chair. When he finally straightened, he flicked a finger at the paper on which he'd written while I was talking. All he said, with a great deal of annoyance, was, "Tomorrow is Sunday."

I waited, refusing to remark on that.

He spelled it out. "That means that the same conductors and porters may not be on duty at the train station. Nevertheless, I will send Hoggett to make inquiries regarding Bock Bach's boarding a north-bound train to Maine. He's quite distinctive in appearance, with his old-fashioned style of dress and the unusual hair style." He touched the back of his head, to indicate the way the professor gathered his gray hair into a small tail.

When I still didn't say anything, he went on, with an edge of defensiveness, "That is the only reasonable explanation. Bock Bach received an urgent message from his brother-in-law saying his sister was gravely ill. He simply shoved his equipment away and hurried to the station, forgetting to relock Popkin's office, not even bothering to leave a note. No doubt Wilcox will hear from him on Monday."

He didn't meet my eyes. So that was the way it was going to be. He was only willing to send Hoggett off to investigate what he himself regarded as "reasonable" interpretations of the events of the last few days. While Quincey was willing to listen to theories, even formulate them, he wasn't going to accept them. If he did, he'd have to take more vigorous action. But I wasn't going to let him get off that lightly. To me, there was a "reasonable" cause to suspect Sylvie was in danger. I hadn't thought of anything to do, except warn her to stay off staircases.

I switched subjects, asking him what he thought of her belief that she could sense others' feelings. He began his answer, which shouldn't have surprised me, with Darwin. "If his theory is correct, one can assume that our language power also evolved over time. So how did man communicate before that? One could trot out all sorts of ideas, but I'm willing to concede that in the dawn of time there was a primitive ability to transfer thought that we lost when we acquired speech. I suspect that Miss Singer has heard that and she knows that you have." He lifted one shoulder in a gesture of dismissal. "Therefore, you'll believe her if she offers that as an explanation. After that, she can even add the inner voice warning her, and you'll accept that as well."

I was getting really angry. I was tired of his close-mindedness. He'd never met her. Making an effort, I brought out one of his favorite terms from logic. "Let's consider, just as a 'supposal,' which we neither affirm nor deny, that she's *not* a fraud."

At my borrowing from his book, he glared. I stared back. He conceded, "Very well, make your case."

"If she doesn't have a psychic gift of some kind, she'd have to carefully research the background of those who were attending the séance. Now, her story about his embezzling father caused Popkin such distress that he—"

Quincey put up a hand to stop me. "That was Bock Bach's father."

"How can you be sure?"

"His mother was Italian, you'll recall him telling us. That phrase, *viola del pensiero*, is Italian for 'pansy.' Miss Singer is extraordinarily clever. While it's unlikely the professor would have related that little touch to anyone, she could have made it up and he'd have assumed he'd forgotten the flowers strewn on the table. She embellished the other stories, as she did this one, and her listeners were all too ready to 'recall' those details in messages from spirits. They all share the longing of the heart for evidence of the senses that these spirits are there. Even Goss was fooled by her embroidery. Lastly, she was sitting next to Dr. Popkin, and when he gasped out his last words, the others thought she was the source since she'd been speaking."

My anger was now on a fast boil. He was insisting that she was a deliberate fraud before I could even explore the issue. That made the exercise pointless.

He went on, "Everything you tell me about her convinces me that she is unusually intelligent and therefore to become involved in this spirit babble, this humbuggery, is doubly offensive. Leonora Craddock and Susanna Bedell are deluded, but honest in their beliefs. You can't persuade me that Sylvie Singer imagines she is receiving messages from the dead!"

I said nothing.

He pinched his nostrils together. "And she plays on their delusions with her flowing robe, loose hair, and lute-strumming. She must be totally unprincipled!"

I wanted to retort hotly that while *he* could afford his principles, Sylvie could not. There was no way she could live at all without sacrificing one or more. I could point out that what she was doing was the least of many evils.

Still, I controlled myself, trying to find words to lay out my belief in her. She needed help. Evil thickened the air like the fog outside. It was hard to catch hold of, but real.

Quincey's voice was heavy with sarcasm. "You see her as threatened. And she is beautiful. This adds to a situation where the romantic view of life, as opposed to the rational, has sprung up. It surrounds us with mystery, happenstance, chance, strange insights. Spiritualism postulates Heaven as another world just next door. Bah! Soon I'll be hearing of entire new universes equally close, if not within the reach of our senses. No reasonable man can bear such drivel."

I spewed out, "Talk about happenstance! Let me

point out the coincidences you're accepting, sir. Dr. Popkin died of a heart attack, brought on by no discernible cause. Because of Miss Singer's words, the question of murder arises. Then a shot is fired near her, but the effigy, not she, is the target. Dr. Bock Bach, who is involved in this discussion of murder, disappears, but he's on his way to Maine to be with his sister and, despite the fact that he is a careful man, he leaves no note to that effect. My skull was almost split by an accidentally loosened banister endcap as I—"

In an injured tone, he broke in, "You yourself said that might have happened."

"And what if there is some crazed Spirit Killer out there? Or what if some calculating beneficiary of Popkin's will is murdering anyone who might suspect him?"

Quincey drew himself up, saying coldly, "There are even more possibilities than that. There is Mr. Goss. Dr. Popkin tried to sell him a piece of land that was liable to flooding. Enraged at that, he poisons the doctor. Then he spins a theory about a Spirit Killer, which would certainly hide his own personal motivation for murder. He also was at the Medical School, and you didn't see him leave. Let us consider Wilcox. Imagine that he's a zealot about his work and feels the professor should have additional money to go on teaching these under-educated medical students about chemistry. He'd benefit personally because the professor would have money to pay him for his work. So he poisons Dr. Popkin for his fortune. However, Dr. Bock Bach begins to suspect him. Then he must lure him away and finish him off."

Leaning back, he made a tent of sarcastic fingers over his paunch as he went on, "Suppose that Gideon Craddock has become deranged at his sister's incessant babbling about spirits and has decided on slaugh-

tering everyone connected with that séance to discourage her. If I had to listen to that woman, I might
consider such a step myself! He, too, was at the Medical School today."

Quincey slammed his hand on the desktop. "Pfui!
We could occupy ourselves by the hour, lengthening
the list of suspects. Would you have me investigate
each one? What *would* you have me do?"

I tried to keep my voice calm. "Take my case seriously. Persuade Gideon Craddock that the Pinkertons
aren't the people we need. He won't listen to me, but
he would to you. Hire Trapper—and let him choose
others—to watch the house itself, not the road and the
shore of the Charles. And by all means, sit in the living room yourself during the séance. You could take
immediate action in case something unexpected came
up while we were in the inner room."

His look of surprised horror couldn't have been
greater if I'd stood up and pitched a newel cap at his
head. Pressing his lips together first, he blew out his
breath and almost sputtered, "Such an intrusion into
the affairs of the Craddocks would be unconscionable!
Outrageous! I've given my advice and it's been disre-
garded. To do anything further, based on mere supposition, would be unforgivable. You can't be serious,
Michael."

My anger was making my vision blur, but I was
going to wait until my words sank in. Maybe, just
maybe, he'd heard them. To me, putting convention
and his own convenience first in this situation was
what was outrageous. One didn't have to be completely sure of a threat to protect others against it. It
was impossible for me to write off such a dangerous
combination of events as coincidence or happenstance. And I was convinced that, in any other kind of
case, it'd have been so for him, too.

At last, he breathed in more calmly. "I must make allowance for the sort of day you've had. Your experience was unnerving, so your emotion is understandable. But as Ovid says, *'Ut fragilis glacies, ira mora.'* Like fragile glass, anger passes away. Yes. You'll be calmer tomorrow, although I see no need for further discussion of this proposal."

That was it. I exploded out of the room.

# Chapter Twenty-six

**E**mily Craddock's eyes were even rounder with surprise. "You did get a message from Dr. Bock Bach? How wonderful! When?"

"He was heard from, let me put it that way," I answered, frustration sharp in my voice. "Maybe. His sister in the far reaches of Maine got a telegraph. It had to be hand-delivered a good distance. By the time she received it—and the news was relayed back to us—the *Independent* had already published the news of his disappearance. You remember that issue also carried Goss's signed article laying out the idea of a Spirit Killer, a theory based on the fact that the professor couldn't be found. The Monday and Tuesday editions sold instantly." I grimaced as I brought out the next sentence. "Then we received word of his telegraph."

This dubious news did nothing to relieve my concern about Sylvie. It was Wednesday. Tonight was the séance. I was tense with inaction, but I couldn't think of anything useful to do. None of my worries had a name, but they muttered and whispered loudly in my inner ear. And my anger, contrary to Ovid, had solidified instead of melting.

Emily and I were standing on the river bank between the Craddock property and Quincey's. The low-hanging November sky mingled with the river's filmy mist which, as it rose, formed looming, half-recognizable shapes. The outside atmosphere was as close and unbreathable as it was in the house.

Still, the ground was dry and here we could talk in privacy. She'd added a conspiratorial note to my invitation, saying she'd be taking the air at ten-thirty by the summerhouse and underlined the time. After two days' rest, my feet felt much better, even if they didn't look it. While waiting for her, I walked up and down, trying to give the impression of strolling about for exercise in case anyone peered out of a window.

When Emily caught up to me, her face was puckered with worry. Even the stylish plume in her bonnet drooped. Her cheeks had lost their pinkness, and the dull brown cloak over her drab brown dress emphasized her sallow look. There was no sign of her cheerful smile. She was obviously in need of a sympathetic ear, but I wanted first to tell her the news.

I went on. "Of course, hearing that the professor was well and had been 'urgently called away,' Mr. Quincey was quite relieved." Actually, he'd been smug. "He sent a note to Mr. Goss, instructing him to make this news a headline today. However, Mr. Goss replied that he felt it was necessary first to find out where and when the message was sent. Anyone can use the telegraph."

"Oh, dear, yes. I hadn't thought of that," Emily murmured unhappily.

"I'm quite sure Mr. Quincey had." And I was also sure he'd thought of the questions that followed from that. Why had the professor taken the time to notify his distant family but not the College authorities? Why not also send instructions to his assistant? A note in his own handwriting would really have been reassuring. Yet Quincey was determined not to discuss the matter, acting as if the editor's investigation was merely routine fact-checking. I just nodded when he told me. Our conversations at mealtimes were limited to the continuing European economic crisis and America's establishment of the gold standard. I occupied myself by considering my new lodgings. I intended to find some next week. Freegift, noticing the leaden words and the heavier silences, served us with downcast eyes.

Earlier, I'd asked him if we'd had visitors—the doorbell often rang—but he said it was messengers coming and going. Quincey didn't say a word about this, either.

Glancing now at Emily's deepening frown, I added, "Of course, the telegraph might well have been from the professor."

Her breath was a hopeful sigh. Her fingers in their brightly embroidered wool gloves rubbed her arms under the brown-wool cloak hard, as if to warm the underlying bones. "It could be, couldn't it? And Dr. Story came yesterday with a suggestion that's made things easier between Aunt and Uncle. Somewhat. Their disagreement about having the séance at our house has been quite . . . heated. Uncle Giddy keeps saying that people would certainly talk if anything . . . unpleasant happened again. He repeats that no suspicion, no breath of scandal has ever been attached to the Craddock name and that he has his position at the College to consider. He won't attend, of course. But Dr. Story proposed an experiment to test Sylvie's psychic powers that he hoped Uncle would take part in. He is to stay upstairs in his study on the third floor and concentrate on a Greek play while we're gathered downstairs. Apparently, it should be one that she's familiar with, that she studied with him as a girl, but Uncle Giddy is not to tell any of us which one and he's to choose it only after we've begun."

"He agreed to do that?"

"Yes. He said the scientific nature of the undertaking appealed to him. And no one at the College would therefore criticize. He's raised no more objections to holding the séance. He told me that he planned to sit in his pedestal chair, wearing his Grecian robe—actually, it's a sheet I trimmed with a gold border, but he's careful to drape it just as the pictures show—and concentrate on the play. Aunt Leo doesn't approve of the idea because she believes this might interfere with the spirits' coming. But she's determined to say nothing further, she says, because Uncle's hostility might have blocked them anyway and at least now he'll be in a receptive frame of mind. Dr. Story is such a pleasant man, isn't he? So helpful and—"

She interrupted herself, putting one hand quickly on my arm. "But you're not to tell Sylvie about the experiment, of course. None of us are. Not that we'll really have an opportunity to do so. On the day of a séance, she keeps to her room, except for time with Robbie. I think she reads. She really doesn't like holding such gatherings, you know, not at all, but Mrs. Bedell is so anxious to get in touch with Mr. Bedell, and she's been such a friend that Sylvie wouldn't refuse."

"How do *you* feel about attending, Emily?"

Surprised at my question, she plucked nervously at the bit of ivory lace trim at the neckline of her gown. "Well, I've said nothing, of course. But it's only been a week since Dr. Popkin passed away. In our dining room. That was hard. I'd much prefer we'd not have another, just yet. I find I can't sleep. And Mrs. Ticknor has been cross because I haven't been eating. Well, some, because her feelings do get so hurt if you don't. Worse, try as I will, I can't concentrate on my needlework." Her gloved fingers sketched an empty square in the air, like a blank canvas, looking at it sadly as she did so. Shaking her head. "Perhaps it's just as well. Aunt says stitchery should show a knowledge of botany whereas I produce fanciful frippery."

She tried for a smile. "Forgive me for my silly complainings. There are so many more important things. Sylvie—" She stopped and then went on determinedly. "And we must look on the bright side. As Aunt said, the doctor himself might get through to us and that would put our minds at ease, wouldn't it? He might even tell us he was mistaken about being murdered. All our worries would have been for nothing, about nothing."

Studying her face, I could see no shade of doubt that spirit communication was possible. The way she spoke about it showed she saw the supernatural as natural. For a brief moment, I found myself hoping no one ever tried to persuade her otherwise. Such faith with its promise of a safe passage into another, better world allowed her to escape her present narrow life with her oblivious uncle and her carping aunt. Nor could I see much chance for change. Her only deliverance from her situation would be marriage, but she'd not meet a suitor since she so seldom went into society. Her own kin who, according to Craddock, would have made real efforts to ensure that the beautiful Sylvie found a wealthy husband, did nothing in plain Emily's behalf. Yet her warm generosity and her face, open as a daisy's, would be as welcome as the sun to some young man.

Then I had a second thought. It was possible that they planned on Emily being a spinster so that she'd look after them as they aged.

Her nervous fingers were never still, and that sign language contradicted the optimism she forced into her tone. "Then, too, Mrs. Bedell is very worried about any further attacks on herself so that if she could be in any way reassured by the spirits, that would be all to the good. Her condition is very delicate. Dr. Haskins comes every day to her and now insists he come and sit in our living room during the séance in case anything over-excites her." Her voice trailed off.

Finally I decided that all this was prologue to something else she wanted to talk about. Apparently she had to find a way to do that. We walked in silence. The day, although edging toward noon, seemed to be darkening by the minute. Over the Charles, the mist, thin as ectoplasm, swirled up and faded. The dried vines scraped the summerhouse lattice wood like restless, bony fingers.

Then Emily turned abruptly toward me. "To be honest, Mr. Merrick, yesterday I didn't think I could go through with it at all. But the invitations have been sent, the arrangements made to Aunt's satisfaction, and the men hired as guards, so I'll have to."

She swallowed hard. "Worse, so will Sylvie. She doesn't sleep at all. I begged her to take the sleeping powder from Dr. Haskins, but she said Robbie found it and poured it all away. He doesn't like medicines, you know. She looks . . . haunted. And you could say she truly is. She hears a voice night and day warning her. And saying something else . . . about a 'shining city.' She thinks she's in danger. Well, that's not how she put it, but she does think it."

"How *did* she express it? You must tell me," I said urgently.

"I . . . I'm not sure she'd want me to. It sounded very much like a confidence. . . . And I tell myself that lack of sleep can affect one's thinking. Tomorrow, after the séance is over, and she can rest, she'll be quite all right."

A tear slid down her smooth cheek. She brushed it

away with a gloved finger, took a deep breath, and went on. "This does no good at all. I'm sorry. It's just that I'm worried witless at the strange things she says. But she does have a favor she wanted me to ask of you."

When she stopped again, I said bluntly, "Does she need money? Perhaps I could—"

"No, no," she answered, horrified. "Nothing like that. She couldn't possibly take money from an unmarried man. How would that look to others?" Each time I talked to Emily, it occurred to me that, while the Chinese bound women's feet with cloth, here their bodies and minds were corseted in stiff ivory. She shook her head. "No, Sylvie needs you to find out whether Mr. Quincey's newspapers are saved somewhere. And for how long."

That was so unexpected that I stopped abruptly and stared at her. "What? Why?"

She twisted her fingers in distress. "Oh, dear. I know it's odd. Very odd. But it seems quite important to her. She wonders if they'd be kept for a hundred years or even two hundred. That's what she said. Please, please ask Mr. Quincey."

Now I was beginning to share her worry about Sylvie. I ran a hand down my beard, glad that it hid my tightened jaw. I answered, "We were just talking about that last week because of the alarming rise in the cost of paper. I know that each issue, from the first, has been kept at the newspaper. He has a clerk who cross-indexes them so that facts in an ongoing story can be checked against earlier statements. Another set of bound volumes of them is stored at his house. Over time, they might well be saved as a matter of historical interest. As to whether the paper itself would survive a passage of years, there's a problem. Up until a few years ago, newsprint for all the papers was made of boiled rags. There are English newspapers made that way that have lasted well over a hundred years, and will probably last another hundred. But now there's a new process for making paper that shreds logs to pulp. It's much cheaper, but it's weaker."

As I talked, I was trying to consider what Sylvie could possibly have in mind. I went maundering on, hoping something would occur to me, at least something that would reassure Emily. "We don't know how long that paper will last, but Mr. Quincey felt he was forced to use it. The rag paper rose to twelve cents a pound and was almost impossible to get. But if the pulped paper were stored properly. . . . You can tell her that much. Quincey wouldn't know exactly, either, although he frets about it." I looked down at her, demanding, "Now, tell me why you think she wants to know."

"But that's what I can't figure out." Her voice rose in distress. "She said she's made up her mind and placed an advertisement in the paper, giving her address! But the only reason I can imagine that she'd do that is to let people know where to reach her if they wanted a séance."

She wailed out the next words. "Michael, *that* makes no sense. She doesn't need to advertise—all of Mrs. Bedell's friends here, and in Boston, would gladly have her come to their homes to do séances. Sylvie could even go to homes on Beacon Hill because she's so different from most mediums, who'd be just ill at ease in such houses. But she doesn't want to do séances! And why would a newspaper have to last longer than a week if she only intends to gather business? All I can think"—her words now were so low I could barely hear her—"is that the balance of her mind has been disturbed."

Another idea came to me. Sylvie had to get her address to someone in the area. But she didn't know where *he* was, either. I could see exactly why Sylvie, under constant pressure to give the séances she dreaded and unable to see a reasonable future, would leave with a "protector." Now that I thought of it, she had probably had one after her husband left, or how had she come by the money to get to Boston? Perhaps she suspected he'd followed her, knew that she was here, but not where. If she published her address, under the pretense of advertising her services as a medium, he could find her. But he'd only need to check for a week, at the most, to find that small notice, not a hundred years. Why had she asked about the newspapers' survival? Now that made me fear Emily might be right. Sleepless, too exhausted to think clearly, Sylvie had begun imagining—

No. I stopped myself. Probably she was thinking very clearly. Coming from her rigid, sheltered background, Emily couldn't accept that her friend would walk boldly out the door with a man who wasn't her husband. To so flout society's rules would be beyond Emily's understanding. No doubt Sylvie had told her, as well as me, about that dark inner voice. It occurred to Sylvie that if she connected that in Emily's mind with her leaving, it'd be easier for Emily to accept. After all, then Emily might come to believe that her friend, privy to spirit voices, had been wafted off to another world. It'd certainly explain the fact that no letters from her ever came. And why should she write? Leonora Craddock would destroy any correspondence from a disgraced woman immediately. Sylvie was trying to let Emily down easily.

Suddenly, a seagull hidden in the mist screamed above, making Emily jump. Her whole body was shaking. In as comforting a tone as I could summon up, I said, "I think I have an idea of what Miss Singer has in mind. I'll call on her tomorrow and we can talk. Please don't worry about this today. Just tell her I'm coming tomorrow. That's important. Send a note right away. Now you have enough on your mind. Try to get some rest. Tonight won't be easy."

Watching her walk back toward the house, her shoulders drooping beneath her somber cloak, I decided that statement was a superb example of what Professor Craddock would call *litotes*. A true understatement.

# Chapter Twenty-seven

**W**HO SENT THAT TELEGRAPH???? The evening edition of the *Independent* blared the news that the wired note, supposedly from Dr. Bock Bach to his sister, had come from Boston, two days *after* the professor had been "urgently called away" from the city. Printed in block letters, it was handed in during a busy time. The clerk couldn't describe the man who gave it to him, other than to say he was shabbily dressed. He only recalled that because he wondered if the man had the money to pay for such an expensive message. But the correct amount was slapped firmly on the counter and then the man was gone.

Newman Goss declared the telegraph a hoax by a murderer in a signed inside article under the headline **SPIRIT KILLER MATERIALIZES.** He noted the timing as "sufficient evidence" that the professor hadn't himself sent it, pointing out that Bock Bach would have left the city immediately. Goss then fleshed out his theory that those who'd attended the séance at the Craddocks were being killed one by one. But he went one step farther: "A dangerous fanatic is prowling, his dagger drawn against all those who gather in hopes of hearing from their loved ones on the other side. Why? Such an idea challenges his beliefs. In his crazed state, he can see only murder as the answer."

After laying out his "proof"—the suspicious death of Dr. Popkin, the shot fired near Sylvie, the odd circumstances around Bock Bach's absence—he expanded: "While it would be quite irresponsible of us to alarm the citizenry needlessly, it is highly possible that any séance-goer is threatened by him. Who knows what such a man is capable of?"

He concluded, "Don't look for a wild-eyed, raving man. He's a clever killer who plots, but he is capable of seizing a chance, then striking fast! This time, the *Independent* was too quick for him. We immediately informed the city that Dr. Bock Bach had disappeared. After our Monday edition alerted him that we were on his trail, and only then, was that very suspicious telegraph sent to the professor's family. We instantly checked on its origin. We will continue to track him. Not one of our newspaper rivals sees the problem. The Boston Police aren't ready to accept that a murderer exists. They see no threat. WE do. Our pledge to our readers is that we'll follow every development in this case so that the citizens can be informed and thus protect themselves."

In the Craddock parlor before the séance, everyone was talking about the article. Although the room was amply sized, we were all gathered in one end, close together around the dim pools of light from the oil lamps. The heavy velvet drapes were pulled tightly against the night, but cold seemed to seep through the walls. A damp draft slid around the room, making the fire jump and sputter. Its uneasy crackle counterpointed the voices, spiked with edgy excitement or lowered in strained anxiety.

Mrs. Bedell, her black pleated turban adorned with a glittery pin that scattered pricks of light, showed both feelings at once. Her face was pinched and still, yet her bejeweled hands and braceleted arms jittered, throwing distracting prisms around the room.

She brought out in a high-pitched tone, "Tonight Walter will tell us what to do. I know he will. But we have no cause for concern, in any case. Do we? We couldn't be more safe with guards everywhere. Coming here, the Pinkerton man made both Sylvie and me sit well away from the carriage windows and wouldn't let us enter the driveway without a thorough inspection of the surrounding grounds."

"And," Newman Goss drawled, "before the cabbie bringing Story and me could even proceed down the road to get here, the man there made him show his license. Then he shone his lantern full in our faces. I was blinded for some five minutes." He spoke, though, with an edgy approval.

That same cab had then fetched me from Quincey's door. We were stopped by a guard at the entrance to the crescent-shaped Craddock drive, presumably stationed there so that he could keep an eye on the thick woods across the road as well. A rifleman *might* be hiding there, but he'd have to crash around and shout to be noticed among those dark trees with scarves of mists winding through them. And even an expert marksman couldn't pick off anyone at the distant front door, poorly lit and partly obscured by the tall evergreen shrubs on both sides and an overarching, broad-leaved maple.

The house itself, once a straightforward three-story clapboarded structure with a gambrel roof, befitting a Craddock ancestor aspiring to be a country squire, had sprouted wings, one on either side. But these additions hadn't been done at the same time and were slightly different, which made the entrance look off center. Moreover, mature trees hid the west wing, but only a few saplings stood in front of the east wing.

The landscaping had been left to Mother Nature, who didn't seem interested in symmetry.

This morning's fog had turned malicious, suddenly clumping too thickly to see at all in one spot, and thinning into wisps in another. But even on a clear night, it would have taken an army of Pinkertons to protect such sprawling property with its orchards and fields that stretched east to the stables, if that's what they had in mind. If Trapper were watching the house . . . But he wasn't. Since the conversation was meant to reassure, I said nothing.

"We're as secure as we'd be in a bank vault," Leonora chimed in with a deliberate nod that didn't disturb the square of lace on the top of her head. "In addition to the guards at the top of the road and the bottom of the drive, there are two men, one at each end of the stretch of river that borders our land. No one can approach the house. If someone should try, the gardener's son Jonah, quite a substantial young man, is sitting with Father's flintlock, still in quite good working order, at the back door. Gladys will be seated at the front entrance, which is bolted, and though a slight girl, she's only required to alert us to any commotion outside, should those men find anything amiss. She has a large bell, ready to hand, to ring for assistance." As she was speaking, it occurred to me that her thin-lipped mouth managed, like Queen Victoria's, to be both firm and prissy.

"And," she added, drawing air deeply through her nose, "everyone has exact instructions. Gideon is to remain in his study until Emily goes up for him. Jonah is not to leave his post, no matter what happens, unless directly summoned. I will not have men with guns wandering through the house."

Goss gave me a significant look and jerked his head toward the front hall, presumably to indicate that his

Colt Peacemaker was in his coat, ready to hand. Then he smiled slightly and patted his stick.

"Now Gladys does know," Mrs. Bedell said worriedly, "that Dr. Haskins will be joining us a little later?" She'd already been assured twice that the Pinkertons were aware of this development. His sleek carriage with the physician's caduceus on the door, drawn by matching gray horses, had been carefully described to them. His note, which warned that he might be kept by a very sick patient, had been delivered early in the evening to her residence. He'd added that he was certain he'd be waiting in the Craddock parlor long before the séance ended.

"Even were this imagined killer a spirit, he couldn't slip in." Leonora gave another emphatic nod, with an acidic look at Goss. Addressing him, she added in a tone of reproof, "I do think that stirring up people by printing such a story was unwise. Certain classes of people, servants and such, are likely to become overwrought. It took me some time to explain to Gladys that your phrase did *not* mean a dead person was harming living people. Now she has the idea that the killer might be lurking under her bed in the attic! I had to promise her that Jonah would look there and in the closet before she retired tonight. Then I had to give her a severe talking to in order to get her to answer the front door this evening. I pointed out that she was much safer down with us than upstairs alone."

All this, I thought, explained why the poor girl went white-faced when I handed her my tall hat and coat but kept my cane. Perhaps she had the idea that I envisioned this demented man bursting through the window glass, and I'd have to ward him off with my stick. I was braced against my chair, as if I expected it myself.

Adjusting his carefully fitted trousers before putting

one knee casually over the other, Goss replied, "I'm sorry, dear lady." There wasn't a hint of apology in his voice, however. He brushed an imaginary speck off the quilted satin lapels of his informal double-breasted black dinner coat. His striped white shirt-front had a high collar with a tiny strip of a silk tie in a small bow beneath it. Tapping the gold head of his stick, as if to reassure himself that he could run through an intruder easily, he went on, "Yet it's my duty to make sure people are alert to this real threat. A number of séances are scheduled for tonight. As they come and go, people have to be watchful, prepared."

"But I understood from your previous article that you felt this disturbed man was directing his anger only at those who attended last week's séance here?" Dr. Story, who'd been sitting next to Emily and conversing in low tones with her, now turned his bright, intense eyes toward Goss. "What persuades you that Spiritualists in general are in danger?"

The editor was caught out. Since Monday, he'd obviously decided anyone who'd ever attended a séance in the entire Boston area was at risk because that would sell more newspapers. Goss wasn't at all disconcerted, though. He smoothly turned the question back to Story. "You're our expert, sir. What do you think such a lunatic is capable of?"

Story pulled at his untrimmed goatee as he thought. "If you will forgive a roundabout answer, I'd have to begin with an explanation. Some people in Harvard's Mental Philosophy Department are suggesting we change our name to the Psychology Department. As the English scientist Thomas Huxley puts it, 'As the physiologist inquires into the way the functions of the body are performed, the psychologist studies the faculties of the mind.' That sounds more scientific than it is. We're only on the threshold of learning about the mind and its diseases."

Although he was in evening dress, he still had his gold pocket watch stretched across his vest, and he fingered its fob, the small gold circle entwined with a fragment of bright red hair. He spoke consideringly, "So I really don't know. I can believe that an individual could develop a monomania and 'demonize' all those who disagreed with him, thus forming a rationale for killing them. And, as you say in your article, he could go about his daily life, appearing to be quite normal. At least for a time." Glancing hurriedly at Emily, he added, "Of course, that's a long way from saying that such a person exists and is doing that."

She kept fascinated eyes on him all the time he spoke. Perhaps she was amazed that any of her uncle's colleagues would reply to a question by saying he didn't know the answer. Or she was imagining the man he described.

Goss also was listening intently. I could see the headline in tomorrow's paper: **NOTED PROFESSOR SAYS KILLER SEES DEVILS!**

The noisy fire crackled. Susanna Bedell's turban gave a startled toss. Her fingers pleated the front of her black silk dress. Emily grabbed for the sofa arm. Leonora darted a sideways glance at the windows. I decided a change of subject was in order. Addressing Story, I said, "Tell us about the experiment with telepathy tonight. You're trying to see if Miss Singer, while in a trance state, might catch a reference to a Greek play that Professor Craddock has on his mind?"

He nodded. "We're really interested in learning anything we can about the nature of the trance state. Can Miss Singer call the spirits to her and speak with their voices? Or is she hearing the thoughts of those in the room? Or both? Is she receptive to the living *and* the dead?" As he spoke, I noticed that his usual air of intense alertness was heightened, his eyes animated, never still.

Remembering the conversation at Quincey's dinner table, I thought Story was capable of genuine scientific detachment. He could hold opposing ideas in his mind. He could see the spirits as very close, touching the transparent wall separating them from us with their weightless fingers, trying to find a way to reach out to their loved ones. Yet he could also look at the idea that instead Sylvie had an odd power to tap into others' thinking. To go further, if I'd said to him, "You know Mr. Quincey believes she puts together these little speeches beforehand based on what she knows about the sitters," Story would have conceded the possible truth of that.

Despite that, I detected a note of longing in his voice when he mentioned those spirits.

Mrs. Bedell's voice was shrill in her plea. "But you do think that Walter *might* get through this evening?"

"What we must do," Story replied, "is keep our minds open to the spirits' coming. Dr. James always noted the atmosphere before a séance. He was very sensitive to it. He felt people had to actively participate to have a good sitting. We must shut out our daily lives and move into their world."

Bending her head slightly in satisfaction, Leonora said, "I've prepared everything carefully, Susanna. Nothing has been left undone—"

The double doors of the parlor were thrown open so quickly that they banged against the walls on either side. Mrs. Bedell shrieked. Story and I jumped to our feet, and he was right behind me as we rushed in that direction. Goss was slower because he was fumbling with the top of his stick.

The young parlormaid, her cap askew, stood there trembling. "Miss Craddock . . . Ma'am. There's a noise upstairs. Loud. A door shutting. Hard. It could be that killer. Coming down the stairs!"

For just a moment, Leonora sat like a stone. Then she let out her breath and stood up, saying sternly, "Gladys, this is very wrong of you. Control your imagination. You've alarmed us all needlessly. You know the master is in his study on the third floor. This evening, in your hearing, I reminded him to make sure the door to his outer staircase that leads to the garden was bolted. No doubt he's doing just that. Keep your wits about you!"

She pointed a finger up the staircase. "To reassure yourself, go up now to Mr. Craddock's study. Tell him that the séance is about to begin." Her breath came out in a long-suffering wheeze. "He may choose his book and commence his reading."

The young parlormaid stood, stiff with fear. Her mouth worked until she brought out, "Go upstairs? *Alone?*"

Emily got up hurriedly. "I'll go with you, Gladys." Turning to her aunt, she added, "I'll remind Uncle again to bolt his outer door."

In a sharp tone, her aunt added, "And tell him again that he is to remain in his study until he is notified that the séance is over."

Leonora sank back down, reached for a fan on a side table, and fluttered it slowly in front of her face. Story moved to sit beside Mrs. Bedell and rubbed her hands, speaking to her in a quiet voice. Goss was still trying to loosen the gold head of his cane. I resumed my seat and gave my nervous system a talking-to.

After a time, we heard the footsteps of the two women descending, Emily murmuring reassuring words. At the bottom of the stairs, she gestured toward the table beneath the foyer mirror on which sat a foot-high brass bell with a wooden handle. When she came into the parlor and shut the doors behind her, she murmured to her aunt, "Uncle is quite prepared and knows what he's to do. He says that we should . . . go ahead."

"What were his words exactly?" Leonora asked sharply.

Emily hesitated, then brought out, " 'Let the follies begin.' "

Leonora rose magisterially. She pulled the thick drapes before the doors in the opposite wall. Throwing them open, she announced, "The séance will now start."

# Chapter Twenty-eight

The flickering candles did little to light the enormous Craddock dining room. Set on low sideboards and high cabinets along the walls, the candles cast their unsteady glow only on the faded flowered wallpaper behind them and turned the heavy furniture beneath into shapeless bulks. The ponderous logs in the fireplace kept both their brightness and their warmth to themselves. The center of the room was dark.

To make our way to the massive mahogany table, we used the glow of the oil lamps behind us in the parlor. Once we were seated, the maid shut those doors and pulled the drapes across them so there was no glimmer of light on that side of the room. Deep-colored textured draperies on the far wall covered the river-facing windows. Since everyone wore sober evening clothes, I could only make out the circle of pale, shadowed faces.

Emily was on my right, Dr. Story next to her, then Leonora Craddock, Newman Goss, and Susanna Bedell. The empty seat between us was for Sylvie, who'd not yet arrived. When she did, we could all join hands in a circle.

After we sat down, no one spoke. The quiet was heavy in the confined air, already weighed down with the musky aroma of frankincense. Despite the sealed-in feel of the room, there was that same slithery chill along the floor. The candles' flare and waver made shadows slide around the room, most just visible out of the side of the eye. Even an unbeliever could conjure up spirits here, imagine them waiting in the unlit corners, behind a wall, not of glass but of hardened air.

But I told myself I'd need to have any spirit appear in a daylit room. A place without a wisp of smoke, without a gleam of mirror. Perhaps then I'd be satisfied. William James said *that* wouldn't happen; such phenomena were always unconvincing. The others in the room, with the possible exception of Story, sat in solid hope.

What made my bones tighten was a tangible evil rising from the darkness. I still couldn't see what form it would take. Or where it would come from. Anybody could strike, and there was every chance nobody would. Maybe, having tried so hard to persuade Quincey that the threat was real, I'd succeeded merely in persuading myself.

A low, muttering wind made itself heard beyond the windows on the far wall. As if frustrated by the immovable fog, it poked through the narrowest crack between glass and wood. The thick drapes billowed just slightly.

We sat waiting in the pressing darkness.

Sylvie came silently through an entrance from the back rooms. In her long ivory gown, with her pale hair cascading around her face and over her shoulders, she might have been one of those ethereal spirits. The dress was of antique lace with loose, belled sleeves. She was luminous in the dusky room. I stood up and pulled out the high-backed chair for her, and as she sat down, she glanced up at me, giving me a brief nod to indicate she'd gotten my message from Emily about tomorrow.

The idea of any help I could bring then didn't seem to comfort her much tonight, judging by the gleam of apprehension in her eyes. It brought back a student production I'd seen of a play by Euripides. Alcestis, the young wife, agrees to die in her husband's stead and, walking away, she looks longingly at the sun as she goes to the gloom of Hades. Sylvie had much the same look as that actress.

In so many situations, she'd shown real courage. She held her head high in gossipy Cambridge where everyone knew she'd returned with a child but without a husband's name. She'd stood steadily before her father's blustery menace. A real bullet whistled by her head, and two minutes later she was calmly holding the smelling salts for her friend.

But Sylvie feared the supernatural. I knew that. She could accept that she had an telepathic ability of some kind. That at least followed Darwin and had a scientific ring. And, although the terrors of childhood die hard, she didn't believe it was the dead speaking through her when she was in a trance. It was the fact that she heard that inner voice. As a child, she accepted it, listened to the stories it told her. As an adult, she could find no rational explanation for it. She might use it to save Emily's feelings if she left, but there was no doubt that she heard it. That was the cause of the upleaping terror she'd shown in Harvard Yard.

Still, as she settled the wide-bottomed lute in her lap and began to play, her fingers plucked the strings with a sure touch. It was an old ballad, the words just out of memory's reach, but the melody sprang lightly up into the air. The next one was slow and calm, and everyone seemed to breathe that way along with it. At last, she began singing the words of "Greensleeves," her voice low and sweet. "Alas, my love, you do me wrong/To cast me off discourteously,/For I have loved you so long—" Suddenly, she shivered, stopped as abruptly as if an unseen hand had grasped hers. She stared down at the lute before her fingers on their own continued playing to the end of the song.

Bending down, she leaned the instrument against the table leg and then put both palms on the table. Everyone else did as well, and we linked our smallest fingers. There was enough light to see that all had done so. Emily's was over mine, and mine over Sylvie's. I was so close to her that I could hear her breathing in the stillness.

She rested her head against the chair's tall back and closed her eyes. The fire in back of her shimmered on her fair hair. After a time, her breaths were as even as a sleeper's.

Suddenly, she sat up and began to speak, but it didn't sound like her. It was a disembodied voice, not a man's, not a woman's, more of an echo in the room. "That night in Rome, in the Colosseum. . . . Curtain over the moon, but it still cast light, couldn't dim the high color of bright hair. . . . Half the giant, crumbling structure was dark, but the clear and silent arena was lit. Behind it the cavernous shadows. Air softened by the passage of so much time . . . we were laughing with the pleasure of the night . . . misquoting the poet on the moon's shine, 'The splendor falls on Roman walls . . . old in story.' Alone, finally, now because of the engagement. The two of us."

The voice had a laugh in it. "See, my love, aren't you glad we came? Doctors *always* too careful . . . what harm can come? We'll be in by midnight."

Abruptly another voice. This one was harsher.

"You're in danger. Do as I ask you! There's not much time."

I swerved to look at Sylvie. Her lashes fluttered, as if she were trying to open her eyes, but couldn't. Her finger trembled and then curled tightly around mine. Susanna Bedell let out a sharp whimper, but no one spoke. Goss's sophistication had slid away, leaving his face open as he stared straight ahead. Leonora wore an intense frown. Emily's lips moved, but no sound came. Story's eyes looked almost clenched shut.

The room was very still when the echoing voice came back with a touch of despair. "The unseen evil, miasma, seeping out of swampy ground. Bad air. Roman fever. Only three days later. Buried in an angle of the wall in a Protestant cemetery in imperial Rome."

Even though the sound died away, the pain in it lingered in the room. Though my skin was prickling, I tried to think. At first, I was sure that tale belonged to Person Story. His fiancée had died before the wedding. He wore that watch fob bordered with red hair, and "even moonlight couldn't dim the high color," as the voice said.

But Goss would have traveled through Europe, could have been engaged, might have come to America to escape grief. His expression was unreadable.

Mrs. Bedell, too, could have had a suitor before Walter. She might have persuaded him to overlook the well-known worries about the fever that came from staying out at night. She was statue-still with staring eyes. A tear glittered on her cheek.

The wind's whine was more evident in the uneasy quiet. The slight sway of the drapes was more noticeable.

Sylvie spoke now more slowly, her head back against the carved chair back. The tone was quiet, as if someone were musing aloud. ". . . remember that play. Bound to. Ending is horrible in a way. Only Euripides would do it. That young wife, heavily veiled, returning from the depths of Hades. Oh, yes. Stands before the husband she died for. Doesn't recognize her. A most unexpected visitor. I—" A pause, then the voice became tremulous. "A knock? Unexpected company of my own. Won't answer. Won't open the door. Oh, has to be one of those men outside. Bound to be. I'll just ask." Then the words are flooded with relief. "Gad, you gave me a turn. Come in, come—"

Sylvie jerked upright, and her hand jumped against mine. Then there was a long silence. Very long. Abruptly, the deeper voice came again, even harsher with urgency. "Wake up. Hear me now. You have to—"

A high-pitched shriek pierced the room. The bang of a door. I turned to Sylvie. Her eyes had struggled open, but her lips were pressed together. It came from the hall. That horrified screech was cut off abruptly. A loud, reverberating thud came, and the clatter of metal.

Mrs. Bedell tried to scream in answer, but all she could do was grasp her throat and stare, wild-eyed. Both Emily and Leonora were frozen in place. I was on my feet. I pointed at Goss sitting with his mouth agape. "Stay here. Have the women stay, too." Story was already flinging open the door to the parlor. I pushed past him and he shoved it shut behind him. We raced toward the entryway.

# Chapter Twenty-nine

The entry hall was in chaos. Hats, coats, scarves, gloves, and canes were jumbled on the floor. The thick wooden coat rack had been toppled, flung on its side, and all it had held thrown down on the parquet squares. One top hat spun slowly on its brim down the hallway. But the brass bell was untouched on the marble-topped side table. The outer doors were tightly shut.

It took us a moment to see it. Gladys's unmoving hand lay outstretched beneath a scarlet-lined black evening cape.

After we'd shoved aside the coats, it took both of us to heave the heavy oaken stand upright again onto its leaden claw-foot base. Crouching down quickly, Story felt for her pulse with one hand and carefully lifted an eyelid with another. A thin line of blood was trickling from her temple. A scattering of freckles stood out starkly on her white, unconscious face, which was otherwise unmarked.

I threw open one of the front doors. The gas lantern, set beside an untrimmed spruce, cast only a small pool of light on the bricked steps. Beyond that, some fifty feet away, all I could make out was a swinging lantern at the far end of the crescent drive. It shone on the gray horses slowly trotting toward it. The Pinkerton man was guiding a carriage to wait at the opposite end of the drive. There was no sign of Haskins, who must have alighted at the entrance. No sign of anybody. In the windy darkness, all I could hear was the clop of slowly moving horses' hooves, the scurrying of fallen leaves.

Whoever had attacked Gladys had gotten away unseen. The guard seemed only interested in moving the carriage away from the front door so he'd have an unobstructed view of it. He must not have heard her scream. He was some distance away, and any sound might have been swallowed by the shrill wind and the carriage's clatter on the gravel.

I whirled back to Story, who was now gently running the fingers of both hands over the maid's head. "Knocked out," he muttered, glancing up at me. "Or fainted. As far as I can tell. The only mark I can find is that lump on her forehead, or what will soon be a lump."

Fainted, I thought. That could have been what happened. Because she heard the carriage, and was expecting the doctor, she'd opened the door when she heard the knocker. Or what she thought was its rap. She was already tense, nearly hysterical, and then she'd seen something unexpected. She screamed, slammed the door shut. Badly frightened, reeling backward, she threw her hand out for support, grabbed a coat and yanked the rack over on top of her. A knobbed branch struck her head. It sounded likely.

Or had someone brushed her aside and raced up the staircase? No. That made no sense. Her frantic cries were sure to summon help. I jerked my head toward the broad staircase with its dim lighting, and then toward Story. He was now leaning back on his heels, again lifting her eyelids.

He glanced to the open door behind me. Hearing a

horse's snort, he said urgently, "Make sure Haskins has his bag."

Stepping out onto the bricked walk, I could now see a tall, cloaked, top-hatted figure outlined against the distant upheld lantern of the guard, hurrying toward us. I shouted the question at him.

Coming nearer, he swung up the black leather case in his hand to show me. Sounding out of breath, he brought out, "Had to go back for the blasted thing. When I got out, I grabbed my spare one instead of the proper one. Coachman couldn't hear me, and I had to chase him half down the drive." He slowed as he came up to the door, clutching his hat in the wind, taking in air. His face was reddened with exertion. "What with those idiots stopping you, shining lights in your face, asking your name, it's a miracle I thought of either—"

I interrupted. "Did you see anyone near this door?"

For answer, he stared at me, still holding on to his hat, then answered, "No. Of course, I had my back turned while going after— Why?"

I sprinted past him, my arm uplifted while still in the light, trying to attract the Pinkerton's attention, waving at him to come forward. Behind me, I could hear Haskins burst out, "Good Lord! Was she attacked?"

The guard wasn't even glancing at me as I ran up. He was raising the lantern up toward the coachman, yelling at him over the wind. "Any blind fool coulda seen I was wavin' you to come on to the end. Why din't ya move the coach—"

I grabbed his arm. "Did you see anyone at the door of the house?"

Startled, he whipped toward me. "Just what I'm sayin' to this idjit driver! He was in the way! How I was s'posed to see the door with him and his horses and that damned great—"

From his seat high above, the coachman yelled down, "Had to wait till the doctor got out, didn't I? And I myself couldn't tell if he'd gone in—"

By out-shouting them both, I found out that neither had had a view of the door. And they'd seen nothing. Dashing back, I could see Haskins and Story lifting Gladys, carrying her into the parlor.

I stopped at the foot of the staircase. Why hadn't Gideon Craddock come down when he heard Gladys scream? Did he think it was part of the goings-on at the séance? Those words about the "unexpected visitor" that Sylvie repeated were at the front of my mind. What she'd heard meant he'd let someone in his outside door. If she'd really heard him. I took two steps up at a bound.

"Wait," Haskins called to me. "She's coming round. We'll soon find out what happened. Bring me my bag." He gestured to me to hurry.

Gladys let out a moan. He took the leather case, saying, "I've a preparation in here that'll work quickly." He knelt down beside the chaise, flipped the side of his silk-lined cloak over his shoulder and pulled the case open. Inside, on an upper tray, there was an array of vials, stoppered bottles, and packets of pills. His vest was unbuttoned, and Haskins pushed it aside impatiently. His color was high, and he was still out of breath. I was catching my own. Story sat beside Gladys, patting her cheeks.

"This will work." Haskins held up one of the bottles. As he pulled out the small cork, he said in a self-satisfied tone to Story, "Ammonium carbonate and ammonia water as usual, but I add an aromatic scent so the sharpness won't so offend the ladies."

At the smell, Gladys lifted her nose away and fluttered her eyelids. Her eyes were unfocused when she opened them. Consciousness came with a rush. She looked wildly at Story, perched on the edge of the chaise, let out a small cry, and squinched her eyelids down tight again.

He chafed the back of her hands, murmuring that everything was all right and that she should tell us what happened.

Gladys started to shake her head vigorously, but the pain stopped her. Instead she pressed her lips together.

I knelt beside the chaise. Deciding that anyone who worked for Leonora would be used to a tone of command, I said firmly, "You must tell us. Think about it. You heard the doctor's carriage coming up the drive. And then?"

"Yes, sir." She turned anxious eyes toward me. "I waited, but the doctor didn't come right to the door, and I figured he's talking to somebody outside. I was gettin' nervous, but finally I heard the knocker. Still, just to be safe, I asked, 'Who is it, please?' And he said, 'It's the master.' When I heard that, I was right flummoxed. You can see why 'cause—" Her voice cracked, and she stopped.

"You mean Professor Craddock?" I asked incredulously. "But he was upstairs!"

"Well, see, sir, but he's got the outside staircase, hasn't he?" She hurried to defend herself. "So I'm thinkin' that he stepped out for a pipe and couldn't get back in. Or I wouldn't of opened the door. Truly. I was bein' careful. 'Cause of that killer. Honest, I was." Then she let out a wail. "But I shouldn't of opened that door. I shouldn't of."

"Was it your master?"

She clamped her eyelids closed and nodded. A tear slid down her cheek, and she choked out, "He's run mad! He has. Soon as I seen him like that, I slammed the door shut. Did it without thinkin'."

"Gladys, are you sure it was him?"

"Oh, yes, sir." She tried to talk but couldn't and instead pulled at her cheeks to indicate the square sides of his beard. "And he laughed, like he does."

"Then why did you shut the door?"

Her lips framed words twice, and she finally managed to sob out, "'Cause he's astandin' there without any clothes on! He was stark naked!"

# Chapter Thirty

None of us said a word. It was quiet except for Gladys' loud snuffling. Haskins abruptly motioned to us and stepped back to a far corner. Story reached into an inside pocket, drew out a folded handkerchief, pressed it into the girl's hand, and followed me.

"Before you go rushing upstairs," Haskins said, "we'd better think a minute." He glanced at Gladys, raised his eyebrows, touched his temple with his forefinger, and looked inquiringly at Story. In answer, he lifted a worried shoulder and said in a low tone, "She was flustered before the séance began, quite on edge. She's naïve girl, she was sitting alone, probably glancing fearfully up the staircase lest a killer come creeping down, and then at the front door, sure there was a killer lurking in the bushes outside. Under those circumstances, it's hard to imagine she drifted off. That rules out her being half asleep and half dreaming. I can't account for her making up such a fantastic tale in any other way. So I'd have to say she's sane enough. She saw *something* that upset her."

"What about Craddock's mental state?" I asked. "He's been so opposed to holding the séance here, he and his sister have been quarreling. . . . A temporary aberration? Gladys said he laughed." I recalled the professor's distinctive cackle. Craddock's self-absorption and the nasty edge to his tongue also came to mind. "Could he have conceived this as some sort of joking revenge, aimed at Leonora?"

Story tugged at his goatee. "I'll go with you upstairs. We'll try talking quietly to him." He didn't add that there was a chance the professor might be raving, might need to be restrained. We were both thinking that. Gladys' story sounded eerily true.

"Wait." I gestured backwards toward the dining room. "We'd better—"

"Good Lord!" Haskins burst out. "Poor Mrs. Bedell. The woman must be in a terrible state of anxiety. Her nervous system cannot take that. In all this, I've forgotten my own patient." He threw off his cloak and put his hat on top of it. His evening clothes were in some disarray, and he began straightening his cravat, buttoning his gold jacquard vest. Catching my glance, he said, "I had to hurry into my evening wear. Last patient kept me much longer than I'd expected." He seemed to be readying himself for his audience. He lightly brushed his hair back with his fingers and ran a hand down his clean-shaven cheeks, which still had a high color. He adjusted his tucked white shirt and inspected his black patent laceless shoes. As he put his clothing in order, he resumed his usual authoritative manner. "I'll make sure everyone's quite calm before they come into the parlor."

"I have an idea," I said, stopping him with a raised hand. His cool gaze at me indicated he didn't need any suggestions, but I went on. "Why not have Emily come out first to sit beside Gladys? You might mention that the maid hit her head and could be a little . . . confused. We don't want the girl blurting out her story as everyone comes back in. It'll give you more time to quiet Mrs. Bedell's fears and make everyone's minds easier. In the meantime, Emily can soothe Gladys. We'll wait here."

Haskins shrugged and opened one of the dining room doors. Susanna Bedell's almost hysterical wail abruptly changed to a welcoming cry at his appearance, and then he shut the door firmly. After a moment, Emily appeared and, seeing the weeping girl, bustled straight to her side. Story gave her an approving nod, and the two of us stepped over the scattered coats and went directly up the stairs.

At the second landing, he stopped abruptly, putting a restraining hand on my arm. "I don't know how to approach the man." His voice was deeply troubled. "What did you make of those words—which could have been Craddock's—that Sylvie came out with?"

Although impatient, I answered, "I wanted to ask you. Let's accept for the moment that she has a genuine gift for telepathy and has really heard his thoughts. The professor is upstairs and he's chosen to read Euripides' *Alcestis*. At the end the young wife comes back from the dead and arrives at the door. He's thinking, therefore, of a visitor who's *really* unexpected. Just then he hears a rapping at his outer door. He's startled, fearful. Who on earth is going to be asking for entrance there? Then it occurs to him that it has to be one of the Pinkertons with a question. Or one of them checking on his welfare. He's been persuaded, like his sister, that the guards are capable of keeping out all intruders. He opens the door. No one is there. He realizes the wind has just rattled the latch. But his quirk of humor sets in. He's dressed in his Greek robe and imagines himself saying humorously, as if to Alcestis, 'Gad, you gave me a turn. Come in, come in.'"

Story ran his hand nervously over his mouth. "So your thinking is that Craddock then, while in this antic frame of mind, decides to continue the joke. He'll go downstairs and knock on the door. But his coming wouldn't be that unexpected to Gladys, who might assume, as she did, that he'd locked himself out upstairs. Therefore, he has to do something quite out of the ordinary. Shocking, in fact. He strips off his Greek robe and stands there naked. Quite a cruel trick on the parlormaid." He grimaced. "You know, it's very possible that the girl has never seen an unclothed man."

Nodding in agreement, I asked, "True, but he's aiming at disrupting his sister's gathering, getting even with her, so to speak. He doesn't even consider the effect on that young girl. Is this possible?"

Getting edgier by the moment, I took a step up. So did Story, but he stopped as he replied, choosing his words carefully. "I myself talked to the Craddocks about the arrangements for this séance. He was adamant that he did not want it held here. His sister was equally determined. Both were very angry. Humor is a loaded gun. It's often used to wound."

The gaslight above us flickered on his face, as if tracing the quick patterns of his thinking. He spoke faster. "I have to say this. I've known Gideon for some years. He taught me Greek as an undergraduate. Although he has his little eccentricities, such behavior is not like him. He's a conventional gentleman. He's in his sixties, but I've seen no sign of a lessening of his mental powers. Yet, there is real tension now because of all that's happened. Too, he does keep several fine bottles of sherry and port in his study. His sister doesn't drink, and he likes a small glass as he reads and reflects. He and I have shared several pleasant evenings together there. Perhaps, tonight, he had more than one glass, thus affecting his judgment, releasing him from the usual constraints. I can see this as an explanation."

Story didn't add, didn't have to add, that the other explanation for Craddock's behavior was much worse. The talk of murder, especially one committed in his parlor, the shooting in the sanctuary of Harvard Yard, and now the presence of armed guards on his property might have truly unbalanced the man.

We went up the remaining stairs at a trot. But some ten feet from the study door, Story paused again. He whispered, "He may already be quite ashamed. If he begins talking about what he's done, let him do it, even if he tries laughing it off. We won't accomplish anything by making him defend his actions. Eventually, if he's quiet enough, we can see him to his bedroom. If not, we may have to get a sedative from Haskins." He ran his fingers through his hair, rumpling it even further. "No matter the outcome, things will be very difficult in this household. Poor Emily. Such a gentle woman." He pressed his lips together. "This won't be easy."

We walked up to the thick, paneled door. I rapped gently at first. There was no answer. I knocked harder. There was not a sound from inside.

With a warning glance at me, Story turned the knob and cracked the door slightly. A lingering odor of fruit-scented pipe tobacco trailed toward us. He cleared his throat and said quietly, "Craddock? It's Person Story and Michael Merrick." There was no response.

He pushed the door all the way open. The book-lined room was pleasant, inviting. Several layers of textured rugs were piled deep on the floor. Apple-wood logs crackled in the fireplace, and there were two leather chairs by the sides. Directly in front of it was a backless chair that looked vaguely Grecian. It was low enough that one could climb on it and deliver a speech in an ancient language.

A cluttered desk stood before thick drapes over windows that overlooked the Charles. There was a pathway between it and an overstuffed sofa that led to an outer door set against a far wall. That sofa caught our attention. On it was a neat pile of clothing—trousers, shirt, vest, and undergarments. Shoes were beneath the sofa. Over its back was flung a white square with a blue-and-gold border, and a braided, tasseled belt. That was obviously the professor's Greek robe. As well as his usual clothing.

We looked at each other. What was he wearing? Had he run naked again outside? There was no place he could be hiding in here. Not a cabinet, closet, or cupboard. I strode to the outside door with Story behind me.

I stopped so suddenly that he pushed against my back.

At my feet, facedown, with his head toward me, Gideon Craddock was sprawled behind the sofa. His thin white arms with knobby elbows were flung forward as if reaching for help. He wasn't wearing anything at all, except for a pair of sandals with narrow leather strips that laced up his stick-like calves. But we were not likely to hear his explanation. The back of his skull was bashed in.

# Chapter Thirty-one

"The killer was outside the séance room, lurking in the bushes, waiting his chance! The entire time!" As Goss paced past me, he leaned down toward me and brought that out in a shocked whisper. This had to be his third pass in front of my chair. Again he added, "Someone from the Other World was trying to tell us! You heard that voice." I kept shooting him warning looks to urge him to keep *his* voice down. He did, but he couldn't stop either his feverish walking or his constant repeating. He was clutching his cane tightly, but his hand still trembled.

Hysteria quivered in the air of the parlor, although the only sounds now were of subdued comments. For a time, Gladys and Susanna Bedell had kept up a steady duet of muffled whimpers and abrupt bursts of untuned screeches. The maid steadfastly refused to go upstairs, although, after sending for the constabulary, I'd recruited Jonah from the back door and he, Story, Goss, and I had searched the house from attic to cellar. Why would the killer hide in the house when he could make an easy escape down the outer staircase? It made at least as much sense as anything else that had happened so far.

The image of a coolly waiting killer, one with a gabbling mind, crouching in the innocent shrubbery unbalanced us all.

Finally, Gladys had been persuaded to lie down on a chaise in the adjoining library and had swallowed the mixture Haskins gave her. She must have fallen asleep since there was not a sniffle from that direction. Mrs. Bedell had also dutifully drunk a powder that seemed to soothe her, although she clung to Sylvie's hand so tightly that she must be stopping the flow of blood. With maddening regularity, she'd fix one of us with a glazed look and repeat quaveringly, "You heard Walter's voice. He kept warning me, saying I was in danger. I'm alive at this moment because of his constant care." Tears would run down her cheeks unchecked, and Sylvie would gently wipe them away.

Although Haskins had urged the same cloudy potion on the other three women, Sylvie and Emily sipped chamomile tea. Leonora sat with her hands in her lap, eyes fixed on the middle distance, in a state of near catatonia. She said neither yes nor no to medication, tea, or brandy. She'd said nothing at all since she'd heard of her brother's naked appearance at the front door.

Emily, Story, and I took our turns sitting beside her, trying to console her, to distract her. Nothing worked. Emily, blinking back her own tears, attempted to involve her aunt with practical decisions about the upcoming day. She pointed out that by afternoon, friends would be making condolence calls. I was thinking that, given the sensational nature of Professor Craddock's death, carriages would be lined along the road all the way back to the center of Cambridge. The funeral would have to be the morning of the next day in Mount Auburn Cemetery. Emily pleaded with her aunt to begin the necessary arrangements. But for once, Leonora had no orders to issue, no commands. I offered help from Quincey's household, asking Leonora's preferences on staff. Her eyes never moved in my direction. Story felt her pulse, chafed her hands. She didn't respond at all. Her cheeks seemed to have sunk slightly; her whole body looked less round, as if air was slowly leaking from her.

She was the only still point in the room. All the rest of us were in motion. Haskins, who'd agreed with surprising lack of argument to the wait for the constables, went back and forth between his patient and the front window, holding aside the drapes, staring into the darkness, and then letting them slip from his fingers. Several times I marched to the front door, stepped out, surveyed the black night, and listened to the shouts of the guards. By doing this, I established several things. That the wind had finally pushed the fog seaward because I could now see the lanterns in sharp outline. That the Pinkertons felt constant activity of any kind was useful. That I didn't have any better ideas than they did. That Quincey should have been sitting in the living room. That I wanted to slam the door shut with a resounding crash. Then I'd once again return to a chair by the fire.

I wanted to talk to Sylvie about her view of the séance, but I knew that would agitate Mrs. Bedell. Haskins wasn't going to allow that. I couldn't even catch her eye. Usually her face was turned toward her friend, but when she glanced up, her look was distant, absorbed, as if she were looking down a remote pathway, trying to see where it went. Surrounded by all of us, in our clothes suitable for a funeral, she was in that white lace dress, fair hair curling down, dressed instead for a quite different ceremony.

Person Story was the only one of us doing anything helpful. When he wasn't soothing Leonora or stopping to look in on Gladys, bending over to say a quiet word to Emily, he refilled the brandy glasses. When he stopped by my chair to add logs to the fire, I took the chance to ask him about the séance. I began cautiously, "I'm sorry if you find this disturbing, Story, but I want to ask if that description of the Colosseum was what you yourself had in mind at that moment."

Picking up the poker, he adjusted a log, stood still for a moment, and then answered slowly. "It was. Or to be exact, it's a description of the picture I was recalling. You see, I was concentrating on Daisy, hoping for a message from her. My fiancée. Her name was Daisy. But try as I will, whenever I do that, it's that night in Rome that comes back to me. The black shadows in the arches and the moon's light on her red hair. Her laugh. The emotion comes back. I should never have let her talk me into taking her there. Even at the time, I knew—" He swallowed, pain in his voice and in his eyes.

Clearing his throat, he set the poker back in its stand, straightened his back, and faced the parlor. "But Dr. James has a vital theory which he calls 'the will to choose.' As I understand it, he's saying that even the luckiest of us have only small control over all the circumstances of our lives. Yet we can choose how we respond to events. This evening I was thinking that I should choose to live in the present, not the past. So I— Pardon me, Merrick, that tray looks a little heavy for Emily." He hurried to take it for her.

Goss kept roaming the room, but his low-voiced asides were now concerned with a different matter. "What has to be done, Merrick, is to put out the afternoon edition as early as possible, and then run an extra in the evening. The headline, bold Roman type, of course, spread across all six columns, will read 'Spirit Killer Strikes Again.' As many exclamation points as the printers can cram in."

On his next tour, he said, "Now the second head will make it plain that my original theory was exactly right. Craddock's murder shows that all those at the first séance are in danger. But I want to work in that the man is brainsick, quite demented. No one who's ever attended one is safe. Inside, on page three, my own article will include Story's phrase that the killer demonizes his victims. No question that Quincey will approve—" Goss brought himself to a full stop. "He doesn't know about Craddock yet!"

"Yes, he does," I answered. On one of my trips to the front door, I'd given the Pinkertons something worthwhile to do and sent Quincey a note. I'd have much preferred to tell him in person because of the nature of the news, but he had to be aware that something was wrong. The river guards, called off their positions, were patrolling the length of the road, their lanterns flashing like distant fireflies. Maybe by morning, when I could give him a full report, he'd have an idea, even with the sudden shock of this loss.

The neighing of horses and the clatter of wheels outside roused us all. Mrs. Bedell's coach had been dispatched with one of the guards to fetch the Cambridge constables, and they'd arrived with a noisy flourish. I went to the door immediately and watched while two blue-uniformed figures bent their heads toward the Pinkerton man who climbed out of the carriage last, still talking. He waved his arm in several directions. Finally, he took his place by the door, and they clumped toward me.

As I accompanied the constables up the stairs, I mentioned to the older man, who'd dressed in such haste that his long tunic jacket was misbuttoned, that my employer, Mr. Quincey, had investigated some of the events preceding this. He chewed on the edges of his bushy mustache and then said in a flat voice, "Owns the *Independent*, right? I read about that Spirit

Killer. And the editor fellow, he's here, too? You work for the paper?"

I agreed, adding, "Not at the moment."

He shot a mistrustful sideways glance at me and nodded. "Mmm. Pinkerton man said you and the doctor found the body. You move anything around? Either of you?"

"No." While Story examined the body, I'd certainly examined the room, but I hadn't moved anything.

"Mmm. Like to talk to you first, then. 'Course, we'll talk to everybody. Separately."

I thought about them trying to speak to Mrs. Bedell under those circumstances. All I said was "Mmm."

At the door of the study, I was dismissed.

Their inspection of the body and the room didn't last long. When they returned, they beckoned me into the dining room. Haskins was on his feet immediately. He introduced himself, adding his credentials at Harvard Medical School. Then he asked for the older man's name.

"Watkins," he replied laconically. He made no effort to introduce the terrier-faced younger man.

Chopping the air firmly, the doctor pointed out that it was essential for Mrs. Bedell to return to her home immediately. He said that she could be questioned tomorrow. Possibly.

"Mmm," Watkins answered, nodding. "We'll take what you say into account, sir. But murder is what we have here. Major crime."

Haskins began a description of the harm the woman would suffer, but Watkins, still nodding and mmming, showed me into the inner room.

He was really only interested in one point. Did I see a lead pipe anywhere in the room, or anything that resembled a lead pipe?

I shook my head. "There are a number of rolled-up scrolls on the shelves, but they look fairly light."

"See anything out of place? Mmm. Anything odd?"

"No. At the entrance of the outer door, there were some grass strands, a piece of an oak leaf. The bottoms of Craddock's sandals were quite clean."

The younger constable, whose straggly blond mustache would never achieve the grandeur of his colleague's, threw in, "Stands to reason there'd be grass or some such, don't it? 'Cuz the murderer, he's hiding in the bushes where he'd be bound to get grass on his shoes. When the professor nips out, then the killer goes right up and he gets behind the door and when the professor comes back, he just reaches out and bonks—"

A thunderous look from Watkins made him clamp his lips together. But I couldn't resist saying, "Something troubles me about that idea. How could the murderer be sure that Craddock would come out in the first place, let alone come back? When you see a naked man sprint past you, and there are guards on the property, why would you think that he'd return alone?"

"Mmmm. No accounting for a lunatic, though, is there, sir?"

I wasn't sure whether Watkins was referring to the professor or his killer.

He went on, "Let's see now. I take it you didn't see anything out of the way as you was arriving. The Pinkerton fellow said they had the whole property buttoned up tight. Mmm. And you didn't hear any noises from outside while you were in this room doing the séance business?"

I shook my head. If he wasn't going to ask what went on during the séance, I wasn't going to volunteer. He could get the account from Mrs. Bedell. Silently, I wished him luck.

"Anything else you want to add? I'd just like to hear it from you instead of reading it in the paper, sir. No point in printin' that we're baffled and then saying that we should instead be lookin' into this or that." His tone was dry.

"Mr. Goss will be writing up tonight's events, not I." I looked at Watkins's bleak eyes. He was clearly out of his depth, but I couldn't imagine what I could say that would be of any help. If he wanted to know about Craddock's mental state, which he didn't seem interested in, he could get a clear statement from Dr. Story. As a matter of fact, Watkins could get a description of the study from him, too. Both Story and I saw the open copy of *Alcestis*, the golden tassel of a sewn-in bookmark spread across the last page. Next to the book was a sherry decanter and an unused glass.

When he nodded in dismissal, I stood up and held the door. Dr. Haskins, supporting Mrs. Bedell, who still clung to Sylvie, entered in a group.

I went outside, deciding that talking to the Pinkerton man had to be more useful than that interview. But he was far more interested in talking to me, especially about the cleverness of the Spirit Killer. He described the elaborate precautions taken ahead of time by his men, which would have made it absolutely impossible for anyone to get by them once they arrived. The gist seemed to be that the man had been hiding on the property most of the day. He himself hadn't seen the professor at the door, repeating that the doctor's carriage was blocking his line of sight.

Then Goss came bursting through the front door, shrugging into his scarlet-lined cape. He stopped beside me. "I'm going back now in Haskins's carriage. Mrs. Bedell's in a state of near collapse! The doctor and Sylvie will go with us, of course. A break for me. I can get to work immediately on getting home. Had to promise Watkins I'd show him the article before I published it. I'm going to have that paper on the streets before noon, Merrick. The extra later. Be sure to tell Quincey." He flew past on his way to the doctor's sleek gray coach, now circling up the drive toward us, and stood impatiently waving the driver to move faster forward.

Mrs. Bedell came tottering out behind him, supported on one side by Sylvie and on the other by Dr. Haskins. Glowering, he jerked his head back toward the house. "We'll leave Mrs. Bedell's coach for Story. I told that fool Watkins my patient was in no condition for questions! Now look at the result."

I followed them to the carriage, and helped Haskins carefully settle Susanna in. She sank back on the cushions, her breath coming in hiccups. As I put my hand out for Sylvie, I said hastily, "Would it be convenient if I called in the morning?"

Brusquely, the doctor answered for her. "There can be no visitors tomorrow. I cannot allow that. No agitation of any kind. Nor can there be any question of even Miss Singer returning here tomorrow. Mrs. Bedell is much more comfortable with her by her side."

He drew me aside. Lowering his voice so that he couldn't be heard, he added with disdain, "It's a question of their safety. Surely you can see that. Both these women were at the first séance. This Spirit Killer, or whatever name you give him, got by your defenses tonight. I'll not give him a chance again. I trust no one. No one will be admitted, take my word for it."

Taking my hand to climb into the carriage, Sylvie pressed it tightly. "I'll send you a note," she said in an urgent voice. "And tell Emily I'll write her first thing in the morning. I couldn't even say good-bye properly since she's with the constables."

I caught only a glimpse of her profile as the coach moved smartly off. I watched as the horses, tossing their magnificent gray manes, passed the swinging lantern of the guard far down the road.

Just as I was turning to go back into the house, I saw a procession on foot, also with lanterns, coming from the opposite direction. As they neared, I could see there was one man in front with his light and another in back. In between there was a tall, black-cloaked figure in a top hat. He was walking with his back rigid, as slowly and deliberately as a soldier executing the Dead March.

It was a night of marvels.

The Pinkerton guard by the door jerked his thumb at the approaching group. "Two of my men. Who's that then they got with 'em?"

"A neighbor," I said. "I'll introduce you to Mr. Quincey."

He stopped before us, both his height and width dwarfing the men beside him. "Michael," he said in a tight voice, "I shall pay my respects to the two Miss Craddocks. I shall also offer them any assistance in our power."

There seemed to be something wrong with his jaw. His words were clipped, forced through thin lips. Then, despite the dim light, I saw his face and understood. His thick brows were drawn darkly together, his heavy chin far more pronounced. Quincey was filled with an icy fury.

He continued, "My visit will be short."

Imperiously, he motioned with a finger to the guard by the door. The startled man threw it open. He walked straight in.

# Chapter Thirty-two

"The one man with a motive, and the arrogance, the quickness, the knowledge, to do it all, couldn't have done it!" Quincey gritted out the words, his tone as cold and bitter as the night air as we headed back along the gravel road. "If from the beginning, I'd accepted that here was a clever and determined killer, I'd have instantly pointed to him. Yet I'd have been wrong. Incredible. I would have been wrong." He whacked at a stone with his stick and it caromed with a *plink* off a nearby tree.

Whirling around in alarm, the Pinkerton man in front of us swung his lantern in that direction. Glaring, Quincey gestured to him to go on.

I didn't reply. At the Craddocks', I'd already given him an account of the events of the evening. He'd listened without a word. He'd seen the upstairs study. He'd said nothing. Now, this remark. He was attempting to excuse himself, implying that no action on his part would have changed what happened. Witnessing his fury at his friend's house, I'd hoped that emotion would move him forward. No. Instead he was outraged because he'd been outwitted.

"It should have been Haskins!" He sent another bit of gravel flying but it landed noiselessly in the road-side weeds.

He said, "For the past week, I've had Hoggett looking into the backgrounds of the people who wouldn't be directly under your eye. Tonight I had all of their whereabouts checked. I was delayed in arriving at the Craddocks tonight because I needed this information. The minister, James Cranch Meeker, attended a dinner on Beacon Hill. I'd already discovered that he doesn't need money and he had little chance of getting it from Popkin's bequest. The other three men are all connected with Harvard, and they'd have united against him.

"And," he went on tersely, "tonight Hoggett played cards at the stables with Josh Singer and his friend Goslip. Osbert Davies sat quietly by, reading his Bible. I even had the evening's activities of young Wilcox, Bock Bach's assistant, traced. He was at a lecture."

I made no answer. Now Quincey was saying that, although he ignored my particular plea for action, he had done *something*. It didn't erase the image in my mind. I saw Craddock's body, naked, his arms outstretched for help. He'd been defenseless. While I wasn't expecting Quincey to confess to crimes of omission, let alone beat his breast, he had to see what went wrong so that he'd take the right actions now. Sylvie needed our protection.

Quincey missed the next piece of gravel entirely. "Haskins is in desperate need of money. Hoggett found that the man owes every merchant, tailor, and bootmaker in town."

There was nothing to say to that. Quincey was easing his conscience by repeating all the steps he'd taken. I'd made plain to him that Haskins arrived at the front door only minutes after Craddock himself was there, alive and well. At least alive. The doctor didn't have the time to kill him, nor did he have any reason to kill him. I'd eliminated Haskins as a suspect early because of his lecture the night of the shooting.

While Quincey was no doubt still maintaining that a student shot at the effigy, I was sure that Sylvie was the target. I was convinced that one man had murdered Popkin, Bock Bach, and now Craddock. He'd also tried to kill Sylvie. And me.

But I had no suspects. All the beneficiaries of Popkin's will were eliminated. That left the Spirit Killer, a nameless, faceless fanatic.

Quincey's breath puffed out visibly in the frigid night. "Despite the barrels of my ink that Mr. Goss has drained in persuading readers that we're faced with an inspired madman, everywhere I see the cunning of reason. This man benefits from these killings."

I stopped abruptly. How far was Quincey willing to go to shift the blame from himself? "You're not suggesting that Bock Bach is really still alive and is skulking about planning on getting rid of the others and just throwing in a few extra people to cover his tracks?"

"No." His answer was very quiet. "When you said he'd left his walking stick in the office, I should have known he was dead. That cane, like his jacket buttons, has the insignia of his university dueling club. He carried it for so many years that it would have become an extension of his hand. He wouldn't have forgotten it."

It was a small admission. Maybe he imagined that now I'd help him extricate himself from the hook of guilt, but he was mistaken. I said nothing.

"But"— he jammed his top hat down so fiercely on his head that the brim almost touched his eyebrows— "I could accept that idea more easily than I can the idea that Gideon Craddock would behave as he did tonight. To remove his clothing—"

I'd already trotted out my theories on that to him. I wasn't sure I believed them myself. Wearily, I threw out one more. "There he is, standing on his pedestal, declaiming Euripides's poetry. He becomes a different person. A heroic Greek. A man free of the usual restraints. He's wearing his robe. As the proverb has it, 'Clothes make the man.' "

He didn't reply. Maybe he was thinking that over. Or maybe he was trying to come up with another explanation for his lack of action. I was surprised he hadn't yet blamed what he'd have called the flim-flammery, the twaddle, and the blather of Spiritualism for misleading him.

As we turned into the driveway, I could see the faintest line of dawn in the east, separating the black water from the blacker sky. The lantern by the door lit the mellow brick of the Georgian facade of the house, showing its beautiful simplicity. I realized I'd be sorry to leave. But I would. I didn't see how I could work with Quincey any longer. He had no feelings for others. He turned everything into self-serving words.

The Pinkerton guard wished us good night and took himself off, his lantern bobbling down the road as he retraced his steps. Quincey, still quiet, opened the door with his key and we went inside.

As I was putting my cloak and hat on the hooks that lined the foyer, he cleared his throat. I turned to look at him. He straightened the narrow tie beneath the stiff collar of his old-fashioned evening wear. Then he brushed at the hem of his double-breasted black jacket. Finally, he said, "Popkin was a solitary man. If he keeled over walking from Cambridge to Boston, if he slumped over his desk or slipped away in his sleep, everyone would have assumed it was a heart attack."

I waited. He was going to come up with some new way to acquit himself so he could sleep.

Still not looking at me, he went on. "Where Popkin

would die wasn't in the killer's control. It occurred at a séance, and Miss Singer overheard his dying words. Yet what I had to pay attention to was the fact that Popkin was himself a doctor. A layman would only have known something was wrong with his body, but a medical man could point to what was wrong. He knew he'd been poisoned. His death had, of course, nothing to do with Spiritualism, let alone the supernatural. It was a straightforward murder. I'm convinced of this. I allowed myself to be misled."

He swallowed hard. "I was wrong from the beginning. One error led to another. Bock Bach's death was preventable. And my own errors caused me to lose a friend of many years."

Now he met my eyes and I saw the terrible regret in his. "A bitter loss. An ongoing loss. And at this moment, I can't even guess who the murderer is. But I won't rest until I know. Together, we'll make sure of Miss Singer's safety."

He turned, went down the hall and into the library, and closed the door behind him.

B

face.
cross
the c
body
its na
Th
half-
see S
Josh
low
disag
Fir
how
have
prom
and
into s
In
The
Quin
hand
my
until
sign

would be slumping beneath the heavy sorrow and sense of failure that weighed down the air. Outside, under a dingy sky, I hurried down the gravel road.

Only a hansom cab stood outside the Craddocks' gates. It'd been there some time because the staked horse had nibbled most of the grass in reach. The only sound was its slow munching. The house, too, was wrapped in such silence that it seemed vacant.

The door opened promptly. It was Freegift standing there. Someone had found him a black butler's coat that was too big for him, and he looked diminished in it. But his back was straight, and the gray fringe of hair over his forehead was neatly brushed. As he took my coat and hat, he said, "Mr. Quincey insisted we come—Mrs. Hingham, that is, and I. She's in the kitchen assisting her sister, Mrs. Ticknor. When we left, *he* was sitting in the library, still in his evening clothes! Wouldn't take as much as a cup of tea." At that, he drew in a desperate breath before saying, "Miss Emily's in the parlor. The professor is laid out in the library." Blinking rapidly, he added, "Amongst his books."

As I came in, Emily rose quickly and came toward me. "I'm so glad you've come," she said, sounding as if she certainly meant it. She was quite alone. Over her shoulder, I could see the polished pine casket on a trestle through the open doors. It was surrounded by Michaelmas daisies, and their sharp autumn smell filled both rooms. Although she was subdued, her hair was neat in its bun and her black silk dress was becoming.

"I apologize for Aunt, who's unwell," she began rather formally as we sat down on the sofa nearest the fire. Then her voice quavered and she said, "Michael, she won't talk to me at all, and if I press her, she turns her face to the wall. That's not like her."

"No doubt it's the shock." I added all the soothing phrases that I could come up with. Emily should surely have someone with her. Just then she said, "I did get a note from Sylvie this morning. A long one."

Her smile was genuine as she reached for an envelope on the piecrust table. "It lifted my spirits." Smoothing the vellum paper on her lap, as if simply touching it gave her pleasure, she added, "She paid me so many compliments, and at the end she says how much having me as a friend means to her. I shall always treasure this and I'm going to make an embroidered case to keep it in."

I wanted to snatch it and read it. It sounded very much like a farewell letter. Why did Sylvie write it this morning? Could she have had an answer that quickly from yesterday's advertisement? Maybe it was just that she knew how much Emily needed comfort. In fact, Emily needed her now. I said, "There has to be some way around Dr. Haskins's concerns. I'm going to Brattle Street immediately, and I could escort her here—"

"Not today, I think, Michael. She says that Mrs. Bedell has been given a powder in the hopes that she'll sleep through the day, and I'm sure Sylvie wouldn't like to leave her. She herself said she couldn't swallow any potion because she wanted to be wakeful. She says she'll spend her day with me in her thoughts." Emily ran her fingers over the envelope again.

"You have loyal friends, and I'm one," I said. "If there's anything you need done, you only have to ask." I meant that, but my anxiety to get to Sylvie was pressing on me.

Lightly touching my sleeve, she answered, "I'm just grateful that you're here. I do wish Sylvie could be as well. But Person promised that he'd return quite early. He's been so very helpful." She was blushing as she said the words. And when the door knocker sounded just then, she looked up in anticipation. It was Dr. Story. The warmth of his greeting to her left me in no doubt that she was in good hands.

I quickly made my farewell.

The hansom cab driver by the gate, staring in boredom at his horse's bent head, was happy to take me to Quincey's door. But before I could alight, the door was thrown open and Quincey came out. Fast. "Stay where you are, Michael. You must leave instantly."

Still in his evening clothes, he leaned over the cab door, the slight breeze making his wiry hair stand wildly upright. His eyes were full of fear. "Did Miss Craddock receive any communication from Miss Singer this morning?" he asked urgently.

"She did. Sylvie said she couldn't come because Mrs. Bedell was meant to sleep for the whole day and—"

He shut his eyes in profound relief. "She got through the night safely. Still, we haven't a moment to lose. Miss Singer is in real danger. I know now. I have the answer. Go immediately to Brattle Street. Don't worry about Mrs. Bedell. She's quite safe. But you must bring Miss Singer and the child back with you. She'll have to stay here with us until we have the killer, but don't tell her that. Just bring them."

I stared at him. "It might be hard to convince her because—"

He waved an abrupt hand. "This is the only way to protect her."

"For God's sake, from whom?"

"*You* told me last night. But if the name comes to you, say nothing. If you say who threatens her, Miss Singer might not believe you. She might refuse to come, and she must. Now if Dr. Haskins is there, tell him to come as well. But Miss Singer is to leave in this cab with you. He'll try to dissuade her. Override any of his objections. When you return with her, then find him. He could be in danger too. That's a real possibility, but he'll certainly dismiss the idea."

"If he does, how in the world am I to talk him into it?"

Quincey frowned, rubbed his chin, and finally said, "Tell him I know the truth. That'll bring him. Now go."

Beckoning the driver to lean down, Quincey gave him the address and thrust paper money in his hand. "With speed," he ordered.

The horse took off so fast that I was thrown back against the seat.

# Chapter Thirty-four

As the cab spun to a stop under Mrs. Bedell's portico, the door flew open. The butler stepped out even faster than Quincey had and sprang over to open the cab door. On my way here, I'd gone over the best approach to get inside the house. "Portman," I said firmly, "I have to—"

"Thank the good Lord it's you, Mr. Merrick! I was just about to send for you. We couldn't think who else might help us. Mrs. Rogers and I—we're just at a loss!" His starched white shirt front had pulled free from his weskit, ballooning up beneath his chin, emphasizing his pouter-pigeon look. A distinctly ruffled bird. He was distraught, urging me with both hands into the vestibule.

Signaling to the driver to wait, I went in. The housekeeper standing just inside the marble hall was frantically fingering the buttons on the pleated front of her gray dress. She wailed out in one long breath, "What *are* we to do, sir? Dr. Haskins gave me strict instructions about not waking Mrs. Bedell, and I doubt that I could if I tried. I looked in and she's sleeping very soundly. But even so, she'd just be more upset, which will make her nervous state worse, and anyway what could *she* do?"

I held up my hand. "What's the trouble?"

They burst out in unison, "Miss Sylvie's gone off!" The housekeeper added, "With Robbie, too."

"How long ago?" I was dumbfounded.

Portman glanced at the housekeeper as he said, "Quarter of an hour." She nodded in agreement.

"With someone? Someone you know?" Now I was cursing Quincey for not telling me whom to guard against. Whatever I'd said last night might have made things clear to him, but definitely not to me. Suppose it wasn't her "protector" she'd left with? Fear rose in my throat.

"Not anyone I've seen before, sir," the butler answered emphatically.

"But Miss Sylvie knew him?"

They spoke again at the same time, but Mrs. Rogers said, "No," and Portman said, "Yes."

He hurried to explain, "You see, Miss Sylvie came down quite early to send off the note to Miss Craddock, and at the time she said she was expecting a visitor whom she had to see, despite Dr. Haskins's directions. When I asked for the caller's name, she said he'd merely say, 'I've come for Miss Singer.' Now, since some of those people from the newspapers say all sorts of things to gain admittance to speak to her, I asked for his description. Miss Sylvie just half-smiled and said, 'I know him, Portman, but I'm not sure I'll recognize him.' Which is an odd thing to say, but I'm thinking she meant that the gentleman might send a messenger rather than coming himself."

Mrs. Rogers broke in, "Sir, I was standing right beside the staircase when she came down with the boy, and I truly believe she'd never seen that man before. Just the way she kept looking at him."

Portman wheeled toward her. "But she did *know* him. Think of the way they got to talking then. Laughing and joking, they were." It was clear they'd already gone over this ground together.

"So he definitely wasn't a messenger," I got out. My

heartbeat was slowing some. Sylvie hadn't left on a false summons of some kind, and she was comfortable with him, whoever he was.

Trying to be helpful, Portman explained, "A foreign man, he was, sir." He thought for a second and added, "From China."

Stupefied, I stared at him. "A Chinese? Black hair? Slanted eyes?" I asked.

"Oh, no, sir," the butler replied quickly. "He looked just like you and me."

Since Portman was short, pudgy, clean-shaven, and gray-haired, and I was tall and lean with a dark beard and hair, I tried for a description. "As tall as I am? About how old?"

He considered. "Almost as tall. His hair was lighter brown than yours and he had no beard, and I've never seen a shorter head of hair. A young man. I should say he was about Miss Sylvie's age."

"How do you know he was from China, Portman?"

"I don't *know*, sir. He didn't say. His English was quite all right, although he didn't talk as if he were from Boston. It was what he was wearing. I understand they dress very oddly over there in China. He had no hat and no coat on a day like this! Not even a jacket, properly speaking. His shirt and pants were all one piece!"

I stared at the floor, trying to imagine such an outfit.

Mrs. Rogers added, trying to be helpful, "A light gray outfit. Sort of silvery. At the time I thought he could have been connected with the theater and was got up for a performance of some kind. Why else would he be dressed so strangely? And he was a good-looking man, like those actors." She glanced at Portman. "I hadn't thought of China."

He nodded sagely. "I understand from a seagoing

person that both the men and the women there wear
pajamas. In the street, during the day, Mrs. Rogers. So
he must have been from there. Now the Englishmen
who've visited at the house dress quite properly. And
even that Frenchman with his jacket so tight at the
waist and the high cravat looked acceptable."

She let out her breath and sought my eyes. "Mrs.
Bedell will be most unhappy with us, but we could
hardly have prevented Miss Sylvie from going. And,
after the first few minutes, she was quite happy to go
off with him." Her plump Irish face was lined with
worry, but both she and the butler seemed more relaxed now that they'd shifted some of the problem to
me, no doubt in the hope that I'd speak to their employer.

Turning to the housekeeper, I said, "You'd better
tell me what made you think Miss Singer didn't know
him."

"As soon as the maid takes up the message that
he's here, she comes right down the stairs with Robbie. Slow, though, because the boy has to hold tight to
the banister. And this man walks right up to the foot
of the stairs. I've never seen a man smile so much. All
the time, she's coming down, she's staring at him, but
no expression at all on her face. Then she walks right
up to him, without a word, looks him in the eye, and
*then* she smiles. 'It is you. I couldn't believe it,' she
says.

" 'I know,' he answers. 'Talk about discourteous
treatment! And after all this time.' But he's laughing
when he brings it out.

" 'I just couldn't believe it,' she tells him.

" 'I know. You used to listen. Then you stopped.'
Then he takes her right by the arm, bold as brass. 'We
have to hurry. There isn't much time.'

"She doesn't move. Just stands right there, holding

on to Robbie's hand. 'We're *both* going,' she said with
no nonsense in her voice.

"He laughs right out loud. 'Did you think I imagined otherwise?'

"So she asks Mr. Portman to get her cloak and Robbie's coat. Miss Sylvie turns to me and tells me there's
a note on her dressing table for Mrs. Bedell and
would I please make sure she gets it."

The housekeeper stopped and looked at me sideways. "Even if it wasn't my place, sir, I did say that
Mrs. Bedell would be very upset at her going. And
Miss Sylvie looks real sad but she just says, 'I'm
sorry.' The boy is saying nothing at all, just looking at
her and squeezing her hand so tight that I'm surprised it didn't stop the blood.

"When Mr. Portman brings out her cloak and bonnet, the man helps her into the cloak and then looks at
the bonnet and hands it back to Mr. Portman. He says
to Miss Sylvie, 'Very pretty, but you won't need it.'
And he bends down in front of Robbie and says, 'We
haven't much time. Do you mind if I carry you?'

"Robbie just shakes his head and he picks him up
and off they go!" Mrs. Rogers shook her own head in
amazement.

While she was speaking, Portman was shifting from
one foot to the other, eager to get a word in, and he
brought out immediately, "While you were going
over it again, Mrs. Rogers, I had an idea. He must
have been someone she knew from here when she
was young."

"Of course," she said, clasping her hands together
in surprise. "That's why she wasn't sure she'd recognize him. Hasn't seen him for years."

The butler caught my eye and gave me a significant
look. "And, if he's been off in China, who knows, sir,
what other arrangements—" Portman stopped and

coughed, still looking at me. "I mean, living arrangements, he might have made?"

It was clear he meant that the man might already be married, but he wasn't going to say that in front of Mrs. Rogers. At least while I was there. They'd discuss it in the servants' hall. She was looking down primly.

Nodding, he pressed his lips together as if he now had the complete explanation. "No doubt that's why the gentleman came on foot. He didn't want me to see the carriage, which was probably around the corner. I might even know who it belongs to. He seemed the sort of man who'd surely have a carriage or be staying with someone who would."

"They went on foot?" I asked. "In what direction?"

"I can't say, sir. I left the door open a bit as they went down the drive. I heard Miss Sylvie ask him if there really was a shining city. He said, 'A city all of lights. I promise.' And I could hear them laughing at something even when they were out of sight. I waited a few minutes and then I ran, fast as I could, down to the end of the drive. They must have taken the next street because there was no sign of them. As I said, the carriage must have been just there. No question about the hurry he was in."

Mrs. Rogers spoke up, her eyes on Portman. "He might have been worried she'd change her mind."

He pursed his lips and then replied, "Or maybe there was a train to catch. More likely," he went on, "a ship." Satisfied now that he understood the events, he began to relax and gave his shirtfront, still almost under his chin, a tug down. He adjusted his weskit over it, straightened his jacket, and then suddenly clapped a hand on its inside pocket. Looking at me in dismay, he said, "Sir, I am sorry. In all the excitement,

I clean forgot to give you the note Miss Sylvie handed me just as she was going out the door."

Still apologizing, he pulled out a square white envelope addressed to me in a flowing script. I ripped it open.

There was no greeting and no farewell. She'd run the last sentence together as one. It read: "As we said, it's hard to believe that we've lived before and will live again. Except on a rare Thursday. This is one. Thank you for your friendship as always. Sylvie."

# Chapter Thirty-five

*Haskins could be in danger.* Quincey's words were jouncing in my head as the cab jolted over the cobblestones at speed on the way to the Medical School. Who threatened him? Why? He benefited from Popkin's will, but so did Story. So why wasn't I fetching Story? Or Cranch Meeker? Or had Quincey already summoned them? I went over everything we discussed last night, trying to figure out what I could have said that gave him the answer. Then I gave up. There was no point in thinking about it anymore. I was going to get Haskins and bring him back.

Worrying about Sylvie was just as useless. The mysterious stranger she'd gone with was someone she knew, possibly her "protector." All I could do was send Quincey a note to that effect and set off for Boston as fast as I could.

As we rounded the corner of Fruit Street, I saw Haskins's carriage just up the road by the hospital, which meant he was nearby. I pushed my way through the double doors of the Medical School. I was barely inside when one of the office doors on the left opened. Dookin came out, clutching his mop, pushing his bucket slowly ahead of him.

At the sight of me, his thick shoulders beneath the too-small jacket stiffened. His eyebrows became one dark line of frown. But the expression on his lumpy

face was hangdog, resigned. He leaned the mop
against the wall and said, "I knowed it. Knowed
you'd be back 'fore the week's out. Soon as I found
'em on the Monday, I says to myself, 'That's what he
was lookin' fer.' There had to be some reason you was
wantin' so bad to go down to the basement. I din't
even tell Mother cuz there's no point in gettin' her
hopes up and then see 'em fall down."

He shuffled two steps closer to me, one hand creeping toward the pocket of his tight jacket. Trying to put
determination into his voice, he went on, "But seein'
as I was the one got 'em from the ashes, when they'd
jist be thrown out, I should be gettin' somethin' for
'em. Fer my trouble in findin' 'em. Took a sharp eye to
spot 'em under the grate. Then it took a fair bit of time
to sift through everythin' at the bottom of the furnace.
There was only eight of 'em, so don't be sayin' I sold
any. That's all that was there. They all fell through the
grate."

I couldn't make any sense out of what he was saying, but he had my attention when he mentioned ashes
and the furnace. Anxiety prickled my neck. "Dookin,"
I said, "I'm in a hurry. Just tell me what you found."

"You know." His enormous hand was now stuffed
all the way in his jacket pocket. "Them gold coins."

Slowly, he pulled out his hand. In his grimy palm,
there was a flattened circle of gold.

Picking it up, I saw still the faint outline of a crossed
sword, the insignia of the university dueling club in
Leyden. It was one of Bock Bach's jacket buttons,
melted on the edges from the fire, but shining.
Quincey was right. The professor hadn't left the
building. At least his jacket hadn't, and he certainly
wouldn't have left that behind on a cold day.

I let out my breath, thinking of blackened bone.

"Where do you put the ashes after you clean out the furnace?"

Dookin drew himself up indignantly. "Out in back. But there ain't no call fer you to poke through the whole heap of clinkers." He shuddered. "Ya don't want ta be doin' that. Dreadful stuff gets thrown in that there furnace. From Dr. Bonner's place where he takes bits and pieces from dead folk. Which ain't right. And I don't look at it too careful. Anyway, I'm tellin' ya, I got all them coins."

"Give them to me. All of them."

With infinite slowness, his hand slid down the length of the worn tweed jacket.

Wearily, I pulled out a dollar and shoved it into his upper pocket. "I have to see Dr. Haskins right away. But I want you to wait here and show me where you put the ashes."

His eyes lit up, and he rubbed the pocket to hear the crinkle of the bill. Cheerfully, he quickly counted seven more buttons into my hand. Then he jerked a thumb toward the next door. "He's in there. 'Least I ain't seen him come out. I been waitin' cuz I do the office floors Thursdays. That's when the clerk usually in there goes to do the hospital's books for him and Dr. Bigelow. Dr. Haskins got a black bearskin rug front of his desk, but I move it a bit and do round the edges. He don't want the shelves touched 'cuz the clerk—"

He followed me, still talking as I went through the empty outer office and knocked on Haskins's door. There was no reply. I pounded, then called his name. Only the quiet answered. I tried the handle. The door was locked.

Dookin was standing by the clerk's desk, piled with neat ledgers. He craned his neck to look around it at the clock in the corner. "That's queer. It's gettin' on to five." He glanced at the early twilight darkening the window. "On a weekday most of the doctors are gone on their rounds by now."

"Could he have stepped next door to the hospital?"

"Might of. But fer a good hour I been listenin' so's I could finish up on time. Well," he turned to go, "you kin try 'im over there. The nurses'll know."

"Dookin. Unlock the door."

He was aghast. "You kin't go in there. What if he comes back? Dr. Haskins, why, he'd have my head!"

"I just need a quick look. I won't touch anything."

He put a hand over his pocket as if afraid I'd snatch the dollar back. His round eyes narrowed as he thought. "I could say I'd opened it to do the floor and you followed me in to look fer 'im. But I'm goin' in first."

He turned the key quietly, put only his head in, and almost whispered, "Dr. Haskins?"

When there was no reply, he stepped in briskly. Over his broad shoulder I could see the thick pile of a black fur rug and velvet, floor-length drapes pulled shut. It was a good-sized room. Totally dark. Dookin turned and reached up for the gas jet inside the door. "I'll just get on with the cleanin'. You kin see he ain't here."

But he was.

When the light sprang on, I could see him in the chair behind a massive desk. His head was thrown back at an angle as if he were staring at the ceiling. Both of his hands were clutching a half-loosened cravat. His mouth sagged open as if gasping for air. He didn't move.

I rushed around the desk, my feet crunching on the broken glass of a jar that had been tipped violently over and splintered on the edge of the mahogany. Reaching for a pulse in his throat, I had to push aside one of his hands, tightened in a death grip on the black silk of his tie. But as soon as my fingers brushed his cold skin, I knew. He'd been dead for some time.

Still, with my hand on his neck, I called over my shoulder, "Get one of the doctors, Dookin. Right away!"

When there was no answer, I spun around. The custodian had quietly fainted on the black bearskin rug.

# Chapter Thirty-six

"We had a Spirit Killer, after all. It was a dead man who killed Haskins. No question about it."

I just stared at Quincey.

He tapped the thin blue notebook in front of him on his desk. His heavy voice was slowed by exhaustion. "Here's the evidence. This is Bock Bach's missing experiment book. He analyzed the horehound drops he took from Popkin's office. They were poisoned."

Now I was glaring at him. If I hadn't been hoarse, I'd have shouted at him. I'd spent hours with the Boston police, saying over and over that an autopsy had to be performed on the doctor. But I had no solid reason for my insistence. All I could point to was the broken jar that had contained the horehound cough drops scattered across his mahogany desktop. They'd only nodded, one after another of them saying stolidly, "Could have been a heart attack or some such, couldn't it, sir? Doctor said maybe, said it looked like it. Poor man knocked that glass jar over in his last spasm."

In an effort to spur them into sifting through the ash heap, I'd also given them Bock Bach's gold buttons. After some discussion, they'd agreed there might be something in that. I'd suggested that they talk to the Cambridge constables because Professor Craddock's murder was related. At that point, they'd begun glancing at me sideways. I couldn't give them a coherent explanation for those three deaths because I didn't have one.

For hours, all the lights blazed at Harvard Medical School. Plodding footsteps went up and down the wooden floor of the hall. Messengers hurried in and out. I repeated what I knew to one police inspector after another.

Now it seemed that what I should have done was tell them to send for Jasper Quincey. He'd have been outraged, and at the time I didn't see any point in his coming. I'd thought they might as well talk to him in the morning when they might or might not listen to his theory. I'd assumed he had nothing to back it up. Now he was looking morosely at the experiment book, which he considered proof.

Catching the look in my eye, he held up both palms to placate me. "I've only had it for an hour. And I had no way to know it still existed. It could easily have been burned. Yet, thinking over what Bock Bach might have done on his last afternoon, it occurred to me that, if he had time, he'd have hidden it after he completed his analysis of those horehound drops. But where? His assistant, Wilcox, told you he'd searched the lab and the office because he himself needed it."

Dropping his hands, he lifted a shoulder. "I had only a thread of hope that it would turn up. Yet I knew the police would shrug away all my words if I didn't have at least *some* basis for laying out my ideas.

"Here's what I did. As soon as I got your message about Haskins, I sent Hoggett to get Wilcox. He admitted he'd only looked in likely places. Obviously, he hadn't gone through every book on those rows of shelves, felt for loose floor boards, or seen what might be taped under a desk drawer. All the time you were downstairs, the two of them were searching. Wilcox told the police that now they had the buttons, he'd look for any last note from the professor. When they saw the widespread array of bottles and jars in the lab and the crowded shelves of books in the office, they were happy to leave it to Wilcox and his 'helper.' Hoggett was the one who found it. But the notes at the end were so cryptic that he could see that I'd have to explain their meaning to official investigators. He brought it here."

"Where was it?"

"Slipped into a stack of very old experiment books that looked just like it." He flipped it open to begin reading.

I rested my head on the chair back. "Spare me the cryptic notes. As tired as I am, I can't think clearly. Not that I can stop thinking, though. Start at the beginning, if you will."

He hauled himself to his feet, crossed to the sideboard, and unstoppered the largest of the decanters. "We'll have the Douro port. It's only fitting."

Handing me one of the glasses, he began while he was still standing. "As I told you, I had the backgrounds of several of these people looked into. Although Haskins's practice paid well, he had extravagant ways. Moreover, he wanted funds for his elaborate new clinic. Under Popkin's will, he could make a legitimate case for the use of magnetic rods to 'prolong man's life span.'

"In the end he was spurred as much by anger as greed, I should think. He owed Popkin for the curio cabinet and couldn't afford to pay him. So Popkin unwisely marched into Haskins's lecture and pointed his finger at him. Almost any man would be offended by such treatment and Haskins, proud as he was, would hardly brook it. I think we'll find there was a piece of jade amongst those curios, possibly valuable but maybe not. That was the motive that occurred to Pop-

kin. He knew he'd been poisoned, and he suspected
Haskins. Hence the mention of the jade piece. A small
Chinese carving, perhaps." He stopped, settled him-
self behind his desk, and set down his glass.

"Haskins might have killed Popkin, but he couldn't
have—" I began.

"Let me go on," Quincey rumbled. "I need the re-
hearsal for tomorrow when I shall have to speak to
the authorities. So much of this is mere conjecture,
and I'll have to say it very firmly so they'll accept it.
Haskins was in an ideal position to poison his colleague. Popkin, despite the way he'd insulted the
other man, still took horehound drops out of the glass
jar on his desk. It's an herb, *marrubium vulgare*, routinely used to soothe coughs. It's also believed to have
other healthful properties. To show that he harbored
no ill will, Haskins gives him a dish of them for his
own office. Now, horehound is so bitter that it'll mask
the taste of any additives. I'm assuming that Haskins
put in digitalis, derived from the foxglove flower and
readily available. It's also extremely poisonous. In
small doses, digitalis reduces the heart rate, but in
large doses it causes the heart to beat wildly, bringing
on dizziness, convulsions, and death. Of course,
Haskins couldn't know *when* one of them would be
swallowed."

Quincey stopped to sip his wine, and I said slowly,
"So, as it happens, before the séance begins, Popkin
slips one into his mouth."

"Exactly. Haskins reads about his extraordinarily
bad luck the next day in the newspaper, and at this
moment, he's really concerned about the threat Miss
Singer could pose. He might believe that she has
some genuine psychic powers, or might assume that
she overheard more than she said. When he learns
about her appointment at Harvard that evening, he

slips a rifle into his tall carrying case of magnetic rods, and goes immediately to the Yard. Mrs. Bedell's carriage is waiting near the Common; Haskins is assured of the way of their return. He waits for a chance at a shot at Miss Singer and gets it. He misses, but just."

Rubbing his forehead as if to ease a headache brought on by recalling his own insistence that it was the act of an irresponsible student, Quincey continued. "While Haskins no doubt sorely regrets that near miss—such a killing doesn't point to him at all—he knows he has another chance. Because of her upset, Mrs. Bedell will need his services, and he'll kindly offer a sleeping powder to her friend, Sylvie, as well. He'll go back to the Medical School and prepare one especially for her, one that ensures she doesn't wake again. But he sees a copy of the *Independent* on that fatal Halloween. He learns that Bock Bach has ordered an autopsy. If there's anyone who can level a finger at Haskins, it's the chemistry professor. Worse, the doctor sees the lights burning in the lab quite late.

"Now what has Bock Bach been doing? After talking with us, he's been thinking. What mimics a genuine heart attack? Digitalis. He knows of Popkin's habit of sucking on horehound drops, and he recalls seeing a dish of them in his friend's office. Bock Bach has a key, goes in, finds a dish of them sitting on one of the shelves and takes them next door to his lab for analysis. You yourself noted the clean circle in the dust of that shelf. He runs his experiment on the tablets."

"Did Bock Bach write all this down?" I asked.

Quincey returned glumly, "No. Would that he had! He just writes out the result, noting the high concentration of digitalis. He adds the revealing sentence, 'I shall speak to Haskins. How shall I do this? Use the drops.' Unfortunately, he doesn't explain what he intends to do with them.

"I can only guess what his unfortunate choice of action was. Bock Bach leaves out all his equipment, although he slips this notebook in a pile of others. Taking the rest of the cough drops with him, he goes down to his colleague's office on the first floor. It's empty, but the door is open and he goes in to wait. He has a little plan. He puts those poisoned tablets into the glass jar on Haskins' desk and sits back. Suppose he intends the conversation to go something like this: 'Popkin mentioned to me that you gave him some of your horehound drops. While they must be harmless, as you keep them on your desk and eat them yourself, let us both try one. That way, there can be no unpleasant suspicions.' The doctor might smile in relief and humor him. When Haskins puts one in his mouth, Bock Bach intends to add, 'By the way, the ones on top were from Popkin's office.' "

At that, I sat up straight. "Bock Bach counts on the fact that Haskins will spit it out fast."

Quincey nodded. "But Haskins was moving very fast himself. He'd gone up the back staircase to check on why those lights in the lab were still on. And he sees from the spread-out equipment what the chemistry professor had been up to. Haskins goes looking for him and finds him sitting in his own office. He doesn't wait for any conversation. A quick blow on the back of the head and Bock Bach is dead."

Grimacing at the thought, Quincey drank his wine as if it could take away the foul taste in his mouth. "Haskins returns to the lab, puts everything away to hide the nature of the experiment, gathers up the professor's coat, turns down the gas jets, and shuts the door."

"To support that," I said, "we at least have evidence

of how his body was disposed of. The police have the buttons. Bock Bach was slight, elderly, and Haskins is a younger and bigger man. In the middle of the night, he could easily take him down to the furnace." I blew out my breath. "A long night for the doctor. No wonder his eyes were red-rimmed when I saw him at Mrs. Bedell's on Saturday. And what's more"—I leaned forward—"he misses his chance to give Sylvie a fatal powder. She does take a sleeping draught, but it was given to her by the young doctor who's called in when Haskins can't be found."

Quincey riffled the edges of the experiment book. "He would, though, be feeling a little calmer that morning. While Bock Bach won't appear for his Saturday tutorials, only Wilcox will be alarmed at that. The young assistant would certainly not report that. And the next day is Sunday. What Haskins can't know is that Newman Goss had an appointment with the professor to get the autopsy results. Nor is the doctor in any position to understand a journalist's driving need to fill columns of print. Since it will sell papers, Goss immediately provides some flimsy speculation on Bock Bach's disappearance. It must have stopped Haskins in his tracks. You can see, Michael, how from this point on his actions began to be determined by what is published in the *Independent*."

I held up my glass in a mock toast. "One always hears about the power of the press. This time I believe it. Haskins sees from the paper that a message from Bock Bach is in order. No doubt the professor had his sister's address in his pocket case. So he sends a telegraph."

Quincey held up a finger. "Keep in mind that from the beginning Haskins was influenced by what he read. He'd act on it. Quite remarkable how circular it was. From the beginning, he accepted Goss's account of Miss

Singer's 'amazing' powers. That aside"—he waved away the doctor's credulity—"he's very shrewd. Moreover, he knows that the newspaper will influence opinion. He's learned from Mrs. Bedell that another séance will be held. When he reads the editor's theory about the Spirit Killer, he sees how to take advantage of that idea."

Pressing his mouth into a grim line, Quincey stopped before going on. "Haskins decides that if someone from the first séance is killed, he himself will be free of all suspicion. The airy idea of a Spirit Killer will become fact. He plans to kill Gideon Craddock."

At that I stood up. "But he can't have done it! Up to this point, I can accept what you say, sir, even if much of it has to be supposition. But not this. Craddock is at the front door only minutes before Haskins walks through it. I was there. He didn't have the time!"

Quincey got up, too. He walked to the fireplace, set his glass on the mantel, turned to face me, and said broodingly, "Nonetheless, Haskins did it. I was baffled, too. I couldn't see how it was possible. Luckily, that remark of yours drew my attention. No doubt the solution would eventually have come to me, but—"

In three strides I was before him. "What? What did I say?"

"You repeated the old adage 'Clothes make the man.'" He sipped his wine wearily. "Reverse that idea: no clothing at all is a disguise."

Still staring at him, I sank down into the wingback chair. "It *wasn't* Craddock at the door."

"No, it wasn't. Once you rid your mind of that time frame, you can see that Haskins can accomplish all he has to do. Gladys said she heard the doctor's carriage and she fidgets, waiting nervously for him to knock. But he doesn't knock. Instead he whips around the side of the building and up the outer staircase. Obviously Craddock will open that door to *him*. Not only does he know Haskins well, he's been told the doctor is coming to the house. Dressed in his Greek robe, Craddock waves him in, perhaps thinking that the doctor plans to wait upstairs for the séance's end rather than in the parlor. Haskins raises a lead pipe and bashes in the back of Craddock's head when he turns to lead the doctor into the room. An unexpected visitor, as in the end of *Alcestis*."

Despite the warmth of the fire, I felt suddenly cold in my bones. I heard Sylvie saying the words. *Gad, you gave me a turn. Come in, come—*

Quincey leaned over, picked up the poker, and gave one of the logs a vicious jab. I couldn't see his face, but I remembered the pain in his eyes last night. He said, "Then all Haskins has to do is strip the body of that robe. While he's still upstairs, he carefully pats on a makeshift false beard cut to match the professor's. After all, it doesn't have to withstand close scrutiny."

Running a hand down the side of my own beard, I shook my head. "No, it doesn't. So Haskins goes back down, strips off his own clothing near the bushes, and knocks on the front door. He stands there naked and grinning. Cackling, in fact. And he gets the reaction he expected. Perhaps even more than he could have hoped for. The parlormaid not only faints, but manages to pull over the coat rack and knock herself out."

"Yes. Then all the doctor need do is hurriedly dress. His cloak will hide any disarray at this point. He runs after his own carriage, puts in the bag in which he's concealed the beard and the weapon, and takes out the proper leather case. He runs back to the door, and there you and Story are, bending over Gladys."

I pounded my fist on the arm of the chair. "In fact, the man calmly arranged his clothing in the parlor right in front of me!" I banged it again. "Said he had to hurry into his evening dress because he was kept by his last patient!"

"Throughout, his coolness is extraordinary. It's matched only by the speed of his actions when he feels in danger. Recall what he did last Saturday afternoon. He's at the Medical School, no doubt to make sure everything that points to Bock Bach's death has been smoothed over. But there you are, asking questions, spending time in the lab, going into Popkin's office. Then, as you and the custodian are at last going downstairs, you tell Dookin that you are going to inspect the basement! Your voice carries right up the stairwell. Haskins probably was standing two flights above you."

I saw again that lead-heavy newel cap crashing on the step directly in front of me and then battering its way down the rest of the stairs. I stretched my chilled fingers toward the fire and rubbed them hard.

Shoving the poker back into its stand, he said, "Oh, yes, I think so, Michael. Now. Haskins sent it plummeting down, intending to kill you—"

Not only was I cold, I found it hard to take in air. I managed to get out, "And he would have gotten away with it. All of it."

"Not only that. He'd have made another attempt on Miss Singer. Quite probably he'd have succeeded. Her son may have feared the doctor's medicines, but she had no reason to suspect them."

The urgent words Sylvie spoke at the séance echoed in my head: *You're in danger. Do as I ask. There's not much time.*

Quincey drew himself up. "I would finally have understood, but perhaps not in time. And even then—" Quincey put out an empty palm.

I had to agree with him. "There'd have been no real proof. Ever."

"Indeed not." Quincey's tone was harsh. "The experiment book only says that there was digitalis in those tablets, and that Bock Bach intended to talk with Haskins. If questioned about that, all Haskins has to do is shrug and say that Popkin could have gotten horehound drops anywhere. An apothecary's mistake. The only real mistake that Haskins himself made was that once, just once, he moved too fast."

Leaning my head back, I considered as I stared at the ceiling. "When he found Bock Bach waiting for him in his office, he should have waited to hear what the professor had to say and then killed him."

"Precisely. Instead, his own death was waiting for him. His own poison in an innocent jar in front of him. Put there by the hand of the man he murdered. Then this afternoon, while he was considering his next move, he reaches in and puts a horehound drop in his mouth."

Quincey heaved a sigh and settled himself into the wingback chair next to mine. After a time, he said sadly, "You know, it was Craddock who wrote those letters to the *Independent* railing against Spiritualism, the ones signed 'Truth Seeker.'"

"He added his own name?"

"No, no. His sister might have found him out, and there'd be no peace in the household. To disguise his handwriting, he even printed them out in block capitals. But I recognized his style. Over the years I received so many notes from him that I—"

He shook his head instead of finishing that sentence. He added bitterly, "If he'd attended that last séance, he'd have been quite safe."

After that, his continuing silence made me think that he'd sunk into black thoughts. But he stirred himself and brought out musingly, "I should have liked to meet Miss Singer. She's a woman of infinite invention.

That charade she performed right before you arrived this afternoon demonstrates that again. A delicious bit of flummery."

"You're sure that's what it was?"

"Certainly. She must have instructed her 'protector' to dress outlandishly. I wonder what put that particular outfit in her mind? The uniform dress of European royalty? They tend to fit tightly in one piece. Or the work of the fantasy writer Jules Verne? That book of his just out had a captain of a ship that could go deep beneath the sea and, since there was little room, I should imagine the character had to dress very sleekly. The book sold well. And I believe he has another work in which a man travels great distances by air. Well, no doubt doing this entertained Miss Singer, but I'm persuaded the act was conceived out of kindness. It would ease the mind of her friend, Emily Craddock, as you suggested. It adds mystery and romance to her going. Miss Singer would hardly have staged it for the benefit of the servants. The butler would have known exactly where she was going and the nature of her relationship with this 'mysterious stranger.' If the housekeeper didn't understand, Portman would enlighten her. And I must admit I'm pleased that Miss Singer is going off to Paris and with a man who clearly enjoys her wit and finds her as beguiling as you do."

"Paris? I didn't mention that."

"You said 'a city of lights,' and the French capital is often referred to that way. But Paris is an ideal place for her. No one there will know her background, or care about it, since she's lovely and dresses modishly."

"You have to admit that she had some telepathic ability. She knew the name of the play Craddock chose."

"Come now, Michael. That was an easy guess on her part. She lived with the Craddocks when she was quite young and then was taken away after a few years. By the time she'd mastered the language well enough to read the literature, there wouldn't have been sufficient time to go over many of the plays. And *Alcestis* is a likely one for the professor to have chosen for a child. It has a great deal of action—Hercules wrestling with Death and so forth. It seems to have a happy ending—a young girl wouldn't have appreciated the exquisite irony of the conclusion. She'd have been bound to remember it. And I'm most impressed with her bringing out, at intervals, that deep voice that cries of danger. An inspired touch, under the circumstances."

I waved a hand, too tired to argue. We both stared at the fire. After a few moments, he said, "It occurs to me that there's no need for you to take lodgings in Boston when you resume your duties at the paper. Since you'll be covering the entire city, there's no way you could be conveniently located to your work in any case. You must remain here. As you know, the west wing isn't used."

I did want to stay, but I was considering my answer.

Before I came out with a reply, he said, "Good. That's settled then." Clearing his throat, he added stiffly, "I enjoy our conversations at dinner."

I thanked him. We continued looking at the fire's dance.

After a long silence, Quincey sat forward, his hands on his knees, and shook his head. "Fantasy always pleases, doesn't it? Ships that go twenty thousand leagues under the sea or float through the air. But we must be guided by reason, by our experience of reality. Another glass of port?"

I nodded. I was thinking of Sylvie and her last words to me: *Thank you for your friendship as always.*

## AUTHOR'S HISTORICAL NOTE

The nineteenth-century movement called Spiritualism—the attempt to contact the dead through mediums—caused enormous excitement in America and in England for years. It started in the 1840s and continued into the twenty-first. As *The New York Times* notes, interest in the movement is burgeoning in the twenty-first: "A growing number of the living are attempting to hear from the dead." (October 30, 2000) The article points out that mediums are now often referred to as "spiritists."

Because I wanted to show this rich history, I compressed time. The book is set in the early 1870's, as the mention of several historical events makes clear. The descriptions of the Boston/Cambridge area, the Harvard campus, the clothing all reflect that era. But, while the actual historical figures in the book are accurately placed at that time, I bring in incidents from their later lives. For example, William James was teaching at Harvard then, and he did study Spiritualism intensely, but the given quotations from him appeared in books published later in his career. I made every effort to show correctly the attitudes of the people of the time toward the movement.

Some readers will also see the similarity of one of the murders in this book to a famous crime committed at Harvard Medical School a little earlier in the century. (The fascinating Parkman/Webster case recounted by Samuel Eliot Morison in *Three Centuries of Harvard*.) I fictionalized only it slightly. The janitor there "solved the case"—not two newspapermen, as I have it. My janitor wasn't so clever.